Praise for *A Blade of Grass*

"*A Blade of Grass* is a novel of the earth. . . . Haunting, intimate [and] compelling."   —*Quill & Quire*

"[The author] writes evocatively . . . about a wild and natural country that seems both authentic and tragic."
—*The Globe and Mail*

"A significant work of post-colonial literature. A gripping read . . . that effortlessly places the reader within the pulsating landscape . . . of South Africa."
—*The Gazette* (Montreal)

"[The novel] is typical of the painterly delicacy of DeSoto's prose. [His] descriptions of farm life are timeless . . . and compelling. *A Blade of Grass* is a bleak, vivid novel . . . where black and white are anything but."
—*The Vancouver Sun*

"A powerful and compassionate story of belonging and betrayal, *A Blade of Grass* is rich in detail and unflinching in its treatment of apartheid."   —Helen Humphreys

"Part historical fiction, part war-survival story, [*A Blade of Grass*] is above all an intimate drama of two young South African women . . . in search of home. DeSoto evokes the elemental landscape with lyrical simplicity."
—*Booklist*

"DeSoto explores the psychological complexity of friendship with absolute authenticity . . . and the richness of character is matched by the exquisite landscape of Africa."   —Catherine Gildiner

LEWIS DESOTO was born in Bloemfontein, South Africa. After moving to Canada, he attended the University of British Columbia, where he received a Master of Fine Arts. His writing has been published in numerous literary journals, and he was awarded the *Books in Canada* Writers' Union Short Prose Award. A past editor of *The Literary Review of Canada*, Lewis DeSoto lives in Toronto and Normandy.

A Blade of Grass

Lewis DeSoto

A Blade of Grass

Harper*Perennial*Canada
A PHYLLIS BRUCE BOOK

A Blade of Grass
© 2003 by Lewis DeSoto. All rights reserved.

A Phyllis Bruce Book, published by Harper*Perennial*Canada,
an imprint of HarperCollins Publishers Ltd

First published in hardcover by Phyllis Bruce Books
and Harper*Flamingo*Canada, imprints of HarperCollins
Publishers Ltd, 2003. This paperback edition 2004.

HarperCollins books may be purchased for educational,
business, or sales promotional use through our Special
Markets Department.

HarperCollins Publishers Ltd
2 Bloor Street East, 20th Floor
Toronto, Ontario, Canada
M4W 1A8

www.harpercollins.ca

National Library of Canada Cataloguing in Publication

DeSoto, Lewis
A blade of grass / Lewis DeSoto. –
1st HarperPerennialCanada ed.

"A Phyllis Bruce book".
ISBN-13: 978-0-00-639280-4
ISBN-10: 0-00-639280-6

I. Title.

PS8557.E84075B53 2004   C813'.6   C2004-900350-X

RRD 9 8 7 6

Printed and bound in the United States
Set in Monotype Fournier

for Gunilla

The World was all before them, where to choose
Their place of rest, and Providence their guide:
They hand in hand with wandering steps and slow,
Through Eden took their solitary way.

—Milton, *Paradise Lost*, Book XII

Part One

The Farm

I

FIRST SHE MUST wash the seeds.

To do this, Tembi places them in an old tin can, salvaged long ago from the refuse heap of the big house—a tin can that once might have contained jam, or peaches, or sauce, but is now scrubbed clean of its label and any residue of sweet or bitter. A vessel of many uses, worn smooth by many hands.

There are five seeds. Each is no larger than one of her own fingernails—pale, pink, oval, the outer husks hard and corrugated with fine ridges that gradually appeared as the seeds dried. She has kept them safe for many days, folded into the corner of a handkerchief tucked in the pocket of her dress.

Cyril brought the seeds. Not like this, hard and dry, but still inside a fruit, a fruit strange to this part of the world, with firm yellow flesh and the seeds deep inside. Cyril, who is a friend of her father, from the time before the Relocation. Cyril brought them, a gift from her father, from the city, from the gold mines where her father works, where he digs the hard yellow metal deep underground. A gift from her father, Cyril said, a gift from a faraway city.

Her father cannot come himself, so he sends this fruit instead, in his place, this fruit offering such surprising flavour, such smoothness on her tongue, and the taste that is there and then not there. And the seeds hidden deep inside.

When the fruit is eaten, every bit of the yellow flesh taken from the rind and the juices licked from her lips and fingers, all that is left are these five pale seeds. Tembi folds them into her handkerchief and tucks this gift into her pocket. Already, while eating the fruit, she has resolved to plant the seeds, in some secret place, and nurture them, and bring forth sweetness out of the earth, so that when her father returns from the mines he will have this taste in his mouth to wash away the bitterness of the gold dust. A gift.

First she must wash the seeds. There is an iron tap outside the kraal washhouse, one that the farmer installed not long ago, so that the women would not have to walk to the river with buckets and pails to fetch water or to wash their clothes. Washing clothes in the river was bad for the water, the farmer said, so he built the washhouse and installed the tap outside. Now the water is drawn out of the deep earth by the windmill in the maize field, the metal blades always drifting in a lazy circle under the soft breeze that blows from the west and the faint regular grind of the pump mechanism, always audible amongst the sounds of birds during the day and the chirrup of the crickets at night.

The water is warm on Tembi's fingers when she opens the faucet, warm from its journey through the sun-heated iron pipe laid across the field to the kraal washhouse, and when she stoops to touch her lips to the spout of the tap the water is warm and tastes of iron. She lets the stream run a minute, splashing on her bare feet, until the water becomes cold and tastes of the dark deep earth.

Tembi unfolds her handkerchief and lets the seeds fall into the bottom of the tin can, then half fills it with water. She cups her hand over the opening and shakes the can, rinsing the seeds, then pours out the water and fills the can again, and shakes the seeds, then repeats the whole procedure, rinsing the seeds until the can is cold in her hand and the seeds glisten in the sunlight, cool and moist.

Above Tembi, the African sky is a high wide arch of blue. The air is hot and dry, the season is new, ready for planting. She raises the tin can and touches it to her brow, shivering at the pleasant little stab of the cold metal on her hot skin. Far above her in the blue arch of the sky, a glint of silver light gleams for a moment and the sigh of a jet's engine mingles with the rustling breeze in the branches of the eucalyptus trees.

Someone is going somewhere, to the faraway world. How does this place where she stands look from up there in the faraway sky? She sees a quilt of ochre and brown and green, and the white farmhouse, small as a page in a small book, and the tiny glint of metal sparking in the sun where the light catches the tin can in her hand.

Tembi turns off the faucet. At her feet the earth is muddy, and she wiggles her toes into the cool, wet soil, and her skin is the same dark color as the African soil when it is wet after the rain.

A shadow moves across the land. Across the quilt of ochre and brown and green, across the hills and the valleys and the rivers, across the maize fields and the veldt grasses where the cattle graze, across the farmhouse bordered by eucalyptus trees and the kraal and the washhouse, across this place called Kudufontein. From the corner of her eye, just on the edge of her vision, Tembi sees the rapid flicker of a shadow on the ground, as if a hand has suddenly placed itself between the earth and the sun. More rapidly than her senses can register, the shadow becomes a sudden dark cloud that leaps from the earth to swoop over her. A metallic shriek rips the sky and the black shapes of two military jets boom and flash over the farm just above the roofs. Like predatory hawks they scream away towards the border, and the booming of the engines slams against Tembi's body, buffeting the air with the acrid stench of jet fuel.

Behind the farmhouse the treetops bend and sway in the hot wind and the doves that roost there fling themselves wildly into the air like bits of torn paper. Tembi feels the trembling of the earth in her legs and in the soil at her feet and in the chase of her heart as it races inside the cage of her ribs. Above her the two metallic specks glint in the far blue heavens. At her feet is the fallen tin can and the spilled water and the seeds scattered in the mud.

She bends to gather the seeds, for she will plant them this day. But first she must wash the seeds.

2

In the kitchen of the farmhouse, in the coolness of the slate floors and the thatched roof, a fly buzzes with noisy persistence towards the sunlight on the other side of the window screen. Grace Mkize, the mother of Tembi, pushes up the mesh and shoos the fly out with her dishcloth. Behind her the kettle on the big iron stove whistles a plume of steam into the air, and Grace slides it off the burner before turning to set out a single cup and saucer, a glass bowl of sugar, and the small china milk jug. From the oven she takes two pieces of toast and cuts off the crusts before buttering them and spreading on a thin layer of Rose's Lime Marmalade. She slices the toast into neat triangles and arranges them on a plate. The teapot is then rinsed with boiling water, two spoonfuls of tea leaves are added, and everything is placed on a tray.

Grace removes her apron, smudged in places with fingerprints, and ties on the clean one she uses for serving, then carries the tray down the hall to the living room at the front of the house. She places the tray on an ebony coffee table before crossing the carpet to knock once on a door leading to a farther room.

"The tea is ready, Missus."

The woman sitting at the desk with the papers and envelopes spread across it, her face half hidden by her thick chestnut hair, looks up at Grace with a distant expression in her gray eyes. "Fine, Grace. Just leave it out there."

Grace hesitates a moment, for she has something to tell the Missus. But the detached, almost dreamy look on the young woman's face deters her.

It is not her place to disturb the Missus when she is busy, even if the matter is important. Perhaps later.

Grace goes back to the kitchen along the dark cool corridor, her rubber-soled sandals making a soft squeak on the slate floor, and hangs up her apron. She replaces it with her usual one, then eases her tired body into a kitchen chair and begins peeling potatoes for the evening meal.

Märit Laurens sits at the desk in the room she calls her office, with a row of small envelopes spread out on the desk, and on each envelope is a small pile of banknotes and coins. She has an open ledger at hand. She is putting together the weekly pay packets for the farm workers. It is one of her duties, one of her responsibilities. The accounts, the correspondence, the bills, the lists, the wages—these are the responsibilities that her husband Ben has entrusted to her. The understanding between them is that he will farm and Märit will look after the house.

She is a young woman, in her mid-twenties, recently orphaned, recently married, recently mistress of this farm in the remote African countryside. And she is still new to all these three states. It is strange to her to know that her parents have died, and even though the grief is starting to lessen there is still pain with each memory, and a hollowness inside her when she realizes that she is without family, without that link to the past. It is strange to her to know that somewhere on the farm her husband, Ben, is busy with his farming, and that he will come later to sit with her at the evening meal when the sun sets. It is strange to her to know this, but not without joy. And it is strange to her to think that this place, this farm called Kudufontein, is now also her responsibility and that she is mistress to the field workers and their families, and to the cattle and the fowl, and the crops and the fruit. It feels strange to call this place her home.

Three months since she came to this farm, six months since she married Ben, nine months since her parents died. Everything happening so quickly. Somewhere in the back of her mind, in the recesses that are not visited except in the small hours before the dawn, is fear that she will not be adequate to this life, to this responsibility. And even farther behind those unvisited recesses, in the place where the soul hides its deepest truths, is the thought that perhaps she has made a mistake with her life, that she has chosen too soon, too hastily, and that her decision to marry, to live on this farm, has not been wise.

In the nearest town, Klipspring, they know her at the shops and at the Retief Hotel as Mevrou Laurens, a term of address with a certain dignity that she appreciates. They ask after her health and that of her husband, and about the general welfare of the farm. A part of her acknowledges these things, and takes some satisfaction in them—the ownership, the belonging, the responsibility to the land and the people. But there is also the loneliness. She pretends a bit about the farming, to herself and to Ben, for she finds it difficult to be really interested in cattle and crops and growing seasons and the price of maize or beef.

She misses the job she had in Johannesburg, even though it was only secretarial work, even though she still lived at home with her parents. At least she felt free then, strolling along the streets after work, stopping to window-shop, to go to a café if she wanted, or to a film.

She loves Ben, and that is enough. Yet why couldn't he have chosen a farm closer to civilization, closer to a city, or to the sea, for if she admits it to herself, they are isolated here, surrounded by blacks and Boers, hard-necked Afrikaaner farmers who trace their settlement of this land back two hundred years and cling to their God-given rights of occupancy with the same tenacity as their forefathers. And now this talk of war on the borders, of guerillas attacking farms.

These are thoughts best not visited, for to acknowledge them, to even consider them, will put a rip in the fabric of her life and cause it to unravel. She fears this even as she hides it from herself.

So Märit raises her eyes to the window, which gives a view of the rock garden where aloes and cacti grow, and down the slope to the orchards, and beyond to the maize fields, and to the river hidden behind the willow trees, and across the grasses of the veldt to the hills blue in the distance, and the high arch of the empty sky. And beyond that lies the border. Where there are rumors of war.

Ben's farm. Her farm. *Kudufontein*. Even the name is new, for when she came here with Ben the farm was called Duiwelskop, which means Devil's Hill in the Afrikaans language, but can also mean Devil's Head, named so because of the koppie, or hill, behind the farm, which at certain times of the morning, when the shadows are long, can look like a head with horns. She said to Ben that she could not think of living in a place with such a name, so they called it Kudufontein, because on her first visit to the farm they had come upon a magnificent kudu buck drinking at the river. The animal had raised its majestic head slowly at the sound of their voices and stared regally at the two interlopers. Ben had shaken his head in admiration and said softly, "There's the rightful owner of this place."

When they took possession of the farm, Ben surprised her one day by painting the new name of the farm onto one of the stone gateposts, so that all who came past would know the new name, and he told the workers that this was the name of the farm from now on and they must call it that always.

Märit sighs and looks down at the papers on the desk. She pushes the envelopes and ledger away and lifts her long thick hair from her shoulders, shaking it loose, then leaves her office and goes out to the living room to drink her tea, and to smoke a cigarette, which she allows herself because she is alone in the house.

Here in this room, between the thick stone walls and the thatched roof above the sturdy beams over her head, she is alone. The furniture is dark oak, inherited from her parents' house. A couple of watercolor landscapes, purchased by Ben, brighten the walls. On the sideboard are a few gilt-framed photographs: her parents, Ben's mother and father, her wedding. It seems as if she has stepped into a timeless past, where life on the land has not changed in a century. Even the radio plays only severe classical music and crop reports between the weather and the news.

She is alone, and because she is alone she fears that she has made the wrong decision, that her life will not change. And she fears the future.

GRACE PLACES the peeled potatoes in a bowl of water so that they won't discolor and covers the bowl with a cloth before she sets it on a shelf in the refrigerator. She washes her hands and removes her apron once again, then takes the clean apron from behind the door and goes down the cool passageway to the living room.

Outside the door Grace listens, hears the sound of a teacup being placed in its saucer, the flutter of a magazine's pages. She knocks.

Märit looks up at the matronly figure of Grace—a woman roughly her mother's age, in her clean white apron, her rubber sandals, the pink head scarf.

"You can take the tray now, Grace. I've finished."

"Yes, Missus."

Grace gathers the tea things. Märit studies the other woman's broad back, a sturdy back, used to work. At the door Grace sets the tray down on a side table and pauses. She takes a breath.

"Missus, I must go away for a few days."

"Oh?"

"Yes, my cousin is sick. She must go to the hospital."

"Which cousin is that?" Märit asks, and hears in her own voice the unintentional adoption of the same tone her mother used in her conversation with the domestic servants. There is a slight undertone of sarcasm in her voice, a hint at disbelief, which she is unable to suppress, for this is a standard excuse, almost a formula, that any domestic servant or worker will use when asking for leave from duties.

Märit asks this question of Grace not entirely out of disbelief, but also because she is less than sure of her own authority in this house. Märit has grown up with servants, and she is used to assuming a superior role when talking to a black person. It is the way things are done in this country. But here on the farm she is the newcomer.

"Why do you have to go?"

"Sofia. She lives in Rooifontein. She is sick. She has a small child, and no husband. I must help her."

"Rooifontein? That's some distance away, isn't it? How long do you need to be away?"

"Only two days, Missus." Grace holds up two fingers. "Two days, only."

"Yes, I can count, Grace. But who is to prepare the meals while you are gone? Who will do the kitchen work?"

"My girl Tembi can do the work. She knows how."

Märit shrugs. There is no point in objecting. If workers want to go they will often just disappear, and give you some excuse days later when they return. A sick relative, a family member arrested for not carrying the proper identification papers—always something.

"I suppose we can manage. But only two days, mind."

"Yes, Missus. Thank you, Missus." Grace bobs her head gratefully and backs towards the door.

Märit feels a sudden pang of guilt, aware of the coldness in her manner, aware that even though this woman works in the house every day, Märit knows so little of her. For a moment she cannot quite remember the daughter's face or even if she has met her.

"How old is your girl now, Grace?"

"Eighteen years, Missus."

Not that much younger than Märit herself. "And how is she getting on?" Märit asks, curious now. "What does she do here on the farm?"

"Tembi is working in the dairy, Missus. She is a good girl. A very clever girl." The lines around her eyes wrinkle in a smile.

"Does she have any schooling?"

"Oh yes, Missus. Before we came to this place Tembi was learning many things in the school. And there is a school here, on Sundays. She is very clever now. She is clever in everything. One day she can be a teacher, or even a nurse in the city."

"Well, perhaps. The city is not always the best place for a country girl. And her father, what does he do here on the farm?" How little she knows of their lives, Märit realizes. How invisible they can be. Even now, after three months, she has asked almost nothing about Grace's life. But she is still a stranger here herself, still unsure. She wonders if she can ask Grace to sit down, to drink a cup of tea with her. But that sort of thing is not done. It would break all the rules.

"My husband is in Johannesburg, Missus. He is working in the gold mines."

"Oh, I see. But you prefer to be here?"

Grace shakes her head. "There is no place for families on the mines. The men live in hostels on the mines."

"But you see him, don't you?"

"The men have annual leave, Missus. So that they can visit their families. We are not traveling to Johannesburg."

"Well," Märit says, drawing back from any further intimacy, from any further knowledge. This is not the time or place to discuss the ways of this country. "Of course you can go to see your cousin, Grace. But only two days, mind."

"Yes, Missus." The relief shows on her face. "Thank you, Missus." She bows her head and moves to the door.

"Oh, Grace?"

"Yes, Missus?" Grace says, turning in the doorway.

Märit points. "Don't forget the tea tray."

"No, Missus," Grace says humbly, bowing her head. "Sorry, Missus."

3

BEHIND THE FARMHOUSE, behind the screen of trees, eucalyptus and a few mulberries, is the kraal where the workers' *rondavels* are situated—circular huts of mud and wattle, with tightly thatched roofs of straw and whitewashed walls—and behind the kraal is the small area of vegetable gardens for the workers—spinach, tomatoes, carrots—and beyond this is the veldt, grasses and shrubs and a few *doringbooms*—thorn trees—and beyond the veldt are the *kloofs* and koppies—the gullies and hills. The orchards and the fields and the river lie in the opposite direction, where the land is fertile. But here are gullies and hills and thorn trees. Here is the koppie called Duiwelskop. It is here that Tembi brings her seeds.

Her dress is a simple cotton garment, blue, patterned with small white flowers, fastened down the front except for the upper two buttons, which are undone because she is hot, and she is alone and there is nobody to look upon her full breasts. Her head is bare, she does not wear a *doek*, as her mother does, for she does not work in the house, or go to town, and so a head scarf is not necessary. Her feet are bare, dusty with dried mud, the soles hard.

It is here Tembi comes, to the hidden side of Duiwelskop, cradling her tin can with its precious cargo of seeds, moist and cool and soft now from soaking in the water. The smooth brow of her oval-shaped face is furrowed with concentration. It is here she will plant the seeds, in this unfrequented place, away from the house and the kraal. Here she will make her garden.

At the foot of the koppie, in the shelter of the rocks, Tembi clears a space. With a hoe taken from the toolshed she slices away the tussocks of tough grass, then with a garden fork she digs into the soil, turning over the clods of earth and breaking them up. Dropping to her knees she uses a trowel to break the soil up further, removing any pebbles and bits of root. Finally, she sifts the soil through her long, slim fingers, meticulously picking out every twig, every hint of weed, every bit of hard stone.

Earlier, she has pilfered a few handfuls of potash and bonemeal from the supply shed, and added some coffee grounds and crushed eggshells. Using her bare hands she works this mixture into the soil, squeezing, sifting, combing, and caressing. Tenderly she does this, for this is her patch of earth now, her garden, her place on the farm. This small piece of the land, measuring not more than a couple of feet in either direction, is hers now.

Tembi makes a trip to the washhouse tap, and returns with a red plastic bucket of water, careful lest she is seen, careful lest she spill a drop, for water will be precious here. She has chosen the place so that the warm morning sun can fall directly on the plot of earth, and in the heat of the afternoon the rocks will cast a cooling shade.

In the gullies beyond the koppie Tembi breaks branches from the *doringboom* trees and builds a barrier around her patch of earth, long sharp thorns to keep out small animals, such as the *duikers* that roam the hills and might wander here in search of tender green shoots. She carries stones and small rocks to build a low wall, artfully placing them to mimic the natural arrangement of the koppie's rocks and boulders. Only a careful inspection would reveal that a garden exists here. But who would care to look? The place is safe.

Her arms are nicked with scratches from the thorns, the muscles in her back are weary, her fingernails are ragged. But her garden is built.

Now she must plant the seeds.

Tembi pokes a hole into the soil with her forefinger, gently, one, two, three, four, five times, each small depression to the same depth, just past the second knuckle of her finger. Then a small scoop of water with her palm to pour into each hole. The seeds are cool and moist and softened from lying in the dampness of the tin can. A pale white seed into each dark receptacle. Then the soil is brushed gently over the seeds, and smoothed, and patted down softly. In each spot where a seed is hidden Tembi places a single tiny pebble. She scoops water again with her palm and wets the earth, and the aroma of the dampened soil rises to her nostrils, like the smell of the countryside that wafts across the fields in the summer when the afternoon rains have fallen and the land is wet and fragrant. The smell of life to come. But today only here, in this place, this hidden place.

She sits back on her haunches. She is alone. There is only the koppie and the empty countryside and the blue sky. Her heart is beating, with pleasure, with her secret knowledge, with anticipation. This now is her own acre of the world, her garden, her farm, her country. Her secret. Here she will grow that which does not as yet grow. From here the sweetness will come. A gift.

4

THERE USED TO BE another place. Not this place, but before this place. Before the Relocation. Grace lived there and Tembi lived there and her father, Elias, lived there. It was the place of their family and the place of their people.

The hills were grass-covered, rich with green grass fed from the streams that ran down the *kloofs* and rolled into the distant valley. The cattle were well fed on the rich green grass, and fat. The maize plants grew tall and the cobs were thick and abundant.

In the mornings a mist covered the hills, and in the afternoons, after rain, a mist covered the hills, and in between the sun was bright on the hills and the birds sang. The fields were fertile, the water was sweet, and in the valley the people were happy.

The name of the place was Ezulwini, The Valley of Heaven.

On a day like any other day, at the end of the summer, a car drove along the winding track through the hills and up to the place called Ezulwini. Because this was a rare occurrence, and because the car was seen for many miles and by many people before it finally reached the village, a large group of onlookers had gathered to greet the unexpected visitor. Because of this, the news that the visitor brought that day fell on many ears all at once.

Two men emerged from the car, one black man wearing a much-worn dark suit and a tie, and one white man, who wore sunglasses and did not take them off.

The village headman came forward, greetings were made, hospitality was offered, food and drink, but the white man shook his head and said, No, there was no time. And so the other man drew a sheet of paper from his pocket and began to read what was written there.

The government had declared that this land was no longer the land of the people who lived there. Another place had been declared their land and all who lived here must now go and live there in that other place.

The headman said he did not understand this declaration. This land was the land of the people and had always been so, and he did not understand what this declaration meant. No doubt it was a mistake on the part of the government.

The man in the suit looked at the man in sunglasses, who obviously understood the language being spoken, because he said, "No mistake," and then added in Afrikaans, *"Maak hulle verstaan."* Make them understand.

So the schoolteacher was fetched, a man who knew something of life in the cities, and he read the paper for himself, and then read it aloud to the village headman, and said, "The government is telling us to leave this place and make our homes in another place."

The village headman shook his head again and said, "I do not understand this government. Such a thing is not possible."

And now the white man in the sunglasses, who had been leaning against his car with his arms folded, became impatient with all this discussion and said to his assistant, "Give him the paper." He turned to the headman and instructed, "Two weeks. You have two weeks to get ready."

The visitors climbed back into their car and drove the long winding track that led through the hills, and the small boys ran after the car laughing in the dust while the village elders gathered around the paper to examine it, as if by studying it further they would understand how their land and their home could be declared not their land and not their home. But they could not understand the reasons, which were formulated by ideologues in the distant cities and on the fertile farms, men and women who had decided that it was the will of God that the races must live separately and that the white race was ordained to remain superior.

After two weeks had passed, the trucks came, and the people were required to place all their belongings on the trucks, then to climb aboard themselves. Their cattle and their goats and their furniture and their tools were also placed on the trucks. A detachment of policemen stood by to ensure that this loading was orderly.

The trucks drove down the long winding track that led through the hills of Ezulwini, The Valley of Heaven, and this time there were no small boys to run laughing after the vehicles. On the following day two bull-dozers were brought up to the empty village, and the huts were knocked down and flattened by the bulldozers and the debris spread across the fields so that the place entered the silence of the hills and lost its name. In other places along the frontier of the country, other villages were being relocated, lives uprooted, new places created while the old places were exiled into silence. It was the command of the government.

The new place had no name, because no one had ever lived there. The government erected huts and installed a water outlet, and then the trucks departed.

In the new place where Tembi came with her mother and father, the soil was hard against the plows and yielded little in the way of crops. The seeds that the government had provided were weak in their growth. The cattle grew thin. During that first winter many of the villagers became ill with influenza. Because the harvest was poor, because the soil was hard, because the seed was weak, some of the young men left the village and made the journey into the city where there was work in the gold mines and the factories. But the money they sent back to their parents and their families from the mines was not enough, and soon other men left for the city. Tembi's father, Elias, was among the men who went to dig the gold out of the mines. The soil remained hard, the seed poor. Then some of the women left the village and went to the towns and the cities to find jobs as house servants, as maids and cooks and washers of laundry.

By the time of the second winter the population of the village consisted of mostly the young and the old—children and their grandparents. In the winter of that year Tembi became ill with influenza and spent long hours huddled in her hut, wrapped in a blanket next to the kerosene stove. Her father sent money for medicine but it was never enough. The inhabitants of the village began to drift from this place without a name, to find work on farms and factories elsewhere. If there was a name for this place it was only Sorrow.

When the winter ended, Tembi's mother heard about a job as a cook on a farm in another district. She asked the schoolteacher to write a letter of recommendation, and she made the long journey to the farm to apply in person.

The Missus at the farm, an old Afrikaner woman who lived only with her husband, took a liking to Grace and said she could have the job and come and cook in the farmhouse and live in the kraal. So Grace left the village, and took Tembi to the farm. Not many months later, the old couple decided to leave the farm because of the Missus's ill health. Their son drove up in his car from the city and walked around the farm, writing down in a book the quantity of cattle, the yield of the maize, the number of workers. He stayed only two days before leaving. The farm was put up for sale.

Those who worked on the farm, who lived in the huts of the kraal, who tended the cattle and tilled the fields and cooked the food, waited to see what would become of their lives, for everything depended on who would own the farm.

The farm was sold to a young man from the city, who came with his young bride. One of the first things he did was change the name of the farm from Duiwelskop to Kudufontein. He organized the men to repair the fences, to whitewash the outside walls of the *rondavels* in the kraal. A contractor from Klipspring came to build a washhouse of cement blocks and install a water tap in the kraal where there had been none before. The young man bought and sold cattle, so that the herd was healthy, and he replanted some of the fields. For three months the farm was a flurry of activity and change.

Now Grace works in the farmhouse, cooking and cleaning. Tembi works in the dairy with the other girls, where they milk the cows and make the butter and the cream.

Tembi has only seen her father once in the past year, when he came back from the mines for two weeks on his annual leave. He sends letters, he sends money, sometimes a small gift. In his letters to Grace he asks her to save as much money as she can, as he will do too, so that one day he can leave the mines, so that one day he too can buy a plot of land for his family, so that he can plant the seeds and till the soil.

For Tembi, life has been broken apart. The people she knew before the Relocation are scattered. Ezulwini is no more. She is a stranger here.

5

Märit appears at the kitchen door, not entering, but hanging back as if she must ask permission from Grace before coming in. The kitchen is Grace's domain. Just as Grace is uncomfortable in the rest of the house, so Märit feels herself to be a trespasser here. She has tried to be friendlier with Grace, the way she was with Miriam, the woman who worked in the house when Märit was a girl. But maybe the laws of apartheid are more rigid here in the countryside, for Grace maintains a dignified distance and sometimes seems puzzled by Märit's attempts to blur the lines between mistress and servant.

Grace looks up from where she is slicing carrots at the table and directs a quizzical glance at the pale face of the woman standing in the doorway. She rises, wiping her hands on the front of her apron.

"Missus?"

"Is there any hot water left in the kettle, Grace? I want to take a flask of tea to my husband . . . to Baas Ben . . ."

"Yes, Missus, I can make it."

"No, no, you carry on with what you are doing. I'll do it." She brushes the hair from her face and moves to the sink.

Grace sits down again and continues cutting the carrots while Märit spoons some tea into the pot and adds hot water, and as the tea steeps she fetches a handful of biscuits from the tin in the pantry. When the tea is ready Märit pours it into a Thermos flask with some milk and a spoonful of sugar. The biscuits she wraps in a sheet of waxed paper before placing them in the pocket of her dress.

Outside the house the landscape seems cloaked in stillness. It is always this way, even when the tractor is plowing, and the cattle are lowing at milking time, and the voices of the farm hands are calling. The sky and the distance make all sounds small and insignificant. She stands on the veranda, feeling herself shrink from the landscape, as if the silence will absorb her as well. When she descends the steps and walks across the gravel driveway, it seems she floats above the earth, not a part of it, her passage hardly disturbing a blade of grass.

She is wearing a light cardigan over her dress, for it was cool in the house, and already the material prickles against her arms as she steps into the heat.

Märit walks down and across the rock garden and past the windmill, through the orchard where the new fruit is still small and green and hard on the branches, until she reaches the edge of the field where Ben intends to plant his almond seedlings.

Ben comes from the industrial north of England, and even as a boy in that country he had looked with longing on the fields, the neat rows of crops, the cattle peaceful in the pastures. Even as a boy he wanted to be a farmer. Not an insurance salesman like his father, selling life policies to factory workers. He has told Märit of a childhood memory of almond trees in blossom, the white flowers swaying in the breeze like the white foam that blows across the waves of the ocean. When Märit first met Ben, before he had this farm, he talked often of this dream of his, for it struck some deep chord in his soul, even though he was a child, and the memory has beckoned to him all his life.

Now he has his farm, where he can plant his almond trees. Märit has no dream of her own for the farm, but she responds to this longing in him, although it unsettles her a bit too, for she likes to think of him as an uncomplicated man, a steady, plain man, without talk of longings and souls. This talk of yearning unsettles her because she relies on Ben to be strong and plain and understandable, the rock against which she can secure her own vague, troubling sense of displacement and anxiety.

As she crosses the plowed soil she stumbles a bit on the hard clods of earth, realizing that she ought to have changed her shoes. But she forgets these simple things often. There seems to be a separation between the house and the countryside around it that she must constantly cross, yet when she crosses that border she does not know how to be, where to go, what to do. She tries to think of herself as a farmer, as a farmer's wife, but the truth is that only in the house can she find some purpose. The land seems to be in possession of the workers and there is no place for her to function.

It's different for Ben. When his father died at fifty from a heart attack, sitting in his car outside a small suburban house in Manchester, Ben realized he could leave. His mother had passed away two years earlier, and now he has no further connection to the drab streets of his childhood. He came to this country because he heard that there was land available, that there were farms to purchase, that the government wanted farmers, especially on the border. Grants were available and the land was cheap and fertile.

This is Ben's dream. To be a farmer. He has come to this country as an immigrant, has learned the languages, has learned the climate and the geography and the history. He has even changed the spelling of his name from Lawrence to Laurens, to an Afrikaans spelling, not so much to disguise his origins—his accent will always testify to that—but as a commitment to a new life, as an accommodation to the place where he intends to live.

It's different for Ben; he is the Baas, they accept him, they rely on him, they defer to him. Ben wants to be here, he wants to farm, to work on the land. And she is here because of Ben, for Ben.

She sees the figures on the far side of the field, and recognizes her husband from the hat that he habitually wears outside. The men are stringing long strands of shiny wire between the posts that were dug into the ground on the previous two days. Fences are a fact of life here: to keep what is yours inside, to keep those who desire what is yours outside. This is a land of separations—between veldt and cultivated, between wild and domestic, between black and white.

Ben glances over as she approaches and straightens up, handing his oversized pliers to one of the workers. He smiles at her. The work stops, the other three men turning to watch her approach. Ben steps forward, a tall man, his face already sun-darkened around his mustache, laugh lines etched at the corners of his eyes, for he is a man who smiles often.

"I thought you might be thirsty. I've brought you some tea." She offers the Thermos to Ben, not looking at the other men.

"Wonderful. You are a godsend, darling." He kisses her, the stubble on his chin brushing her cheek, and she smells the soil of the country and the hot air and his perspiration and his tobacco. The smell of him, which she knows now.

He turns and says to the men, "We'll take a rest now." They sink to their haunches, setting their tools aside. One of them produces a little bag of tobacco and begins to roll a cigarette.

"Good afternoon," Märit says to them.

"Missus." They smile, they nod their heads. She does not know their names, and there is nothing she can think of to say to them.

"What have you been doing with yourself?" Ben asks.

"Accounts. Talking to Grace. Nothing much, really." She does not say that she is lonely. "Grace wants a few days off to visit a sick cousin."

"Does she? Well, that's good. That's fine. We can fend for ourselves, can't we?"

"Of course. Grace has a daughter, Tembi, who will come in to help."

"Good. Excellent." He unscrews the cap of the Thermos and pours some tea into it. "Want some?"

"No, it's for you." She watches him drink, the way his Adam's apple moves as he swallows, a glint of perspiration on his neck where it disappears into his shirt. She wants to put her hand there, to feel the pulse of his energy. She looks at the men, then away.

"I brought some biscuits too. Are you hungry?"

"Famished." Ben unwraps the waxed paper, then hesitates and looks over at the men, who are sitting on the ground regarding Märit with mild curiosity. "I'll have the tea first," he says, and puts the biscuits in a pocket.

"Sorry, I didn't think to bring enough for them too."

"Oh, they'll be all right."

She knows he is embarrassed to eat the biscuits in front of the men. And she knows that he will share the biscuits with them when she leaves.

"How is the work going here?" Märit asks.

His face lights up. "Fine, fine. But there won't be enough wire to enclose the whole field. I'll have to go into Klipspring and get some more."

"Today?" Today, she hopes—now—so that she can ride with him into the town, so that she can speak to people, so that she can sit on the terrace of the Retief Hotel and drink something sweet and cool, with ice in the glass.

"No, there's no hurry. I'm waiting for that shipment of seedlings to come in on the train. Tomorrow."

"Oh."

Ben replaces the cap of the Thermos and screws the cover back on. He glances over at the men waiting patiently. Märit senses that he wants to get back to work. He is always eager to get back to work; his energy for the farm is boundless.

"Well," Märit says. "I'll see you at supper."

"Yes, darling. I'll see you then." He smiles and touches her arm lightly. "What will you do now?"

"I'm going to take a walk." She gestures vaguely at the countryside around them.

Ben kisses her again, on the cheek this time, and squeezes her hand.

As if this is their signal to resume work, the men rise to their feet and nod to her as she passes. She walks on, away from the house. And when she looks back she sees Ben handing out the biscuits to his helpers. Märit envies the men, because they have their work, because they have their place on this farm, but most of all because they have his company.

She waves, but Ben does not see her.

THE SILENCE RETURNS. Almost before Märit is out of the men's sight, the sounds fade behind her—the sound of their voices, the sound of their tools, the sound of Ben's voice—and then she hears only the birds and she is alone.

This is wild country. The farms are miles apart, the towns even farther. She cannot place herself exactly, not geographically, not spiritually. This is not like the place where she grew up, where the gardens that lined the suburban streets were lush from the sprinklers that hissed their mist every morning and evening. Not like the city, where nature took the form of manicured parks behind wrought-iron fences, where the signs on the gates read "Whites Only." Not like the stretch of coast where she went with her parents on a holiday, where sugarcane plantations grew right up to the railway line that separated the strip of beach and hotels from the rest of the country. Not like the farm where she went one summer when she was sixteen to stay with a school friend, in the wine country, just outside the city, where mimosa grew abundant and there was a swimming pool.

This is a wild country with a history that Märit does not understand—a contested history, of which she has only a vague understanding. In the schools she attended, history begins with the arrival of a ship at the Cape, when a white man claims the country. Before that it is a history of other people, whose story is considered unimportant. They have no history. She knows that her education has been stilted, that her thinking is conventional, that her life is unremarkable. She knows all these things, but the knowledge does not make it any easier to stand here under the weight of the silence.

This is a wild country—perhaps it belongs only to the animals.

There are animals in the valleys and the forests and on the veldt. She has not seen them for she does not venture into those places, but she has heard the stories, told by the farmers who come to visit Ben, who sit in the living room with coffee and rusks and sometimes a glass of apple brandy. Stories of the leopard that took a child from a village in the middle of the night, of elephants drunk on marula berries rampaging through fields of maize, of the baboons that invaded a house when the owners were absent and pillaged the kitchen and left excrement on the table.

Märit talks to Koos van Staden, the nearest neighbor, about animals, because she wants to see them; like a tourist from the city she wants to see wild animals. This is the wild country around here and she wants to see the wild animals and the real Africa.

"No, Mevrou," van Staden says, laughing in a good-natured way at her innocence and naïveté, "you won't see much around here anymore. This is all farming country now, the wild things have been driven away into hiding. They are out there, and they see us, but we don't see them.

"But," he says, "sometimes a troop of baboons will come down into the mealie fields, usually if there is a drought. They like the mealies." He laughs again and says, "I remember when I was a kid and my father still ran the farm—in those days we had quite a problem with the baboons. There was a troop of them that lived in the hills and they would wait until just before we harvested the mealies. I don't know how they knew, but they would come down out of the hills in the early morning and ruin the whole field. It happened regularly.

"They are very clever animals," he continues, "but they can sometimes be damn stupid. Now, what your baboon does when he gets to the mealie field is pick a couple of cobs and stick them under his arm, but then instead of taking those off with him to eat somewhere he picks a few more, and of course he doesn't have any way to carry them, except to tuck them under his arm, which he does. And he goes through the whole row of mealies doing this, so that by the time he reaches the end, he still has only two or three cobs under his arm. And in his wake are all your mealies lying on the ground. You can imagine what happens when a troop of twenty of them get into the fields.

"My old man used to go up into the hills with his rifle and spend the whole day up there. I would hear the shots, but when he came back he would only shake his head. A baboon is clever that way—he knows what a gun is, he knows when you are after him, and he hides.

"But we finally got rid of those baboons. Not with guns or fences or anything like that. One of the old black workers on the farm told us what we should do. So, we built a kind of trap and put some nice food in there, food from the table, and early one morning we heard a terrible noise and when we ran out there was a baboon in the trap. Very angry too. He'd eaten the food, of course, but now he wanted to leave and he was screaming his head off. And there, just on the other side of the fence, we saw his brothers and sisters shouting to him. They have their own language, you know, and they look out for each other, just like people.

"Well, my father wasn't going to let him go, not just yet. First he sent me to get the can of paint that we had set aside, a can of whitewash, the same thing you use to whitewash the walls. We couldn't use brushes on that baboon in the trap, he was much too angry, and you know they have teeth that can rip your arm to the bone. No, we just threw the paint over him. When he was covered in white paint we opened the trap and stood back.

"He was out of there like a shot, charging across the veldt to his friends. As soon as they saw him they all fell silent. And then they started to run. The closer he got, the faster they ran. And he was screaming at them to wait for him, but they just ran from this strange white baboon. They'd never seen anything like it before, so they ran away.

"We heard him up there in the hills, screaming for them to come back, and his voice growing fainter, but those other baboons didn't want anything to do with him. I believe they thought he was a ghost. A white baboon ghost."

These are stories meant to tease her, to frighten her the way one frightens a child, to make her admire the brave farmers.

Once, in the deep hours of the night, soon after she had come to the farm, Märit sat up in bed awakened by the whining howl of a hyena, half laughter, half mad keening. She wanted to reach out to shake Ben awake too, and tell him that a wild animal was on the farm, but the howl of the hyena, the madness and lust in the eerie laughter, held her transfixed where she sat clutching the pillow, listening to a sound that seemed to come from inside her own throat. Her neighbors, the farmers, have no sentimental notions about the animals. They are practical men and women, intent on growing their crops, on taming the wild, on being successful farmers. There are guns to keep the animals away. Their guns are a solution. And the animals are hidden now, in the wild country.

Märit walks on, into the silence, where the shadow of the koppie that is called Devil's Head throws a long shape across the ground at her feet. With the farm behind her and the wild country all around she feels like a trespasser, with a trespasser's sense of apprehension—as if this land is not hers, as if she has no right to be here.

But is this land not hers to walk? She owns it, does she not? Her money and Ben's has paid for her right to walk here. It is hers to walk.

She stops and looks back the way she has come. There is nobody in sight. There is always someone when she walks, always someone busy with some task, and if she stops to watch she feels herself an interloper. There is always someone there, wherever you go, in the whole country. So many strangers. They are always watching you, gauging your purpose, your intent towards them. And they are wary of you, not unfriendly, but always deferential, unforthcoming. Because to be in their presence means you want something—information, labor, identification papers. Her attempts at small talk are always awkward, unsuccessful, making the workers nervous as they apprehend her own nervousness. Conversation ceases when she appears, and only resumes with nervous laughter when she has gone on her way. She never knows what to say. Ben can talk to them—he can talk about work, about the farm—and he can work with them so that they accept him, if not as one of them, at least as a man. He has an easy rapport, and speaks their language, albeit imperfectly, but they laugh good-naturedly at his mistakes and his jokes. But she cannot talk to them. Nor does she ever visit the kraal, where the women are. It is too intimate there, too different from the way she herself lives. Their lives are hidden. And she is hidden from them.

She has never really known one of them as a friend, only as a servant.

They are not natural in her presence. Because of the differences. Because the color of their skin is different from hers. Everything is based on that distinction. She brings a discord into their lives. She is always a stranger. Color is the marker—here on this farm, in this country, across this whole continent.

Only in the house is she at home, between the walls. Only there. She might own the farm and all the land, but only in the farmhouse is she at home. Sometimes not even there.

The realization comes to Märit that she fears them. She is uneasy in their presence, because they are so many. In the city you don't notice it so much, but out here it is she who is different, she who is the stranger.

And do they fear her? They give her respect and deference, and they probably fear her too. Because she owns the land, because she can do what she likes, even order them off the land, take away their homes if it came to that. She can burn the crops or let them rot in the fields. She can sell or not sell. She has authority over their residence permits and their livelihood. She can come and go. They cannot.

But even so, even so.

Märit clambers over some rocks at the base of the koppie, and comes upon what looks like a little garden. Someone has closed off a piece of the land, here in this barren place, and tilled the soil and built a barrier of rocks and thorn scrub. Even here, she thinks, is the attempt to fence off, to enclose, to possess. But the effort is pathetic, like some child's attempt to mimic a garden.

She bends down to touch the soil and a small green lizard darts away into a crevice. Märit recoils. Even here some creature watches you, and waits for you to leave. The clods of dark soil crumble and trickle through her fingers. And who owns this? she asks herself. Me? Ben? The child who built this garden? The lizard that watches from the shadowed crevice? Or none of us?

6

SHE WALKS ON AWAY from the koppie, into the long yellow grass, and the coarse texture of the grass brushes across her bare legs. She stops, looking down at her pale skin, wary of snakes, because she is only wearing sandals that leave her ankles and calves exposed. Always something to fear, to watch out for.

The terror of snakes has haunted her from childhood, ever since that time when her father took her to the Snake Park in Durban. Until then, Märit had never seen a snake up close, but she had an instinctive revulsion to them. When her father asked Märit and her mother that day if they wanted to go to the Snake Park, her mother shook her head adamantly and said, "I won't be going near any snakes, thank you very much."

"And you, Märit?" her father asked.

"Yes, I'll come, Daddy," she said. Even though she was afraid. But she wanted to show her father that she trusted him, that she was brave.

Märit remembers the name of the place, the FitzSimons Snake Park, on Lower Marine Parade, the long road that runs along the beach, and how when she got out of the car, her hands were damp and her armpits wet from the humidity and from her nervousness. She could smell the sea air and hear the booming of the waves on the beach not far off. She remembers that she asked her father as they stood in the parking lot, "Maybe we should go to the beach instead and collect some shells for Mommy?"

Her father raised his eyebrows at her, and she said quickly, "After we look at the snakes." She wanted to please him, to be brave for him.

The Snake Park was more like a zoo, with tortoises, a wire enclosure where bats hung in a tree, a pool where an old crocodile floated in the murky water. There were no snakes. Then Märit's father said to her, "Come, we can go and see them milking a snake."

"Milking?" She imagined a snake with teats, like a sow, with a row of nipples along its underside.

"It's just an expression. They take the venom from the snake and use it to make a serum, so that if you get bitten, they can inject some serum into your blood and you won't die."

Her father took her hand and led her to an enclosure, a patch of grass surrounded by a narrow ditch of water, where two men stood on either side of a large wooden box. One of the men had in his hand a long pole with a sort of clamp on the end. His assistant opened the box and the man reached in with the pole. After a moment he withdrew the pole and a long black wriggling snake was held in the clamp.

"That's a mamba," her father whispered. "Very poisonous."

What if it gets loose? she thought. "Snakes can swim, can't they?" she whispered. What if it got loose and came towards the crowd and swam across the moat?

Now the man holding the pole handed it over to his assistant. He drew a small glass jar from his pocket and moved towards the wriggling snake held in the clamp on the end of the pole.

"He's going to put the jar by the snake's mouth and make it bite," her father said. "The venom will go into the jar."

The man reached out and grasped the snake behind the head, and the assistant released the clamp. The long writhing black body coiled back and forth. Märit thought she could hear an angry hissing noise, like air escaping from a punctured tire. The fangs were exposed, protruding from the snake's mouth, and they fastened onto the lip of the glass jar.

But then something went wrong. A sudden coiling, whipping motion from the snake, and the man lost his grasp on the jar, which fell to the grass. Märit saw the fangs sink into the man's hand, into the fleshy part just behind the thumb.

He screamed in pain and flailed his hand in the air, with the long black snake hanging there, fangs embedded in his flesh.

Märit screamed too, then pulled away from her father and ran. She ran along a graveled path, not wanting to be trapped in this place, with the snake loose, and she imagined the snake loose now, swimming across the ditch, into the crowd, coming for her. There was a small building just ahead, and she dashed for it. She would be safe inside and there would be someone to help her, someone to catch and kill the snake.

She blundered into a room with a dimly lit interior. There was a faint animal smell in the air. A movement flickered ahead and Märit jerked back, turning to flee. Her motion brought her full tilt into a thick sheet of glass. The impact stunned her, exploding her vision in a flash of bursting light. As she put her hand to her forehead, rubbing the bump that was already forming, she saw the snake.

Behind the glass, in the dim room with its murky yellow light, a cobra had reared up, the whole upper body swaying back and forth, the wide hooded head swollen out like a fan. And at the top of the engorged hood the small reptilian face was watching her with black eyes that were almost on a level with hers.

Märit could not move—her body trembled but she could not move. The sinuous body of the snake swayed slowly from side to side, and she followed it with her eyes, and the other black eyes held hers. The swaying stopped abruptly, the hood seemed to enlarge, to become even more engorged; the mouth opened wide, revealing the pink interior and the stretched muscles of the jaws and the yellow fangs. In a motion that was too fast for her to register, the snake struck.

The reptilian head banged against the glass, once, twice, towards her face, and from the pink mouth a whitish liquid spurted out onto the glass window. The swaying head of the snake shuddered, and it reared and spat again, the thick liquid spattering onto the glass.

Märit screamed and screamed. She was screaming when her father found her, and she was still screaming when he lifted her in his arms and hurried out to the car with her.

She remembers the long walk on the beach afterwards, her father carrying her in his arms, and the cool salty wind off the ocean, and an ice-cream cone, and then a bottle of cream soda that she held in both hands so long that the liquid lost its fizz and chill until it had the flavour of warm syrup.

But afterwards, for a long time afterwards, her parents had to check her bedroom before she would enter the room to sleep, and she would make sure her father looked under the bed and beneath the pillow and behind the dresser before she would go to bed.

Even now Märit does not like to go barefoot, even in the house, especially at night, and she is always wary when she walks in the long grass.

7

MÄRIT ARRIVES at a fence, the barbed wire that marks the border of the farm, the limits of what she owns, the territory where she may walk without being a stranger. A fence to keep others out, and to keep her in. A frontier. She paces along the fence, glancing through the strands of wire to the other side. If she crosses and continues walking, how long before she reaches another country, the real frontier, where there are rumors of war? She will not be welcome there. If she crosses that country and goes to the next she will not be welcome there. Or in the country beyond that. In all the miles and acres of the whole continent it is only here, on this side of the fence, behind the wire, that she belongs.

Märit searches on the ground for a sturdy stick, then uses it to separate two strands of wire, the way she has seen Ben do, making a space wide enough for her to step through. Her thick chestnut hair falls across her face and she pauses a moment to gather it back, fastening the tresses into a rough bun with an elastic from her pocket.

The trees are the same here, the soil, the sky, the air all the same as on the other side of the wire. But she is different. A trespasser. She walks farther in, until the fence is no longer in sight. When she reaches a conical mound of dried mud, a termite mound in the shade, she sits down and removes her cardigan, glad to feel the air on her bare arms. Silence closes in on her. But then she picks out the sounds of birds, the chattering of finches, the soft call of a dove, then the flash of tawny brown and white as a hoopoe sails through the branches of an acacia, a wriggling grub in its long beak.

In this unknown country, this wild place, she is nobody, she is unknown. She is not Märit, not Mevrou Laurens, not the farmer's wife, not the new bride, not the girl who lost her parents, not the Missus, not the one who walks and is watched. Here there is nobody to see her. She is nobody. Here is a place to forget and be forgotten.

She sees the shrubs and trees and the long grass, but her mind takes no notice of what is there as her consciousness drifts into a state of half awareness, as she forgets herself and her trespasses. Her eyelids droop like those of a cat, the world dissolves in a haze of light. She is free of the burden of her self. She is alone. She is nobody.

Time has no substance when she lapses into these states. Time stops, becomes nonexistent, as if she steps out of the flow. She is aware, but her usual consciousness is suspended. It is not a state that could be characterized as happiness, yet she is happy, after a fashion.

A rustle sounds in the trees nearby, the movement of leaves, the sharp snap of a twig breaking—the motion of another presence on the earth. Märit rises quickly to her feet. She hears the careful tread of footsteps, stealthy, then silence. The birds have ceased their chattering.

All the fear rushes back, all the awareness. She is not alone, she is watched. Her eyes move across the screen of brush, peering into the dappled green and brown. Nothing. Nobody. Her heart flutters rapidly in her chest.

Nobody, yet she is watched. She feels it in the silence and the suspension that fills the air. Her ears strain to catch the slightest sound, the slightest movement. And it comes again, the furtive footsteps.

"Who is it?" she calls.

The movement stops. She feels herself watched, seen by the unseen.

She decides to run. All her muscles tense for flight.

In that moment as she poises to flee, a face peers at her from among the leaves. Dark eyes meet hers and hold her transfixed.

The footsteps shuffle again and the face pushes forward through the leaves. A long muzzle, a white chevron down the bridge of the nose, large almond-shaped eyes.

The animal steps into the clearing. A kudu, jaws slowly chewing, shell-like ears swiveled in her direction, brown eyes focused upon Märit. A long sigh of relief shudders through her chest as she breathes again.

The fear drains from Märit, flowing away like water, and she is left trembling and grateful. Only a buck, only an animal. Only a kudu, studying her with cow-like eyes. The antelope steps into the clearing delicately, dainty for an animal of that size, for it is almost as big as a horse. Above the mild brown eyes, and the shell-like ears turned in her direction, are corkscrew horns, heraldic, regal, like a royal headdress. On the tan hide, thin white vertical stripes are like further emblems of royalty. A bearded fringe dangles below the animal's chin, brushing its neck.

Recovering from her fright, Märit is left grateful and trembling, seized for a moment with an almost overwhelming desire to embrace the kudu. Could it be the very same kudu she saw that first day she came to the farm with Ben, when they disturbed one as it was drinking at the river? Kudu-fontein, the name of this farm, given for the presence of this animal.

Märit remembers a picture she saw as a girl, in a book of paintings, of a walled garden and a lady in white kneeling before a white unicorn that had the same expression on its face as this kudu. The desire to embrace the animal, to touch it, comes upon her again.

Märit feels herself in the presence of some wise and beneficent dignitary, a creature from mythology, something priestly and good. And in this presence she feels herself also to be good and wise and without malice or harm. Slowly she lowers herself to her knees and folds her hands before her chest, in a gesture of prayer, of worship. The kudu dips its head and looks at her, wide black nostrils flaring slightly to take in her scent. She smells the kudu's breath, a scent of warm grass.

She looks up into the creature's eyes and sees no guile, no malice, no fear, only the kudu's knowledge of itself. She sees its soul. And her own soul is tarnished and flawed in comparison, compromised in some manner that she fears will never be purified.

Gently she reaches up to touch the bearded fringe, to stroke the chevron of white across the nose, to be taken up onto that strong back.

She is emptied of doubt, of trespass, of fear.

"I am Märit," she whispers.

The kudu ceases chewing for a moment, then emits a soft pant, like an answer, and again she smells the warm scent of grass, the very breath of the animal.

She stretches her hand forward, wanting just one touch, and she feels the warm breath on the tips of her extended fingers. Then the kudu steps back, and the regal head reaches up, and the wide shell-like ears swivel away. It turns without looking at her and moves back into the trees, unconcerned.

The soft thud of the footsteps fades and the rustling of the leaves fades, and the silence returns.

The tears that come to her eyes are hot and bitter, and filled with great sadness. Some great opportunity has passed. As if the hope of grace has been offered, then withdrawn from her forever. She remains kneeling on the ground, head bowed, hands clasped.

Eventually, Märit rises to her feet, a supplicant whose prayers have remained unacknowledged, and she is chastened and disappointed. She rises and brushes away the dust from her knees and turns again to the way she has come, to the farm, to the fence, to the house where she must live.

As she walks slowly back to the house Märit recalls a story she once was told of a traveler who lived amongst the Bushmen of the desert, those nomadic wanderers who slept under the stars and carried nothing and left nothing behind, moving with the winds of the seasons. The traveler asked them one day, How is it that you never become lost? They had no maps and there were no roads, no signposts, yet the Bushmen moved unerringly to where there was water, and food, moving like the breezes of the desert.

They laughed at the question, for it was strange to them. How can we become lost, they said. The birds know us, the animals know us, the wind knows us. At night the stars see us and they know where we are. So then, how can we become lost?

But nobody knows me, Märit thinks. And I am lost.

8

THE DAY is dark. The hour is early, too early to even be called morning. The sun has not risen, the world is still immersed in the silence of night. Only a single bird in the darkness, calling with a cry like water falling on stone, announces that daylight will come, that this darkness too shall pass.

Grace stands with Tembi next to the gate, where the driveway to the house meets the dust road that winds through the veldt and past the other farms until it eventually meets the paved road to Klipspring. From here Grace will walk to Klipspring, and there she will take a bus to Postberg, and there she will take another bus to Rooifontein, and from there she will walk to visit her sick cousin Sofia in the hospital.

Because it is a long distance to walk to Klipspring, and because the bus to Postberg leaves early in the day from outside the station, she must leave here while the darkness of night still lingers, before the morning light touches the sky.

Grace carries her handbag, the good black one, and a small overnight case. She wears her Sunday coat and hat, her going-to-church clothes. But her feet are bare, her shoes placed neatly in the top of her suitcase. She walks barefoot because it is easier to walk these dusty roads unencumbered by shoes, because she wants her shoes to remain free of dust until she reaches the town limits of Klipspring, where she will put them on, and straighten her hat and brush down her coat and present to the world the image of the respectable, employed woman that she is, not some wanderer come in from the countryside.

Tembi shivers slightly in the predawn chill, standing close to Grace. "Mother, I want to visit Sofia in Rooifontein and see her baby." There is a pleading in her voice, a child's tone that she has not used in many years, the yearning of a child to be taken along on a trip, to participate in the adventure of leaving home.

Grace shakes her head sharply. "You must stay here and work in the farmhouse. I told Missus Märit that you will help her with the cooking and cleaning."

"Why can't Missus Märit clean her own house and cook her own food?"

"Don't talk this way, my daughter. My work is in that house, and now I must go away and you must do that work for me. You must keep my position there for me. If you don't, they will find someone else."

Grace has worries other than what Tembi desires at this moment. She worries about her cousin Sofia, about the small child, about there being no husband, about what happens if Sofia has to stay in the hospital. She worries about the long walk in the darkness, and whether she will miss the bus. She worries about the money she will spend on bus fares and medicines. She wants to hurry now, to be on her way, to allay her anxiety.

But she is also glad to linger here a moment, glad that Tembi has risen with her and walked down to the gate with her, and carried her bag this short distance.

The sand underfoot smells damp from the dew that falls in the night and there is a faint aroma of wood smoke in the air even though it is too early for any cooking fires to have started.

Tembi shivers, shifts Grace's suitcase to her other hand and hunches her shoulders, for she has only pulled on her thin cotton dress before coming out.

Grace looks at her kindly, with the affection of a mother for her daughter. "You should have stayed in bed longer, my *piccanin*. Or at least have put on a pullover." She rubs her hand briskly across her daughter's shoulders. "And why are you so thin? All that porridge I feed you, you should be as plump as a heifer, but you are like a gazelle instead."

"I am strong now, Mother." Tembi says this as a statement of fact, as if there is no question of her being otherwise.

Grace smiles in the darkness. "Yes, you are. You are strong. I know this."

"When will I see my father?" Tembi suddenly says.

"Father visits later in the year. When the mines give him his holidays. You know that, Tembi."

"Why must my father always stay in the mines?" There is still something childish in her tone, the belligerent insistence of a child demanding answers.

"Why? My daughter, you ask me that?" Grace shakes her head. "So that you can have food for your breakfast. So that you have a warm pullover on cold mornings. So that we can pay the schoolteacher for your lessons. So that you can have sandals to wear instead of going with bare feet. That is why."

"But why do we need extra money? Doesn't the Missus pay you enough? You should ask her for more. And my father should work here on the farm. Ask Baas Ben. He has money." All her impatience with her mother's stolid, accepting ways comes out in her complaint.

"Do you blame me, Tembi? Do you blame me for this life?"

The girl scuffs her foot in the sand and shakes her head.

"Come then, daughter, give me my bag. I must go."

She takes the bag and leans forward to place a kiss on Tembi's cool forehead. "Things might be different one day, God willing."

"How will they be different? Is God going to change things for us? Is that what you expect?"

"Hush, child. I won't hear such words from you," Grace answers, stepping across the cattle grate that lies between the road and the driveway. "You must look after everything while I am gone. All right?"

Tembi pouts.

"All right, Tembi?"

Tembi suddenly reaches for her mother's warm hand and holds it to her cheek and presses her lips to the calloused palm.

"Go well, Mother," the girl says.

"Stay safe, my child," comes the reply from the darkness.

* * *

ELSEWHERE IN THE DARKNESS, as the dawn approaches, there is a celebration, or rather the tail end of a celebration. The occasion is the return of two young men who have just the day before come back to the district after completing their two years of national service in the army.

They are local boys who have grown up in this district. Their return has been cause for a party, especially because they were both fortunate enough not to have been sent across the border on one of those quiet little incursions that the army makes—punishing raids against exiles and dissidents who don't adhere to the creed of apartheid—expeditions, unannounced to the public but nevertheless common knowledge, that always result in a death or two and leave many other deaths behind.

A party, for two young men who returned home without being shot at, without having to shoot at anybody, without having to kill anybody. Although they were ready, as they told their friends, and it was too bad they didn't any action, too bad they weren't sent out on a raid. They were ready, and can be at any time they are called. Ready to do what has to be done. But the truth is they are farmers' sons, more suited to cultivation and husbandry than destruction, for all their bravado, and they are glad to be back on the land, to be home.

They drive home now, Carl and Eugene, neighbors, friends since childhood. The party began at the farm of Carl's parents, with swimming, then a *braai*—a barbecue—with beer in a big iron tub filled with ice and all the neighbors from the other farms there to welcome the two young men home. Later the young people go into Klipspring to the Retief Lounge at the hotel and there is more drinking, until the party becomes too rowdy and they are refused service, so they go on to The Roadhouse, just outside of Klipspring, where you can buy a drink after hours and no questions asked, where they close the place down. By then it's just Carl and Eugene who decide to drive to Eugene's house, because he says he has a bottle of brandy there and will cook bacon and eggs as the sun rises.

They pile into the car after a small argument over who is to drive, who is the least tired, but it is Carl's car so he drives. The night is dark once they are away from the lights of Klipspring, but Carl knows the route, he is familiar with these roads that wind across the veldt between the farms.

The headlights sweep across the vegetation and the strange half-light they create is melancholy, but familiar.

Grace hears the sound of the car's engine as she walks along the road in the stillness of the dark and her heart lifts with the knowledge that she is not entirely alone. Perhaps the car will stop for her, she thinks. It is probably a farmer transporting something to Klipspring, to the railway station for the early freight train, and he will stop for her, because the farmers in this district sometimes stop for a person walking on the road, even if you are black, and they let you sit in the back of their trucks—unless you are walking out on the main road where the traffic speeds by too fast to even make out a face and nobody stops because nobody knows who you are.

Grace sets her case down in the dust and listens, unsure in which direction the car is traveling, but just the sound of human life out there lifts her spirit. To be alone in the darkness is to be lost in the world. A brief arc of light flashes across the veldt, then disappears. The vehicle is some distance away, she decides, and she lifts her case and walks on. The sound of the engine comes and goes. She wants it to be traveling in the direction of Klipspring, even if just a little way, for her legs are tired and she is uncomfortable in the darkness, afraid of animals, even though it has been years since so much as a hyena has been sighted in this district. But she does not know this, for this is not her district, and so she is afraid of the darkness.

Her breathing is labored and she holds her breath a moment, so that it will not sound in her ears, so she can listen for the car. The sound of the engine is louder, and Grace thinks she sees the lights again, coming from the direction of the farm, and she is glad because that means the vehicle is heading in the same direction as she is. She turns to wait for it.

In the car that travels alone towards the dawn, Carl's eyes droop for a moment with happy exhaustion. He is happy to be home, away from the war, back in his own country.

Grace sees the bushes at the side of the road light up in sudden detail, every leaf clear and frozen in the white light as if painted by a flash of lightning. The roar of the engine shatters the stillness, and in a moment of disorientation Grace realizes that the car is immediately behind her. As she turns, the left fender hits her on the hip, breaking the bone on impact, and Grace is flung to the side of the road and something else breaks inside her as she falls. A deep pain rips in her chest, a pain that pulls the darkness of night down deep into her body.

"*Fok!* What was that?" Carl grasps the steering wheel in both hands and slams his foot on the brakes as the suddenly swerving vehicle slews towards the bushes. The rear of the car fishtails to right and left in the soft sand, then rights itself before the vehicle comes to a stop.

Carl looks in the rearview mirror and sees only swirling dust in the red glow of the brake lights.

"I think it was an antelope," Eugene says, because out of the corner of his eye he saw a dark shape, a quick leaping shape just as the car bumped.

"You think so? Did we hit it?" Carl gets out and walks around to the front of the car and looks at the hood, which is unmarked, then he walks back a few paces down the road and peers into the darkness and sees nothing. The dust settles.

"Hello?' he calls. " Anybody there?" No sound, no movement. There is only the night.

"Well, it didn't do any damage, whatever it was," Carl says as he gets back in. "It must have been an animal of some kind. Did you see it, Eugene?"

"An impala or something," Eugene says. "What else could it have been?"

"It could have been a person," Carl says, because at the moment of impact he thought he saw a face. He rubs his eyes and looks out into the darkness.

"A person?" Eugene says disbelievingly. "But what would a person be doing out here at this time of the night?"

"Up to no good, probably," Carl says, and chuckles. "All the honest people are in bed by now."

"Except for us," Eugene says, and twists in his seat to look through the rear window. "Maybe you should look again, Carl."

He gets out and walks back along the road a few yards. "Anyone? *Elkeen daar?*" A scuffling in the grass, some small rodent darting away. In the distance the faint barking of a dog.

"Nothing," he says when he returns to the car. "It must have been an antelope."

The dust hangs in the faint light of approaching dawn as the car drives off.

9

As dawn touches the kraal, Tembi leaves her hut and makes her way along the path from the kraal to the kitchen of the farmhouse, as her mother does every morning. She knows what needs to be done, for Grace has instructed her, and even though she will be alone in preparing the breakfast on this day, the tasks are not unfamiliar. Often she had come with her mother, and sat at the kitchen table with a mug of hot tea and a rusk for dipping while Grace went about her morning duties. But Tembi has never been into the other rooms of the house, not even when the Missus and the farmer were away. Grace has never allowed that. When Tembi asked why, her mother replied, "This is not our house," in a tone of finality that cut off Tembi's curiosity. Tembi has had to content herself with only a glimpse through the doorway into the dining room, and down the corridor to the other rooms where Missus Märit lives.

Today Tembi has been instructed to prepare the breakfast and to take it into the dining room. When breakfast is ready, she is to ring the little silver bell that sits on the sideboard. She is to wait in the kitchen until the Missus and Baas Ben are finished and then clear away and wash the dishes. After that, if Missus Märit does not require her to do anything else, she is to go to her regular work in the dairy.

In the kitchen Tembi lifts her mother's apron from the hook and ties it around her waist. The edge of the apron dangles to her knees and she loops the strings twice around her waist. After she scrapes out the cold ashes from the big iron stove and loads it with fresh wood and a few pieces of coal, Tembi stands shivering next to the open stove door until the fire is blazing, then she fills the kettle with water and sets it on the stovetop.

What comes next? She runs over the sequence of instructions Grace has given her. Porridge, then eggs, then tea and toast. The porridge that she measures into the pot is not the coarse maize that she herself eats, but something much more finely ground, although the proportions of water and grain are the same. While she slices bread for toast she keeps an eye on the porridge, so that when it boils she can shift it off the direct heat and let it steam for a few minutes. The bread goes onto the grill rack in the upper part of the oven to toast.

After giving the porridge a quick stir to make sure there are no lumps, Tembi counts out the cutlery, two of everything: knives, forks, spoons, teaspoons, cups and saucers, plates, side plates, egg cups, napkins. All of it is loaded onto a tray and carried into the dining room. She takes a table-cloth from the sideboard and sets the table, one setting on each side. Then the salt and pepper shakers, sugar bowl—and make sure there is enough sugar—then milk from the fridge for the porridge, poured into a small jug, finally HP Sauce, butter, marmalade.

The toast! She runs back into the kitchen and pulls the grill rack from where a tendril of smoke is drifting. One of the slices is burned. So she cuts another from the loaf and slides it onto the grill. Another quick stir of the porridge before moving it to the side of the stove away from the heat. Now the water in the kettle is boiling and she must pour some into a pot and add two eggs to boil and watch the little clock carefully so that the eggs cook for just the right amount of time, not too soft and not too hard. While she stands at the stove watching the hands of the clock, Tembi chews the burned slice of toast and counts off in her mind all the steps she has taken, to be sure she has not forgotten anything.

The tea is made last. A splash of boiling water into the teapot, swirl it around, pour it out, add four spoons of leaves, pour in the boiling water, carry the pot into the dining room. Don't forget the tea strainer. Now spoon the porridge into the blue serving bowl, place the lid over it, set it on the table.

Tembi takes a moment to run her eye over the table. Everything in place, nothing forgotten.

While she has been setting out the breakfast, other sounds have been audible from the interior rooms of the house: the gurgle of the cistern as a toilet flushes, a murmur of voices, the heavy tread of the farmer, then a radio voice, in Afrikaans, reading the weather. Tembi takes the little silver bell from the sideboard and extends her arm in the direction of the interior of the house and shakes the bell. Then she retreats to the kitchen.

When she has waited a few moments, and heard the Missus and Baas Ben sitting down to breakfast, Tembi pours herself a glass of tea and slips out the back door, which she leaves ajar so that she will hear if they summon her.

The early sun casts a pool of warm light onto the side of the house, painting the white walls orange like the glow of a flame, and she sits on the kitchen steps in this warmth, holding the warmth of her glass of tea in both hands, and because it is early in the day and because she has risen before the sun and she is tired, she closes her eyes a moment.

The summons sounds into her sleep like the warning blare of a car's horn on a deserted road, and a voice calls, "Grace!" and Tembi leaps to her feet. The glass of tea drops from her hands and cracks into two pieces on the steps, the dark liquid spreading across the cement steps.

The bell from the dining room rings again, and the voice calls, "Grace?"

Tembi runs into the kitchen, to her mother, for the voice is calling her mother and she expects to see her mother, standing there at the stove as always, but it is Missus Märit who stands there instead.

"Oh, Tembi, it's you," Märit says. "Sorry, I forgot Grace wasn't here today. Are you all right? You look like you've seen a ghost."

Tembi shakes her head. "I am all right, Missus."

"You can clear away the breakfast things now."

"Yes, Missus. I will do that."

Afterwards, after she has washed the dishes and put them back into the cupboards, and shaken the crumbs from the tablecloth and folded it away, and swept the kitchen floor, Tembi slips out of the kitchen. There on the back steps are the two pieces of her drinking glass, two pieces exactly like each other, for the glass has broken right down the center. Her first impulse is to take the broken glass and throw it away in some unseen place, for she doesn't want the Missus to know of her carelessness, but instead she fits the two pieces together, so that they are a whole, and she holds them in her hand, together as a whole, and makes her way back along the path to the kraal.

WHEN DAWN APPEARS in this part of the country it begins with a thin line of deep red along the horizon, like the red coals that lie in the heart of a fire. The sky changes from black to gray. What was unshaped darkness now is revealed as the silhouettes of acacia trees, shrubs, the gentle rise of a koppie. A faint color creeps over the veldt, and the grayness is infused with the tans and the olive greens and the reddish dust that is the color of Africa. The dew that lies on the grass gleams like silver. Birdsong fills the branches of the trees. The sunlight spreads across the veldt like golden honey.

On the road between Kudufontein and Klipspring two feral dogs, thin-shanked, scavenging, scent the body lying in the dust. They scramble across the ditch and circle warily, sniffing at the suitcase and the handbag and the supine figure. One of the dogs, bolder, fastens its teeth around a corner of Grace's overnight bag and drags it away. The other chases. There is a brief snarling and tussling between the two dogs and the bag breaks apart under the ripping teeth, spilling the contents into the dust. A blouse is shredded, and a brassiere. One dog grasps a shoe in its jaws and lopes swiftly away. The other returns to the body and noses it, then makes a quick cringing nip at an area of exposed flesh. But some noise disturbs the dog and it snarls from the side of its mouth before slinking off after its companion.

A bicycle approaches at a leisurely pace. A man named Griffiths Mthali is cycling to his job in Klipspring, and he sees the ripped valise on the road and the torn clothes, and he stops his bicycle and stares at these objects. He turns his head and surveys the veldt, the trees, the bushes. Then he dismounts and bends to study the objects in the dust, but does not touch them. He walks to the side of the road and looks down into the ditch and sees the body lying there. He touches the woman's face, which feels cold under his fingers, and he sees the dried blood on her lips and nostrils. With a cry of alarm he runs back to his bicycle and pedals furiously towards the town.

The duty constable at the police station in Klipspring drives out in his van to rediscover the body and examine it. He suspects murder. In the absence of any witnesses and any further evidence, he handcuffs Griffiths Mthali in the back of the van and radios to his sergeant for instructions. The sergeant drives out in another van, the corpse is inspected further, then the body is loaded into the back of the second van and taken into Klipspring. The doctor arrives later to examine the body. Griffiths Mthali is questioned, threatened, and left in his cell for some hours. At last a tentative conclusion of accidental death is reached. Pending further investigation, Mthali is released from his cell, with the advice not to leave the district.

A telephone call is made to Mr. Ben Laurens, employer of the domestic servant named Grace Mkize. Death is announced.

The two young men who celebrated that night as they drove along the dark roads, who thought themselves lucky to have returned safely from the war without killing, who now sleep off their celebration into the late hours of the day, will never hear of the death of a domestic servant on an outlying road. The death of Grace Mkize will not be remarked upon in the privileged world of these young white farmers as they go about their ordered lives.

10

First he must plant the seeds.

Ben Laurens tips his hat back on the crown of his head and crouches and lifts a handful of freshly dug soil in his fingers, lets it rest in his palm, then trickles it back onto the earth. The men have gone back to the kraal for their midday meal and he is alone now. Shortly he too will return to his house for lunch. But in this moment, before he goes up to the house to join Märit, he wants to be alone and savor the realization of his dreams.

One day there will be a row of almond trees growing along this fence, this newly erected fence where the wire is taut and shiny and the posts are still clean and unweathered. One day he will walk in this very spot with his wife and their children and there will be the scent of almond blossoms in the air to greet them.

In Ben's shirt pocket is a small glass jar with a screw top, and inside the jar is a handful of soil—reddish, loamy, rich.

When he first came to this country he would often drive up to the border country and meander along the back roads, studying the farms he passed. One day he stopped the car and got out to smell the air, and as he inhaled the aroma of the veldt, the sweet grass, the sun-warmed soil, he had the sudden feeling that he had come home. Taking the empty bag which had contained his sandwiches, he walked a few yards from the road and scooped a handful of the rich soil into the bag. When he returned to his small apartment in Hillbrow, he poured the soil into a glass jar and set it on the mantelpiece. In that jar was the soil of Kudu-fontein, the beginning of his garden, of his farm.

Land is cheap here, especially so near the border, the troubled border, but that is why Ben can own a farm here, where so many are unwilling to risk a belief in the future. He rises to his feet and rests his hands on the shiny wire, careful of the barbs, and lets his eyes travel the width of his land. He is not naïve, he knows the risks, he knows the history, he knows that there are many who look upon him with envy, perhaps with hate. But Ben is also an idealist, and he believes that if he is fair, if he is just, if he is generous, then he will be understood, not resented, even respected. One day the ways of the country will change, and fair, just men who can farm well will be appreciated, even desired.

So he does not trouble himself too much with politics. He is careful in his dealings with the other farmers in the district, he is careful in his dealings with the workers on the farm, he is careful with the land.

Now he is in the place where he always wanted to be. Now he has what he wants. But first he must plant the seeds. He takes the jar from his pocket and shakes the soil out, onto the earth.

As he turns his hand brushes carelessly across the barbed wire and one of the barbs catches the fleshy mound at the base of his thumb. A sharp jab. He jerks his hand back and the barb pulls, digging into the flesh.

It is nothing, a small cut only, the kind a farmer grows used to in his labors. Yet when he looks down at his palm the drops of blood oozing from the cut fascinate him, the redness of the blood, so dark. A trickle runs across his palm as he tips his hand and the drops fall to the soil, down to the place where he will plant the seeds. He watches as the blood drips into the soil, darkening it, mixing with it.

A slight tremor passes through Ben, a pulsation of cold, as if someone has called his name. He looks up, startled, but he is alone.

He reaches into his pocket for a handkerchief, which he uses to dab at the cut as he walks up to the house.

THE STRIDENT PEAL of the telephone startles Märit. The phone does not ring often in this house. She hesitates with her hand over the receiver as the bell shrills again, then lifts it to her ear.

"Kudufontein Farm," she says.

"This is Sergeant Joubert in Klipspring. Can I speak to Meneer Laurens?"

Märit leans to look out the window. "He's in the fields. Can I help you, Sergeant? This is Mevrou Laurens."

"No, excuse me, Mevrou, but I must speak to your husband."

"Well, I can take a message to him if it's urgent. He can call you back."

"If you can fetch him, I will wait, Mevrou. It is important."

"All right. Just a minute." She puts the receiver down on the table and steps out to the veranda to call Ben.

When Ben comes to the phone, Märit listens to the one-sided conversation, to Ben's questions—"What?" "How?" "When?"

She paces back and forth, watching his face as a deep frown creases his brow.

"Yes, yes, of course. Thank you." He reaches up and takes off his hat, as if he has just remembered he is still wearing it.

Ben listens a moment longer, staring down at his hand, where Märit notices a thin red cut across the skin. "All right. I'll come now." He replaces the receiver.

"It's Grace," he says.

"Grace?"

"An accident of some kind. They think she was hit by a car."

"How badly is she hurt? Where did this happen?"

He reaches out a hand and rests it on her arm. "She was killed, Märit."

Märit's gray eyes widen. "Killed?"

"She is dead. Her body was found at the side of the road not far from here early this morning. The police are pretty sure it was a car that hit her."

"But don't they know? Who reported it?"

"A hit-and-run." He sits down and rubs a finger back and forth across his palm. "They don't know."

Märit glances towards the kitchen and lowers her voice. "Oh my God. Her daughter. Tembi."

"She was the one who served us breakfast this morning?"

"We have to tell her. Oh God."

Ben rises to his feet and touches Märit on the arm again. "Not just yet. I have to go into town first, to the police station. I have to talk to them."

"She was going to see her sister—no, her cousin. Who would do such a thing? Oh God, Ben, what can we do?"

Ben folds her into his arms, stroking her back, lifting the heavy coils of hair from the nape of her neck and stroking the cool skin of her neck. "I'll talk to the police. We have to be sure it is Grace before we say anything." He looks at his watch. "I'll drive in now. I said I'd come immediately."

"I'll come with you."

"Are you sure?"

"I can't stay here. I have to know." She walks quietly to the kitchen and sticks her head through the door, but there is no sign of Grace's daughter.

"Tembi?" Märit calls softly. Opening the back door she peers out, but does not see the girl.

When she rejoins Ben, he says, "There is her husband as well. He will have to be contacted."

"If it is Grace."

Ben nods. "We will have to find out where he works."

"In the mines," Märit says. "Grace said something about him working in the mines in Johannesburg."

"We will have to ask the daughter."

"If it is Grace."

THEY ARE BOTH SILENT on the first part of the drive as the car takes them along the sandy road towards the junction.

"Where did it happen?" Märit asks, her eyes on the brush and ditches on the side of the road.

"The sergeant didn't say. On the road near the farm is all he told me."

"Somewhere along here?"

"I don't know." He concentrates on his driving.

Two figures appear ahead, two men, one carrying a paper parcel in his hands.

If he were alone Ben would stop and let them sit in the back of the pickup, as he usually does when he drives into town and sees Africans on the road. There is no bus between the farms and the towns, and no worker can afford a car. Usually he stops. But not today.

"Don't drive so fast," Märit says as they pass the two men.

Ben eases his foot off the gas pedal until they turn onto the paved road, then speeds up again without being aware of it.

Three months on the farm and he feels that he is moving forward at last, and now this. He looks sidelong at Märit. "Did you get to know her at all? Grace, I mean."

"Not really."

"I just wondered—the two of you together in the house. You know, if you became friendly in any way?"

"We talked a bit, but I didn't know her. Or anything much about her. Just that she had a daughter, and that her husband worked in the mines."

Her tone is distant, causing Ben to glance at her again. Märit's own parents passed away not so long ago. Ben remembers this same withdrawn, distant expression on her face in the days afterwards. He wonders if he had proposed marriage impulsively, out of concern, pity even, and the desire to make her happy again after her loss. Sometimes he doubts that he can make her happy. Sometimes it occurs to him that he might have brought her into a place to which she is unsuited. Perhaps he has made a mistake, perhaps they both have.

In those first months of courtship he had believed she shared his dreams of a farming life, away from the city, away from the prospect of a faceless life in a faceless office, becoming faceless oneself. In those first months of sexual enthrallment perhaps they had both believed the wrong things about each other. What he had taken to be something distant in her, something hidden, is instead something closed. He fears sometimes that he will never know the depths in her.

"It doesn't remind you . . . does it?" Ben says, "The daughter . . . losing her mother. I understand how it could affect you. . . ."

She gives him a wan smile and moves closer on the seat. "No, it doesn't. I'm all right. I just worry about Tembi."

The telephone poles spaced along the side of the highway speed past and she counts them unconsciously, following the dip and rise of the wires, the way she did when she was a girl traveling somewhere with her parents.

Märit reaches for Ben's hand and holds it in her lap, running her fingers across his. "You've cut yourself."

"On the fence."

"Does it hurt?"

"No." He shrugs. "A little." He does not tell her about the blood dripping into the soil, or the inexplicable sadness he felt at that moment.

"I'll put something on it when we get home. You don't want an infection setting in."

Märit watches the dip and rise of the telephone wires. A single white cloud drifts in the blue sky. The tires hum on the road, on the empty road.

At the police station in Klipspring the sergeant is waiting for them. He shakes hands with Ben and greets Märit before explaining the circumstances.

"The body is here, in the back," he says. "If you would come through and identify her?"

Ben looks at Märit. She shakes her head and says, "I can't. I'll wait outside."

Märit puts on her sunglasses against the glare and lights a cigarette. How do you tell someone that her mother is dead? Who among us can announce Death? Who will announce it now to Tembi, to her father, to the workers on the farm?

Ben steps out into the sunlight at last, his face pale, his mouth drawn into a thin line.

"Is it . . . ?" Märit asks.

"Yes." He takes the cigarette from her fingers and draws deeply. "They think a car hit her as she was walking in the dark."

"What will happen now? What will we do? We have to contact her husband. We have to tell Tembi."

Ben gives the cigarette back to Märit. "The police will do it. They'll contact the mine and notify Elias."

"Elias. I didn't even know his name. But how will they find him?"

"The records are on file here. Everybody is on file. They will notify him and he'll come home."

"And Tembi?"

"A native constable will go to the farm and talk to the bossboy—

Joshua." When Märit shakes her head, Ben adds, "It's better. They have their own ways. We can't just call Tembi into the house and tell her. She needs to be with those she knows, with her own kind."

"I suppose so. But what about the body?"

"It will go back to the farm later today. Let them deal with it, Märit. They have their ways. I'll talk to Joshua later about the costs and the burial. We can't do much more now."

Märit nods and climbs into the pickup. Ben starts the engine and says, "We'll go to the hotel and have a drink. I think we both need it. Let the constable go out to the farm and talk to Joshua first."

"I can't understand how someone could just drive off and leave her lying at the side of the road. She might still have been alive. How could I let her walk into town like that in the dark, alone?"

"I didn't know," Ben says. "I didn't think of it."

"No, we didn't think of her. We didn't ask."

11

AND SO THE DAY of the burial arrives, on a day of late spring sunshine, on a farm in the remote countryside.

There will be no work done in the fields this day. Instead, on the banks of the river there is a singing of hymns and the chanting of prayers. The Reverend Kumalo leads the procession, enrobed in the sky blue cloth of the Living Water Assembly Church, walking at a stately pace with a wooden cross held aloft. Behind him, a donkey pulls a cart with the coffin. The women follow behind the cart, wearing their Sunday clothes, each with a blue sash tied across the waist. The men come after, many of them wearing their work clothes, for they have no special clothes for such an occasion. They have doffed their hats, and hold them clutched in their hands.

The women wail. Their ululations, high and piercing, banish the sound of the river, the rippling and running of the water across the rocks, banish the cooing of the doves in the branches of the eucalyptus trees and the chatter of the finches in the reeds. For why should the river laugh on such a day, and why should the birds sing? The women wail, and in their midst is Tembi, who neither wails nor cries but walks in silence.

At the rear of the procession as it wends its way up from the riverbank to the cemetery near the koppie come the white man and the white woman. A little apart from the rest. Strangers here. He wears a dark suit and tie and carries his hat loose in his hand like the other men. The woman is dressed in a sober, dark blue dress with a white lace trim at the sleeves. Her handbag is black and she has draped a rectangle of black gauze across her hair. She walks with some difficulty on the rough track, the heels of her shoes catching in the uneven ground.

The procession makes its way up from the river, across a field, and to the foot of the small hill where the cemetery of the people rests. Here the dead of the farm cease their labors. And here another place in the earth has been prepared.

The women sing.

> In the land of ageless days, lies a valley four-square
> It shall never pass away and there is no night there.
> Ku yosulw' inyembeẑi, nokufa neẑinsiẑi
> Ayibalwa iminyaka, ubusuk' abukho.
> God shall wipe away all tears, there's no death, no pain, nor fears
> And they count not time by years, for there is no night there.

The procession halts while the coffin is hauled down from the cart. The hymn singing ceases.

The Reverend Kumalo stands with his head bowed and his eyes upon his Bible until silence falls. He makes a gesture with his head towards the waiting men. The casket is lowered, the soil is heaped upon it.

The Reverend Kumalo speaks a short prayer and then looks towards the white man expectantly. Ben Laurens is not a religious man; he attends the church in Klipspring on Sundays, but only out of a desire not to offend his neighbors, who consider church attendance a sign of a man's moral standing. He realizes now as he steps forward that he knows no prayer suitable for the occasion. Jumbled fragments heard in church move through his head, mixed with bits of poems and psalms learned at school. He is one of those men who never thinks about God, or the scope of the infinite, or the difference between what he knows and what is unknown in the universe. Privately, he thinks of religion as a childish activity. There is birth and there is death. In between is life for the living and that is the end of it.

But at this moment he must say something to these faces watching him—expecting him, he assumes, to define why and how death came, and what can be done about it. He tries to remember what was said at that other funeral he attended, when Märit's parents were buried. So far from here, in such different soil. He can recall only a portion of a psalm, and he recites those words that he remembers.

"'Yea, though I walk through the valley of the shadow of death, I shall fear no evil: for Thou art with me; Thy rod and Thy staff they comfort me. . . . Surely goodness and mercy shall follow me all the rest of my days, and I will dwell in the house of the Lord forever.'"

Silence follows this recitation. The faces that look at his are neither friendly nor hostile. Ben turns to the Reverend Kumalo, who nods his head slowly in approval.

"Grace was a good woman," Ben says. "May she rest in peace." He has no other words to offer.

A moment of silence follows, a long moment, before Ben realizes what is required of him now—his absence. He seeks out the faces of the daughter, Tembi, and the husband, Elias, and inclines his head to each of them, then he turns and takes his wife's arm and they depart.

The farmer and his wife walk back alone across the field to their house behind the trees, while the funeral party makes its way to the kraal, where the mourners will mourn. Because the farmer and his wife feel themselves strangers here today, on their own land, because they have a sense of not belonging here today, although they do not acknowledge it openly to one another, they agree to drive into Klipspring. At the Retief Hotel they will sit in the comfort of the dining room, with its linen tablecloths and heavy silverware, with the framed prints of faraway landscapes on the walls. And there they will talk of other things and not of death.

On the hillside, next to the grave, Tembi does not join the wailing of the women or the singing of hymns. She wears a white blouse under a dark pinafore, and around her waist is the light blue sash that her mother wore on Sundays. A light blue *doek* is knotted turban-like on her head.

Tembi's face is impassive, rigid, and her large brown eyes show nothing of her sorrow. Something in her heart prevents any outward expression of grief. Neither sorrow nor regret shows, but in her heart is the realization that tears are finished now. She watches the spadefuls of reddish earth as they fall onto the coffin. It is good, rich earth, suitable for growing. She thinks of the seeds in the earth and how they come up each season after the winter. Why should a human soul not do the same? Will her mother grow into life again in that rich soil, like the seeds, if tears fall upon them like rain? The thought is childish, she tells herself, and she is no longer a child. She can never be a child again. The time of childish things is finished, and there is no growing of souls in the earth when the winter is done.

In the kraal the slaughtered calf is on the spit. There are many to feed. The jugs of milky sorghum beer are passed around. The Reverend Kumalo doffs his fine sky blue robes to reveal an ordinary business suit underneath, a little shiny at the seat and with a discreet patch on one elbow. He receives the envelope of banknotes, passed on from Ben Laurens via Joshua the bossboy. There is also a bottle of brandy and two plump chickens given by Grace's husband, Elias.

The women hang up their hats and put on aprons to prepare the food. The men roll cigarettes or light pipes and drink the milky beer that is passed around in gourds.

Tembi stands a little apart and looks at her father. Her father is here. But who is he? This man who sends money, who pats her cheek affectionately, who visits once a year, this stranger of her blood?

Even before the Relocation he had become a stranger. When she was but a child he went to work away from home, leaving early on Monday mornings with some of the other men from the village for his job in the sugar mill, and because the hours were long and the mill was a great distance away, he shared a room in the town there, only returning to his home on the weekends. And then he was tired, and wanted to sit in the sun or tend his small vegetable plot.

After the Relocation there was no work, nor was there farming. The land was too dry and too hard to take the seeds. Already some of the men had gone to the mines in E'Goli, the city of gold, because when there is no work there are always the mines. Elias left to work in the gold mines in Johannesburg. But in E'Goli a man must live in a hostel with other men, and send his money home, and only visit his family during the weeks allotted to him. And if he stays away longer than his allotted time, or wants more days with his family, then he loses his place in the mine, for there are always others waiting. Some men take town-wives whom they can visit on a Sunday, for who can be alone fifty weeks of the year? Other families are created, and men become strangers to their wives and their children. Yet when asked, a man will say that this place or that place in the far country is still his home. But Elias only knows his home for two weeks in the year, and the home that he thinks of is now in that place called memory. On this farm called Kudufontein he is a visitor; he knows this as he receives the condolences of those who live in the kraal. His home is not here.

The sorghum beer makes him a little drunk, it clouds his grief and softens the thoughts he has about what his life is now that he is without a wife, and the beer softens the loss that he feels when he sees his daughter, who has become a young woman while his gaze was elsewhere, while his eyes were upon other things. He looks across at Tembi where she pours beer from a calabash. Some young man will want to marry her soon, and then that young man will find that there is not enough work on the farms, so he will go off to work on the railways, or in the mines, or somewhere else in the cities, for who can truly be satisfied to live here and be paid in salt and sugar and a portion of the harvest, and a handful of coins?

Elias drinks more beer to cloud these thoughts. What else can he do? he asks himself. That is the way things are.

Tembi watches her father, always aware of him. This man in his new city clothes. But his face is not as it once was, it is not the face she remembers. The face of her father is now in that place called memory. This man is not the person she remembers.

She remembers the glad laughter that sprang from his mouth when she would run down the hill to greet him as he came up from the bus stop, his arms filled with parcels and his face so eager for the sight of his family at the end of a working week.

She remembers sitting in his lap, as a small child, while he ate his mealie-pap and stew, and how he spooned morsels into her mouth as she rested in the crook of his arm, half asleep in her happiness.

She remembers the long road to the place where the bus stopped, when he went off to the mines, and she remembers walking with him, dragging at his hand to slow him down, to prevent his going. She remembers how he sent her back after a while. She remembers the long road to the bus that would take him to the train that would take him to the mines in the city. A tall man on the road with a suitcase in one hand and a swing in his step. And even as he walked away from her he faded, like a mirage in the summer heat, wavering at the edges, losing shape, becoming a blur, becoming a memory. This man, this stranger. Her father.

Tembi takes a plate of food from one of the women and brings it to her father.

"Will you eat, Father?" She waits while he sets his gourd of beer down and accepts the plate in both his hands.

"Thank you, daughter."

He holds the plate on his lap and looks up at Tembi. She stands above him now, she is a woman, no longer the girl who sat in his lap. "My daughter," he says.

A light appears in her eyes. "Yes, my father."

He shakes his head and says no more. His eyes are bloodshot with tears, his throat is closed, his heart is locked, his thoughts are dulled—with beer, with distance, with loss, with sorrow—all the things that fill a broken heart. He looks away from the light in his daughter's eyes, a dying flame that he cannot rekindle.

"I am sorry, daughter," he says. "For everything. For our lives."

"Yes, Father," Tembi says, and lets her hand rest on his shoulder.

And in this moment, this moment of touch between father and daughter, her hand on his warm shoulder, she knows that he will not come back after today. Tembi knows, with a sudden knowledge of the inevitable, that he will not come back. He will walk down the long road into the mirage one last time, a man with a suitcase in his hand, and his shape will become a blur and not come back. This man, this stranger.

12

AFTER THE BURIAL, after the funeral, after the grieving, life must go on.

In the weeks that follow, the small boys must herd the cattle to pasture in the fields. There are the maize crops to attend, the fences to be maintained. In the orchard, where apricots and peaches grow, the farmer must spray the fruit against the depredation of insects. In the vegetable garden, the women must water the soil and pull the weeds. In the chicken coop, the eggs must be collected and brought to the house. And in the dairy, where Tembi usually works with three other girls, the milk must be poured into cans and the butter churned. Life must go on. The dead are buried and the living must labor.

Ben Laurens must work his farm. Märit Laurens must work too, in the house, because there is nobody to cook and clean, to do the work that Grace used to do, for Tembi has not come to the house in the two weeks since the burial.

Nor does Tembi return to her duties in the dairy with the other girls, to the cool shed with its warm sweet smells and the liquid gurgle of milk pouring from the big silver cans, to the thick cream clotting in the tubs and the regular grind of the butter churn. From this she is excused, for she is without parents now. And if at mealtimes she sits silent with her plate, and barely makes answer to the conversation, she is excused, for she is without mother and father now, and mourns, and her life is a question.

Tembi goes to the grave of her mother and lies on her back across the prickly dry grass, gazing up into the faraway sky, where sometimes the trails of jets seem like indecipherable writing on the blue of the sky. Sometimes a bird alights on the ground nearby and scratches in the grass for insects, not noticing Tembi in her stillness. Sometimes a thin trail of ants tracks across her outstretched arm, where she lies so still, lost in the sky. In the distance cattle low, the windmill turns, the beat of a hammer sounds, voices call, the breeze moves through the willow trees on the riverbanks and life goes on. Underneath her body the earth seems to vibrate softly and steadily with the pulse of life. Tembi thinks of her mother, lying in the bosom of this living thing that is the earth.

When she rises and leaves her mother to the earth, Tembi goes to the secret place behind the koppie, to the dry hard place where the earth does not mourn. Here is refuge.

Here she finds the place in the rocks where the sun falls and warms the earth. Crouching down, she examines the soil, her eyes searching for signs of growth. With the tip of her index finger she tests the moistness of the ground. Although the garden is damp and free of weeds, and no animal has been digging, there is still no sign of any growth.

How many days has it been since she planted her five seeds? How many days has she come with her pail of water to let the thirsty earth drink? She counts the weeks. Already the season is turning from spring to summer. Will anything grow here? Is her desire to make the fruit come up out of the earth a foolish notion, a waste of time, leading only to disappointment?

In secret, Tembi brings a small pail of water from the washhouse and carefully lets the earth drink, so that the soil turns dark and moist, and gives off that scent that rises after the rains. She presses her finger on the soil and it is soft and warm, like a living thing, like the flesh of a body. The small area on the surface of her finger, where it touches the earth, where it touches the living body, is the place that binds her to the earth, that anchors her.

Tembi scoops a little more water into her palm from the pail and lets it trickle onto the soil. And a little more. And again, five times in all. Once for each seed hidden in the embrace of the earth's body.

Setting the empty pail aside she leans her back against the flat, warm surface of the rock, shuts her eyes, and dozes. The sun moves in its slow eternal arc across the sky, and when the sunlight touches Tembi's face, she wakes, dazzled by the light, dazzled by the brightness that falls on all living things.

When she opens her eyes to see her garden, to see all living things, Tembi sees also a small lizard motionless on the flat rock not more than two feet from her hand. A tiny green creature no larger than one of her fingers that watches her with its small black eyes, black like river pebbles. The green color down the lizard's sleek back is green like the shoots of new grass in the spring, and there is a thin dark green, darker like a eucalyptus leaf in mid-summer, down the center of its back. Like a line drawn with a thin paintbrush. The lizard's belly is pale green, and so are the insides of the legs, and the part under the mouth, where a faint beating pulse quivers. All as green as the grass and the leaves.

The small black eyes are like the pebbles in the river, alert, glistening like jewels, and she knows the lizard watches her. When she blinks, the lizard makes a quick dipping movement of its head, dainty and quick, like a leaf moved by a puff of wind.

A longing comes over Tembi; she wants to stroke her finger across the smooth underside of the mouth, the way one would stroke a cat. She wants to feel the beat of the creature's heart, the pulse of the secret heartbeat of the earth, the vibration in all living things.

Tembi raises her finger gently, but the lizard flicks its body around—a flash of green, quick as the blink of an eye—and it is gone into a crevice of shadow. Gone into the earth.

13

THERE IS ANOTHER PLACE where Tembi can go, another refuge.

Along the sandy road that borders the farm she walks, past the fences that enclose the fields, to a small plot of land set back from the road, where a small church stands. A church built once by a farmer in the district, when travel to the town was more difficult. But it is a place of worship no longer in use, for there is now a bigger church in Klipspring, where the farmers and their families pray on Sundays, and even the farm workers prefer the outdoor worship led by the Reverend Kumalo of the Living Water Assembly Church.

So the church stands empty of prayers. The building has fallen into disrepair, the roof leaks, and many of the windows are broken, the glass replaced by sheets of scrap wood. But the building is not without use.

On Sundays, on the day when there is no work to be done, some of the children from the neighboring farms come to the church, the children of the workers, but they do not come to worship, for this building is now a school. It is not a proper school, like the one in Klipspring for the white children, a sturdy brick edifice paid for by the government, where there is reading and writing, arithmetic and history. In this school, standing back from the sandy road, there are no set lessons, there is no official curriculum, and there are only a couple of shared textbooks. Attendance by the pupils is intermittent, for it is not required by any government regulation, and what child would not rather play by the riverbanks on a Sunday, when there is no work to be done on the farms? Who would not rather hunt for weaverbird nests in the willows, or find the hive where the bees hide their honey?

But Tembi attends anyway. The teacher is a man called Mr. Simon, who works in the post office in Klipspring as a sorter of parcels in the back room of the post office—a man who has attended three years of high school himself, and is thus considered educated by the workers of the farms.

Mr. Simon is paid by the parents of the children who come to the school on Sundays, and when there are few children his pay is paltry, but still he persists, for he teaches not to be paid but because he is a man with a vision of the future, of a time when it will be necessary for the children of farm workers to be able to read and write.

Tembi attends the school every Sunday. She loves the books Mr. Simon reads from, she loves her own ability to read and to write out the exercises Mr. Simon sets. There are few books in Mr. Simon's school, but there is the Bible, which he always brings with him, and he reads the stories to Tembi and he explains to her how the words are so beautiful, how they tell of the deepest longings of those who wander in exile.

She loves to hear him talk, for Mr. Simon has traveled in the country, has been to Johannesburg and Cape Town and Durban. He tells Tembi about the ocean, the crashing waves, the smell of salt in the air, the feel of hot beach sand under bare feet. He tells her of the outside world.

On this Sunday, Tembi walks along the road that skirts the farm. From the kraal the wood-smoke scent of cooking fires lingers above the trees, the weaverbirds chatter in the willow trees; from somewhere across the river drifts the haunting refrain of voices singing a hymn.

Here is the old church, the school. A small building with a peaked roof, once painted blue but now bleached by sun and rain and wind. A simple wooden cross still stands aloft on the steeple.

Tembi mounts the steps to the front door and reaches for the handle. Then she sees the chain looped through the door handles, and the iron padlock. The school is locked. But why is the school locked? she wonders. Why lock this door when there is nothing inside to steal? And where is Mr. Simon? She grasps the chain in her hands and pulls it and tugs at the door. Why is the school locked?

Tembi steps down from the little porch and walks around to the side of the building, to one of the windows that still has glass, that is not boarded up. Rising up on her toes she grasps the windowsill and peers into the building.

This is a church without an altar, or pews, or stained-glass windows. There is the chair where Mr. Simon sits, where the altar once stood, and there is the small blackboard he uses. There is his table, salvaged from a kitchen somewhere. There are the two benches for the pupils. And there are the books that Mr. Simon brings, and in those books are doors that open something in Tembi, and the doors lead to a road down which she can travel, and she knows that at the end of the road is a gift she will one day grasp. She knows this. It is why she is at the school today.

But where is Mr. Simon?

Tembi raps on the window with her knuckles, then after a moment goes around to the front door again. She shakes the chain and pulls at the lock. Their purpose defeats her. Why is the school locked?

As she stands there, a shiver moves across her shoulders, as if someone has touched her, as if she is not alone, and she turns slowly to look.

Within the deep shadows under the trees a man on a horse is watching Tembi. He is dressed in a khaki shirt and shorts and long khaki socks that come up to his knees. On his head he wears a wide slouch hat of the kind favored by older farmers in the district. But he is a young man. The stock of a rifle shows in the scabbard next to his saddle.

He says nothing, sitting very still, watching her, and his horse is very still too, its head held high from the pull of the reins clutched in his hand. A young man, with a scraggly blond beard.

Tembi recognizes him. He is from the neighboring farm. She thinks he is the son of old Koos van Staden. He sometimes rides his horse across the fields here, galloping through the cattle so that they scatter and the small boys have to round them up again.

He gives a quick kick to the horse's flanks, and it trots forward across the clearing towards Tembi, and then he pulls on the reins so that the horse halts, obedient to him.

He smiles down at Tembi, but she sees that his eyes are without a smile in them. "Class is dismissed," he says.

Tembi does not understand his words. The language she understands, yes, for he speaks in Afrikaans, which is the language between the farmers and the workers everywhere, but it is the meaning of them that she does not understand.

"Where is Mr. Simon?" she asks. This is his school, he will tell her why a chain and padlock bar the entrance.

"Mr. Simon? Who is this Mr. Simon?"

"This is his school. He is the teacher."

The horse drops its head to nibble at a tuft of grass and the man jerks the reins taut in his hand. The horse throws up its head and shows the whites of its eyes.

"Oh, it's Mr. Simon's school." His lip curls. "And what does this Mr. Simon teach you in his school? Huh? That all this land belongs to you, that it will be yours one day, that you people can drive us off? Hey?"

The horse makes another attempt to nibble at the grass and he yanks the reins hard so that the bridle bites into the horse's mouth.

"Well, this school is closed. For today and forever. So you can just *voetsak* off."

Tembi recoils at the word. It is an insult, used only on dogs.

She shakes her head and mumbles, "I will wait for Mr. Simon."

He kicks at the horse's flanks, forcing the animal forward, towards Tembi, and the big head of the animal pushes her back against the door. The padlock digs into her back. The young man smiles at Tembi again, but again there is no smile in his eyes.

He leans down from the saddle, close to her. "How old are you, *meidjie*?" He reaches out to touch her breast. Tembi slaps his hand away.

His heels dig in at the horse's flanks, forcing it towards Tembi, and its hooves scrabble on the steps, plunging down inches from her bare feet. She sees the animal's big frightened eyes, the whites showing, and she smells the sweet grassy smell of the horse's breath and the thick smell of its sweat.

"I told you," the young man hisses down at her from between clenched teeth, "class is dismissed. There is no more school for you here." The big head of the horse is pressing her against the door, and it turns its head away from her, showing frightened eyes.

Tembi screams. The horse rears back in alarm, almost unseating the rider.

As the man struggles to bring the horse under control, Tembi leaps from the porch, landing with a jarring thud that tumbles her to her knees. Then she is quickly up and running. Without a backward glance she is across the clearing and into the trees.

"You little nigger bitch!" he shouts after her.

Tembi runs between the trees and back to the sandy road, where she pauses, looking right and left. If a car passes, if someone is walking on the road, she can call for help.

Then she hears the thunder of the horse's hooves drumming on the ground and she runs across the road and down towards the river. The reeds are thick and high along the riverbanks as she plunges into them. Birds scatter, chattering in alarm. The thunder of the horse's hooves is behind her.

She flings a glance backwards, does not see the rider, and throws herself flat between the tall reeds, flat on the mud.

The horse gallops past, then a moment later charges back. Tembi lies with her cheek pressed against the mud and breathes with shallow gasps through her mouth. The earth stills under her as the reverberations of the horse's hooves move upriver. And there is no sound, not even the birds.

She breathes hoarsely and begins to raise her head, then freezes as she hears the soft tinkle of a bridle, the soft chink of metal. The deep panting of the horse is very close. Tembi holds her breath. She waits. She hears the breathing of the man. He is waiting too. She closes her eyes and holds her breath and presses herself into the mud, willing the earth to swallow her.

When she can no longer contain her breath, when it feels as if she is under water and will drown if she does not raise her head and suck in the air, when it seems she must rise up and be found, she hears the horse move away, the jangle of the bridle.

A hard voice shouts out, "Class dismissed!" The man laughs harshly.

The horse splashes through the river and scrambles up the opposite bank, and the faint vibration trembles on the earth as it gallops away.

At last Tembi breathes. Her breath comes quickly, becomes a shuddering in her chest and then a sobbing. The tears flow down her cheeks and fall upon the mud.

Who can she tell, who can she turn to for help? Mr. Simon will never come again. The doors of the school will never reopen. The books will remain unread, closed to her. The man on the horse is the law, the iron law of this country, and there is no recourse for her. She must accept her lot; always in this country, this life, she must accept her lot.

She weeps. Tembi weeps for what is taken from her. She weeps for what will never be.

14

In the farmhouse there is no help now for Märit with the cooking and the cleaning; she must do these things herself. In the three weeks since Grace's death, Tembi has not appeared in the kitchen, and Märit cannot bring herself to go and find her and ask her to work in the kitchen. Since the death of Grace, Märit prepares the meals, which is easy enough as there is only herself and Ben. She sweeps the house once a day and carries out the kitchen scraps to the compost heap and airs the bed linen. All the tasks that Grace used to do. There are many tasks, more than she had realized, and some of them she does not do, like the polishing of the silverware or the washing of the windows.

All her life others have done these tasks for Märit. When she was a girl, living in her parents' house, there was a cook, and a housemaid that came in twice a week to do the cleaning. On Mondays a woman came in to wash the laundry. Her parents were not wealthy by the standards of the country, but even so, it is normal in this country to have servants, for there are so many people who seek work, who will do menial tasks so that they might have a job.

Today is Monday, laundry day. And Märit must do the washing. There are the clothes, the bedding, tablecloths and napkins, kitchen towels, bath towels. And Ben's shirts. He likes to have a clean shirt every day, even if he is going to be doing messy work around the farm, and he likes to change into a clean shirt after he comes in from his work before he sits down to dinner with her.

In a small room just off the bathroom there is an electric washer, powered from the farm generator. The soiled clothes are kept in a big wicker hamper next to the washing machine. Märit lifts the lid of the straw hamper and is about to reach for the clothes—actually has her hand extended, not paying much attention because her eyes are on the powder in the machine—when she looks down and sees something, and recoils immediately.

Her first thought is that something obscene has been deposited on the clothes, something dark and coiled, like excrement, as if someone has intentionally placed this filthy and horrible thing on her laundry. Then the dark coils move, and a small flat head shows itself, and a thin tongue flickers. A snake.

Märit springs away from the laundry basket and sucks in her breath. She still has the wicker lid to the laundry basket in her hand and she holds it in front of her, like a shield.

The head of the snake stands higher, rising from the thick coils, and the tongue appears again from the flat lips and flickers at her.

Her body goes rigid with fear. She wants to scream, but her throat is dry and locked. As the snake slowly uncoils it watches her with flat eyes.

She knows it will come out of the laundry basket, and uncoil onto the floor, and slither across the slate towards her, and strike at her, into her bare flesh. She feels naked, exposed, vulnerable. Her feet are in sandals, her legs bare, her dress thin.

But she cannot move, for her body is rigid, and her throat is locked, and her bladder is suddenly full, so full it could burst. The snake rustles and slithers on the clothes and its head dips over the side of the hamper, and still it watches her.

She knows the danger she is in, she knows this is a mamba: quick, aggressive—and poisonous.

The long black body unwinds and the head slides over the edge of the laundry basket and the snake slowly begins to lower itself to the floor. And still the eyes watch her, and still Märit cannot move, as the snake drops to the slate floor, making a soft meaty sound. The head rears up, flat and black above the swollen thick length of the extended body, and the tongue flickers at Märit.

Her fear is something terrible, holding her like iron as the snake slithers towards her. She watches it with deadly fascination, the obscenity of it, yet she cannot stop her watching or her fascination. Then the mamba seems to coil into itself, the coils rippling, the muscles gathering with tension, and Märit knows that it is readying itself to strike.

Only then does the fear that holds her break into panic, and she springs backwards, slamming into the wall, then turning to the door, and out of the corner of her eye she sees the flash of the black body extended its full length and the mouth bared and the fangs snapping at the spot where she stood a split second ago.

Then she is running, down the long corridor, and across the vast expanse of the living room, and across the veranda, and down the steps, lifting her feet high, with small cries of distress coming from her throat.

In a moment she is outside the house, and there is nobody around, and she must go for help, but she is safe here, in the middle of the lawn, where nothing can approach without her seeing it. She must go for help and find somebody to kill the snake, find Ben, but there is nobody here, and she is afraid to run in the long grass in her bare legs, and her bladder is full to bursting.

Märit watches the house, she watches the door, which she left open, she watches the darkness beyond the door, where the snake will appear, for it is in there, in the shadow behind the door. If she was brave, if she was a true farmer's wife she would find a shovel, that one, leaning against the wall in the flower bed, and take it and kill the snake. But she is not brave.

When she opens her mouth to call for someone, to call for help, her voice croaks in her throat and all she can do is watch the house and wait for the snake.

And then there is someone, a person, just crossing to the side of the house. Tembi.

Märit tries to call out for help but her throat has seized up. She forces her tongue against her teeth. "Tembi!"

Tembi stops and looks over.

"Tembi! Quickly, come here." What is the word for snake in their language, Märit wonders. "*Slang*," she whispers in Afrikaans, and then remembers the word, one of the few she knows. "*Nyoka!* There . . ." She points.

Tembi's eyes widen as she looks at the house.

"A mamba, in the laundry room. Mamba! Get someone, get the men."

Tembi looks at the house, frowning, unsure.

Märit tries to still the quivering in her voice, takes a deep breath and speaks clearly. "Tembi, there is a snake in the house, in the laundry room. Fetch someone to kill it."

"In the washing?"

"Yes, for God's sake. Go and find the Baas or one of the men. Quickly!"

Instead, Tembi moves to the shovel standing in the flower bed, grasps it, and slowly climbs the veranda steps, then enters the house.

"Don't," Märit cries in a choked voice. And still she is frozen where she stands.

Nothing happens. Tembi has disappeared.

Now Märit hears the sound of a vehicle, and here, coming up the driveway is the pickup truck, with Ben at the wheel, Joshua the bossboy next to him, another one of the workers sitting in the back.

Ben sees her, waves, then stops the truck and gets out.

As he walks closer he sees her face, and his step quickens. "What is it? Märit, are you ill? What's wrong?" His arms are around her, and she wants to collapse, to give in to her fear, to let him take over.

"Tell me what's wrong, Märit."

She takes a deep breath. "There is a mamba in the laundry room and Tembi has gone in there."

Ben shouts to the men in the truck, *"Nyoka!"* points to the house, then runs up the steps. The two men dash after him, Joshua swinging a hammer in his hand.

For a moment Märit is alone again, still standing alone on the lawn, and the house has swallowed her husband too now. She hears voices shouting, then silence. And the dark door of the house holds only shadows.

It is Tembi who emerges. She walks down the steps slowly, the shovel in one hand, her face dazed, slack. In her other hand hangs the limp form of the snake, like a length of rope. Then the two men emerge, and some moments later Ben follows. He strides quickly across to Märit.

"It's all right now, darling. She's killed it. It's dead."

Joshua takes the snake from Tembi and holds it aloft. The head is a bloody pulp. He brings it to Märit. "Dead," he says.

Märit turns her head away.

"Quite a specimen," Ben says. "Must be at least five feet long. The skin could make you a nice purse."

Märit shakes her head. "Take it away," she says through clenched teeth. "Burn it!"

Ben jerks his head at Joshua, who retreats to the truck with the snake.

"All right now, darling?" Ben slips his arm around her shoulders and squeezes. "Nothing more to worry about. That Tembi is a brave girl. She had the thing dead already when I went in. A very brave girl."

Märit nods. She feels nauseated. "Did you make sure there wasn't another one around? They travel in pairs, don't they?"

"That's an old wives' tale," Ben says. "Yes, I did check, there's nothing. Why don't you go in and have a strong cup of tea—you look like you need one."

"What about you? Don't you want to come in?"

Ben looks at his watch. "Ah, the thing is, I have to drive into Klipspring. We've got to get some bags of potash; I want to do the fertilizing before dark. Do you want to come with me? You could have your tea at the hotel, do a bit of shopping."

"No. No, I think I'll stay here."

"Well, I have to get going. Don't worry, darling. It's just one of the little travails of living in the country—snakes and bugs and that sort of thing." He kisses her on the cheek, then gets into the truck where the two men are in the back, talking excitedly, holding the snake between them.

And she is left alone.

The tension in her body breaks; she sinks to her knees on the lawn. A trickle of hot liquid on her inner thigh, then a stream, and the urine pours down between her legs, splashing on the grass. She wants to lie down, right on the lawn, and curl up. But Tembi is there, urging her to her feet, grasping and tugging her arm.

"Come, Missus. Come inside."

Märit rises, dabbing at her legs with the edge of her soaked dress. "I'm sorry," she murmurs.

"Come inside now, Missus. You can wash. I will make you tea."

In the bathroom Märit pulls off all her clothes and bundles them into the bathtub. She wipes herself down with a damp washcloth, then goes through to the bedroom and finds clean clothes.

Tembi is brewing tea in the kitchen, in the African way, very strong, each cup with an added dollop of tinned condensed milk she has found in one of the cupboards.

Märit comes in and says, "We can have it in the living room. Bring your cup."

Tembi follows, into this unknown part of the house.

"Sit with me," Märit says, as Tembi diffidently stands near the door with her cup in her hand. "Here." She pats the couch. She finds her cigarettes and lights one, drawing gratefully at the smoke. "Look at my hand, it's still shaking. God, I hate snakes."

"You were frightened."

"Terrified. I don't know what I would have done if you hadn't come along."

"A mamba is a dangerous snake. We always kill them. These snakes are bad." She reaches for her tea and sips.

"I peed myself out of fright. What must you think of me?"

"I was frightened also."

"You? Hardly. You just marched straight in there and killed the snake."

"I saw it on the floor and I hit it. But I was very frightened. I don't like snakes."

"You were my savior, Tembi. Honestly. And I'm sure the men were very impressed."

Tembi looks down at her cup. "I was frightened." She sighs as a tremor quivers through her.

Märit smokes in silence, calm now. After a moment she says, "Tembi."

"Yes, Missus." The shy smile again. "Yes?"

"I'm sorry about your mother. About what happened. The accident."

Tembi nods her head gravely.

"Where is your father now?"

"He has gone back to the city. To his job in the mines."

"Have you any brothers and sisters?"

"I am alone."

"I lost my parents too, you know. I am also alone."

Märit falls silent again, smoking her cigarette. Then she leans forward and stubs it out in the ashtray. "And do you like your work here on the farm? It's in the dairy, isn't it?"

Tembi shrugs. "Yes."

"How old are you, Tembi?"

"Eighteen, Missus."

"Oh, that's right." Märit remembers asking Grace. "When is your birthday?"

"May sixteenth, Missus."

"Close to mine. May twenty-third."

Märit studies the girl across from her—the young woman who sits with her hands clasped in the lap of her thin cotton dress, her sturdy legs tucked half under the chair as if to hide her dusty feet. There is a melancholy in the dark brown eyes that glance at Märit every now and then. There is not that great a difference in their ages, she realizes.

Märit takes a deep swallow of the sweet milky tea. "Thank you for the tea . . . and for helping me."

"Yes, Missus."

"Don't call me 'Missus' all the time."

"No. What must I call you, Madam?"

"Not 'madam' either," Märit says with a smile. "Call me by my name—Märit."

"Yes."

"Say it."

"Märit, Missus."

Märit laughs. "Just 'Märit.'"

"Yes."

"Say it."

"Märit." Tembi looks down, shy. "It's a nice name, 'Märit.'"

"Tembi, would you like to come and work here in the house? You can do what Grace used to do, cooking and so on. Would you like that? I can show you what to do—it's not hard work, much easier than in the dairy. And you will earn more as well."

Märit is leaning forward now, towards Tembi, and there is a plea in her voice. She wants more than just help in the house. An intimacy has opened between her and this girl, not so much younger than herself, perhaps not even so unlike her.

For Tembi, the offer is unexpected, and she asks herself why it is made. Is it because Märit is afraid to be alone in the house when her husband is at work on the farm? Is it something else? She wonders how it would be to work here. Her job in the dairy is not difficult, only the making of butter and cream. But she often feels out of place there, in the company of the other girls, for she is still a relative newcomer. And because she has more schooling than the other girls she feels herself apart, unable to join in their easy ways with one another or their childish talk. It is not possible to talk to the other girls of the thoughts in her head.

But here in the house will it be different? Will she be able to talk to Märit? There are books here, she has seen them, and there will be times when she is alone, when she has the house to herself and she can read the books. Cooking and cleaning do not take up a whole day.

"Tembi?" Märit says softly.

Tembi raises her eyes and looks directly into those of Märit. She sees the plea in Märit's face, she hears that Märit is asking her for friendship. But is such a thing possible? How is it possible? She starts to shake her head slightly.

Märit's face is full of yearning, full of loneliness. And that yearning echoes something that Tembi feels as well. It is something she recognizes in herself.

She sighs. Then she makes her decision. "Yes, I can be here, Märit," she answers.

15

AND so Tembi comes to work in the house, to replace Grace, to help Märit.

The following evening she assists Märit with the preparations for dinner—steak, boiled maize on the cob, and a bean salad. Märit slices tomato for the salad while Tembi fries the steak at the iron stove.

"Is this ready now?" Tembi asks. "I don't know if the Baas wants it very cooked or not."

Märit leans over and pokes at the meat with a fork until the juice trickles out. "You can take it off the heat now, he likes it red. Is the maize done?"

"It's boiling."

"All right, just let it rest in the pot for a while. Come, I'll show you how to make a dressing for the salad."

Märit demonstrates by pouring a spoonful of oil into a bowl and slowly adding a bit of vinegar. "Just mix it together well," she says, handing the fork to Tembi. "Faster," she adds as Tembi stirs the mixture. "You need to beat it together so the oil mixes." She puts her hand over Tembi's to increase the motion.

A drop of oil splashes across Märit's hand. "Oh! I'm sorry, Missus."

"Never mind. Here, you'd better wear this apron. Let me tie it for you." Märit knots the strings of the apron and pats Tembi on the shoulder. "Why don't you cut the bread instead—Ben likes a lot of bread with his supper. I'll finish the dressing." She turns Tembi around by the shoulders and smiles. "And call me Märit, not 'Missus.'"

When the food is ready they both carry the plates into the dining room. There are only two places set at the table, one for Märit and one for Ben.

Märit is suddenly aware of this disparity—but it is usual, she reassures herself, for Grace never ate with them either. House servants do not sit down to meals with their employers.

Märit looks away, embarrassed. "Thank you, Tembi. I'll ring the bell when we are finished." She leaves the room to fetch Ben.

Ben, as he always does, eats hungrily for a minute or two without speaking, then, when the first urgency of his appetite is assuaged, he sits back and takes notice of her. Märit does not mind this, she thinks of it as something masculine, and enjoys watching him in those first moments. He is the same way with her, when they are alone at night—direct, urgent to take possession, to have her, and only then becoming aware of her own desire and needs. To see his appetite at table is to remind her of the way he is in private, and suggests a promise of other appetites later.

"Did you get all your business done in town?" she asks as she cuts into her steak.

"I met van Staden, you know, our neighbor on the next farm, and mentioned the snake. Seems his own wife found one in the house too. Also a mamba. Nine feet at least, he said. And he's heard of other incidents. For some reason there are more snakes around this year."

Märit looks down at her steak, the thick meat as the knife slices into it, the pink juices. She remembers the thick body of the snake, hanging limp in Tembi's hands, and the bloody pulp of the crushed head. And she remembers her fear. She sets down her cutlery and pushes the plate to one side, reaching for a slice of bread instead. "Let's talk of something else."

"Of course. I was thinking that when the harvest is done this year . . ." He looks at her plate. "Aren't you going to eat your steak?"

"I'm not hungry. You have it." Märit slides the plate across to Ben. "You were saying . . . ?"

"Yes, when the harvest is done, why don't we take a little trip? We could go to the coast. Durban, maybe?"

"Oh, Ben, I'd love to. Or even better, Cape Town." Anywhere civilized, anywhere away from here, she almost says.

"Yes, I thought you'd like the idea. We need a little holiday."

Märit's appetite reappears and she serves herself salad. "It'll be lovely. We can swim in the ocean, and eat seafood, and go to the movies."

When they have finished eating, Märit rings the silver bell that stands on the table next to the sauce bottles, a signal to Tembi in the kitchen that she may clear away the dishes. Ben rises and pats his pockets. "Have you seen my tobacco pouch?"

As he turns towards the door, Tembi enters with the tray and there is a small collision. The tray is knocked from Tembi's hands to the floor. Both she and Ben crouch to retrieve it at the same time. In the action of squatting, Tembi's dress rides up her thighs, revealing the shadowed declivity there, and at the same moment Ben, in reaching for the tray, brushes her knee with his hand.

They both look at Märit. Tembi's face darkens with embarrassment, with a kind of apprehension, almost shame. Ben rises to his feet with a sheepish grin and hands the tray to Tembi.

"Sorry, my fault."

But in the moment before Ben rises, Märit has seen another expression on his face, in that moment when his hand brushed Tembi's knee and his eyes dropped for a split second to the shadow between her partly open thighs. An expression of fleeting swiftness, disappearing in the instant that he turns to Märit with his abashed grin. But she has seen it, and she recognizes the look, for it has been on Ben's face before, when he has looked at her as she rises from the bath, or as she sits on the edge of the bed to put on nylon stockings, and his eyes drop with that almost glazed look to the juncture of her thighs. She has never minded, for it is proof of his maleness, and proof of her allure.

Ben smiles sheepishly and says, "I'll just go and find my tobacco. Shall we have our coffee in the lounge?" He turns away, assiduously not looking at Tembi.

Märit remains in her chair as Tembi gathers the dishes and puts them on the tray. She sees the bare feet, clean but somehow very naked, and she sees the way the thin cotton dress moves across the buttocks and rests on the full breasts, rounder than her own. As Tembi leans across the table, Märit smells the faint female perfume of her body.

Märit pushes her chair back abruptly and strides out of the room, down the corridor to the bedroom. She opens her closet and rummages around on the shelves.

When she has found what she wants she returns to the kitchen, where Tembi is standing at the sink. Märit drops a pair of sandals on the floor. "Try those on."

Tembi wipes her hands and crouches to slip on the sandals, and again her dress slides up, showing her strong thighs. The sandals are slightly too small for Märit and not much used. Tembi's feet are smaller than Märit's but with a similar shape, narrow with long toes, and they slip into the sandals comfortably.

"They fit," she says with a smile. "Thank you, Missus."

"I don't want you to walk barefoot when you are in the house." Märit thrusts a pale blue cotton housecoat towards Tembi, something she bought in Klipspring to wear when cleaning the house but has not used more than once or twice. Tembi slips the coat on and buttons it up. The hem falls to mid-calf.

"We are the same size," Tembi says. "Thank you, Missus."

"Wear it when you are serving. There is no need to walk around half dressed. And bring the coffee through to the living room."

Tembi drops her eyes at the coldness in Märit's voice and nods. "Yes, Missus."

Ben is sitting at the radio when she enters the living room, his hands on the dial, tuning in to the evening weather report. Märit sits in her own chair and lights a cigarette, inhaling with quick, irritated little puffs.

When Tembi brings in the coffee tray, Ben glances over at her once, then bends to the radio, twiddling the dial to find another station. Static fills the room.

Märit pours the coffee. "Do we have to listen to the radio?"

Ben switches it off. "How are things working out with Tembi?"

"Fine."

"Nice to have someone young around the house."

"Is it? She isn't that much younger than me."

"No, no, I didn't mean that. I meant younger than Grace. She used to be a little dour sometimes. Made you feel that you shouldn't leave things too untidy. It sometimes felt as if she ran the house, not us. Not you, I mean."

When he looks over at Märit, she glares at him, and a quick flash of understanding passes between them, a moment of shared knowledge between husband and wife. There is an unspoken admission on his part that he has looked with lust at Tembi, and an unspoken admission on her part that she saw this. But neither Märit nor Ben can speak of what they know. To do so will admit that mistrust can exist, that fidelity is only a contract, sometimes broken.

"Well," Ben says, "it can't be easy for her, losing her mother like that, and her father off in the mines. It's good that you've done something for her."

Is it? Märit wonders. And who will it be good for?

16

IN ANOTHER PART of the country, north of Kudufontein, across the border, at first light, when the birds have begun to call out the new day and the animals stir in their sleeping places, when farmer and worker alike still lie abed, two men are already busy at their task.

In the darkest hours of this night, when the fields and the veldt lie silent under a faint moon, they come across the border. Not at any checkpoint, with passport and customs control officers in attendance, nor on any road or path, but instead crossing the line at an anonymous and lonely place, where cutting the strands of barbed wire that straddle the land is easy, and unnoticed.

Each man carries a cheap canvas knapsack across his back, and they walk fast and silent, for their task requires darkness, and they must return across the border before daylight, which will bring helicopters, and soldiers on horseback with trackers searching out footprints.

They are in the peaceful grassland now, in the farmlands, the land that the white farmers call their own. But the two men have brought an opposing view—what might be called a disputation of ownership. Their petition is in the form of plastique; a cheap, lightweight explosive that is easy to use, and deadly. This is a petition that will give voice to many mouths, and will not go unnoticed.

Each man also carries a land mine in his knapsack. These devices are small and crude, but then their function is simple. Once buried in the sand of a country road, their pressure pads will be triggered by the weight of a vehicle, and the explosives will ignite, spraying hot shards of metal in all directions. That is their sole function—to explode, to destroy, to kill. The handiwork of clever men in distant places: scientists, politicians, financiers, ideologues. The men come now in the bird-sound–rich dawn to the radio tower on the outskirts of the sleeping town, the town called Klipspring. Once more they cut strands of barbed wire, in this country of fences, working in silence, without wasted gestures or unnecessary words, for they have trained in these actions and rehearsed them. At the base of the radio transmitting tower the plastique is packed against metal struts, and fuses and timers are set, then the men go back through the gap in the fence, closing it behind them.

They walk to the road, some two hundred yards from the turning to the tower, and there bury the two land mines beneath the soil of the road. So that when the tower explodes, and the soldiers inevitably come speeding to the scene in their Jeeps and trucks, they will encounter a second deadly petition.

And now the two men disappear into the bush, back towards the border and their homeland, their home-in-exile, hoping to be there before the helicopters come, and the patrols, and the mounted soldiers with the trackers who can follow footprints almost as fast as a fleeing man can make them. But even there, across the line, who can be safe? For this is a war, and in times of war who can have a home, even in exile? Who can be safe?

17

EVERY WEDNESDAY Märit drives into Klipspring with Ben. It is the day for shopping in the town, for lunch in the Retief Hotel—a day away from the farm.

Today Märit wakes as Ben steps from the bathroom and stands in front of the mirror to dress. The curtains are drawn wide, because that is the first thing Ben does every morning when he rises, open the curtains to assess the weather—a farmer's habit—and the morning light falls across the floor in a broad swath that illuminates him as he stands in front of the mirror. He is still naked, still a little damp from his morning bath, his clothes laid out on the chair next to the wardrobe.

Märit lies in the warm sheets, where the scent of her husband's body lingers, and the warmth of his body is still with her under the sheet, and she looks at her husband so slim and strong as he stands in the morning light, and he is beautiful to her.

"Come back to bed for a little bit," she says.

Ben smiles at her in the mirror as he fastens his watch to his wrist. He always puts his watch on first, before he dresses. He turns to look at Märit and says, "We don't really have time."

She looks down the length of his body and her desire is hot in her loins. Since they have come to the farm his body has grown stronger and more muscular. He seems bigger to her now, even down there, between his legs where her eyes linger.

Märit pulls the sheet back to reveal herself. "I'm yours," she murmurs.

"Shameless," Ben says, smiling, but he does not come to her, reaching instead for his trousers and slipping them on. "We really don't have time to waste this morning. I have to get the pump dismantled before we go to town, I didn't get round to it yesterday. And I want to pick up my seedlings before the railway station closes for lunch."

Märit stretches, cat-like, and gives him a veiled look. Ben crosses to the bed and sits down next to her. He looks at his watch. She grasps his hand and puts it on her lower belly.

"Märit, we have to get going. We don't want to be late. And the maid will be coming in to call us to breakfast any minute."

"Send her away. We have time."

He rises. "No, really, we don't."

"Don't you want me?"

"Always. Tonight, I promise." He reaches for his shirt and completes his dressing. "Up you get now, darling," he says from the door as he goes out.

Märit lies with her hands clasped between her thighs. Her frustration makes her want to shout. She moves her fingers into her wetness, then pulls them away. She has never been able to do that, to herself, it seems wrong somehow. Kicking away the sheets she sighs and rises from the bed.

From the closet Märit brings out her blue silk dress, the one with the cinched waist and the wide skirt and the scooped neckline that shows off her throat and shoulders. The dress that she wore with Ben on their honeymoon in Durban. She wonders if he will notice. But then she changes her mind and lays the dress across the unmade bed and selects instead a cream-colored suit and half-heels of a slightly darker color than her suit. A leather handbag completes the ensemble.

When she appears in the kitchen, hair brushed, makeup applied, Ben is standing at the stove sipping a cup of coffee. Tembi is there, giggling shyly at something Ben has just said.

"I thought you were in a hurry to get the pump dismantled," Märit says. "Aren't you the one who is worried that we'll be late?"

"Just going." He sets his cup down on the counter and leaves by the back door, still smiling at his joke with Tembi.

"The Baas and I are driving in to Klipspring today," Märit says.

"Yes, Missus." Her eyes linger on Märit's suit.

Märit pours herself a cup of coffee and takes a fresh package of cigarettes from the carton in the cupboard. "I won't be back until late this afternoon, so you'll have the whole morning to clean the house. Leave the bedroom, though, you don't have to clean in there."

"Yes, Missus."

Märit has never liked servants in her bedroom; even as a girl in her parents' house she did the tidying there herself. It is the one intimate place she wants to keep private.

"I think it might be a good idea for you to polish the silverware today. Do you know how to do that? Do you know where the cleaning things are?"

"Yes, Missus. I have seen my mother cleaning the silver. I can do it."

Märit turns her back. "Right. See that you do a good job."

Outside, she waits impatiently next to the pickup truck. Ben is not in sight. She regrets that she still has not yet learned to drive. If she could, she would get behind the wheel and start the engine and drive towards the gate so that Ben would have to come running after her. She walks around to the side of the house and smokes a cigarette.

THE WEEKLY TRIP into Klipspring is something Märit enjoys and looks forward to, a high point breaking the monotony of the week. Ben will collect the mail, and she will make the rounds of the shops and then meet him at the hotel for lunch. Afterwards they will sit with a coffee and brandy on the bougainvillea-shaded veranda at the back of the Retief Hotel while Ben reads the newspapers and she smokes, dreamily, looking at the gardens. Often there will be people there they know, neighbors, acquaintances, for Wednesday is town-day for most of the farmers, and she and Ben might join another table for conversation and perhaps a second brandy.

She has a fondness for the hotel; it was where she stayed with Ben when they came up to the district to look at the farm the first time. When she thinks back on that occasion she remembers less of the farm than of the two long afternoons in the hotel room, the shutters drawn, a whisper of a breeze cooling the perspiration that their lovemaking had drawn out on their skin. She remembers the cold, cold beer that Ben ordered from room service, and the feel of the glass on her naked belly. She remembers how the first sip had seemed to make her instantly drunk. She remembers taking the cold liquid in her mouth, and holding it there until her lips were cool, then taking the heat of him into her cool mouth. She was shameless.

Sometimes she wishes that Ben would suggest they take a room at the hotel in Klipspring for the afternoon, instead of returning to the farm. But she knows that is no longer possible, she and Ben are known here now. There would be gossip. She knows that she could not come down into the lobby afterwards and see the knowing glances. But she wishes that she and Ben were free in that way again.

Ben is already waiting for her in the pickup outside the house. He has loaded the machine parts into the back of the truck and washed his hands. He has on a blue denim shirt and a dark blazer.

Märit is silent in the cab of the truck as they set off. She has decided to be a bit cold to him, to let him feel her displeasure of the morning. For the first few miles she says nothing, and he wisely holds his peace, but after a while she relents, for she does not want to spoil the day; the grass is yellow in the sunlight, casting violet shadows, and at the foot of a rocky outcrop she sees a splash of pink and white flowers.

"I think we're going to have a good summer," Ben says. "There's been a lot of rain this spring."

"Look," Märit exclaims, pointing as a large blue bird flashes across the road, "a kingfisher." As she speaks the engine cuts out. Thinking that Ben is going to stop to look at the bird she says, "We don't have to stop."

"I didn't. Something's wrong with the truck." He applies the hand brake and turns the ignition key. Nothing happens.

Ben gets out and opens the hood. Märit follows and stands next to him. After removing his jacket and handing it to her he rolls up the sleeves of his shirt and reaches into the engine. "Try and start it," he says after a moment. She lays his jacket down on the seat and gets behind the wheel. Her efforts are fruitless. There is nothing but a clicking sound.

"Try turning the headlights on," Ben calls.

She flicks the switch and gets out. Ben shades his hands around the glass and peers at the lamp. "Nothing."

"What's wrong?"

"I don't know. It must be the battery. There's no power at all." He _releases the catch for the hood and closes it gently, then looks up and down the road.

"Perhaps someone will come along and give us a lift," Märit suggests.

"Unlikely."

"What shall we do?"

He glances at his watch. "Van Staden's farm is over there a few miles. I can cut across the fields and see if someone can give us a hand."

"Won't he have gone into Klipspring? They usually do on Wednesday."

"I can get one of the farm boys to bring over a tractor and give the battery a boost. If it is the battery. Otherwise we can tow the truck back to the farm."

"I'll come with you."

"It'll be hard going in those shoes across the fields. Why don't you wait here?"

"How long will you be, do you think?"

"A half hour? Maybe longer. It depends if van Staden usually leaves the keys to the tractor where somebody can find them. I don't know how he is about that. Some of the farmers won't let their workers use the machinery when they're away."

Märit taps a fingernail against her teeth. "No, I think I'll go back home. Who knows how long all this will take? I can walk back to the house."

He looks down at her feet. "In those shoes?"

"I'll stay on the road."

"I'm sorry," Ben tells her. "I know that you look forward to a day in town."

She leans forward and kisses him. "Never mind, it's not your fault."

Ben takes his jacket from the front seat and locks the doors.

"Sure you'll be all right?" he asks Märit. "It's quite a long walk."

"Of course I will. And don't forget about tonight."

"Tonight? What's on?"

"What you didn't do this morning."

Ben laughs and shakes his head. "You really are shameless. I'll see you back at the house."

18

AFTER THE PICKUP TRUCK has disappeared down the driveway and clanked across the cattle-grate, after the sound of the gate closing, then the whine of the engine fading, there is silence in the house.

Tembi has not been alone in the house before; always Märit was nearby, or the Baas.

The sounds of this house—the tick of the pipes in the water heater, the thunk of a piece of wood settling in the stove, the creak of the roof as it is warmed by the sun. She hears nothing else, nothing from the fields and the kraal, nothing of the birds or the leaves rustling in the eucalyptus trees, nothing of the river burbling across the stones.

The silence gives Tembi the sensation of illness—the illness of childhood, when she lay with influenza in her mother's hut, in the shadows, in that other place where she once lived, and the world with its sounds receded into the sliver of light that was the window, abandoning her, and she was forgotten.

Tembi puts down the can of Silvo she is using to polish the knives and forks, drops the soft yellow cloth, pushes her chair away from the table, and leaves the kitchen to go into the main part of the house.

In the living room she takes off the housecoat that Märit has given her, then kicks off her sandals and sits on the couch. The silence is oppressive, so she moves to the big radio that Baas Ben listens to in the morning, for the news and the weather, and turns the knob. The loud voice of a man speaking in Afrikaans fills the room, and she recoils slightly, then twists the knob until she hears music. For a moment she stands there, head inclined to the unfamiliar sound, trying to imagine the strange and faraway place where this music is made, then she turns the music down a little and crosses to the bookshelf.

The titles on the spines of the books, the words there, are as unfamiliar and strange to her as the music, from the same faraway place. Some she knows—a dictionary, a Bible—but most are strange. She pulls down *The Book of South African Birds*, and pages through the illustrations. She recognizes some of the birds, the shapes and colors familiar to her from the fields and gullies around the farm.

She sets the book back on the shelf and takes down another, with the word *Durban* on the spine, the name of a place that she has heard of, and this is a slim book, much leafed through. Pictures of the sea, and yellow sand beaches, and people with colorful bathing suits. But only white people are on the sand and in the waves. Except for one photograph of a smiling black man with many necklaces of shells, holding up a handful of bananas. Tembi wonders if this place Durban is only inhabited by white people.

But it is the pictures of the sea that she lingers over, wondering if the water is the same as that in the river, sweet and soft, but the sea is so blue, with white waves, and the river here below the willow trees is dark green, sometimes brownish after heavy rain, and there are reeds and trees along the banks. The sea is wide and flat and blue, and she wonders how the taste of the salt water would be on her tongue. She imagines that at night she would be able to hear the sea inhaling and exhaling, like the rhythm of her own breathing, how it rises and falls like the flanks of some sleeping animal in the moonlight.

The sound of an engine breaks the silence and Tembi darts quickly to the window. She peers down the driveway but there is no car. At the opposite window she sees the tractor chugging across a field, with the recognizable figure of Joshua the bossboy in the seat.

Clutching the book in her hand, Tembi walks down the hall and opens the door to the bedroom. She stands on the threshold and looks in, where she is forbidden to enter, where Märit has told her not to enter. Immediately she sees that this is a woman's room, and the first impression is that this room is like Märit: the colors, the scents, the textures—the secrets.

On the bed where the sheets are tousled she sees the sheen of a blue dress. Light throws itself back from a mirror on the dresser, sparkling through an array of perfume bottles. And the smell, of soap and powder and flowers. The smell of luxury. The smell that white women have—flowery—like roses and milk and honey.

She feels like someone who stands in front of a shop window where a cream cake rests on a stand. But always unobtainable, always on the other side of the glass. In her life, and the life of her mother and father, in the life of those people who have the same color skin as she does, there are no rooms like this. Her room has a hard earth floor, she sleeps on an iron bedstead that creaks and groans with every movement, she must sit on a wooden chair at a rickety table. There is no mirror full of glittering reflections in her room, only the small hand-mirror that reflects more shadow than light.

Tembi steps into the room. And she sees another person there in the mirror—a stranger—like a stain amidst the finery. A shabby stranger, a person of dirt. She turns away in dismay from the wretched sight of herself.

She runs her fingers across the jars on the dresser, the glittering bottles of perfumes and creams. She removes the stoppers and smells the contents, and the smell is too rich, too intense, too unfamiliar. Her own sharp smell is that of sweat, wood smoke, cooking odors, earth. In one bottle of perfume the scent reminds her of the first roses that come after the dry winter, and she tilts it over her wrist, the liquid splashing over her skin and onto the carpet. The room becomes a garden of roses as the perfume coats the air.

Now she touches the blue dress on the bed, a blue the color of the sea in the book, and she strokes the soft material for which she has no name. And when she lifts the dress in her hands and lets it caress her cheek there is no weight to the material, it is light, like the mist is light. She wraps the cloth around her, a soft blue mist, and turns to see herself in the mirror.

Is it only the dress that changes her? she wonders. And if Märit lived in the kraal, and wore the clothes that Tembi wears, and did not have her creams and perfumes, how would she look? How would she be changed?

She wonders if it is only the clothes that make a difference between her and Märit. In another country, not this country, would there be a difference? If she lived in a house like this one, and also went to town in a car, and also had a husband, where would be the difference between her and Märit? Only in the skin color is there a difference. And in the way that Tembi must live.

Tembi stands in front of the mirror and unbuttons her dress. She lets it fall to the floor and surveys herself, her reflection, naked but for her panties. If Märit stood here now they would be the same. Then she reaches for the dress and draws it over her head. And it fits her as if made for her body, except a little tight in the breasts because she is fuller there than Märit.

She looks into her own eyes in the mirror and sees herself as someone new. The woman in the blue dress is not her, she is not yet that woman. In that image behind the glass Tembi sees something she has not yet become. But will. She makes that promise to herself.

19

Märit walks away from the truck, back in the direction of the house, turning every now and then to look at Ben as he moves across the veldt to van Staden's farm. Once, he turns to look back at the same time as she does, and they wave to each other. Then the road curves and when she waves a last time he is lost to sight.

Rather than being disappointed by the turn events have taken, Märit finds herself enjoying the walk—as if she has been given an unexpected day off. There is no obligation upon her now, she doesn't have to be at home, where there is always something that needs to be done, nor does she have to play her role in town, for it is something of a role to be the farmer's wife, to sit with neighbors on the veranda of the hotel and listen to the gossip of the women, and answer their questions, which although phrased politely are prying and inquisitive of her personal life in a way that sometimes offends her. There is no one amongst the neighboring women with whom she has made friends. She is too different from them. And she senses that they pity her a little, that they condescend to her, as to a child, and that they think of her as too young and fragile, too inexperienced to make a success of the farm. Sometimes she thinks they want her to fail.

Her musings are interrupted by a sudden flash of familiar blue—the kingfisher again—once more darting across the road the way it did in front of the truck. Into the trees it flashes, twice more, closer to her, back and forth before disappearing. Märit leaves the road and turns towards the trees, following the kingfisher, until she sees it again, perched on a branch overhanging the river.

The river is wide here, but shallow, dotted with rocks that the water foams around as it flows swiftly downstream in the sunlight. Märit crosses the shingle of pebbles and finds herself a seat on a flat rock at the edge of the shore. She slips off her shoes, setting them on the rock, and lets her feet touch the surface of the moving water. A little shock of cold makes her shiver, but then, as her skin accustoms itself to the temperature, she moves her feet deeper, up to the ankles, savoring the coolness.

The kingfisher darts away, a flicker of blue feathers above the water.

Suddenly she wants to swim, to sink into that swift stream and feel the current against her body. The desire is like a thirst. She has no bathing suit or towel, though—and what if she were seen? But there is nobody about; the screen of trees hides her from the road, and in the other direction is open veldt. If someone were to come she would see them. The thought of removing her clothes is both a fear and a desire.

The kingfisher flies back, dipping just above the river, free in its world.

She unbuttons her jacket and slips it off. Then she unfastens her blouse and opens it so that the sun touches her belly. She divests herself of her brassiere, her skirt, her panties, and steps quickly into the shallows, feeling the cool swift water rise up her calves, then over her knees and thighs as she goes deeper. She crouches and immerses herself up to her shoulders, gasping at the cold.

The river tugs at Märit's body, gently, insistently, like a caress, urging her to submit, to give herself to the current. She clasps her arms around a rock that rises above the water, pressing her face and her shoulders and her breasts against the warm smooth stone as one would embrace a lover, and the silky motion of the river strokes her flanks and smoothes over her buttocks. Märit submits, shutting her eyes, giving herself.

Then awareness returns, and anxiety, and the realization of where she is. Raising her head, she glances back to the rocks where her pile of clothes is gathered. How foolish to do this. What if she were seen? Releasing her embrace of the rock she scrambles back to shore, the river tugging at her thighs as if not wanting her to go. Her wet skin soaks her blouse as she slips it on. With the skirt in her hand she sits back down on the warm rock.

The sun will dry her. Extending her limbs to the light and the warmth she leans back on her elbows. Beads of moisture speckle her pale skin and glimmer in the patch of hair between her thighs. Her eyelids droop, then shut as she basks in the heat of the sun.

If Ben were here it would be different, she would not be half anxious, afraid of being seen, she could give herself over completely. Her thoughts turn towards the events of the morning. She wanted him so much when she woke up and saw him naked before the mirror. If he were here now they could swim together; she could clasp him, instead of unyielding stone. Märit realizes that she has never been naked outdoors with her husband. The closest they ever came was in Durban, when they swam in the ocean together, separated only by the cloth of their bathing suits.

Every now and then she half opens her eyes and looks around, confirming that she is alone, unseen. She is aware of the nearness of the road, of the possibility of being seen, of the fact that she is breaking the rules.

When she shuts her eyes again, a sudden memory surfaces, something long buried, like a shadow hidden in the deep current of the water. She remembers water, her skin wet and naked, and that other skin—black skin and white skin, naked together. She remembers the rules being broken.

IT WAS THE YEAR that Märit turned fifteen—a period of transition from childhood to something else, not yet adulthood—but she sensed the differences in herself even if she did not understand them.

Märit's parents arranged for her to spend a few weeks with a girl named Sondra at a farm outside the city. She did not know Sondra, she did not want to go, but her father told her that it was a chance to widen her experience, and her mother told her that it was better than being cooped up in the city. Sondra was the daughter of her parents' friends, a girl who went to a different school, a girl who was older than Märit. One morning Märit overheard her mother on the phone discussing the holiday—there was a mention of Sondra's "crisis," of "difficulties" being over, of Märit's presence being a good influence on Sondra.

From the first day it was obvious that Sondra regarded Märit as a burden to be endured. Sondra was polite, but distant, and once away from the presence of her parents, she ignored Märit completely. Friendship, confidence, intimacy were out of the question.

The place was not a farm, but a large suburban house transplanted to the countryside, reached by a long and bumpy sand road that wound down from the main highway. There were gardens, orchards, a swimming pool surrounded by rose beds. The rooms were dark, shadowy, silent. A grave servant came in each day to clean. Sondra's father departed early to his job in the city and her mother was frequently away from the house on various errands of her own. Sondra spent her time reading magazines at the side of the swimming pool, stretched out in a deck chair with her eyes hidden behind dark glasses.

All of Märit's efforts to know Sondra were rejected. The other girl remained hidden behind an impenetrable wall. The friendship that their respective parents had hoped for did not develop. Märit retreated into silence, counting the days until she could return home.

During the long hours of the day she wandered around the gardens and sat by the pool reading, sometimes slipping into the water when she was hot. The only other person that she ever saw was a boy who tended the gardens and cleaned the swimming pool. His name was Dollar. He was black. A boy her age, dressed in khaki shirt and shorts, dragging the hose around, pushing a wheelbarrow, skimming the fallen leaves from the surface of the swimming pool.

At first Märit barely took notice of him, then she watched him, interested in his presence. Sometimes he looked back at her and smiled shyly. After a few days he began to nod and mumble a greeting to her.

Out of necessity, out of desperation, Märit turned to him for company.

They were reserved at first, not sure how to act in each other's company; she was of the house and he was of the garden, she was white and he was not.

Sometimes, when Sondra was not in her usual place at the pool, Dollar would crouch next to Märit where she reclined in her deck chair and share an illicit cigarette with her. Sometimes he would cut a sprig of mimosa from the garden and present it to her.

One very hot day, when the cement flagstones burned her feet and there was no shade, and she could find relief only in the blue water of the swimming pool, Dollar appeared, pushing a wheelbarrow loaded with soil. Perspiration stood out in glistening beads on his face and the shirt on his back was dark with sweat. When he saw Märit in the pool he stopped and looked at the water with such longing in his face that she impulsively called out, "Dollar! Come and swim."

He lowered the wheelbarrow, then wiped the sweat from his brow. His expression was doubtful.

"Come on, Dollar." Märit splashed water at his feet, where it immediately evaporated on the hot flagstones.

His eyes moved up to the house, hidden behind the rosebushes, and he laughed nervously.

"They're not here," she said, meaning Sondra's parents. She did not know where Sondra was.

He looked towards the house again, then came around to the shallow end of the pool and bent to unlace his sneakers. He sat down on the edge and let his legs dangle in the water.

"Yes, it's nice," he said to Märit.

She swam a lazy breaststroke towards him. "It's nicer if you're all the way in."

He directed another look towards the house.

"Come on," she called. "Nobody is around."

"No, I'm not knowing how to swim, Märit."

"I'll teach you."

"Okay." Dollar unbuttoned his shirt, bundled it to one side, and slipped into the water up to his chest. Briefly he shut his eyes, gasping with pleasure. The moisture beaded on his shoulders and chest and danced with reflected blue light from the pool. Märit turned on her back and kicked lazily around him.

"Show me how to do that, Märit. You can teach me."

"Here, put your hands on the side of the pool," she said, moving next to him. "Good, now move your legs like this, like a pair of scissors."

"Like a frog!" He imitated the sound of a frog croaking.

"Pay attention, Dollar! Now you have to do the same thing with your arms. This way, as if you are opening curtains. And remember to keep your mouth closed." She pushed away from the side of the pool to demonstrate.

After one or two spluttering attempts he found a rhythm, and paddled back and forth across the shallow end, head held high, a smile on his face.

"It's easy, Märit! You didn't tell me it can be so easy to swim. Now I can race you!"

"Hah!" Märit kicked away with a powerful stroke. To her surprise Dollar kept up, and she increased her pace. As she moved past him he grabbed at her ankle, and they both went down in a tangle of limbs, then surfaced laughing.

"You cheated!" Märit exclaimed, grasping his shoulders and trying to push him down. His arms came around her waist and lifted her, spinning her body. Her thighs wrapped around his waist as she struggled for supremacy, and in that moment of contact she was suddenly aware of him as a boy, a man, and of her own body, her breasts on his chest, the warmth of his skin under her hands, and the firmness of his body against the juncture of her thighs.

Märit looked into his eyes. The smell of him was sweet, like the earth in the garden, like the mimosa in the garden. Despite the cool water she suddenly felt heat pulse through her.

A shadow fell across the blue water of the pool, across Märit and Dollar. They both looked up at the same time.

Sondra stood looking down at them in her white bikini and her dark sunglasses. "The pool is not for the use of the servants, Märit." Not an angry tone, but condescending, sarcastic, as if speaking to a child who ought to know better. Sondra lifted her sunglasses and said, "Dollar, go back to your work."

Dollar released Märit and scrambled out of the pool, hunching over as he retrieved his sneakers and shirt. As he stood up, turning his back to them, both girls noticed the bulge at the front of his shorts. Märit glanced at Sondra quickly, long enough to see the direction of Sondra's gaze.

"I really don't think you should be playing with the garden boy, Märit," Sondra said with a faint smile curling her lips. "Even if you find him attractive. It's improper."

"Sorry," Märit murmured, her face going hot and the water of the pool suddenly cold against her skin.

Märit avoided Dollar after that, swimming only when he was not around, and if she saw him when she was in the garden she walked in the opposite direction, succumbing to a peculiar feeling of shame.

A couple of days after this incident she telephoned her mother and demanded to return home.

The day before her departure she felt feverish, oppressed by the sudden heat, the cloying smell of the mimosa, the monotonous drone of the bees. Kneeling at the edge of the pool she dipped her fingers in the cool water and brought them to her flushed cheeks. The very air seemed to hang on her like a fever.

She noticed that Dollar had left the hose running in one of the flower beds and the muddy water was trickling in a slow stain across the cement towards the swimming pool. The faucet was located next to the little cabana that housed the deck chairs and cushions—a musty little room that Märit avoided using, preferring to put on her bathing suit in the house.

As she reached to turn off the tap a muffled mewing sound came to her ears. She turned to look for the cat, for that is what it sounded like—sometimes she had seen a cat that drifted around the periphery, a cat without a name that fended for itself, occasionally coming into the kitchen for scraps.

Märit cocked her ear, and the mewing was there, not plaintive, but steady and insistent. Kittens, she thought, the sound was just like that of kittens. Perhaps there were kittens hidden in the cabana. The idea pleased her; she could ask to take a kitten home with her. But when she tried the door of the cabana she found it unaccountably locked, with no key in the door. She moved to the little window on the side of the building.

The window glass was dirty, obscuring the interior of the cabana, but the mewing was louder now, high-pitched and urgent. Märit pressed her face against the glass, eager to see the kittens.

In the shadows a shape moved, something pale and too large to be a cat. Märit could not understand what she was looking at—the shape was like a pale cloth moving back and forth. She peered closer, cupping her hands on either side of her face and pressing against the window. And then she realized what it was—the naked back of Sondra.

But why had Sondra locked herself in the cabana? And why was she rocking back and forth like that, making kitten noises?

Märit raised her hand to knock on the window, and at the same time Sondra arched her back and her breasts were visible, paler than the rest of her skin, and a hand reached out from the shadows and stroked one breast, then a head stretched forward to kiss the breast, and the moaning rose loud from Sondra's throat.

Märit pulled away in fright. But she did not call out.

Slowly she leaned forward and pressed her face to the window again. Dollar was reclining on the cushions strewn across the floor of the cabana, his shorts around his ankles as Sondra straddled him. Märit watched as his head lifted forward to kiss Sondra's breasts, and she saw Sondra rise into a crouch, her buttocks milky white below the tan lines of her bikini, and Märit saw Dollar's erect penis enter the place between Sondra's thighs.

Märit shut her eyes and clenched her fists over her ears. She stumbled away from the cabana, pressing her knuckles hard against her ears, shaking her head from side to side. She didn't want to see, she didn't want to hear. Nothing, nothing, nothing. The shame, the awfulness, the obscenity of it. She didn't want to see, she didn't want to hear. Inside herself she felt the violence, the pleasure, so that she wanted to cry out. The fever was inside her, burning.

Oh, the betrayal! The beasts! The jealousy burned in her face. She hated Dollar and Sondra. As she ran blindly from the cabana, shaking her head from side to side to banish the image of what she had seen, she knew that she could not—because she wanted to be there, with Dollar, in place of Sondra.

20

THE SOUND of a vehicle on the road brings Märit back to a sudden awareness of her surroundings. The images of the swimming pool, of the cabana, and of Dollar, flee as she looks up, realizing that she is half naked.

Hurriedly she pulls on her skirt and stuffs her brassiere into her handbag, all the while listening to the sound of the engine. What if it stops— one of the neighbors, the van Stadens? How will she explain herself, sitting here dripping wet, half dressed?

By the time Märit reaches the road the vehicle is not in sight; there is only the faint sound of the receding engine as the dust settles. It could have been Ben, she tells herself. The engine sounded familiar. He must have found assistance with the truck and got it fixed, and he is probably going back to the farm to fetch her. She sets off at a brisk pace, carrying her shoes in her hand.

The walk back to the house takes little more than a half hour, but when Märit reaches the house she doesn't see the truck in the driveway. She wonders if Ben has parked it already in the garage.

The radio is playing softly in the living room as Märit enters from the veranda. She leans against a chair for a moment, rubbing at the soles of her aching feet.

"Ben?" she calls. "Are you back?"

Draped across the couch is the housecoat that Märit asked Tembi to wear when cleaning the house. Then she sees Tembi's sandals lying on the floor.

A quick accumulation of images tumbles through Märit's mind—pictures, not thoughts—Dollar and Sondra in the cabana, Ben crouching next to Tembi to retrieve the fallen tray in the breakfast room, the look on Ben's face. Märit stands a moment, frowning at the discarded housecoat on the chair, at the sandals kicked negligently off, aware of the soft music on the radio.

"Ben?"

Without calling out again she walks softly on bare feet down the corridor to the bedroom. The door is ajar. On the bed Märit sees the rumpled sheets, Tembi stretched out in a position of abandon with one arm flung to the side, wearing a blue dress, Märit's own blue silk dress from Durban, the one she wore on her honeymoon. The air in the room is thick with the scent of roses.

"Ben?" The images in Märit's mind twist into a tangle of limbs and bare skin entwined on the sheets.

Tembi raises herself from the bed, eyes clouded with sleep. Märit shouts, "What do you think you are doing in here? Get up!"

MÄRIT'S HAND closes around Tembi's wrist and jerks her upright, dragging her across the bed. She tumbles to the floor as a blow lands across her shoulders. Her arm feels as if it is being wrenched from its socket. The voice is shouting at her.

Tembi manages to scramble away across the floor and half rises to her feet. But then Märit is grabbing and flailing at her again. She cowers under the blows.

"How dare you wear that dress!" Märit shouts. "How dare you!"

Tembi cannot think, she cannot gather her thoughts in this sudden onslaught. Märit is pushing her out of the room, along the corridor towards the kitchen, grabbing and slapping at her, shouting all the time.

"This is not your house! That is not your dress! Get out, get out!"

Once they are in the kitchen Tembi manages to pull away. "Let me go!"

Märit is pale with rage, two bright red spots burning on her cheeks. Her hand grasps the bodice of the dress and pulls. With a ripping sound a long tear appears down the front. Märit grabs at the cloth, tearing it off Tembi's body.

The dress falls away, leaving Tembi naked except for her underwear.

"Leave me alone," Tembi screams, shocked out of her surprise and fright at last. She pushes at Märit. "Don't touch me!"

"Who do you think you are?" Märit shouts. Her hand flies up and slaps Tembi hard across the cheek. "Get out of here! This is not your house!"

The tears of pain and shame are sudden and hot in Tembi's eyes, blurring the room around her. She falls back against the kitchen table, stunned. It is not the pain of the slap on her face that silences her, but the astonishment. She has never been struck before, never been touched by another's hand in that way. Not even as a child. The violence shocks Tembi, the perverse intimacy of the violence—to be touched in this manner by a stranger.

And still Märit is shouting and pushing at her, shoving her towards the back door. Tembi stumbles down the steps, and the door slams with a bang behind her.

The world swims. A pain throbs in her chest, lodged deep in her heart. She falls to her knees in the dust, sobbing. The blow across her face still burns, pulsing with the beating of her heart. She feels again the flat, smacking sound of Märit's palm. The violence of it. The obscenity of it. The shame.

Clutching her arms across her exposed breasts she runs hunched over back to the kraal, away from the house.

21

AT THE VAN STADEN FARM Ben has managed to find someone to help him start his pickup truck. He considers whether to return to the house and fetch Märit or to press on to town. A glance at his watch shows him that there is time still to collect his seedlings from the station, but only if he drives there directly. He decides to phone Märit from the station and explain to her. They can always come back to Klipspring tomorrow.

After completing his errand at the station, Ben drives out of town with the two dozen seedlings sitting in a tray next to him on the seat, the loamy smell of the earth that they are packed in filling the cabin. In his mind he sees the row of almond trees that will develop from these seedlings, he sees the blossoms waving in the breeze, he sees the future. Ben smiles to himself and begins to whistle.

All around him is the veldt of Africa, his home. Rolling down the window he inhales as the scent of the countryside flows into the car. He would know this particular smell anywhere; if he was a sailor on board a ship in the darkest night and a brief whiff of this land came on a breeze he would know this smell. It is in him, in his clothes, on his hands and hair, embedded in the very pores of his skin. He knows this smell in the morning when the earth is wet from the dew, he knows it after rain, when the dust has been washed from the air and a slight mist hangs on the ground and the earth is newly washed.

The grass flows across the veldt, undulating over the dips and rises; the trees stand dark and green; the hills and koppies rise and fall, the mountains are soft and blue in the distance.

In his heart Ben feels that this is home. He has known it since he first saw this landscape. When the neighboring farmers talk of blood and soil, Ben understands what they mean, even though he is a recent arrival, and was not born in this country, and does not have any history of farming in his family. Even so, he understands that he belongs here. His soul has recognized this place, and the longing that was in him has been stilled.

Above the treetops on the right hand side of the road, the girders and aerials of the radio transmitter are visible and Ben realizes with a guilty start that he forgot to call Märit from the station. He pictures her walking along the road in her elegant clothes—he is proud of her when she accompanies him to Klipspring—but if he imagines her out here on the veldt, she seems misplaced and out of her element. He really should have remembered to phone her.

Ah well, he thinks, nothing to be done now, and he'll be home soon anyway. He feels no urgency to hurry, for if the truth be told, he is happiest like this, alone in the veldt under the clean sunlight, in company with the breeze and the scent of the earth.

As the pickup follows a curve, Ben sees a small herd of impala standing in the middle of the road. He is not driving very fast and it is easy enough to slow the car to a halt. The antelope raise their heads, black-tipped ears swiveling towards the truck, short tails flicking from side to side, alert to him but not alarmed. The herd is clumped together, a mass of tawny brown hides with heraldic antlers above them like branches. Ben is close enough to see the dark liquid eyes, which remind him of the cattle on the farm.

When he leans out of the window for a closer look at the animals, heads turn to regard him, muzzles lifted to his scent, ears twitching. Then the herd of impala sets off at a quick trot. Because the brush is thick on either side, the herd stays on the road, and Ben drives slowly behind them.

The road forks—in one direction lies Kudufontein, to the right is the radio tower, and beyond that the border. The impala take the right-hand road. Ben follows in the truck, mesmerized by the grace and delicacy of the thin legs and the tawny hides and the outward curving horns, all bathed in golden light and purple shadows.

As the herd of antelope passes the radio tower, Ben increases speed slightly to keep up and the herd takes fright, breaking into sudden long stretching leaps that are like water shooting over a falls, that are like a ballet, that defy gravity.

Ben hears the thudding of the hooves on the road, and smells the dust they kick up, and he is one with them, leaping and stretching through the air, his heart running with them.

As the underbrush clears, they veer off across the veldt in one smooth flowing motion.

And here on this quiet stretch of country road, where earlier that morning two men paused in the dawn, the wheels of Ben's pickup truck roll over the device those men have buried in the sand, the weight of the vehicle triggering a fuse, which detonates an explosive charge that rips upward into the engine of the truck. The gasoline in the fuel tank ignites with an instant searing heat. The truck becomes a sudden ball of flaming metal as it skids off the road into the underbrush and explodes.

Across the veldt, the herd of impala leaps high above the grass.

22

INSIDE THE HOUSE Märit pulls the sheets from the bed and bundles them into a heap on the floor. She flings open the window to dissipate the cloying smell of perfume that fills the room. With the bundled sheets in her hand she marches through to the laundry room; she has half a mind to take them outside and burn them, but she stuffs them into the washer and sets the temperature to the hottest setting.

Her blue dress is still lying on the floor in the kitchen, her torn blue dress that will never be worn again, not by anyone. She pushes the dress into the rubbish bin under the sink, then washes her hands. As she dries them she remembers the sound of the slap she delivered to Tembi's face, remembers the feel of it on her palm, and the look of shock in Tembi's eyes. Good, she thinks, good. Tembi deserved it, deserved to be thrown out half naked like that. Let her go back to the kraal and tell the others what she had done, sneaking into the Missus's room and wearing her clothes and sleeping in her bed. Let her go back naked and ashamed.

In the living room Märit pours herself a glass of gin with trembling hands, adds a spray of soda water, then takes a big swallow. The taste is vile and she pours in a few drops of lime cordial and stirs the liquid with her finger. Her hand is trembling, she notices, and her whole body is coiled tightly like a bale of wire.

With her drink in hand she stands at the window and lights a cigarette.

When Ben gets back, she will demand that he do something about this. He is too casual with the workers as it is, and now they think they can treat her as a familiar. They have to learn to respect her. But what can he do? He will think she is overreacting. And she can't explain to him that she thought for an instant that he was in the bedroom too. It is her own fault for letting Tembi have the run of the house.

Where is Ben? He should have been back by now.

She paces back and forth as she smokes, sipping occasionally at her gin, and slowly calms down as the alcohol uncoils the tightness within her.

She finishes her drink and goes to the cabinet to make another one, then stands sipping it at the window. Shadows from the eucalyptus trees are beginning to stretch across the lawn. Where is Ben? She wonders if she should telephone the van Staden farm and ask if they have seen him. As she turns away from the window her eyes fall upon Tembi's housecoat, still lying across the couch.

Suddenly a great sadness descends upon Märit, as if the long shadows have come into the room and enveloped her, like a cloak of sorrow. Why is everything so wrong? When she looks out the window at the farm it is a meaningless place—what does it have to do with her? If she were to leave tomorrow, who would care, who would remember? Even Ben, how long would he care? After a while he would find himself a real wife, who could bear him children, who could work next to him on the land.

She hears again the sound of her palm slapping Tembi's face, what an ugly sound, flesh striking flesh, and she knows that she was wrong in what she did. But she had been confused, everything mixed up in her mind.

It was an overreaction, from the surprise and the shock, from the fear that Ben was in the house, had been in the bed, and the revulsion that thought had given her. And the fear. She sinks down on the couch and bows her head, covering her face as the tears come.

At last she rises and goes through to the bedroom, where she rummages around amongst her jewelry until she finds a bracelet made of blue stone beads—the same color as her dress, another purchase from her honeymoon in Durban—a gift from Ben, bought one afternoon at the Victoria Street Market.

Clutching the bracelet in her fist Märit leaves the house and follows the path that leads to the kraal. The sun is high but the shadows under the trees are thick. A smell of wood smoke fills the air. At the edge of the kraal she pauses, hearing voices. A group of women are standing over the communal fire pit, tending to the big cast-iron cooking pot, one of them stirring the contents with a long wooden spoon. A few chickens peck in the dust near the huts. To one side, outside the washhouse, a man bends over a tap, shirtless, with his head thrust under the gushing water. There is no sign of Tembi.

The women notice her presence and turn towards her, expectantly, ceasing their talk. The man at the tap raises his head, also turning to her with the same air of expectation. A small child wanders over towards Märit, half timid, half curious, his eyes fixed on the blue bracelet dangling from her fingers. Just a little boy, with a smear of mud across his cheek and a patched sweater that is too small for his frame.

"Do you know Tembi?" Märit asks.

The boy nods his head.

"Is she here?"

He shakes his head, his big round eyes held by the gleam of the blue stones in her hand.

Across the clearing the women watch her. The man at the tap has turned and stands with his hands resting on his hips. The beads of moisture glisten on his shoulders in the sun. He returns her gaze without embarrassment, curious, alert to her presence. His skin is wet, smooth, and silky. Just like Dollar, she thinks, the thought rising to her awareness unbidden.

There is no welcome in the faces that watch her, only curiosity, only wariness. She is unable to go forward towards the huts, to cross an unmarked line in the dust.

Märit shakes her head and looks down at the boy. "Give this to Tembi," she says, thrusting the bracelet towards him. Then she turns and walks back to the house, overcome with a sense of being outside of the life in the kraal, of not being welcome there. She walks back to the safety of the house, a sense of shame upon her.

23

A FAINT PLUME of yellow dust appears above the road that runs past the farm called Kudufontein, a familiar sight to those who live in this district, a signal of the passage of a vehicle between the farms that lie along these sandy roads in the back country near the border.

From the window of the house Märit watches the column of dust as it approaches, fast-moving, thick, perhaps more than one vehicle, someone in a hurry to be somewhere. Is it Ben? she wonders. For some reason she remembers a line from a Sunday school Bible lesson: "By day in a pillar of cloud, to lead them the way; and by night in a pillar of fire."

Two cars come slowly up the drive towards the house—the old blue Mercedes of her neighbors, the van Stadens, and behind it a white Land Rover with dark-tinted windows. There is no third vehicle, no red pickup truck, no Ben.

Märit draws back slightly from the window, her eyes fixed on the Land Rover, on the sinister dark windows.

The cars come to a halt on the driveway in front of the house with a loud crunching of tires on gravel. For a moment nobody alights from the vehicles, nobody reveals himself, while beyond the two cars the plume of yellow dust slowly revolves in the still air, then settles back towards the road.

It is Connie van Staden who first appears, easing herself from the Mercedes, patting away the wrinkles in her dress: a middle-aged woman in dark clothes, dressed formally, dressed in the way one would on a Sunday visit to church, not in the more casual manner of a visit to a neighbor. Her husband, Koos, appears next, unfamiliar to Märit in his suit, but still wearing his ever-present slouch hat. Connie says a word to him across the roof of the car and he takes off his hat. They both peer at the house for a moment, then turn their attention to the white Land Rover.

The driver's door swings open and a policeman in a gray uniform steps out, settling his cap on his head and flexing his knees to free the cloth of his trousers from his crotch. Märit recognizes him—the sergeant from the police station in Klipspring, a big, boyish man with a soft face. Sergeant Jonker—no, Joubert. He looks at the house before nodding to the van Stadens, and all three turn to look at the Land Rover expectantly.

The man who gets out from the passenger side is a stranger to Märit. A stranger in mirrored sunglasses and civilian clothes: a light-colored safari suit, knee socks, tan desert boots—the uniform favored by government officials during the summer months.

Märit draws back from the window as the man looks up at the house. She notices the posture of deference the sergeant takes with this stranger, and the way that Koos and Connie van Staden look to him, waiting for him to take the first action. Märit keeps her eyes on this man in his safari suit, with his eyes obscured behind the reflective sunglasses. He seems sinister, ominous, foreboding creating an aura around his body. She knows he brings bad news.

As he mounts the steps Märit moves even farther back into the room. She does not want to meet this stranger at her door, she does not want to admit him to her house—if she does not let him enter, he will go away with his news untold, and whatever has happened will not have happened.

The stranger lifts the brass knocker on the door, the knocker in the shape of an ox head, and lets it fall three times, summoning her.

Märit stands paralyzed, staring at the door.

The knocking sounds again, this time made by a hand, bare knuckles on the wood, and she knows it is the stranger who knocks, summoning her.

Her footsteps take her to the door, each step weighted with dread.

As she opens the door the stranger steps back, his hand raised to knock again, his hand lifted as if in a fist against her. Startled, he lowers his arm and steps away from Märit. It is Connie van Staden who steps forward now, her mouth squeezed into a grim line.

"Oh, Märit, Märit." She lifts her arms to Märit, opening them to embrace. "Oh, Märit, I'm so sorry to come like this."

The fear and the pity in Connie's eyes cause Märit to retreat, away from Connie's reach—she does not want to be embraced by this fear and this pity.

Her throat is tight but she forces the words out. "What has happened? It's Ben, isn't it? Tell me what's happened."

Connie wrings her hands together. "Oh, Märit, it's terrible! I don't know what to say."

Her husband clears his throat and looks down at his shoes and puts his hands behind his back and avoids Märit's eyes.

She turns to the stranger. "Is it about Ben? What's happened to him?"

The policeman steps forward, removing his cap. "Mevrou Laurens, I'm Sergeant Joubert. We met before, you remember, in town, with your husband, when you came to the police station . . ." He does not finish his sentence.

Now the stranger removes his sunglasses, and Märit sees his eyes, which have no fear, which have no pity or concern, but which are watchful light blue eyes, regarding her with curiosity.

"Our news is not good, I am afraid, Mevrou. Perhaps we had better go inside, where you can sit down."

He speaks English to her, but with a thick Afrikaans accent, the words clipped and guttural.

"It's Ben, isn't it? I know it is. Tell me what has happened to him." She puts a hand on the door frame to steady herself against the sudden weakness in her legs.

Connie takes Märit by the elbow. "Come, it's better that we go inside," she says, and Märit allows herself to be led to a chair.

The others sit, except the stranger. Märit looks up at him, waiting.

"There was an explosion earlier today at the radio tower outside Klipspring. I regret to tell you, Mevrou Laurens, that your husband was killed in that explosion."

The air goes out of Märit's lungs, as if this man has punched her in the chest.

So there it is—Death. She knew it was Death the moment she saw this stranger get out of the Land Rover. He has the air of Death around him. He is someone used to talking about Death.

Märit tilts her head back and tries to breathe. The meaning of the words sinks in. Then she grasps—at hope. "By the radio tower? But Ben wasn't at the radio tower. He went to the station. Why should he be at the radio tower? That's in the other direction. There must be a mistake." She swings her head from face to face, searching for confirmation.

Sergeant Joubert takes a deep breath. "I'm sorry, but there is no mistake, Mevrou. I knew your husband. I recognized him."

The reference to Ben in the past tense is like a door slamming shut on hope.

The stranger sits down now and crosses one leg over the other and looks at her with his watchful, curious expression, without visible sympathy in his pale blue eyes.

"Who are you?" Märit demands angrily, turning on him, because who else is there to blame except this man who comes with Death. "What is your name?"

"Forgive me, I did not introduce myself." He slips a laminated card from his breast pocket and places it on the polished surface of the coffee table. "Gideon Schoon. Security Branch—Defense Forces." Märit ignores the card, and after a moment he retrieves it and buttons it into his pocket again.

"What is this to do with you?" Märit says. "Ben wasn't at the radio tower. He went to the station to fetch a load of seedlings." She shakes her head, trying to grasp everything that has been said. "What explosion?"

"A bomb was planted at the tower, sometime last night we believe. A terrorist action. It appears that the terrorists also buried a land mine on the road near the tower. Your husband was in his truck, on that road. Evidently his vehicle triggered the land mine, killing him in the resulting explosion."

She can't form an image to go with his words. "Killing him . . . ?" she mutters. Then she looks at Connie and Koos van Staden, and at the sergeant. "Where is Ben?" she appeals to them. "I want to see him. I don't believe any of this. It doesn't make any sense."

"First it is necessary for me to ask you some questions, Mevrou," Schoon says. "Then we can take you to see your husband."

"Are you sure it's Ben?" Märit asks the sergeant, ignoring the other man. "How do you know for sure?"

"It was his truck, Mevrou, the red pickup."

"There are other trucks like that."

"I'm sorry, but it was him. I recognized him . . . the body." He looks down at his hands, shaking his head.

Connie van Staden rises to her feet and puts a reassuring hand on Märit's shoulder. "Can't these questions wait, Captain Schoon? It's not the right time now."

"Time is of the essence," he replies. "I intend to apprehend these criminals." He leans forward to Märit. "Now, the road your husband was on, Mevrou Laurens, it does not lead to this farm. There is a fork outside of Klipspring that branches away towards the radio tower and the border. Can you tell me why your husband would be on that road, traveling in the opposite direction from his home?"

"He went to the station, to fetch seedlings that he had ordered. He wants to plant almond trees. He would have come straight home."

"Do you have acquaintances over there?" Schoon asks. "Maybe he was going to visit someone? Does he go that way often?"

"No," she says slowly, shaking her head.

"No? Let me ask you this, Mevrou. Do you or your husband have contact with any persons across the border? Did he ever travel there? Did you go with him?"

"Where? I don't know what you are talking about."

Schoon studies Märit a moment without speaking.

"Did your husband get on well with the *kaffirs* who work here?"

"That is not a word Ben uses. Neither do I!"

"Very well," Schoon comments with a shrug. "Let me put it this way— what was your husband's relation with his workers? Did he discuss the political situation with them?"

"Ben treats the workers well. Fairly. With respect."

"And you, Mevrou? Do you socialize with the blacks? Do you have them into the house?"

Märit does not answer. She looks at Schoon's hands, which are small and thick, with strands of fine dark hair growing on the back of his fingers, and the sight of his hands fills her with revulsion, almost a sexual revulsion against his maleness. There is an over-sweet smell of hair oil around him. He seems to her not a man, but some kind of animal, compact and thick-bodied, in his safari suit and his knee socks, and with his small hyena-like eyes.

She wants to stand up from her chair and order him from the house, this announcer of Death, this scavenger. But her limbs feel heavy, leaden. And what is the use, what will change? Märit stares past him, through him. It doesn't matter—nothing matters. What is this man to her? Nothing.

"How would you describe your husband's political sympathies, Mevrou Laurens?"

"Ben is a farmer." She cannot bring herself to use the past tense. Nothing of this is quite real to her. Ben will come back. This strange interrogation is only a dream, outside of reality.

Schoon waits for her to continue, and when she does not, he jerks his head with a small gesture of irritation. "Ja, we know that, but did he favor the present way of life here, did he want change, did he work with anybody from outside? Have there been strangers visiting him? Does he know about explosives?"

Märit turns on him angrily. "Why are you asking me all these questions? Where is my husband?"

"I need to know these things, Mevrou Laurens," Schoon answers, unperturbed.

The faces look at Märit expectantly, as if some revelation on her part will explain away everything.

"Ben is a farmer, that's all," Märit says.

Then Koos van Staden clears his throat apologetically and says, "If you don't mind me saying this, Captain Schoon, I knew Ben Laurens, and I think you are barking up the wrong tree here, so to speak."

Schoon runs a finger across each side of his mustache. He turns his head to look at Koos, then at the sergeant, who sits gazing down at his hands sheepishly. Schoon focuses his attention on Märit again. He takes a deep breath and softens his voice as he speaks. "We are all on the same side here. These terrorists, these criminals who come into our country at night like cowards and plant their bombs, killing innocent people, they are the enemy. Innocent people, Mevrou, like your husband. I don't have to tell you that we are all in danger—anyone who lives on an isolated farm is in danger. You might not like me, because I have to bring the bad news and ask the questions, and I accept that—but I have to ask them."

Schoon looks around the room again. "With your permission, Mevrou, I will have to bring a team in here and question your workers."

And if I refuse, she wants to say, but does not because she sees the utter disregard for her opinion in his eyes.

She feels very tired and heavy, and she feels old, so very old and so very far away from these three strangers in her house. None of this makes sense to her. Yet at the same time a terrible, final certainty has descended on her.

"I don't care what you do," Märit mutters.

Ben is gone. Ben is dead. Without him the farm means nothing to her. She suddenly feels an intense loneliness. If only her mother were here, to hold her, to tell her that everything will be all right. But she is alone in all the world now.

Connie rises and touches Märit's shoulder. "We will take you to him, child. Come now," she says softly, holding out her arms, "we will take you to him."

24

IN KLIPSPRING, a town of tidy gardens and small houses on quiet streets, there is a church on Wolmarans Street, a plain white church with a black spire, surrounded by neat lawns behind a wrought-iron fence. It is to this church, to the small graveyard behind the church, that Märit has allowed them to bring Ben.

She has allowed them to bring him here because she is numb, lethargic, moving with the great weariness upon her. Ben should be buried on the farm, but Connie van Staden tells her this is for the best, and Predikant Venter tells her this is for the best, that Ben should be buried here in hallowed ground, amongst his own kind, and not on the farm.

She has allowed them to bring him here, rather than to the farm, because she is weary, and cannot see beyond the requirements of each moment, each daily task of washing herself, and dressing, and sitting in the car, and stepping from it onto the grounds of this church. She cannot see the future.

The sun is a hard yellow disk in the sky and the clods of earth next to the grave turn gray and dusty in the heat, and the people gathered around the grave give off a smell of perspiration and perfume that is turning stale.

Märit stands silent in her dark clothes and her veil. Her thick chestnut hair is drawn into a tight bun on her neck, so tight that it pinches and pulls the skin of her scalp. In the hard sunlight the face of Predikant Venter is sallow, and the farmers and their wives shift uncomfortably in their formal dark clothes. Perspiration trickles under heavy cloth, on the pale flesh hidden under heavy cloth. The words drone from the lips of the Predikant, the way they drone when he speaks in church on Sundays.

Now is the time of burial. Märit does not weep. Weeping will come later. All she knows now is that she has crossed a river, and everything that she once called her life has been left behind on the other side. That place will now be called the past. And what happens from now on will be called her life. There is a before and an after. Everything will be different now.

In the hard sky a hawk drifts on the current, up there where the air is cool. And somewhere unseen beyond the neat town, the drone of a tractor is faintly audible. And here a body is placed in the earth, and covered up, and everything will be different after this.

The dry soil falls upon the coffin and Märit looks away. It is unbearable to think of his body in there—not even a body, just mangled flesh.

Märit does not weep. But as the clods of earth thud onto the coffin in its cavity in the earth she wants to step forward and say, No, not here, he would have wanted to lie in the earth on the farm, on his own land. It was all he wanted, to have his own land.

AFTERWARDS, when the procession of cars carrying neighbors and acquaintances has driven out to the farm, throwing the columns of dust into the air, and the women have set out food and made coffee, and the Predikant has said his platitudes, and Connie has hovered around Märit like a mother hen—after all this, Märit can only wait for them to be gone from her house.

But the women watch her, to know how she is affected, how she is bearing up. Because what if it happened to them? It could have been one of us, they think. What will happen to us? We can't hold out like this forever. There are those who wait just across the border, and in our own towns and cities, in our own houses. They will not go away, there are too many of them, a whole continent just waiting to fall upon us, to drive us out of our country. But where can we go?

The women look at Märit and wonder why she does not weep, why she does not show her grief. The generous amongst them tell themselves that she is in shock, poor thing, and the ungenerous think to themselves that she does not weep because she is cold, or she did not love him, she is a cold one, never quite friendly, never making an effort to fit in. Not one of us.

They want her to weep, for their own fear. And they ask themselves what she will do now. She cannot manage the farm on her own, a frail thing like her, not on her own. She will have to sell. She will leave them and go back to the city.

Märit waits for them to be gone. She does not want to share her loss and her grief with these strangers. She does not want to eat their home-baked cakes and drink the coffee they have made, or listen to their voices, to their regrets and their condolences, or to feel the eyes of the women upon her, or to see the somber men plotting revenge.

The men stand on the veranda, in their dark suits that are only worn for church, for weddings and funerals, smoking their pipes, passing around a surreptitious flask of brandy, and their eyes move casually across the fields and the orchards and the cattle in the distant field. How much will the farm bring on the market, they wonder, and they do calculations in their heads, comparing the worth of this farm with the worth of their own land. But now is not a good time for buying and selling, not now.

The men mutter amongst themselves, quietly, so that the women may not hear. What is the government doing? they ask. This death has been a death of one of their own. For them, Ben was one of their own. What are the police doing about these terrorists who come across the border like thieves and burn the farms? Where is the army? Somebody has to put a stop to it—if not the government, then they will do it themselves, for they are an independent and hardy people, like their Boer ancestors, ready to fight for the land. We have made this land and we will not be moved, they say. The young van Staden son wants to saddle up his horse and ride to the kraal this very moment. We will take care of it, he says. The guns must come out now.

On the farm there is no work being done this day. In the kraal there are low voices and careful movements. The children are scolded if they laugh too loud, and they fall silent under the worried frowns of their elders. In the kraal the people wait, for everything can change now.

DUSK ARRIVES at last, and with it silence. The doves fall silent. The long shadows from the eucalyptus trees creep across the lawn and across the rose garden, the long shadows stretch across the veldt as the sun fades and weakens. The long shadows cloak the house, the empty house where Märit sits waiting for darkness.

She drinks from a tumbler of gin and lime cordial, the bottles on the table next to her with her cigarettes and lighter. She sits waiting for darkness in her funeral dress.

I am a widow now, she tells herself. But was I ever really a wife? I wanted to be. That was the state which Ben found me in—waiting. Waiting to be a wife. Because I wanted to get away from home, and from my dreary job, and from the sameness of my life. I wanted life to begin, real life. And I thought that when I found a man, when a man found me, my life would start, my real life.

My mother liked him, she liked his manners, he was charming to her. She liked Ben because he was gentlemanly, he held doors open for women and stood when they came into a room. Sometimes he brought her flowers. But Mother had her doubts, not about him, but about me, about me living up here. She told me I wasn't suited to be a farmer's wife. She had her doubts about me, and when I disagreed, she said that she knew me, knew the deeper side of me that I didn't even know myself yet. I came here for Ben, because of Ben, because I was married and thought it would be a good life and that I could do it.

Märit stretches out her arm and reaches for her glass of gin, feeling the slackness in her body. The white walls of the room have faded to gray, the outlines of the furniture are blurred, the landscape beyond the windows has receded under a cloak of darkness as night falls. Near the river the croaking of frogs begins. A cricket chirps outside the window. The distant pulse of the generator beats.

I have walked upright today, Märit thinks. I have held my head up when I wanted to fall upon the ground. I did not weep. Once I was a married woman and now I am a widow because my husband is dead. Now I am without family, without children, without friends. Now I am alone.

Dusk becomes evening, and evening turns to night. The only light is the glow of her cigarette and the periodic flash of the lighter. The glass of gin is steadily emptied, and replenished.

It matters little now if I smoke too much and drink too much. What does it matter now? Who is there to care?

I came here for Ben, because I thought I loved him, but I don't know if I loved him. I decided I wanted to get married and I did. And Ben wanted me. He wanted a wife. But did he love me? We made love, but was it love? He liked it, liked me. And I enjoyed being enjoyed. He was different in bed, not so well-mannered. Hungry. Like me. We were different in bed, two other people, or maybe we were our real selves. There was something desperate in our lovemaking, some desperation to meet each other that made it so intense, because in the daylight we did not really meet, and we both sensed it, and we were afraid to know that.

Märit reaches for her cigarettes and finds the package empty. She rises to her feet, stumbling against the side of the couch, unsteady, her head spinning. On her way to the kitchen through the dark house she bumps into the walls; her body seems not to belong to her, to be some clumsy object attached to her self.

In the kitchen she turns on a single lamp and finds the carton of cigarettes and fumbles one out of the package. The taste in her mouth is sour when she lights it, and she tosses the cigarette into the sink. She is hungry. From the shelf she takes down a can of baked beans, then spends a long minute scrabbling in the drawer for an opener.

Standing at the counter she reaches into the can and digs out the sauce-covered beans with her fingers, stuffing them into her mouth, ravenous, swallowing, barely chewing the sticky mass.

Her fingers taste of tobacco, and the wetness across her lips makes her think of Ben's hands. She remembers his hands vividly. A man's hands can arouse tenderness, or revulsion. They always seem so naked, so intimate. Unlike the face, which can be a mask. But the hands are just hands and they cannot be disguised. A man's hands reveal who he is.

Ben's hands were sure, confident. Quite soft at first, but when he started farming, the skin on his palms toughened, but they were soft still, like the fine leather of kid gloves. And there were always little nicks and scrapes on his fingers, cuts from a tool or a piece of wire or just a scrape against a stone—the marks of his life on the land. His hands changed as he changed.

Yet his hands always remained gentle, and sure, and gave me pleasure.

She draws her hand across her mouth and licks the sauce from her fingers. *That time when he put his hand between my legs and drew it across my mouth and kissed my own wetness from my lips.* She licks her fingers and stuffs them into her mouth. *When he put his mouth on me, and kissed me between my legs, and then kissed me on my mouth. I wanted that. I liked it when he did that, but I was too shy to ask him, to say the words.*

And that last morning, when I did ask him, and he was in too much of a hurry to get to town, too eager to get the seedlings for the almond trees that he thought he would see grow on his land. And then he never came back.

Märit slumps against the counter. She lets the can of beans fall to the floor and raises her dress, sliding her hand down the front of her underwear, like her husband had done, clutching at her own flesh the way he had clutched at her.

She presses deeper, clenching on her fingers, wanting the strangeness of it to fill her, to make her remember, to make her forget.

She crumples to the floor, curling into herself, a cry of distress escaping from her throat.

25

THE HOUSE STANDS SILENT through the afternoon and into the night. Long after darkness has fallen a single light flicks on in the kitchen, but no movement is visible. The house stands silent, as if abandoned.

In the kraal, across that unbridgeable distance that separates house and huts, there is a different kind of silence—the low murmurs of gloom, of worry, of fear for the future.

The matter of the death of Baas Ben is the only topic of conversation. This death, and the manner of its coming and its meaning for the future, is being discussed all across the district, in the farms and the town, in the hotel and in the houses, and especially here in the kraal on the farm called Kudufontein.

There has been no work on the farm this day. Joshua, the headman, has known without being instructed that there must be no work today. Those who look to the single light burning in the kitchen window of the house have tribulation in their hearts. What will become of the farm, of their work, of their lives? Everything can change now.

They have watched the coming and going of the cars, have heard the voices talking, have seen the men standing on the veranda. And when Joshua walked to the house, hat in hand, to offer the condolences of those who live and work on this land, the men turned hard faces to him and sent him away.

Nobody stirs from the kraal. The cattle go untended, the soil is not tilled, the crops are not watered. When the cars have gone, and the women in their Sunday dresses, and the men in their dark suits, and the

Predikant, tall in his black hat, only then does something of the weight lift from the kraal.

Shadows lengthen, twilight falls, night and gloom descend. In the kraal they light fires and cook the evening meal and talk in low voices. And they watch and listen for a sign from the house.

Where is the Missus? they ask. Why is there not wailing and lamentations? Does she sit in the darkness, alone with the spirit of her dead husband?

Tembi watches too, and wonders. Joshua, the headman, says to Tembi, "You must go there, up to the house. You must see what she is doing."

"I cannot." Tembi shakes her head. He does not know why she cannot, and she will never tell him, but she cannot go to Märit. Even though Märit has lost her husband, Tembi cannot go to her, because her face still burns with shame where she has been slapped, and her heart is hard against Märit.

"You must go to her," Joshua insists. "You must tell her that we are sorry for Baas Ben, and you must tell her that we are sorry for her. And you must ask her what will become of the farm."

Like the white farmers and their wives, he too doubts that Märit can run the farm now. He too knows that she is weak, alone, without a man. Without a man, a woman like her cannot run a farm.

"You must go to her," Joshua says. "Is not your work in the house? You must cook for her and not let her sit alone in the darkness."

Tembi shakes her head. "No, I will not go there."

"Yes," Joshua says, and then a sly look shows in his eyes, and he speaks louder, so that the others around the fire pit may hear as well. "Doesn't she favor you, doesn't she take you away from your place with the other young women and make you her favorite? Your life is easy in that house, your work is nothing compared to ours. This is so. She favors you, and you must go to her now and tell her we are sorry for the Baas and you must ask her what she will do with this farm."

Again Tembi shakes her head. "No, I cannot go there. She does not favor me."

"She favors you. Did she not send you a gift? Did she not send you a blue bracelet with that little child? She favors you."

"No," Tembi says.

Losing patience, Joshua grasps Tembi by the arm and pulls her away from the fire. He pushes her away from the circle of light. "Do what I tell you. Go there! Go and talk to her."

Because Tembi has no mother and no father to say otherwise against the authority of Joshua, she leaves the kraal and walks into the darkness where the night crickets sing. She stops some distance from the house and looks at the square of light that burns in the window. She stands between the kraal and the house, alone in the night, belonging to neither the house nor the kraal. Tilting her head she looks up to the stars, so many of them crowded together, like houses, each burning its own lamp in the darkness. Tembi has heard people say that when a person dies her soul becomes a star in the heavens. Perhaps that is why there are so many. Is her mother, Grace, there too, holding a candle of light against the darkness? Is Baas Ben there too now? Or do they only lie in the deep soil, without light forever?

I cannot go to the house, she thinks, as she looks again at the single illuminated window. Märit has banished me. She has struck my face and banished me, so that I had to skulk through the trees to my hut, shamed and naked, creeping like a jackal.

Yet I cannot go to the kraal either, for they have sent me out into the night. Where can I go? There is only my garden, hidden behind the thorns and the rocks, but I cannot go there either. How can I sleep where the wild animals hunt at night?

She thinks of Märit alone in the house, alone in grief, and pity touches her heart. She knows what it is to be alone in grief and have to sit with the knowledge of death. She thinks, If Märit would appear at the window now, and see me, and forgive me, and beckon me to come to the house, then I would go.

Tembi looks at the stars, sparkling with blue light, and she remembers the bracelet that Märit sent, that is now tucked away into a little box in her hut with her few precious things. Pity is in her heart, and forgiveness, so she walks forward along the path and ascends the back steps and presses her ear softly to the door, holding her breath.

She turns the handle, swings the door open, puts her head in, and whispers, softly, afraid to break the silence. "Missus? Märit? It's Tembi."

No answer comes and she swings the door wider, stepping into the house, because this is the only place she can go on this dark night. The dim bulb burns in the ceiling, casting a yellowish light on the table and counter. The rest of the house is dark and silent. Tembi steps forward, then looks down and screams.

Märit's body is slumped across the floor by the sink, her dress pulled up to her waist, a smear of red across her mouth and across the pale skin of her thighs.

Tembi screams and falls against the door, then stumbles back into the night. Her first thought is that those who killed Baas Ben have come back and murdered Märit. She runs for the shelter of the trees and cowers in the darkness, too afraid to move, too afraid to run to the kraal and call for help. She cowers and stares at the lighted doorway.

The night, which has fallen silent at her scream, slowly comes to life again—the crickets resume their chirping, the frogs croak down by the river. A glimmer of firelight shows from the kraal.

Tembi waits, her eyes fixed on the splash of light coming from the open doorway, and the night goes on about its business, unconcerned; the crickets chirp and the stars move on their slow passage through the heavens. And when there is no movement from the kitchen, she thinks, Perhaps there has been no murder, and nobody is hiding in the house. Then another thought occurs to her, a thought almost as terrible as murder—maybe Märit in her grief has taken her own life.

Gathering her courage, Tembi leaves her hiding place and slowly climbs the back steps, and peers in through the door at the body on the floor. Fear and nausea rise in her mouth, sour on her tongue, and she bites her lips against it as she crouches down to touch the body gingerly with the tip of one extended finger. And then Märit groans.

"Aah!" Tembi falls back on her haunches in alarm, jerking her hand away.

A groan escapes from Märit's red-smeared mouth.

"Märit! Märit, are you hurt?"

"Tembi," she murmurs, and her breath is strong with the reek of liquor. Märit moans softly and turns on her side and opens her eyes.

"Tembi. You are the only one left," she says with a strange bitterness in her voice. She shuts her eyes again.

Tembi strokes Märit's face. "What has happened to you, Märit? What happened?" She strokes Märit's face and her fingers come away coated with a dark, sticky fluid. "You are bleeding, Märit." Then Tembi's eyes fall upon the half-empty can of beans on the floor, and she touches her finger to her lips, tasting the sticky bean sauce.

"Märit, you are not hurt?"

Märit retches and coughs. "I'm sorry, Tembi." Her voice is slurred, tired.

"You are not hurt, but I think you are drunk."

Märit mumbles something indistinguishable.

"You mustn't lie here, Märit. You are on the floor. It's not good. Come, you must get up."

Slipping one arm beneath Märit's shoulders Tembi raises her from the floor, with the other hand pulling the dress down over her thighs.

She struggles to get Märit to sit up, then urges her to stand. "Come, you can lie down in bed. Come now." Märit's hair is matted and smells of stale tobacco smoke.

They stumble along the corridor and into the coolness of the bedroom, where Tembi lets Märit subside onto the bed. She switches on the bedside lamp, and Märit groans, shielding her eyes against the glare.

"I feel sick, Tembi."

"Yes. I know." Although Tembi has never been drunk in her life she has seen drunkenness, sometimes when the men drink too much of the home-brewed beer, and how after the laughter and the loud voices and the falling down they become slack in their bodies, and speak in this same slurred weary tone, and wake up with the sickness on them.

She fetches a basin from the kitchen and fills it with warm water in the bathroom, and gathers a washcloth, then sits next to Märit on the bed, gently wiping away the smears of sauce, cleaning Märit's face.

Märit sighs, sighs like a child as the cool cloth moves over her face. She puts up her hand and lets it rest on Tembi's, pressing it against her forehead, and her eyes open with a sudden expression of clarity in them.

"You must forgive me, Tembi," she says clearly. "I didn't mean it."

Tembi nods. "Yes."

"Say it. You mustn't hate me. Tell me."

"I don't hate you. I forgive you, Märit."

Märit smiles, and then the veil falls over her eyes again and she closes them and seems to fall into sleep. Tembi rinses the cloth and smoothes it over Märit's face.

Then, as if ministering to an invalid, she unclasps the catch on Märit's dress and removes it and then her underwear. She unfastens Märit's brassiere and tosses it onto the chair. She rinses the cloth in the basin of warm water and wipes away the smears on Märit's thighs, cleaning her, cleaning her the way one would minister to a child.

And when she is finished she rises and takes up the basin and stands a moment looking down at the naked woman in the lamplight. The sight is strange to her; she has never seen a white woman naked. The pale skin, the smallish breasts, the pubic bush that is the same chestnut color as Märit's hair. Despite the differences in the color of the skin, and the color of the hair, and in the different curves of the body, Tembi sees only a woman. Only a woman, she thinks. Like me.

She pulls the sheet over Märit and then empties the wash basin in the bathtub.

"Sleep," she whispers. She feels so tired herself. She will go back to the kraal, and she will tell them only that the Missus is asleep, and that there is nothing to be said about the future and about what will become of the farm. She is tired now and wants to sleep herself.

As Tembi bends to turn off the lamp, Märit opens her eyes and says, "Don't leave me alone. Lie down next to me. I'm afraid."

Pity and tenderness are in Tembi's heart. She turns off the lamp and stretches out on the sheet, and Märit curls herself against Tembi's back, molding herself against Tembi's back in the way that a child clings to her mother, and she murmurs with the plaintive voice of a child, "You are the only one left, Tembi."

26

A BELL RINGS, strident, insistent, and Tembi jerks upright, startled out of sleep by the persistent ringing. For a moment she does not know where she is, this unfamiliar light in this unfamiliar room—and this stranger lying curled up next to her. The bell continues to ring. The telephone, she realizes—such a strange sound to hear in the morning, for never has she woken to this sound; there are no telephones in the kraal.

Slipping from the bed she hurries along the passage to where the black telephone sits on a small table. She has never spoken before on a telephone, although there have been times when she was in the house, when she was in the kitchen with her mother, and the phone rang, and Grace would go to answer the summons.

She stares at the phone—how sinister it seems, with a life of its own. Tembi tries to cover the telephone with both hands, to still its noise, but the urgent, repetitive bell insists. She lifts the receiver, and the noise ceases immediately.

A small voice is speaking. Tembi presses the receiver against her ear.

"Märit?" the voice says. "Märit, is that you? It's Connie van Staden. Hello?"

"Hello," Tembi answers softly.

"Who is that? Märit?"

"This is Tembi."

"Who are you? Are you the *meid*?"

"Yes."

"Let me speak to the Missus."

"The Missus is sleeping. She is very tired."

"Oh. Is everything all right there? Is your Missus all right?"

"Yes, she is all right."

"Well, don't wake her. Tell the Missus that I called. Connie van Staden. Can you remember to do that?"

"Yes, I can remember."

"Don't forget. Make sure you tell the Missus that Connie telephoned."

"Yes."

With a click the voice disappears abruptly. Tembi listens a moment longer, and it seems to her that she hears a sound like the wind, a whisper of voices in the wires that run on poles alongside the roads, voices whispering to each other.

Märit sleeps still, undisturbed by the noise of the phone, curled into herself with the sheet pulled over her head.

In the kitchen Tembi cleans out the cold ashes from the stove and sets new kindling and fresh coal. She puts away the leftover dishes of food that were brought by the neighboring women. She fills the kettle for tea, and sprinkles a handful of maize meal into a pot of water for porridge. This is her job. It is her job to cook and clean in the house. While the water boils she puts away the gin and cordial bottles and empties the overflowing ashtrays and opens the windows to let out the stale cigarette smoke.

When she brings the breakfast tray into the bedroom, Märit is still asleep, her head turned away from the beam of sunlight coming through the window. Her tangled hair frames a face that is pale, thin, a deep frown creasing her brow. Tembi sets the tray next to the bed and draws the curtain across the window, softening the light. She decides not to wake Märit. Better to sleep. Whatever pain is in Märit's dreams will be less than waking to know her husband is dead and that her life is now something other than what it was before.

ON THE FARM, work has resumed. Joshua has set the usual routines in motion, for the life of a farm cannot stop too long for grief. The cows must be milked, the weeds in the vegetable beds must be kept down, the cattle must be herded to pasture by the small boys, the watering of the crops must continue. The sun does not cease to move across the sky because of a death. Death is something that happens, a small pause in the turning of the wheel.

Joshua contrives to keep the house in sight throughout the morning; he finds tasks that will allow him to continually have a view of the doors. And when he sees Tembi appear from the kitchen door he hails her, gesturing with his arm for her to come to him.

"Did you speak to the Missus? What does she say?"

"She is sleeping still."

He looks up at the sun, already high above the land, and shakes his head disapprovingly. "She must talk to us. Now this farm is in her hands. Everybody is waiting to know what she thinks." He turns away and stands with his hands on his hips, surveying the farm. An idea is forming in his mind. He knows that Märit cannot run the farm—he can do it himself, even better than Baas Ben did. Does he not do it now? But for this he needs Märit to be the one who stands at the head of the farm, who negotiates in those matters where he has no authority.

"You must stay with her," he tells Tembi. "You must look after her, and when she wakes you can tell her that everything on the farm is good. You can tell her that Joshua is making sure of everything. And then you must come and tell me, so that I can speak to her."

Tembi nods.

"Go back to the house. It's better that you speak to her when she wakes. Tell her that the farm is good and she can stay here now and that I will run the farm for her. Go now."

Märit still sleeps, but the deep frown is not on her face any longer, there is a calmness there now, still pale, still drawn, but whatever dream had furrowed her brow is gone and she rests.

Tembi does not wake her, but takes the breakfast tray away and closes the bedroom door gently and goes through to the living room. She switches on the radio, and although the dial lights up there is only static on the whole wavelength. She takes down one of the books from the shelf, any book at random, and settles herself onto the comfortable couch with the breakfast tray.

The hours pass. Every now and then Tembi gets up and looks in on Märit. Märit sleeps—deep in the sleep that protects her. Tembi does not prepare any lunch for Märit, but eats instead by herself in the kitchen—bread and jam and cheese. She makes more tea and returns to the living room, to the comfortable chair and the books.

The sound of a car outside the house brings Tembi out of the places in the books. From the window she sees that it is the small white car that belongs to the Missus from the next farm, the same woman who telephoned earlier. Tembi has seen Connie van Staden before, visiting, sometimes with her husband, and she saw her as one of the last to leave when all the people came to the house after the burial of Baas Ben.

When Tembi sees her step from the car, a sudden impulse strikes her and she acts without thinking, without wondering why she does what she does next, or even what the consequences might be.

A few quick steps take her to the front door, where she turns the key in the lock, then she rushes to the bedroom and closes the door there, then runs down the corridor to the kitchen, and from the outside locks the door, pocketing the key.

On silent feet she creeps around the side of the house and pauses behind the hydrangea bushes, where she can be unobserved but still see the woman.

Connie van Staden has brought something in a basket, which she takes from the back seat of the car. She hooks the basket over her forearm and glances up at the house. And Tembi studies her, seeing a sturdy, capable woman who looks at the world with confidence, who can manage the world, who knows what is necessary.

Connie mounts the steps of the veranda and knocks on the door.

Tembi steps from the side of the house and stands at the foot of the stairs, and as Connie raises her hand to knock again, Tembi clears her throat to make herself known. Connie spins, startled.

"Who are you? I didn't see you standing there."

"I am Tembi, Missus."

"Are you the one I spoke to on the phone? Are you the *meid*?"

"Yes, Missus."

Connie nods, dismissing Tembi from her attention. Shifting the weight of the basket on her arm she taps at the door again, then tries the handle, frowning when she finds the door is locked.

"Where is Mevrou Laurens?" she says to Tembi. "Isn't your Missus home?"

Tembi shakes her head. "She is not here."

"No? Do you know where she has gone?"

Tembi makes a vague gesture. "She has gone to walk on the farm."

"For a walk?" Connie says, looking beyond Tembi, a tone of disbelief in her voice. Then Connie moves along the veranda and peers in through the window.

And if Märit should appear now, Tembi wonders, if she should appear and open the door and Connie should say, Your *meid* told me you were not here—then what will happen? Tembi does not know why she has lied, why she has locked the door and pretended that Märit is not in the house. Is it to protect the grieving woman, to let her sleep away her grief? Or is it to keep Märit to herself, to keep her away from her neighbors? Tembi does not want the world to come into the house, neither the town nor the kraal. She wants the house to contain only Märit and herself.

Connie descends the steps. "Which way did Mevrou Laurens go?"

"I do not know, Missus. That way." Her gesture encompasses all possible directions.

Connie now sets her basket on the ground and fixes Tembi with an intent look. She seems to contemplate whether all is as it should be—the habitual mistrust of mistress and servant—then her face changes, she relents, and says, "Is the Missus all right?"

"Yes."

"You know what has happened. The Baas is dead. But is she all right? Is she very upset?"

"Yes, she is sad."

"But is she very upset? Does she weep? Does she eat? Is she herself? She hasn't gone off to do something silly, has she?" Connie gazes in the direction of the koppie.

Tembi says, "No, she is sad, but she is herself."

"Well, that's good, then. That's as it should be. Are you looking after her? You must, because this is a difficult time for your Missus. Very difficult."

"I am looking after her."

"Good. And the farmworkers, they are not using this as an excuse to be lazy, are they?" She is suddenly stern. "If there is any laziness or shirking, then my Koos will be round to set matters right. If anybody tries to take advantage, there will be trouble for them. Do you understand that?"

Tembi nods.

"Yes, well." Connie looks down, noticing the basket at her feet. "I've brought some things. A casserole, some peach brandy. You can warm up the casserole for her dinner." She lifts the basket. "We'll take this through to the kitchen now."

Tembi shakes her head. "I have no key to the house. It is locked." She reaches for the basket. "I will give this to the Missus when she comes back."

Connie hesitates a moment, then lets the basket go. "Don't you take anything from it. And be sure to tell the Missus that I was here. And tell her to telephone me. Mevrou van Staden. Connie. Can you remember that?"

"I can remember. I will tell her."

Connie gets back into her car, and Tembi sits on the veranda steps with the basket next to her as the car drives off. She waves when Connie looks back. She sits there until the car is out of sight, and the dust plumes rise from beyond the trees, moving away with the passage of the car. She sits there until the dust settles again and the air is clear in the distance and the sound of the car has faded away. Then she takes the basket, walks around to the back door, and goes into the house.

The casserole that Connie has brought is a stew of potato and carrots and chunks of beef. There are thick scones wrapped in a cloth, still warm to the touch, a small jar of apricot jam, and the peach brandy, homemade, in a bottle without a label.

Tembi stokes up the fire in the stove and transfers the stew to a pot. She butters the scones and spreads them with jam, then makes tea and pours a measure of brandy into the cup.

Märit is awake when Tembi brings in the tray. She is sitting up in bed, wearing a nightgown and a black knitted shawl draped across her shoulders. Her long hair is a disarray of tangles.

"I thought I smelled food. Have you been cooking? Did you make this for me?" Märit looks up at Tembi, her eyes sunken and ringed with black.

"The other Missus was here. Connie. She brought you this food."

"Connie van Staden? I didn't hear her. What did you tell her?"

"That you were sleeping. She will come back."

Märit falls silent, slowly lifting spoonfuls of the stew to her mouth. Then she looks up and says, "But you must eat too. Where is yours? Bring a plate in, Tembi, and eat with me."

They sit together in silence, Tembi perched on the edge of the bed. When Märit is finished she puts the plate aside and drinks her tea, then sighs and closes her eyes and lies back against the pillows.

After a while, without opening her eyes, Märit says, "What am I going to do, Tembi? I don't know how to live now. The farm, the workers, you, everything. What am I supposed to do?" Her voice quavers. "I don't know anything about running this farm."

"You can go on like before. But you will be the Missus of the farm now."

"Alone?" Märit opens her eyes. "How can I manage this farm on my own? Without anybody?" She imagines the long days in the now-empty house, and the long hours of the night, and no end to it. Ben is gone. The thought is terrible to her.

"No, you can. If you want to. I can help you."

"You are kind, Tembi. Kinder than I deserve. But I don't know. Maybe I should go back to the city."

"If you want to."

"I don't know what I want." She puts her cup aside. "Everything is broken. I don't know what I want." She runs her hand through her hair, clutching at it, and closes her eyes again. She sees in her mind the somber gathering at the church, the black suits, the smell of perspiration and perfume. Ben is gone. Her body trembles with the knowledge. Yesterday it was possible to live, even the funeral was possible to endure, because there was a purpose in her actions and a reason. But today there is no reason and no purpose, and tomorrow, and the days after that. They have no reason or purpose.

Tembi gets up to clear away the lunch tray.

"Tembi?" Märit says in a small, hesitant voice.

"Yes."

"Would you like to come and live in the house? Here, with me. You can move into the other bedroom. It can be yours." Märit lies motionless, almost rigid, not opening her eyes.

Tembi sets the tray down on the edge of the bed; the pity and the tenderness are in her heart as she looks down at Märit.

"We can share," Märit says, still with her eyes closed. Her voice quavers with an appeal, with an appeal to hope. "We can share the house."

Tembi stands at the foot of the bed, thoughtful, for a long while. The pity in her heart and the hope in Märit's voice make her want to say yes. The frown across Märit's pinched and pained brow makes her want to say yes. The quivering lip makes her want to say yes.

But to come into this house, to live here, is that not a betrayal of her people? Will she separate herself from the rest of the workers who live in the kraal, who sleep in huts, who bathe in the washhouse and cook on the open fire?

Yet, she is in exile already, separate from the others in a way that she cannot quite define but feels no less acutely. Because she reads, because she has more schooling, because she thinks thoughts that others scoff at or dismiss, she is already separate. Her mother is gone, her father is gone. She is alone, like Märit. And she does not want things to remain the same in her life; she wants the future to be different from the past.

Tembi knows also that to live in this house will mean a kind of freedom and comfort, an elevation of her place in the world.

When she bends to take the tray again, Märit opens her eyes, meeting those of Tembi with an intimate intensity.

Will there be friendship? Tembi wonders. Without friendship there can be nothing.

"Yes," Tembi says. "I can be here."

A sigh escapes from Märit's lips and her whole body relaxes. "Thank you, Tembi," she whispers. "Thank you."

"I will go to the kraal and fetch my things. But what must I say to the others? What must I say to Joshua about the farm?"

"You can tell them that the farm will continue. Except that I will be the Baas now."

Märit speaks these words, but she does not know if they are true.

THERE IS NOT much that Tembi has in the hut where she lived with her mother—a couple of dresses, one pair of shoes, some underwear, a few books, a photograph in a cheap tin frame of her parents on the day they were married. Her mother's belongings are in a metal trunk, which Tembi has not opened since she packed it after the funeral. She has no makeup, no creams or perfumes, only a brush, a bar of soap, a comb, a toothbrush. All her belongings fit into a single cardboard suitcase. The last item she takes is the blue bead bracelet, which she fastens around her wrist.

Before going back to the house she makes her way down towards the river and up to the ridge where the graves are, and here she stands before the resting place of her mother.

"Is this the right thing to do, Mother?" she asks. "What do I leave behind forever if I go to live in Märit's house?"

The breeze rustles softly through the willows, the doves murmur in the shade of the leaves, the water burbles over the stones.

Tembi crouches down on her knees and places both palms flat on the ground, as if it could speak to her, and she feels the turning of the earth under her hands.

And now there is one more thing to do before going to the house. She fetches her plastic bucket, fills it with water at the washhouse tap, and makes a circuitous path to the koppie and her garden. Every day she waters, without fail, no matter what happens, because here is the one thing that she knows—that the seeds will grow into fruit. Carefully she pours water in each of the five places where her seeds lie, and lifts a few fallen twigs and leaves. She places her hands flat against the ground, and feels here too the turning of the earth, and the earth tells her that the seeds are coming to life within the soil.

On her way back to the house she skirts the kraal, because there are people there now, the work of the day is finished, and wives are united again with husbands, children with parents, the cooking fires are being lit, the scent of wood smoke is in the air. Tembi skirts the kraal—for what can she say to anybody now except that she is leaving something behind for something unknown?

But Joshua is waiting for her on the path, a hand-rolled cigarette dangling from his lips. He is waiting for her, and she wonders how he knew she was coming this way. How much does he see? He raises his chin when she appears, half greeting, half summons.

Before he can speak, Tembi says, "I have spoken with Missus Märit. Everything will stay the same on the farm. She will take the place of Baas Ben."

Joshua removes his cigarette and spits between his feet. He shakes his head, disbelieving. "You told her that I can manage this farm? That only I know what must be done here?"

"Yes."

"And?"

"She says that is good. She is going to stay on this farm and work."

"Mmm! And you, you are going to look after her in the house?"

"She has asked me."

"Yes, that's good." He studies her with a long calculating look. "Then you will come and tell me what she is thinking. And I will tell you what to say to her."

Tembi says nothing. Joshua jerks his chin again, a dismissal, and she goes on her way, aware of him on the path watching her, looking at her back as she walks. Tembi does not know his thoughts, but she fears them nevertheless.

27

Tembi sets her bags down in the hall and taps at Märit's door. The sweet fruity smell of shampoo greets her as she enters and a dampness wafts from the direction of the bathroom at the other end of the room. Märit is sitting up in bed with her long hair combed but still wet; next to her on the night table is a glass and the bottle of peach brandy that Connie van Staden brought earlier. She has a photo album open on her lap.

"You are awake?"

"Yes, come in, Tembi. Is everything all right at the kraal—did you get your belongings?"

"Yes, I have my things."

Märit's eyes fall on the blue bracelet, and she looks pleased, but says nothing.

Tembi steps farther into the room and perches on the edge of the bed, her interest piqued by the photo album.

Märit turns a photograph outwards so that Tembi can see it. "This is on the day that Ben and I got married."

Tembi bends to look, seeing Ben in a dark suit, smiling, squinting slightly in the sun that falls on his face, and next to him Märit in a dress, white like almond blossoms, a bouquet of red roses in her hand. She too is smiling, but frowning at the same time, as if with conflicting emotions.

"It seems so long ago," Märit says, "a time from a different life. How quickly things can change. How quickly we change. I look at this person in the picture and I hardly recognize her. I see someone who doesn't know the first thing about herself."

"But now you know who you are."

"No, I don't. I only know I'm not the same person as the one in the photograph. And that the world is no longer the same place."

"I have a picture too," Tembi says, and gets up to fetch it. She returns with a small gilt frame and presents it to Märit. "My parents, also on their marriage day."

The young couple sit side by side in chairs in what must be a photographer's studio, a painted backdrop of an African landscape behind them. The husband, upright, proud, in his new suit, holding a hat in one hand. And the young wife with her hand resting lightly on her husband's forearm, her round, smooth face glowing.

"How beautiful Grace is," Märit says. "Were they happy together?"

"Yes. For many years our life was good. But then—" she shrugs— "but then we had to leave the place where we lived, because the government said we must go, and the new place was no good and there was no work and so my father went to the mines in Johannesburg. And then we came here, to this farm, where my mother could work."

Märit shakes her head and looks down. She knows only vaguely of the events that take place when the government decides on a new policy to further its aims. These policies barely affect life for the privileged, of which she is one. How little she really knows, she realizes, of the lives of the invisible people that surround her.

"Do you have any photos of yourself, Tembi?"

"No. We had no camera."

"Well, I do, and I am going to take a lot of photos of you. You can start your own album, like this one. And I'll show you how to work the camera so that you can take your own pictures. We'll take lots of photos together."

Tembi looks up and nods, seeing not Märit, but the past, the lost past. But there will be no pictures of the past, Tembi thinks. Only memory will remind her of her mother, and her father, and the place where she was born. When the past is lost, how can the present find its way?

Märit reaches for the glass of peach brandy. When she speaks again her breath is sweet with the aroma of fruit. "I've made up the bed in the spare room for you. And put out towels in the bathroom. Would you like to have a bath, Tembi? Use some of the foam bath."

She rises. "Yes, I can have a bath."

Bubbles appears magically when Tembi pours the pink liquid into the stream of water gushing from the faucet, and she is careful to measure out only one capful. Even so, she thinks she has put too much in, and she lessens the force of the stream from the tap, alarmed that the bubbles will spill out onto the floor. When she takes off her clothes, wearing only her bracelet of blue beads, and catches sight of her dark skin in the fogged-up mirror, dark in this white room, the sight is strange, seeing herself in this room, and she lights the candle that stands on the windowsill, then turns off the overhead light.

It is like a warm river when she sinks down into the foam, like being in a shallow pool by the river, where the rocks have been warmed by the sun, and the smell is like flowers.

She lies there listening to the soft pop of the bubbles, and then hears the gentle pattering of raindrops on the window, and soon the gentle rustling in the thatch of the roof, the sound familiar to her because in her thatched hut in the kraal the rain makes the same comforting whisper, and she is warm and safe and the gentle rain falls on the earth.

At last she rises, wrapping herself in the fluffy towel, and opens the window a crack to allow the scented steam to escape, and the night air that wafts into the room at the same time has the sweet smell of rain and peace.

Tembi carries the candle through to the spare bedroom, her room, and finds the crisp white sheets turned back, the soft pillows plumped up, and a clean nightdress draped across the patterned quilt. She turns off the lamp so that the light is dim as she buttons the nightdress. Then, with the candle in hand, she moves through the house, turning off the lamps, making sure the doors are bolted. When she pauses at Märit's door to say good-night, the room is in darkness, and she moves away silently.

But as she goes she hears a subdued sobbing, like the rain pattering on the roof, a whisper that all is not at peace here. She steps into the room, shading the candle with her palm. Märit is turned on her side, facing away, and when Tembi moves closer she sees the photograph clutched in Märit's hand, and the shaking of her shoulders as she weeps.

"Märit?"

"Don't go, Tembi," Märit whispers. "Stay with me again tonight. I'm afraid to be alone."

So Tembi slips beneath the sheets on the other side of the bed and blows the candle out with a puff of breath, and Märit turns to her in the darkness, like a child, pressing her face against Tembi's breast. Tembi slowly strokes away the tears on Märit's cheeks, gently patting her on the back with a soothing motion, until the sobbing ceases and Märit is calmed, and Tembi feels sleep stealing over her own limbs.

Sometime in the night Märit wakes to the sound of rain and to a sense of desolation. The quilt has slipped to the floor and she reaches down for it, shivering in the chill of the room, then pulls the quilt close around her. The rain beats against the window, the world hangs in suspension, without time, without destination, without purpose.

If only there had been a child, then everything would be different. Her life would be different now if she had a child to love, even with what has happened. She would have someone to love. But nobody needs her now. If she were to die in the night she would slip from the world unremembered, her life unremarked in its passing. Nobody would miss her.

She lies with the quilt pulled up around her eyes, in desolation, in weakness, and when she turns, seeking comfort, her hand touches the unfamiliar body next to her, and she remembers, and with a small cry of anguish buries her face against the softness of Tembi.

Tembi drifts out of her slumber to feel the desperate clinging of the other woman. She strokes Märit's back with a soothing, circular motion.

Märit presses herself tighter against Tembi as if to bury her grief in the living flesh of another body. Her hand touches the warm skin, the soft fuzz of the hair—a stranger, but not a stranger. In the darkness they are the same.

The rain falls on the fields and the trees and on the calm water of the river, making small circles on the surface where the drops fall. The rain falls on the hides of the cattle that stand slumbering in their enclosure, and on the coats of the wild animals that shelter on the veldt under the acacia trees. The gentle rain falls with soft sounds on the straw thatch of the roofs in the kraal.

When Tembi wakes she dresses quickly and silently, and slips from the house without disturbing the sleeping Märit, and goes into the new morning, where the long shafts of the sun touch the cool places that still have the shadows of night lingering. And she too has the lingering of the night shadows upon her, the new morning upon her also.

Dew is still on the ground, the moisture from blades of grass brushing her ankles as she avoids the path to the kraal and strikes off in a direction that veers around the collection of huts. A thin blue haze of smoke hangs over the kraal; the morning cooking fires are already lit. In the chicken coop, Dik-Dik the rooster is calling out to the new day.

She would like nothing better than to settle next to the fire with a mug of hot tea as the women cook the morning porridge, talking idly while they stir the big pot and the smells rise to mingle with the wood smoke and there is that easy, lazy morning mood.

Instead, Tembi gives the kraal a wide berth. She does not want to see anybody, to hear their questions, to feel the subtle exclusion that her presence brings. And neither does she want to meet Joshua. She walks through the dew-wet grass to the only other place where she belongs— the garden behind the koppie.

In secret, Tembi comes with her pail of water to her garden, her refuge. A low screen of thin cloud hangs over the land, not bringing rain, but softening the sun and the heat. She sets the pail down and bends to scoop a little water in her hands, then dribbles it over the soil. And there, on the moist black soil, she sees five green shoots. Her heart gives a leap of joy as she falls to her knees.

Can it be? Five green plants, so pale, so new. She brings her face close to the ground and the damp scent of the earth rises to her nostrils. Five green shoots, coming up from the earth. So small, smaller than the tip of her little finger as she strokes it across the seedlings.

Her seeds have taken nourishment and sprouted, have come forth into life, into the brightness that shines on all living things.

With her knees clasped against her chest for warmth, she sits on the rock that is still chilled from the night, but the sun is warm, and the yellow light falls on her garden. She raises her head and looks across the veldt, unable to see the house, yet aware that soon she must go there.

Tembi knows that she is linked to the woman who lies sleeping in the farmhouse, linked with an as yet inexplicable bond. Her allegiance now is with Märit. And her destiny is there too, equally inexplicable and unknown.

What must Märit be to her now, and what must she be to Märit?

When the sun has warmed the rocks where Tembi sits, and banished the lingering shadows, and burned off the dew from the grass, when the grass lark has started singing, and the haze of smoke no longer hangs over the kraal, and the sound of a tractor starting up echoes against the koppie, Tembi at last rises—reluctantly, because only here does time wait for her, only here can she be without the world. Reluctantly she walks back towards the house, towards Märit—reluctantly, but also with expectation and not without hope.

Part Two

The Land

28

MÄRIT MOURNS.

In the weeks following Ben's death she seldom leaves the house. She is between two worlds—the past and the future—the present has no shape or meaning for her. Tembi prepares the meals and does the cleaning in the house. She tries to draw Märit out of the distant place she has retreated to, but Märit's replies to her questions and comments are listless, uninterested, and her gray eyes look upon Tembi as upon a stranger. Sometimes she ventures outside, but never very far from the house, only walking for a few minutes around the garden before coming indoors again to lie on her bed. Sometimes she sits in one of the wicker chairs on the veranda for long hours, smoking cigarettes and staring into the distance. And when Tembi calls softly to her, she does not turn her head.

Once, when the telephone rang and rang, Tembi went through from the kitchen to answer it and found Märit standing in the corridor looking down at the instrument. When Tembi reached for it, Märit shook her head. Now when the telephone rings nobody answers its call.

The farm has a life of its own, as if it does not need this sad woman who drifts along its edges, and life progresses with the momentum that was in place before the Baas died. Under Joshua's supervision the crops are tended, the cattle are herded to pasture, the milking is done, the maintenance and repairs are carried out. But he keeps a worried eye on the house, and he sees the woman sitting there on the veranda for long hours, the woman who does not acknowledge him when he approaches and doffs his hat and says, "Missus?"

Joshua arrives at the kitchen door and calls Tembi out and asks her what the Missus thinks, what she says. But Tembi can only shrug. "She is sad in her heart" is all she can say. Joshua takes off his hat and slaps it against his thigh with irritation and glares at the house before striding off across to the kraal.

Märit remains shut off with her memories. She remembers when they came to tell her that her parents were dead. A boating accident on Hartbeespoort Dam, where they had gone for the day because her father wanted to fish, and he had tried to convince Märit to come along, and she had said no, because she wanted to spend the day with Ben. He had dropped her at the house just after sunset, and her parents were not home yet. Then, less than an hour later, the knocking at the door. A police officer standing on the steps, a frightening sight, making her heart race because she knew it could only be bad news. When he took off his hat she knew it was something terrible. Then the mumbled words, apologetic, as if it were somehow his fault. She remembers the policeman standing in the Sunday dusk, how he could not meet her eyes, how she had sensed that he wanted nothing more than to blurt out the news and flee.

She had feared that it was Ben, that something had happened to him on his way back to his apartment in Hillbrow. She had felt relief and shock in the same moment. And perhaps it was that sense of relief that made her turn to Ben so entirely in the weeks after her parents' death. It was with relief that she said yes when he asked her to marry him. It was with relief that she allowed herself to be swept up in his plans to buy a farm, to become a farmer. She was without direction, without a home, and Ben steered her towards what was lacking in her life.

But now it is Ben who is dead.

In this time of Märit's mourning and her remembering, Connie van Staden visits the house. Tembi brings tea and cake on a tray to the veranda where Connie sits talking to the silent Märit. And when the tea and the cake are finished Connie walks into the kitchen and looks into the pantry and opens the cupboards and shakes her head. After that, she speaks to Märit again, almost scolding, as one would speak to a sulking child, then she puts Märit into her car and they drive away from the farm.

In Klipspring, Connie takes Märit to the office of the *advokaat*, where there are legal papers to review and sign. The lawyer informs Märit that the farm is hers now, debt free. If she wishes to sell, he will be glad to assist her. Connie frowns at him when he says this and he mumbles an apology. Then Connie takes Märit to the shops, and Märit walks behind her, silent, clutching the folder of legal papers in her hand. She lets Connie choose the supplies of food, the toiletries, acquiescing to every choice Connie makes.

When the trunk and the back seat of the car are loaded, Connie takes Märit by the arm and leads her up Kerkstraat, to the church, to the small graveyard, where the new granite headstone is bright in the sun. Märit stands there only a moment, shading her eyes, imagining the shattered remains of her husband's body enclosed in the pine coffin beneath the ground, before she turns to Connie and says, "I want to go back to the farm now."

Later, when she sits alone on the veranda and watches the outlines of the distant hills soften under misty clouds, and smells the wood smoke from the cooking fires in the kraal, and hears the cooing of the doves in the eucalyptus trees as they settle down for the night, she realizes that this is what her life is now. This farm. Now she is truly alone. An orphan and a widow.

29

Märit wakes to the chirrup of a cricket, close by, perhaps in the thatch of the roof. Chirrup, chirrup. Then a pause, then the sound repeated. She listens to the beat of the two notes, to the little echo that lingers in the moment of silence between the beats, like a waiting. How persistent it is, she thinks, always calling like that, solitary but determined with its hope and its will, this small voice.

Rain has been falling in the night but has ceased in the early hours of the dawn, leaving the earth wet and new as the sun rises. A mist hangs over the fields for an hour or two, then burns off and the earth is new again.

Märit wakes with the acute sense that a veil has lifted from her eyes and a weight from her body. When she rises from the bed and stands at the window the light has a clarity that was not there before. Everything is clear and defined, without illusion—everything is only what it is, nothing more, nothing less. She realizes what accounts for the difference between today and yesterday—fear has left her.

The nutty aroma of coffee is coming from the direction of the kitchen, and there is a pot on the stove when Märit enters, but Tembi is not there. Märit calls her name once, then pours herself some of the coffee, and from a tin in the pantry takes a couple of *boerebiskuit*. She carries her breakfast back to the bedroom and sits down on the stool in front of the dressing table.

Her reflection confronts her: hair in disarray, face still wrinkled and soft from sleep, but with something else in the features that was not there before. Märit sees herself, revealed with the same clarity that illuminates the landscape.

She lifts her chin, almost in defiance, and runs her hands through her tangled hair. Is that me? she wonders, lifting the thick weight of the reddish brown hair, the weight that is always upon her shoulders. A weight made up of all the years of shampooing, and combing, and arranging, ever since she was a child. So that she would look nice, so that she would be presentable, so that she would be attractive. And her mother always saying those words, always noticing Märit's hair, making sure she was presentable, attractive. Sometimes it had seemed that Märit's hair belonged more to her mother than herself. Once, when Märit grew tired of her hair and wanted to cut it, her mother said to her, "You have a plainness in your face—you need to accentuate your features. Without your hair you will look ordinary. You need it to look nice."

People did admire her hair, and the other girls at school were envious, and when she started working and went into the city to her job, men often looked at her. And she always made sure she looked nice, as her mother wanted her to be.

But what a burden and pretense it is, Märit thinks, as she sits at the dresser surrounded by her perfumes and creams and mascara and lipstick—all the accoutrements necessary to make one's self look nice. All of this is a shell, a mask that allows her to be in the world, to be like everyone else. A mask to hide the woman within, until she disappears beneath the weight of her own appearance and wears only her own vanity.

The sight of her reflection does not please Märit. What she sees in the mirror seems false, a disguise. Yesterday's woman.

A sparkle of light bounces from the mirror, a gleam from the wedding ring on her finger. Märit looks at the gold band curiously, then works it loose over her knuckle, surprised at how easily it comes off. She remembers the moment this ring was placed on her finger, where it has remained until this moment. What import it carried then, yet how little it weighs now. She opens the dressing table drawer and drops the ring amongst the other bits of jewelry that lie there. And now everybody will look at her and know that she is a woman alone.

"A widow I will be," she says, then gives an involuntary shudder at the words, as if they are a betrayal of Ben and almost a curse upon herself.

Her reflection looks back at her—timid, but determined.

Rising from the stool Märit walks to the kitchen, rummages around in the cutlery drawer until she finds what she wants, then comes back to confront her image—this time with a pair of scissors in her hand.

Her hair is heavy as she tilts her head, grasping a thick handful, and the shears are heavy in her hand as she brings them forward and slices through the long hair. The bite of the blades sends a tremor through her whole body.

So easy. She tilts her head in the opposite direction and feels again the satisfying motion of the shears biting into the thick hair. So easy.

She bends her head forward so that she can reach the back, laying the shears close to her scalp, and severs another thick plait of hair. Then with quick motions she chops at her hair, and the clumps fall on her shoulders and on her lap and on the dresser amongst the glittering bottles and jars.

With a strange fascination and her heart racing at the boldness of what she is doing, she watches herself in the mirror as the blades slice through the coils and strands with a satisfying crunch that resonates all the way through her body. On the dresser and on the floor and littering her lap, the hair shines in the clear light.

A different face seems to emerge as the hair falls away from her head, a strange face, plain yes, smaller somehow, naked. A face she does not know, but a face that she recognizes as her own.

At last she ceases, for now there is only an uneven stubble across her skull, and she sits looking at the new face with her heart still racing, with her hair in untidy heaps all around her—the debris of the past.

Her hands touch the stubble, reminding her of the feel of Tembi's hair and of the new growth in the fields after the rains and after the plowing.

"Me," she says, to the mirror—to herself.

Märit bathes, washing the past from her skin, marveling at the feel of the stubble on her head as she rubs shampoo into her scalp. Drying herself, she stands in front of the long mirror in the bedroom with a mixture of anxiety—for what has she done so rashly?—and yet a feeling of triumph.

She sees herself—naked and unadorned, nothing more than herself. She smiles at the transformation, at her bravery.

Märit begins to search through her closet for something to wear, something that is appropriate to her new self. All her clothes are from another time, suitable only for a different person.

A patch of bright green on a top shelf catches her eye, on the shelf where those items that will never be worn more than once are folded away. She shakes out a length of cloth, a sarong-like garment, bright with red and green and black and yellow, all mixed in a pattern of leaf shapes. She remembers buying this in the Indian market in Durban, on her honeymoon.

The colors had seemed appropriate to the hot winds and the smell of the salt sea in the air and the spicy cooking smells from the food stalls. She had worn the sarong on the beach, with a wide straw hat, and felt herself to be something exotic.

But when she came here, to the farm, where the colors were tan and ochre, and gray-green in the trees, the brightness of her sarong was only garish, unnatural—and how could any respectable farmer's wife wear such a garment? Only the women in the fields wore clothes like this, and the women walking in the dust at the sides of the roads with baskets balanced on their heads and babies bundled on their backs. Only the "Africans" wore such garments.

Märit shakes out the folded cloth and wraps it around her midriff twice and up across her chest and ties two ends together in a firm knot. Her shoulders and her back are bare, like those of the women who work in the fields.

She runs her fingers across the stubble of her hair, not much longer now than Tembi's. A pang of melancholy falls over her as she remembers the loneliness of her childhood, her longing to have a companion, a sister whom she could confide in, and stand with in front of the mirror like this, marveling at the changes that came with growing up. Always in her girlhood there had been that sense of absence, the long hours alone, waiting for something or someone. Perhaps that is why she married so quickly, so willingly.

She is dressed now. She will not bother with shoes. She will go barefoot, like Tembi, like the women who walk barefoot along the sides of the road in the dust. And now she turns her back on the mirror, for she will not gaze anymore upon her reflection. She will see herself only in the eyes that look upon her, and if by chance she glimpses her reflection in a window, or in a limpid pool in the rocks, or in a fragment of mirror, she will know herself, unadorned.

The heap of shorn hair lies on the floor near the dresser, like a shed skin, never to be worn again. Märit sweeps up the strands with a dustpan and gathers the clumps into the wastebasket. In the kitchen she lifts the lid on the stove and is about to tip the hair into the fire—a final gesture—when she thinks better of it, not wanting the house to fill with the odor of burning hair. Better to burn it outside in the *braai* pit.

Outside, underneath the wire grill on the barbecue, there is dry kindling ready, arranged into a neat pile with a few twists of old newspaper. She remembers the time Ben used this *braai*, when he invited the neighbors for a barbecue not long after he took possession of the farm. The men stood out here with their cans of Castle lager amidst the smoke and smell of grilling *boerewors* and *sosaties* and thick mutton chops. The women gathered in the kitchen, preparing potato salad and chutney. They were curious about her and asked many questions, and Märit was shy among them. Those same women will really talk about her now, she knows.

Let them talk, Märit thinks as she strikes a match and touches it to a twist of newspaper. A thin stream of white smoke issues from the kindling, and she bends to blow at the glowing wood until the small flame expands with a crackling sound and the fire leaps alive.

Märit half expects Ben to appear from the kitchen carrying a plate of steaks and offer to help her, as if they were about to start dinner on the grill. She would then fetch him a glass of beer, and stand next to him as the meat sizzled and smoked, and he would put his arm around her and tell her how happy he was to be standing here, on this spot, doing this very thing.

But he won't appear. Never again. Märit purses her lips and blows fiercely at the flames, and she tells herself that the stinging in her eyes is from the smoke and not from her tears.

The heat is quick and sudden as the dry wood catches, and she steps back as the flames grow. Then she reaches for the wastebasket and takes out a handful of hair. The soft coils are sleek and smooth in her fingers as she holds them folded in her palm a moment—a brief moment of regret—before she tosses the hair into the flames. The quick crackle and hiss sends an acrid smell into the air, a singed smell that makes her crinkle her nostrils.

Now she lifts the basket and shakes all the remaining hair into the fire, and the smoke is thick as the flames burn the hair black, and the smoke stings her eyes, but she welcomes it, for it burns away the old Märit.

The hair burns rapidly, crackling, the way fire does when it moves across the pastureland in the winter when the farmers burn off the old growth.

As the smoke subsides, and the acrid singed smell is replaced by the clean wood-smoke smell, as the last evidence of her long chestnut hair is carried up into the blue sky as faint ashes, as Märit turns away from the flames, Tembi appears.

Tembi's eyes go wide at the sight of this stranger here, and her glance flickers to the fire and back, and then her mouth falls open in recognition.

"Hauh!" she exclaims softly. "Märit, it is you!"

Märit smiles. She sees herself now not in a mirror, but reflected in the face of another.

"I do not know you," Tembi says. "You have changed yourself!" Tembi steps closer, shaking her head in wonderment. "Your hair, your clothes, everything is different." She reaches up a hand and lightly touches Märit's head. "Your hair, it's short like mine now."

"Is it all right?" Märit says, suddenly doubtful. "Do I look strange? Am I ugly?"

Tembi shakes her head. "So different. But the same. Not ugly, no."

"We will be the same now," Märit says. "Like sisters."

Tembi nods her head, her smile changing to a more solemn expression. "You have done this to become new."

"Yes. We are going to live a new kind of life. Both of us. This farm will be ours, and we will make it work. I don't know much about farming but I will try. And you will help me. If you want to, that is."

"Yes, I can help you," Tembi answers. She knows that her destiny has changed, and that it lies here now. "I don't think it can be so hard to look after cattle and grow things."

"Together we can learn what we don't know."

"Come," Märit says, linking her arm with Tembi's, turning her back on the dwindling flames.

30

A FEW DAYS LATER Märit asks Tembi to relay a message to Joshua, who relays it to the rest of the workers, who leave their tasks and come to the sorting shed, which is only a cement floor sheltered by a corrugated tin roof supported by wooden posts. They gather here, squatting on the floor, for there are no chairs or benches, and the small children run amongst the adults, and Joshua stands to one side with his arms folded.

When Tembi arrives to tell Märit that the workers are waiting, Märit, suddenly nervous, says, "What should I say to them?"

"What you said to me. That this is your farm now. That you will run it."

"Will they believe I can do it? I don't know if I believe it myself. Really, I don't know much about farming. Ben did everything. All I did was the accounts."

"You can learn it. The people here, they know what to do—just like before, they can carry on with their duties."

Märit touches her shorn hair and looks down at her bare feet. "Maybe I should change my clothes. They won't understand this . . . the way I look now."

Tembi smiles. "They don't know who you are now. Maybe that can be good for you."

"Maybe." Märit takes a deep breath.

They are waiting for her, gathered in the shade under the corrugated sorting shed roof—the buzz of conversation, children scampering around, calling to each other, the smell of tobacco, of earth, of sweat, of labor.

It is a child who first sees Märit, and points, shouting out what sounds like a cry of alarm before running back to his mother. A hush falls over the assembled workers. The conversation dies as the faces turn towards Märit. She steps onto the cement floor, into the silence.

Who are they? What are their names? How little she knows of them, these who labor on this farm, who bring the bread to her table.

On the faces she sees astonishment, curiosity, apprehension, tiredness—and some faces present to her only an impassive blankness. She does not know what they think. But they all wait now as she stands before them, for she has commanded that they leave their work and come away from the fields, from the kraal. And she holds their future in her hands.

She looks across at Joshua, the only one standing, and he frowns at the assembled workers as if to ensure their continued silence.

She is afraid that the words won't come, that her throat will seize up and freeze the words. She takes a breath, trying to calm herself and appear determined. "I am going to run this farm now," she says.

The murmurs, the sighs, the small exhalations of astonishment, a few heads shaking in disbelief. But mostly there is curiosity.

"You . . . all know what has happened—that Baas Ben was killed. You know how it happened . . ." Her voice falters for a second.

Her words brings a responsive moan from the gathering, and she waits for silence before continuing. "I will run the farm now. Things will go on as before." Will they believe her? Will they respect her? Is it true what her neighbors said—that the men will not give their loyalty to a woman?

"If you think that I can't do it, then you are wrong. If you think that because I am a woman I can't do it, then you are wrong. You will give me the same respect that you gave to Baas Ben. And if you cannot, then you must leave this farm. If you think that you can take advantage of me because I am a woman alone and without a husband now, then you must leave this farm. If you cannot help me to run this farm, then you must leave. I say these things to you now, at the beginning, to give you a choice. Because if you cannot accept me, or work for me, you must leave."

She pauses, waiting for a reaction, running her eyes across the faces that look straight back at her.

"Because I do not know so much about the running of a farm, you must help me. We must help each other. Otherwise, all of us will lose."

There are nodding heads, murmurs of agreement. She notices glances directed at Joshua, who stands with his arms folded across his chest.

"Joshua is the bossboy still, and it is to him that you must go with your questions and your problems about farming matters. I will rely on you, Joshua."

He nods his head, as if there is no question about this matter. The expressions on the faces tell her that they are not against her, but nothing more.

"This is good land, this is a good farm, and I know that we can make a good life here, for us all."

There is more confidence in her voice than in her heart, for she still doubts the future, and her own abilities, but like the hopeful faces that look up to her, Märit wants to believe that her words are true. It is all she has—hope.

THE FOLLOWING MORNING Märit rises early—she has set her alarm clock to ring just after first light—for on this first day she wants to be on the land when the workers begin their tasks, and to show them that her commitment is the same as theirs.

She wears her sarong and ties a kerchief around her head, a bright yellow *doek* that Tembi gave to her. In front of the mirror she practices putting on a self-confident and assertive expression. If she cannot convince herself, at least she can give the appearance of assurance. Tembi joins her in the kitchen a little later, when the coffee is brewed and the toast is made. They carry their cups and plates out to the veranda.

"I want Joshua to walk with me around the farm this morning," Märit says. "I want to start learning about everything that is done here during a normal day—all the different tasks. I'm going to ask Joshua to show me around. Will you come?"

Tembi nods, sipping her coffee, then sets the cup down on the railing. "I don't like Joshua."

"Why not, Tembi?"

"I don't know. . . . He doesn't like me."

"He's not very friendly, I know, but Ben thought he was a good worker."

"Maybe we don't need him anymore."

"I think we do. Neither of us knows enough to run the farm. Joshua does. We need him."

They begin in the dairy, where the cows are milked and the butter is churned and the cheese is cured. The young girls work here, and they greet Märit and Tembi—"*Goeie more*, Missus. *Sawubona*, Tembi!"—and they giggle a bit at the way Märit looks in her sarong and her short hair and her bare feet. Joshua glares at the girls until they fall silent.

Märit asks their names, and tries to commit the faces and the names to memory.

The small boys, the *piccanins*, herd the cattle out to the distant pastures where the grazing is good, and Märit stands to one side as the boys come down the track from the cattle kraal where the animals are penned at night, and the boys whistle at the cattle, flicking willow switches at the brown flanks of the beasts, urging them forward. Märit marvels at the docility of the cattle, for they are the big Afrikander breed, with long horns, and the boys are small.

Joshua counts the cattle as they pass, dabbing his finger in the air as he reels off the numbers to himself, and he shouts at the boys not to dawdle as they turn to gape at Märit and Tembi.

The women of the farm are at work in the fields of maize and sorghum, moving through the rows with long-handled hoes, digging up the moisture-stealing weeds that seem to arise overnight. Women who are like her. Except she can never be one of them, because of the color of her skin, because of the laws of this country.

In the sorghum fields Joshua allows himself a smile. "*Ubhiye,*" he says, raising his hand in a drinking motion. "For beer." This Märit knows—how the grain is fermented to make the sour, milky beer that is considered as much a food as a libation.

Joshua continues the tour, a little swelled with pride, his tone condescending when he talks to the other workers. He points out the irrigation ditches that are fed from the windmill, and the vegetable garden, and the chicken coop, and the fruit orchards.

Much of this is already familiar to Märit, but nevertheless she is overwhelmed. There is so much to know about growing seasons, when to harvest, when to fertilize, when to repair, when to buy and when to sell. How little she has known of all this, of the people and the land.

The sun is almost at its zenith by the time Märit thanks Joshua and returns with Tembi to the house.

On the way Tembi says, "He didn't look at me once. He likes to think I am not here."

"We need him," Märit mutters, her thoughts on the immensity of her ignorance. How will she manage? She could sell up easily. The farm would bring in a good price. There would be enough cash for her to settle again in the city.

But what about Tembi? Märit knows that in the city they could not sit together for their meals, they could not walk down the street together as equals—and if she appeared dressed like this on a street in Johannesburg she would be laughed at, ridiculed, even spat upon. She shakes her head. Leaving is not an option.

She will stay here—this much she owes to Ben, and to Tembi. This much she owes to herself.

31

THE SOUND OF A CAR on the gravel driveway brings Märit to the veranda door. She recognizes the little white Opel that belongs to Connie van Staden. Instinctively Märit steps back, into the shadows of the doorway.

"Tembi!" she calls. But there is no answer.

Two women get out of the car, Connie from the driver's side, and from the other side, Eloise Pretorius, from Bokvlei, the farm that lies to the west of the van Staden place. Märit hardly knows Eloise Pretorius, having spoken to her only a few times in town—but of course she was at the funeral, and spoke kind words to Märit, and offered any help that was needed.

To Märit's surprise, a man gets out of the rear seat. She glimpses a dark suit, white shirt, tie, and for an instant she thinks it is Gideon Schoon, the one who was here before, the policeman from the Security Branch, but then she recognizes the angular form of the pastor—or, to give him his official title, Predikant Venter of the Nederduitse Gereformeerde Kerk.

In the days since Ben's death the Predikant has appeared often, usually with Connie, here suggesting a path of conduct through the intricacies of the funeral, there offering a quiet word of comfort and advice. He is a big man, broad-shouldered; a pipe smoker, with that sweetish masculine smell of tobacco on his clothes. A kindly, calm man, but there is another side to him that Märit has seen revealed on those few occasions when she attended the church and heard Predikant Venter preach his Sunday sermon. From the pulpit he is a fierce moralist, strict in his directions to the congregation, clever at finding biblical quotations to emphasize his exhortations. Yet face-to-face he is charming, given to smiling often, with laugh lines radiating from the corners of his eyes. Away from the church he favors the khaki clothes and slouch hat of the local men. He could be mistaken for a farmer, except for his hands, which are without the rough and calloused surface that results from working the land.

Today, though, he is dressed in his dark suit and he carries a Bible, and the two women are dressed formally as well, and Märit knows that this is an official visit.

If she could, Märit would step back and shut the door and let their visit be in vain, but it is too late, for even though she stands in the shadows, the Predikant has seen her, and his eyebrows come up in surprise.

Märit steps forward onto the veranda, into the sunlight.

Both Connie and Eloise Pretorius stop in their tracks.

"Märit?" Connie says. "But it is! *Heere God!* My God, what has happened to you?"

Märit walks down the steps and smiles, and the women frown, as if more than her appearance is peculiar.

"What is the matter, Märit?" Connie says, approaching with outstretched hands, solicitous, concerned.

"There is nothing the matter. Good morning, Predikant." She nods. "Mrs. Pretorius."

Connie is shaking her head, almost wringing her hands. "But your hair, my child. And what are you wearing? Who has done this to you?"

"Nothing, nobody. I am myself."

She gives them her strange smile again. Eloise Pretorius looks over at the Predikant and her mouth flattens into a sharp line.

"I don't understand, Märit," Connie says.

"Please come in," Märit says, gesturing for them to go ahead of her. Eloise Pretorius reaches into the car and brings out a plate covered with a cloth. Another casserole? Märit wonders.

In the living room there is a moment of awkwardness—the two women still shocked by Märit's transformation, the Predikant rubbing the leather binding of his Bible with his thumb, uneasy.

"Please, sit down," Märit tells them. Connie and the Predikant do so, Eloise Pretorius remains standing with the covered plate in her hand.

"I've brought you something—*koeksusters*," Eloise says, and she can't prevent her tone from suggesting that she now regrets this gesture.

Märit takes the plate and lifts a corner of the cloth, seeing the twists of fried dough, sticky with sugar. She touches one with her finger; they are still warm.

"Freshly made," Eloise says, as if answering a challenge.

"Thank you, Eloise. I'll make some coffee."

The two women follow Märit into the kitchen. Connie speaks, freely now that she is out of the presence of the Predikant.

"Märit, I don't understand why you have done this to yourself. I know that this is a difficult time, with you losing Ben, but I'm worried about you." Her eyes are kind; she wants to help, despite her misgivings. She wants Märit to open up to her, the way any other woman would do after such a tragic occurrence. Even if they are not quite friends, they are neighbors, and neighbors must help each other in difficult times.

"Don't worry, Connie. I haven't gone mad with grief or anything like that. I decided to cut my hair, that's all."

Eloise speaks up. "But why do you want to dress like a *kaffir*? Do you think you will be able to go into town looking like this, to show yourself? *Heere God*, but everyone will laugh at you."

Märit turns to face her slowly, taking in Eloise's own appearance: the lipstick, the carefully coiffed and sprayed hair, the string of pearls too large to be real. The way Märit used to look herself. But Eloise looks doll-like, unreal, and very much out of place.

"You should try a change yourself, Eloise. It's far more comfortable this way. Just think, no more weekly visits to the hairdresser, no more tight, uncomfortable shoes, no worrying if your dress matches your handbag."

"There are certain standards any civilized Christian woman should maintain," Eloise retorts. "You'll soon find that out if you persist in going around dressed up like a kitchen *meid*."

"All right, all right," Connie says, "let's not argue about it. We are here to help. Märit, why don't you go in and talk to the pastor, it's rude to just leave him sitting alone there. Eloise and I will make the coffee."

Märit knows they have planned this visit, or perhaps it was the Predikant who asked the two women to accompany him, but whatever the plan, she knows they have come to advise her, to tell her how to live, to instruct her in the ways of their world, to bring her back into the fold.

She looks at the two women—capable, strong, hardworking. Despite their flowered dresses and their lipstick they can still roll up their sleeves and get their hands dirty if need be. Even Eloise, for all her pretensions to beauty.

She knows they see her as neither strong nor capable. To them, she is something of a hothouse flower, out of place here on the veldt. Behind her back they will shake their heads and they will gossip about her with the other women in the district. She is not strong enough, they will say, she cannot run a farm, she is too highly strung, they will say. And now she is dressing like a *kaffir*.

As if divining Märit's thoughts, Connie says, "What will you do now, Märit?"

"About what?"

"About the future. The farm. Have you given any thought to your position now?"

"I will manage," she answers.

"Yes, of course, but my Koos can come over, just to check on you, until you decide what to do."

"I don't need checking on."

"Märit, my child, you don't know how hard it can be. I know Ben is not long gone, and I mean no disrespect, but without a man around you cannot run this place."

"You could sell," Eloise Pretorius says. "This farm would bring a good price. I know there are one or two people who have their eye on the land. I mean, you probably will sell, hey? Connie is right, it's too big a farm for you to manage."

"This is not the time to talk of selling," Connie interjects sternly. But the thought is there—Eloise has voiced the obvious, what everybody must be thinking now that more than a month has passed since Ben's death. They all expect Märit to give up the farm.

Märit shakes her head. "The farmhands will continue with the work, just as before. It's not going to be different."

"What about your bossboy?" Eloise asks. "Can you trust him? What is his name . . . Joshua, isn't it?"

"You know him?"

"He used to work for us. My husband had to let him go."

"Oh? Why?"

"He's the cheeky kind. Always answering back when you tell him to do something. One of those who thinks he is better than he is."

Märit shrugs, and Eloise goes on. "You have to be careful with the likes of him. Especially now. They will try to take advantage of you, and find any excuse not to work. And another thing—don't think the men will take orders from a woman, especially if there is not a man in the house. Especially that Joshua. They think it's beneath them to listen to a woman, even a white woman. And even if you are mistress of this farm, they will not take you seriously. They'll try to rob you blind," she adds with a certain satisfaction. "Just you wait and see. Isn't that so, Connie?"

Connie shakes her head unhappily. "It will be difficult for you, Märit. How will you manage?"

"Don't pity me. I will manage."

Predikant Venter is waiting for her, seated comfortably, the Bible resting on his knees, an easy smile on his face as he half rises when Märit enters.

"Please, sit," she says. "The coffee will be ready in a moment." She takes a chair opposite him and reaches for her cigarettes. "You can smoke if you like. Would you like a cigarette?"

"Thank you, no, I prefer my pipe. If you don't mind, Mevrou."

"Of course not."

The Predikant takes a moment to prepare his pipe. Märit watches as he tamps tobacco from a leather pouch into the bowl with his thumb and forefinger. The same way that Ben used to do. When the pipe is lit he exhales sweet, aromatic smoke and looks up.

"I suppose Connie asked you to come and talk to me," Märit says.

The Predikant examines his pipe, taking time to answer. "Connie means well, Mevrou Laurens." He looks across at her again, his eyes seeming to know her. "May I call you Märit? I think we know each other well enough now."

She nods.

"Connie means well. And, yes, she did ask me to come along on this visit. But she means well, Märit. So do I. And perhaps our concern is not without reason?"

"I'm fine."

"I'm here not only as a pastor, but also as a neighbor, a kinsman you might say. I offer comfort and advice."

"I don't need them."

"I think you do, Märit," he says softly, inviting her to confide, to bend to him, to give up her resistance. "You have changed, and that is understandable—the shock, the grief, I understand. You are not the first to lose a loved one. But your situation is unique here. You are alone, without family, still something of a stranger in the district. You must try to see things in a realistic manner, without the clouds of emotion."

Märit shakes her head at him and smokes in silence.

"Let me put it this way, Märit. Most of the people in this district have been settled here a long time, blacks and whites. Why, my own family goes back to Voortrekker days, when the first farms were founded in this area. There is an order here, a system of living, an understanding of sorts—between us all, farmers and workers. Despite the troubles on the border, this understanding functions—"

Märit interrupts him. "And you think that me walking around dressed like a *meid*, as Mrs. Pretorius puts it, will upset your understanding, your order?"

He fiddles with his pipe, tamping at the tobacco with a matchstick. "I am not here to judge you, Märit." He indicates her shorn hair, her African sarong, and her bare feet. "If this is the form your grief must take, then so be it. My concern, Märit, is with you. With your place among us. With your soul."

How similar the Predikant is to that policeman, Gideon Schoon, Märit thinks. Both with their confident reasoning, their concern, their cold-hearted resolve.

"When my husband died, Predikant Venter, I died as well. Mevrou Laurens died. And out of that death I have been reborn as someone other."

The Predikant permits himself a gentle smile. "Reborn into Christ, I hope."

"Christ has nothing to do with it. This is my own decision."

"I hope you are not turning your back on God."

"What God? I see no God anywhere."

"Be careful what you say, Mevrou, you are venturing close to blasphemy." He speaks softly, but she sees the hardness in him, the hardness that appears when he stands in the pulpit and preaches to the farmers.

"Is this God's plan for you, Mevrou? Do you think this is what He wants from you?"

Anger rises in Märit, at this man's easy presumption to speak for her. "Really, Predikant? Which God is that?"

"Yours and mine. Is there not only one God?"

"I don't know. Unlike you, I am not on intimate terms with Him."

"Nevertheless," he says, smiling a little smile of triumph. "Nevertheless, He is on intimate terms with you."

"And where is this God? I don't see Him."

"He is all around us, Mevrou. But it is not for us to see His face, only to know His actions."

"I suppose killing my husband was one of His actions?"

The anger blazes quickly in the Predikant's eyes, but he maintains his reasonable tone. "To everything there is a purpose."

"Is that why we live the way we do? Pretending everything is fine, with a war on our borders, with every man fearing his neighbor? Even I know these things, although I pretend, along with everyone else, that things are fine. Even I know that there is something terribly wrong in this country. I see it every day in the eyes of those who work on this farm. Ben didn't die at the hand of any God, he died because our neighbors are at war with us."

"Even though you seem to feel it necessary to abandon God, He will not abandon you."

Leaning forward, Märit grinds her cigarette out in the ashtray. "I have no need of your God, Predikant Venter. Nor of you."

His face darkens, and she sees the anger in his eyes, the hardness, for she has dismissed him, as a priest and as a man.

He gets to his feet. "You may tell Mevrou van Staden and Mevrou Pretorius that I will wait for them in the car."

When the two women come in, Connie bearing the tray and Eloise carrying her plate of *koeksusters*, they see Märit sitting alone, her face flushed, and Connie looks around, bewildered. "Where is Predikant Venter?"

"He is waiting for you in the car."

"What do you mean?"

"I think that he found his visit here was a waste of time."

Eloise clutches the plate of pastries closer to her body and immediately steps out of the house.

Connie sets the tray down, shaking her head. "What have you done now, child?"

Märit rises and takes Connie by the hand, leading her towards the door. "I know you are kind, Connie, and that you mean well, but I don't want help. I am going to do this on my own."

"Child, you don't know what you are saying. This is a harsh world."

"I know that already," Märit answers.

She stands on the veranda and watches the car pull away, the Predikant sitting upright, looking straight ahead, Connie shaking her head and waving, Eloise Pretorius turning to direct a last malevolent stare at Märit.

32

THE LIFE of the farm has a rhythm of its own. Momentum and habit turn the wheels of the days. Each morning Märit wakes to the alarm clock, and after breakfast on the shaded veranda she walks the farm—sometimes with Tembi, sometimes alone. Always Joshua is there, even if she does not intentionally seek him out; even if she leaves the house earlier than usual, he always materializes at her side, as if he knows her movements.

And so she learns—of the maize and the sorghum and the cattle. She tries to remember the names of the workers. She inspects the kraal where they live. They become used to her—she hopes.

Momentum and habit turn the wheels of the days and Märit tries to set her own actions in tandem with the rhythm of the farm. The days pass, the weeks pass. The maize plants reach high, the fruit in the orchard ripens.

Sometimes, when she is alone, before Joshua has appeared, Märit thinks of Ben, and how she ought to have walked the farm more often with him. Perhaps then the distance that was always there between them might have been bridged. But he did not want her next to him on the land; he wanted her to be in the house, protected and pampered, unsullied by dust and grease. He wanted her to stand above what he saw as crude labor.

When she thinks of him now she cannot feel any presence next to her. His image fades with the days, and sometimes she forgets him entirely, then recollects her lapse with guilty admonishments. But sometimes she says to herself, Why must the dead accompany the living? All her memories and recollections will not change the fact of Ben's death, of his permanent absence.

In the afternoon, when the midday sun has lost its brilliance and strength, Märit works with Tembi in the flower garden next to the house. She weeds with a long-handled hoe, like the women in the sorghum fields do, and she crouches to dig her hands into the fertile soil—for must she not also work the land if she is to be mistress of this farm?

When dusk falls Tembi begins to prepare the evening meal and Märit retreats to her office. Over the past weeks she has sat here almost every night, sorting through papers—invoices, bills of sale, tax notices, the house deed, letters to suppliers of machinery and seeds, brochures, correspondence with the veterinarian, crop rotation plans, weather charts that calculate annual rainfall over the years, circulars from the Agricultural Board. There is so much to know.

No visitors come to the farm. Once or twice the telephone in the house rings, but neither Märit nor Tembi answers. The sun warms the farm, and warms Märit, so that her arms and her face lose their pale color and take on a hue like that of the grass on the veldt. The muscles in her arms and legs grow strong and fill out. She stands upright, head erect, and the old distant look is not in her eyes as often as it used to be.

Tembi does not go to the kraal anymore. She has moved all of her belongings to the house, and the room where she sleeps is now her own room. Once or twice she has wandered into the dairy, to talk to the other girls who work there. But she senses the change in the tone of their chatter, their sudden diffidence in her presence; she hears the lightness return to their voices when she leaves.

On one of these visits a girl named Onika says to Tembi, "How long will the Missus be alone like this? When will she take another husband?"

Tembi shrugs. Onika persists. "What is the Missus thinking? What do you see in her face, what do you hear when she speaks?"

"I don't know what she thinks."

Onika shakes her head, disbelieving. "Joshua says that the Missus will not be able to learn this farming. He says she will have to sell if she cannot find another husband."

"You don't know her," Tembi retorts. "You don't know anything about her."

Onika shakes her head again. "The Missus is like one of those bright flowers in her garden. When the soil is dry and the sun is hot, she will wilt."

Tembi retreats, wondering if there is truth in these words, and from outside the dairy she hears the lightness return to the voices of the girls, the laughter.

And if Tembi encounters other workers, they too ask her questions, for they wonder about their jobs, about their place on this farm. They too doubt Märit. But Tembi can give them no answers. She no longer belongs with them.

And so she remains close to the house, cleaning, cooking, helping Märit in the flower garden, and she seldom ventures out with Märit in the mornings to inspect the fields.

When night falls Tembi is happiest, for then she sits after dinner on the veranda with Märit in the darkness under the thick sky of stars, and they talk. Märit tells of her days as a girl, of her school and her parents, of how she met Ben, and of her honeymoon in Durban.

Tembi recalls her own childhood in the place beyond the mountains. She tells of her father leaving to seek work in the gold mines, and how the winters were hard when the crops failed and there was no maize or sorghum to eat.

Tembi listens to Märit, and she says, "All these things you speak of, I have never seen them. My own life seems so small. I have seen nothing."

"One day we will go together and see all these places," Märit reassures her.

"You will take me to Durban," Tembi asks, "to visit the ocean?"

Märit nods. But the future is beyond her at the moment. It is vague; she is too much occupied with each particular. Tembi considers the questions that the girls in the dairy ask her, and she looks into Märit's face. But Märit is still a stranger to Tembi. What is in her heart, Tembi does not know.

Still, they can share this small world here on the veranda under the stars, and for now that is enough.

ONE MORNING the alarm in Märit's bedroom does not ring and she sleeps through the hour when she would normally walk her rounds of the farm. It is Tembi who wakes her, bringing coffee and rusks on a tray to the room.

Märit sits up with a start, glancing at the clock and then out the window where the day is already bright.

"It doesn't matter today," Tembi tells her. "Nobody will mind if you don't inspect the farm today. Here is coffee."

Märit takes the cup and sips, then grimaces at the taste. Tembi says, "There is no sugar in the coffee. We have no more sugar."

Märit drinks anyway.

"We need other things too," Tembi says. "Not only sugar but coffee soon, and salt, and cigarettes for you."

"We'll go into town and do some shopping today," Märit tells her. For a split second it is on the tip of Märit's tongue to say, Ben will drive us, but then she remembers. "I'll telephone Connie van Staden and see if she will drive us in."

But later, when Märit lifts the receiver to dial, she hesitates, picturing the day—sitting in the car next to Connie, with Tembi in the back seat. And after the shopping Connie will want to go for tea and cakes at the hotel, and Tembi will have to wait outside. Or will Connie even want to be seen with Märit now? And there will be other women there, who will stare at her and whisper disapprovingly.

Märit does not want to subject herself to the well-meaning attention of Connie—the sympathetic questions, the advice that will surely be forthcoming. And the pity. Behind the generosity there's pity. Märit does not want it.

From beyond the open front door she hears the sound of an engine— Joshua driving the tractor. Everywhere she looks, Joshua is there. His presence is insistent, almost aggressive, and she senses that he does not trust her on any matter relating to the farm. Sometimes she feels that it is his farm, that he controls and manages it. Märit defers to him, in spite of herself, in spite of the growing dislike she feels towards him. And the truth is that she is a bit afraid of him, for he is stern and humorless.

She watches the tractor moving back and forth between the sheds and an idea occurs to her.

"Tembi," she calls. "We will go to town today—on the tractor."

"But can you drive that machine?"

"No. But I've seen how Ben handled the tractor. I'll practice a little bit first."

"And you can teach me!"

But first they must wait for Joshua to finish whatever it is that he is doing. Märit sits down at the kitchen table with pen and paper and writes out a list—besides the sugar and cigarettes and other staples, she needs shampoo, face cream, deodorant, bath oil, sanitary pads. After considering a moment she crosses out the list of cosmetics and writes instead only one item—*soap*.

The women remain in the house throughout the morning, both listening always to the sound of the tractor engine.

What is he doing that takes so long? Märit wonders. She cannot bring herself to go across to Joshua and tell him that she requires the tractor. The tractor does not belong to Joshua, it belongs to her; there is no need to be afraid of him. But she is afraid of him, and so she will wait.

At last, when it is almost noon, the tractor falls silent. From the veranda Märit and Tembi watch Joshua striding up from the orchard towards the kraal.

"He will go now for his midday porridge and beer," Tembi says.

"Come," Märit tells her.

They steal across the lawn and past the rock garden and skirt the peach trees, making for the shed where the tractor is kept. Märit keeps glancing backward to make sure they are unobserved. When they reach the shed they find the door is shut and fastened with a padlock.

"I didn't think he would keep it locked," Märit says.

"Now we can't drive the tractor. Unless you ask Joshua for the key."

"There is another key, in the office, hanging inside the cupboard door. I'll go back and fetch it."

"I can go," Tembi says. "What does it look like?"

"There is a whole bunch, fastened with a strip of leather. Just bring them all."

In the house, on the hooks behind the cupboard door in the office a great many keys are hung. Tembi takes a moment to find the bunch fastened with the leather thong, then closes the door and hurries back through the house. As she passes the passage leading down to the bedrooms a sudden sound catches her ear. She pauses and listens. The sound is there again—the creak of a wooden drawer sliding shut.

"Märit? Is that you?" Tembi moves along the passage to Märit's room. The curtains are drawn against the light and her eyes take a few seconds to adjust to the gloom.

"Märit?" She sees the figure in the room and recoils with a gasp.

Joshua is standing at Märit's dresser; one of the drawers is still open.

"What are you doing in here?" Tembi demands, her voice shaking, for she too fears the stern presence of Joshua. "This is the Missus's room. You can't come in here."

Joshua slides the drawers shut with his knee and steps away from the dresser, glaring at her. Tembi retreats from him. She is afraid of him and she clutches the bunch of keys behind her back.

"You think this is your house now, eh?" he says. He steps closer, moving his bulk between Tembi and the door, and she shrinks away from him.

"What are you doing here?" she demands again, her eyes moving to the dresser. "What are you taking from the dresser?"

He is close to her, so that she can smell his sweat and the pungent tang of gasoline.

"Because you are the *meid* in the house you think you can tell me to get out?" Joshua says.

Tembi is afraid of him, but still she says, "You are stealing!"

Joshua lifts his arm quickly, and she ducks, thinking he is about to strike her, but he grasps her around the throat, his big hand enclosing her neck, lightly, though, until she tries to break free, and then his fingers tighten. The skin of his palm is calloused, rough against the softness of her throat. His eyes are bloodshot, with a gleam in them, and she wonders if he is drunk, but there is no taint of alcohol on his sour breath. There is only the smell of gasoline from his hand.

His hand drops away from her throat and Tembi gulps a deep breath.

"If you say anything to her . . ." Joshua threatens in a hoarse whisper, and his hand darts around her breast, squeezing, "I will cut this off!" His eyes bear down at her, and he squeezes harder until Tembi cringes with the pain and whimpers. Then he drops his hand and goes away, leaving behind the sour odor of sweat and gasoline.

Tembi sinks down on the bed, cradling her aching breast until the pain subsides. She hears the sound of the kitchen door slam shut, and she waits, and then she rises to her feet, retrieves the keys from the bed, and leaves the house.

"Did you find the keys?" Märit asks when Tembi reappears.

Tembi turns an apprehensive eye back up to the house. "I don't think we should take the tractor."

"But why not? It belongs to me. If I want to use it I will. And don't you want to learn to drive it?"

Tembi shakes her head. She wants to tell Märit what has just happened. But she is afraid. What will Joshua do if she tells? She fears that there is something evil and violent in him. And if she tells, what can Märit do against him, what can two women do against him? He has a kind of power on this farm that Märit does not have.

"Is it Joshua you are worried about?"

"I don't like him," Tembi answers.

"Never mind Joshua. Give me the keys." Märit holds out her hand.

Tembi says nothing, only waits as Märit unlocks the doors and pushes them wide open to reveal the tractor. The smell of gasoline and oil hangs thick in the confines of the shed.

Märit climbs up onto the tractor and settles herself in the seat, placing her hands on the big steering wheel. She remembers riding with Ben, standing next to him as the tractor jolted across the veldt, his hands capable and confident as he worked the controls. He'd asked her if she wanted to drive the machine, but she was happy to stand behind him with her hands on his shoulders and her body leaning into his strong back.

Her feet find the accelerator and the brake, she presses down on the clutch, which is stiff and takes more effort than she expects. Using her right hand she works the heavy gear lever through its positions, remembering how Ben did it.

"We can walk to town," Tembi calls up to Märit.

"No." Märit turns the ignition key and presses the starter button.

The engine coughs and erupts into life with a roar, filling the shed with oily exhaust smoke. Märit struggles the gear into position and releases the clutch slowly as the tractor trembles under her, the large steering wheel vibrating between her hands. She lets the clutch out a little farther and presses her other foot down on the gas pedal.

The clutch springs up under her foot and the tractor lurches forward out the doors, narrowly missing Tembi. For a moment Märit has the tractor in her control as it veers to the left, and then the pedals seem to lock under her feet and the big round steering wheel convulses violently, spinning with a will of its own. Märit jams her foot down on the brake, sending the tractor into a sharp turn. The right wheel grinds against the side of the shed with a terrible shearing noise and the tractor shudders to a halt. A puff of smoke spurts from the engine with a smell of burned oil.

Märit slumps forward over the steering wheel and puts her hands over her eyes.

"Märit, are you hurt?" Tembi clambers up next to her, shaking at her shoulder.

"I'm all right." She slams her hand on the steering wheel. "Damn thing!"

Märit climbs down with trembling legs. "It doesn't matter."

A shouting from the direction of the kraal interrupts them, and Joshua appears, arms flailing in the air as he runs towards the house.

"What are you doing with this tractor? This is for my work!" He turns on Märit, furious. "This is for working, not for women to play with!"

He bangs on the side of the engine cowling with the flat of his hand. "Look what you've done! Breaking this tractor. Stupid. Stupid." Spittle flies from his mouth as he shouts. "Now I'm going to have to fix it. How I'm going to do that, eh, tell me?"

The women cower under his anger and he advances on them, shaking his fist in the air. "Who says you can take my tractor and break it like this? Stupid!"

He is truly furious, striding back and forth, slamming his hand on the engine cowling, then turning to shake his fist at them. The spittle has gathered in a white froth at the corners of his mouth.

"That's enough!" Märit shouts. "Don't you dare talk to us like that!

Did you pay for this tractor? Is it yours? You are employed to work on this farm, nothing more."

Then his tone becomes apologetic, almost wheedling. "But this is for my job. How must I do my work now without a tractor? You tell me the answer to that." His anger gets the better of him again and his voice rises. "You think you can fix this tractor?"

"Don't concern yourself so much with what I can do, Joshua. See to your own business."

He looks sideways at her, unsure, his expression shifting between the accustomed deference to white authority and a still undecided limit to his own power. Märit knows this is a crisis of authority. If he wins, then she is lost.

She puts her hands on her hips and glares back at him defiantly. "Since the tractor is broken, you can find something else to do. You don't need to ride up and down on it all day as if this is your farm. And if you don't like the way I do things here, then you can leave. Do you understand?"

He looks away, not meeting her eyes.

"Do you understand?" Märit repeats.

"Yes, Missus," he mutters, still not looking at her.

"Good. Then go and see to your own work."

He marches away, shaking his head.

"Come," Märit says, taking Tembi's hand. "Forget about him."

As they go up the veranda steps Tembi glances back, just in time to see Joshua as he rounds the corner of the house, and he too looks back, with a sly, calculating expression on his face.

33

BECAUSE THEY NO LONGER have a vehicle, because Märit does not want to ask her neighbor for help, because they are two women alone, they must walk to town.

"Maybe it will be hard for you," Tembi tells her. "But I am used to walking."

"I don't mind walking. In fact, I want to walk. If others can do it, so can I."

"You must wear shoes," Tembi advises.

"You're not wearing any."

Tembi laughs. "Because my feet are strong. I have always walked without shoes."

"Then I will too."

"You will need a *doek* to cover your head. I will give you one of mine." She returns from her room with a rectangle of red cloth, which she fastens over Märit's head, tying it in a knot at the back. "It's not because of your hair or anything. Women always wear a *doek* when we go to town, so that we can look respectable. It's our way." Tembi fastens her own head-covering, of the same red hue but more faded. She stands next to Märit in front of the mirror, considers their appearance, then slips off a few of the copper bracelets she wears on her left wrist and slides them onto Märit's hand. "There . . . now nobody can look at us and think we are just wanderers on the road. We are respectable women."

"Like sisters," Märit answers.

Tembi fetches a couple of straw baskets from the pantry, while Märit retrieves the cash box from its place in the office and takes out a handful of banknotes. Tembi brings Märit's sandals from the bedroom and tosses them into the basket. "Just in case."

The road is a sandy road, of a light, yellowish sand, sometimes rust-colored in stretches, and it winds between the flat-topped acacia trees and the long grasses of the veldt that are a pale ochre color at this time of the year and ripple like water in the light breeze.

Märit feels the ground under her feet, the way the sand falls across her toes, the occasional small stone pressing into her sole. Her feet are less soft with each passing day, for she never wears shoes now.

The touch of the sand reminds her of childhood, the freedom of being without the heavy black shoes she was required to wear to school, and today, like a child given an unexpected holiday, she feels the same freedom, the same pleasure, with its faint echoes of guilt.

Above the koppie the tall finger of rock rises into the sky, casting its elongated shadow across the road towards the women.

"The Duiwelskop is almost touching us," Märit remarks.

Tembi looks up quizzically and Märit points at the koppie. "That rock, and its shadow. The Devil's Head. Duiwelskop."

"We don't call it that," Tembi says. "We have another name, *Isitimane*, in the Zulu language."

"*Is-i-ti-mane*," Märit tries out the pronunciation. "And what does it mean?"

"Sometimes, the girls are putting together a string of beads to give to a man they want to love, or they can wear it themselves to show people something. They put different colors of beads next to each other, to tell a story, because each color can mean something. What you want to tell to the man you can say with the beads. The white bead is called *ithambo*, bone, that means love, or the red one, *igazi*, blood, means tears and longing. *Isitimane* is a color in the story."

"Which color?"

"The black bead is called *isitimane*, shadow. When a girl puts it in a necklace it shows that she is sad or disappointed." Tembi looks up at the koppie. "This rock is throwing a shadow of loneliness." As she says this, she falls silent, recalling that early morning when she stood here at the farm gate with her mother, who walked away into the dawn, into a different kind of shadow.

Looking up at the koppie Märit wonders at the fact that two separate languages have both found words of darkness and isolation for this outcrop of stone. Will this farm always lie under the shadow of grief and loneliness and disappointment?

Märit turns and points at the sign that Ben painted on the post of the gate. "And what about the farm itself? I know it was called Duiwelskop before we named it Kudufontein, but what do your people call it?"

"*Lebone*—that means 'light' in the SeSotho language. Like a candle. I don't know why they call it that. Maybe a light against the shadow of Isitimane."

They walk on, away from the shadow that hangs over the farm. The river is to one side, behind a screen of willow trees where small green weaverbirds dart between the bulbous nests hanging from the branches.

The road curves away from the river, flanked now by the sorghum and maize fields of the van Staden farm. Just above the tips of the sorghum a long-tailed blackbird flaps with a strange, ungainly grace, the long tail feathers trailing across the grain.

"I know the name of that one," Märit says. "*Sakabula* bird."

"Widow Bird," Tembi says.

"Like me."

Tembi glances at Märit's face. "Are you sorry for how your life is now?"

"I don't think about it much. What can I do about what happened—about the past? Nothing. I want to go forward, like this road."

"Every road moves in two directions."

"Not today. Today this road only goes to Klipspring."

"Yes. And we call the town *Pulane*. That means 'rain.' It rains more in the town than on the veldt. That is why everything is so green there. All the jacaranda trees, and the flowers."

Märit mouths the word silently. Everything in this country is called by more than one name. It all depends on who is doing the naming.

Tembi touches Märit lightly on the arm. "We can go to the place in Pulane where your husband is buried. I can visit him with you."

"You are a good person, Tembi," Märit says, touched by this solicitude. "Where does your goodness come from?"

Tembi shakes her head.

"No, I truly believe that. There is a goodness in you that I don't have. I know that you have a good heart, and I'm lucky that you're my friend. I feel that I don't deserve your friendship."

Tembi looks down, embarrassed. "You are good also, Märit. And strong. You will find these things in yourself even if you cannot see them now."

They walk on in silence, Märit thinking about the town, about the grave in the small cemetery. If she thinks about Ben, when she allows herself to, and knows that she is a woman alone, then doubt and fear come over her. And then she knows herself to be weak.

She turns to Tembi. "Do you think about your mother? Do you miss her?"

"I feel sorry for her, that she had to die."

"Do you feel sorry for yourself?"

"No. Because I can live, I can be here in the world. And I know that my mother dwells in the House of the Lord. Maybe that is better for her. But I am here."

"*We* are here," Märit says emphatically, linking her arm with Tembi's.

Just before they reach the junction to the tarred road that leads to Klipspring, where the sand road becomes tarmac, they hear the sound of a car approaching from behind and they both step to the side of the road, turning to look back.

The car slows, and there are two white women in the front seat, women Märit vaguely recognizes from seeing them in town, perhaps they were even at the funeral, but she does not know them, not their names or on which farm they live.

Märit raises a hand in greeting, in hope of being offered a ride into town. For a moment it appears that they will stop to offer a ride, but then the eyes of the women in the car move between Märit and Tembi, and there is confusion on the faces, and startled apprehension, and the car quickly accelerates to the junction and turns onto the main road. As it turns, a child's face appears in the back window, a little girl with a round, serious, plain face, and a small doll clutched in one hand. Märit waves and smiles wistfully, for the image of the face in the window reminds her of her own childhood, of interminable journeys alone in the back seat with only a doll for company and her parents engaged in a conversation that either ignored her or excluded her. She sees her own boredom and loneliness in that child's face. And so she waves.

The child does not wave back, or smile, but instead sticks her tongue out at Märit. Not playfully, but with an expression of malice that is all the more shocking because it is on the face of a child. Märit drops her hand, chastened.

The sudden dust thrown up by the car envelops Märit and Tembi. Tembi, practiced at avoiding dust thrown up by passing vehicles, tucks her head in against her shoulder while cupping a hand over her nose and mouth, but Märit coughs and splutters, tasting the dry texture of sand in her mouth.

She remembers how many times she drove past people walking on the side of the road and never gave a thought to the dust thrown up by the car, and never gave a thought that one of them might be tired and in need of a lift. Those who walked on the side of the road were invisible, mere fixtures of the landscape. There were two worlds; some walked, some did not.

Märit spits out the dust from her mouth. "I need to drink some water."

"There is no place for water on this road, you must wait until we reach Klipspring. Unless we go back to the river."

"No, let's go on." She wipes a hand across her lips. "I can wait."

"I have a *naartjie*," Tembi says, producing a small tangerine from her pocket.

Märit peels it, the citrus tang pungent in the dry air, dividing the fruit before passing half to Tembi, and tosses the skin into the grass, where it is bright and orange amongst the yellow and brown *khakibos*. The juice is sweet in Märit's mouth, but also acidic, and it leaves her throat with a faint ache and her thirst accentuated.

The road is flat and straight, glaring with a metallic sheen as it rises to a distant ridge. On the veldt the *doringboom* is the only tree that grows, all thorn and leathery leaves. This is unfarmed land, hard, dry—a land of thirst and stone. In the distance ahead, mirages shimmer on the road like promised pools of water.

Märit turns to look back at the long road and sees a dark, moving blur in the distant, wavering mirage where the road merges with the pale sky. When she looks over her shoulder again a few minutes later the blur has taken on a shape, and as it approaches becomes a figure on a bicycle.

Märit stops.

The cyclist draws nearer, and Märit sees it is a black man, wearing only a pair of faded trousers, pedaling hard with his head down. He does not look up as he sweeps past the two women with the soft sound of rubber tires on tarmac, and Märit only has a quick glimpse of his face, which is clenched with effort, his features glistening with sweat.

Tembi looks up, surprised, as he passes, and stops to watch his bent back and pumping legs until his receding form is a smudge in the distance that merges again with the pale sky. Neither woman comments.

A few minutes later a gray van appears from the same direction, traveling very fast. As it whips by with a crackle of static, the long radio antenna on the roof bent almost double in the slipstream, Märit sees the uniformed policemen in the front seat of the vehicle. Hot gusts of gasoline fumes buffet Märit's face.

"Are they chasing that man?" Märit looks at Tembi inquiringly, but the reply is only a shake of the head. "Some trouble. I don't know."

The whine of the engine slowly fades into the dry silence. Cicadas buzz with a monotonous drone in the grass. The women walk on.

When they finally crest the ridge, Klipspring is visible below them—a small town of white walls and green trees and the silver flash of tin roofs and the glint of the railway line twisting across the veldt towards the foothills. The tower of the church rises over the center of the town, marking Wolmarans Street. Beyond the town lie the blue hills, and beyond the hills is the frontier—another country.

"Not far now," Tembi announces.

"I have to put my sandals on." Märit takes them from the basket and pauses a moment to fasten the straps around her ankles.

As they descend, longing for the relief from the sun that will be found in the shaded streets of the town, Märit looks up to her left, to the back side of the ridge, where a farmhouse is situated. It is one of the oldest farms in the district, called Geelblom, Yellow Flower, belonging to a family named Potgieter. Märit has always admired the house, with its attractive facade of high gables and a shaded pergola in the Cape Dutch style. She admires it every time she visits Klipspring, this prosperous house on prosperous land.

But what she sees now, in the midst of the ochre grass and the green of the trees, is a black scorch across the slope. Where the house had been is a ruin of blackened walls and rafters.

"Look!" She grasps Tembi's arms. "The house. Oh God, they've had a fire."

"The fields too." Tembi points to a burned scar seared across the land.

A chill trembles across Märit's skin, as if the sun has been blotted out by a dark cloud.

The day suddenly seems filled with omens: the accident with the tractor, that child pulling a malicious face, the desperate man on the bicycle, fleeing from something. And now this. Isitimane is upon the land, the darkness of fear. Something has fallen out of the day, leaving a hollow feeling in her chest. Standing here with Tembi on this open road, Märit feels small and exposed—both of them, small and exposed and defenseless.

"Maybe we should go back," Märit says. Their own house is unguarded, defenseless. Anything could happen.

"Come," Tembi says, taking Märit's hand, for she sees a sudden despair in Märit's face. "Come, we can get something to drink in town. Aren't you thirsty?"

Märit allows herself to be led away from the sight of the burned house, but the image lingers in her mind, and she thinks of her own house and fears for its isolation and fragility.

As the road leads into the town the municipal sign appears. KLIPSPRING Pop. 1200. A familiar sign—but there has been a recent addition. Across the bottom someone has written in thick painted letters, *Slegs vir Blankes*.

Märit knows what these words mean, she has grown up with them, seeing the same phrase on public park benches, on buses, over the entrance to shops. A sign that is common throughout the country. *Slegs vir Blankes*—For Whites Only.

Märit moves on quickly, not wanting Tembi to see the sign. "I'm so thirsty," she says, as they enter the silent streets lined with jacaranda trees that shade the neat, whitewashed houses, each behind its painted wrought-iron fence enclosing a tidy garden—roses, aloes, protea, pots of red geraniums standing on polished steps, sometimes a peach or apricot tree shading the flowers.

As they walk Märit notices Tembi glancing from side to side apprehensively.

"What's wrong?" Märit asks.

"It's so quiet. I don't see anybody."

"They're all probably sleeping off the effects of lunch."

Tembi shakes her head but makes no further comment.

In the garden of one of the houses that they pass, no different from all the others, Märit notices a tap just next to the fence. "I must have some water," she says, lifting the gate latch. She opens the faucet, bends to splash the cool liquid on her face, then fills her mouth with refreshing water.

"Märit." A low warning comes from Tembi.

A woman is standing behind the screen door, watching them.

"Goeiemiddag," Märit calls, wiping her chin with one hand and raising the other in a wave of greeting. "I was thirsty."

The screen door swings open, the woman's lips move. Behind her, Märit sees the dog.

Edging through the door in a stealthy prowl is a big tawny colored animal with the stiff hair along the ridge of its back standing up in a taut brush. The dog doesn't bark, but the lips of its muzzle are pulled back to show teeth, and its eyes are intent on Märit as it slinks down the steps.

"Märit!" Tembi screams as the dog charges.

Märit leaps back, just managing to slam the iron gate behind her. The dog throws itself against the fence, snarling with fury.

"Vang haar, vang haar!" the woman at the door shouts. "Get her!"

Tembi screams again and pulls Märit back, and they race down the street. Behind them the furious snarls of the dog echo with the rattling of the fence as it throws itself repeatedly against the wire.

Only when they have reached a turn in the road do Tembi and Märit pause to catch their breath.

"There is something wrong in this town," Tembi pants.

"All I wanted was a drink of water." Märit holds her heaving chest.

"And where are the people?" Tembi adds. "Usually there are black people walking on the road, or looking after the gardens, or working in these houses to do the cooking and the washing. But today, nothing, no people. I don't understand."

Märit recollects the ominous addition to the sign on the outskirts of town, "Come on, we'll see if there is anybody in the shops."

The street leads into Kerkstraat, named after the church that stands at its head—the church where Ben is buried. On the nearer end of the street the shops begin. But there are no people on the streets.

The first shop, set apart a little from the rest, is Patel's Haberdashery, which is owned by an Indian family. There are two entrances: the main one that fronts onto Kerkstraat and is used by the townspeople, and around the side a smaller door that leads to a counter where Mrs. Patel serves the black customers. This section of the shop is screened by a hanging bamboo blind. Mr. Patel presides over the front counter.

"I want to buy some cloth in Patel's," Märit says. "Something for a new sarong." She wants to buy Tembi a present as well.

She automatically makes for the front door, but Tembi hesitates. "I don't want to go in."

"Don't you want to choose something?"

Tembi shakes her head, glancing up and down the empty street.

"I won't be long," Märit tells her. "Wait here for me."

There are three people in the shop—two women at the counter fingering a bolt of cloth, while Mr. Patel, the rotund proprietor, stands before them with a pair of scissors in his hand. He looks up, a ready smile on his face, for he is always welcoming to the women of the town. But the smile dies as he takes in Märit's appearance—the dusty feet, the housemaid's kerchief on her head. The conversation stops as the other women turn to stare at Märit. They mutter low words to each other and look her up and down, then move a little farther away as she approaches.

Mr. Patel turns back to them, speaking loudly with a kind of forced enthusiasm. "This is pure linen, Mevrous, sent to me specially from Johannesburg. And the price is exactly what you would pay there. I don't add on anything for shipping and handling. What do you think, Mevrou Botha? Nice, no?" While he speaks his eyes make little darts in Märit's direction. The women have turned their backs towards Märit. She waits, running her eyes across the bolts of cloth stacked on shelves that reach to the ceiling.

The shop door opens, the little bell on the handle tinkling, and another customer enters.

Mr. Patel directs his attention to the new arrival. "*Goeiemiddag*, Mevrou Pretorius! *Hoe gaan dit met jou?* How are you?"

Märit nods a greeting to Eloise Pretorius. "Good afternoon." But Eloise looks away, crinkling her nose slightly as if some smell has offended her, and moves to stand at the far end of the counter with the other two women. Mr. Patel shuffles after her. "And how may I help you today, Mevrou?"

Märit steps forward. "Excuse me, Mr. Patel, but I think I was next."

Everyone turns to look at Märit. A sheen of sweat is glistening on the shopkeeper's round face. He withdraws a large white handkerchief from his pocket and mops at his forehead, frowning hard at Märit while simultaneously flashing a nervous smile at the three women. He scuttles down the counter and hisses at Märit. "There is nothing here for you. You must go."

"Are you refusing to serve me?"

Mr. Patel lifts the hinged part of the counter and walks around to stand next to Märit, glancing at the women with a little apologetic shake of his shoulders as he wrings his handkerchief in his damp hands.

"Nobody wants trouble, Mevrou," he whispers. "My other customers . . . Please."

"If you can serve them, you can serve me too. There is nothing wrong with the color of my money."

"Please, I have standards to keep up. This is a respectable place." His voice drops to a barely audible whisper. "Come back, after closing. I have to think of my other customers. Please, Mevrou, after closing." He takes her by the elbow, urging her towards the door.

Reluctantly Märit allows him to edge her to the door, for she is shocked, dazed, and before she knows it Patel has swung open the door and, while not quite pushing her away, has managed to hustle her out of his shop.

She stands on the sidewalk, in the hot light, conscious of the dust on her legs and the smell of her own sweat. The outline of the church shimmers in the heat. The light bouncing off the cement pavement is bright and hard and it pains her eyes, and she shuts them as a wave of dizziness washes over her.

"Mevrou Laurens?"

Märit opens her eyes on the stern visage of Eloise Pretorius.

"Yes?" she answers, squinting.

"Let me give you some advice, Mevrou. You have everybody's sympathy after your tragedy, but there are some of us who might see your presence here as an insult. Bringing your *meid* into town as well—in the face of the new regulations. And dressing like a *kaffir* yourself. Some of us might see that as intentionally provocative. Especially after what's happened."

"What are you talking about?"

"Klipspring has been reclassified as a whites-only town, as you should know. You are lucky that both of you haven't been arrested."

"What? Why?"

"The Potgieter farm—you know what happened there? You must have seen it when you came into town."

"They had a fire. I saw the house."

Eloise shakes her head. "No, Mevrou Laurens, they didn't have a fire. The farm was burned, intentionally, as well as the crops. And the cattle that weren't driven across the border were killed. Their throats were cut."

"The Potgieters? What happened to them?"

"They were here in town, at a church meeting. Lucky for them."

"But who would do such a thing?"

"Who do you think? The same people that put the bomb in the road that killed your husband. The same people who want to drive us off our land." Eloise jerks her head across the street. "Them. That's who."

Shading her eyes against the glare Märit takes a step back and turns to look at Tembi, who is standing in the shade of a tree.

"You think she doesn't know about it?" Eloise says. "They all stick together. You'd be wise not to trust any one of them, Mevrou. You'd be wise to keep an eye on your own farm."

"Tembi is not like that. I would trust her before any of you."

Eloise Pretorius narrows her eyes. "Do you know the term *kaffir-boetie*, Mevrou?"

Märit translates the words into English, not in their literal meaning, but in the sense that she has heard the term used. "Nigger-lover."

"That's right. I'll give you another piece of advice, Mevrou Laurens— you don't want to be a *kaffir-boetie* in this district right now." With these words Eloise turns her back on Märit and steps back into the shop.

Through the plate-glass window Märit sees the women nodding their heads at Eloise Pretorius, and Mr. Patel dabbing his white handkerchief across his forehead. And when the women look out at Märit, and she sees their faces, she sees the contempt in their eyes.

She wants to shout out something, some reply, but the words trip in her mouth and she can only glare through the window. Then she hurries across the street towards Tembi.

"I cannot remain in this town one moment longer," she exclaims through tight lips.

"Yes, I don't like it here," Tembi says. "I don't want to stay here."

"We'll go home now."

Märit only looks back once, to the church spire, solid and unmoving above the roofs. She did not visit Ben's grave. But it is too late now, too late for that.

34

THE TWO WOMEN walk the long road back in silence, each withdrawn into the exile of her separate thoughts.

They walk back past the burned farm, and down the long, straight road across the veldt. They walk through a landscape where no birds sing and the ground is not soft and the shadows are not cool. The thorns are sharp, the stones are hot, the rivers are dry.

When at last they reach the farm, weary, dusty, thirsty, Tembi strides off in the direction of the kraal without saying anything, and Märit is too fatigued to even notice.

Tembi, sick at heart, goes to the only refuge she knows—the garden behind the koppie. In all the change and trouble, this is the only constant. But weariness and disappointment are upon her, and like Märit, she is stripped of illusion. She too feels shame, for the words painted on the sign outside Klipspring were clear to her; she too knows the meaning of the phrase. On the streets of the town it seemed as if hatred oozed from the very sidewalks and walls.

Tembi walks to the patch of earth she has nurtured. Where is the fruit? Nothing will come of her efforts. And even if something grows here, what is the purpose? She is close to despair.

And there, in the secret place amongst the tender green leaves, she sees the pale new flowers, one on each plant, pale yellow petals unfolded to the light. Her heart rises from its despair as she crouches down and presses her face close to the new flowers, inhaling their delicate vegetable perfume.

Her heart rises from despair, because the living earth still lives. In the dry, hard places the earth lives still, in secret, and does not mourn. And the fruit will come now.

IN THE HOUSE Märit turns on the cold tap in the bathtub and adds a sprinkling of Epsom salts to the water. Kicking off her sandals she slips her aching feet into the bath. The soles of her feet are patterned with a mosaic of small cuts and abrasions, and she sits on the side of the tub with her feet under the stream of water.

As the water discolors from the dust on her feet she begins to weep silently. Tears of exhaustion, of frustration and disappointment trickle down her cheeks. And shame.

When she thinks of how she was hustled out of Patel's, and of the venom in Eloise Pretorius's lecture outside the shop, Märit feels only shame. Her desire for a life on the farm, for a good and useful life, is nothing but an illusion—the dreams of a naïve child. Her neighbors in the district care nothing for her, they have only contempt. And those who live in the kraal, who work the land, are strangers—a nation of strangers who fear her, who envy her, and who perhaps too have only contempt for her.

Märit dries her sore feet and retreats to her bed. She pulls the quilt over her body and up to her eyes. Her world has shrunk, and only here, wrapped in the quilt, is the last refuge, the last illusion. She lies like this for a long time, in a daze of exhaustion that gradually, through physical inaction, becomes a kind of weary equilibrium, even a calmness.

Life must be faced, she knows this, but the fading light and the pools of shadow that gradually fill the room are a refuge and a safety. She is unwilling to stir, reluctant to face the world again.

All she wants is sleep, to retreat into unconsciousness, but her repose, while inanimate, is restless, and a different kind of unease begins to assert itself—something specific to the room—so that at last she cannot ignore the unease. She sits up, her eyes moving across the familiar furnishings.

There is something in the air, some smell that is different from the scents that usually inhabit the room. Nothing is changed outwardly, as far as she can see, her eyes trailing across the dresser, the mirror, the clothes draped over the chair. Yet there is a dislocation, as if every object has been shifted slightly from its usual position, as if the room has gone out of focus and them come back into clarity with a slight misalignment.

Rising from the bed Märit paces across the room, her hands lightly touching her belongings. She stands at the dresser, looking down at the cosmetic bottles and jars, and once again she is struck by the inexplicable perception that everything is misaligned. She opens the drawers, one by one, and imagines someone else doing the same thing, opening the drawers and placing their hands on her apparel, her nightgowns, her underwear.

As she bends to the last drawer, a clump of dried mud on the floor catches her eye, and she lifts it carefully into her palm. The mud is hard and gray, a little crumbly around the edges, and imprinted deeply in the center is the ridged zigzag pattern from the sole of a boot.

Someone has been in the room during her absence. Could it have been the police? she wonders. Has she become an enemy to be investigated secretly? Has that man from the Security Branch come back, and crept through the house, writing things down in a notebook, making a report on her?

Märit drops the clump of mud into the wastebasket next to the dresser. And now she is aware again of the faint foreign odor in the room—something familiar yet strange at the same time, the origin of which sits just at the edge of her awareness, hidden, like an intruder.

Troubled, Märit lies down once more, but only for a few minutes before she hears a sound from the direction of the kitchen. Thinking that Tembi has returned to the house, and eager to be taken out of her weary solitude, she rises and makes her way down the passage.

Joshua is in the kitchen.

"What are you doing here?"

He turns, slipping something into his pocket—she thinks it is a package of cigarettes and her eyes move to the carton on the shelf.

Märit looks down at his feet, not bare like so many of the other farmworkers, but shod in a sturdy pair of boots, with a rim of dried mud around the edges of the sole.

"Why are you in the house? Have you been into my bedroom while I was away?"

Joshua does not answer. There is a new expression on his face, as if he is weighing some course of action and calculating the consequences.

"Get out," Märit says. "You are not allowed in this house." The look on his face makes her suddenly afraid.

Joshua moves past her, not to the kitchen door but farther into the house. As he passes she recognizes the odor that lingered in her bed-room—the smell of motor oil and old sweat, the smell of him.

"Where do you think you are going?" Märit calls. "I told you to get out." Märit hurries into the living room where Joshua has paused, survey-ing the room with an air of exaggerated interest.

Joshua turns to face her. "You think you can keep me out of this house?" His voice is hoarse, his eyes bloodshot, and Märit wonders if he is under the influence of some drug. "You think you can tell me what to do?" He shakes his finger at her. "Soon it's you who won't be allowed to live here. I know more about this farm than you do. I know everything about this farm. You don't know anything. This should be my farm now."

He reaches into his pocket and brings out a package of cigarettes, slowly unwrapping the cellophane before he extracts a cigarette and lights it. He inhales and blows smoke into the room.

"Get out!" Märit screams. He flinches, and this gives her courage to advance on him. "Get out! Right now! You are not to come back into this house."

He retreats through the door and onto the veranda, then turns upon her. "You think you can make me leave? You? A woman? How?" His eyes move down her body in a mocking glance.

Märit backs away into the living room, then rushes to the little office. She pulls open the desk drawer and reaches to the very back, where a key for the tall cupboard hangs on a hook. Her fingers scrabble at the keyhole. She jerks the cupboard open and lifts the shotgun out. With a quick movement she folds the barrels down, sees that the gun is not loaded, and reaches for the box of cartridges on the top shelf. She inserts a cartridge into each barrel, then, just as Ben had shown her, moves the safety catch to the off position with her thumb.

Pointing the gun in front of her Märit advances through the room and out to the veranda. Joshua is standing a few yards away from the steps with his back to her and his hands on his hips, surveying the farm.

"You will leave this farm today," Märit says. "By sundown. Your employment here is finished."

Joshua does not even turn around.

"Do you understand?" Märit demands. "You are nothing on this farm anymore."

In reply, Joshua leans to one side and ejects a stream of saliva onto the ground.

Märit raises the shotgun and fires.

As Tembi reaches the back door and is about to mount the steps, the sudden bang of a gunshot rocks the air. A second later the faint echo returns from the hills. Tembi stops in her tracks, turning towards the echo, not sure from where the shot has come. Then a second shot crashes from the front of the house.

The first thing Tembi sees is Märit standing on the veranda with a shotgun in her hands and an expression of grim determination on her face. Strands of white smoke hang in the air, tainting it with the burned smell of gunpowder.

"What happened?" Tembi cries. "Are you hurt?"

Märit motions with the gun barrel. A few yards from the veranda Joshua lies face down on the ground. "He was in the house, in my bedroom."

"You've killed him?" Tembi exclaims.

At the sound of her voice Joshua rolls over, then sits up and pats himself all over. Gingerly he rises to his feet, testing his limbs.

Forming her words clearly and slowly, Märit says, "By the time the sun is below the trees I want you off this land. Next time I won't shoot over your head."

Joshua glowers at the two women.

"Go!" Märit orders, waving him off with the gun.

* * *

199

THAT EVENING, as the sky darkens to a navy blue and the sun is nothing but red streaks over the hills, the women hear a banging at the front door.

"It's him!" Tembi cries, jumping up from her chair.

"Hold the gun," Märit orders, pointing to the shotgun that stands near the door, loaded and ready. She waits until Tembi has positioned herself before opening the door.

Joshua is there, looming in the doorway.

"My pay," he demands with one hand extended.

Märit has the envelope ready. She has already calculated his wages. Joshua grasps the envelope and takes a moment to count the money, then he slips it into his pocket and steps away. "Today you pay me," he mutters. "But tomorrow I will pay you. Both of you!"

Märit slams the door shut and slides the bolt home, then leans against the wood, listening as his feet descend the steps.

"I'm afraid of him," Tembi says.

Märit takes the gun from Tembi's trembling hands. "Don't worry. He won't be back."

THE NEXT MORNING Märit sets out on her usual round of the farm. Immediately she notices that every glance is directed at her with curiosity and anxiety. The workers move with an air of indecision, as if they are unsure what to do.

Märit seeks out Bodule, one of the men whom she has marked out as being capable, and the one who would have been her choice as foreman if it were not for Joshua's prior claim.

"Bodule, I must talk to you," she says, beckoning him away from his companions.

"Yes, Missus Laurens." He removes his hat and stands patiently.

"I have told Joshua to leave."

"This is true, Missus. You have told him."

"He was in the house, stealing. That is why."

"Yes, Missus. That is a bad thing, stealing."

"Can you take over as bossboy?"

"I can do that, Missus. Yes."

"I don't want anything to change on the farm just because Joshua has left. In fact, things should be better now."

Bodule nods his head sagely.

"Well," Märit says when Bodule makes no move to leave. "Back to work, then."

Bodule looks down at his hat. He takes a breath. "Missus, I must tell you."

"Yes, Bodule?"

"There has been some other stealing. The cattle."

She mistakes his meaning and answers, "The cattle? Have they been into the mealies?"

"The cattle have been stolen, Missus. Come, I will show you." Bodule puts on his hat and leads the way.

The grass in the upper pasture has been trodden down into a path leading to the fence. The wire has been cut and peeled back.

"Somebody with a truck," Bodule explains. "They have come in the night and cut the wire and taken cattle away."

Shocked, Märit stares at the cut wire. "But didn't anybody hear them? How could this happen?" She turns on him angrily. "You must have heard something."

Bodule looks down and shakes his head. The anger leaves Märit as rapidly as it came. With a shiver of apprehension she remembers the burned-out farm on the ridge into Klipspring. Even if the workers heard something they would have been too afraid to venture out.

"This means ruin." Unsteady on her feet, she sinks down to her haunches. Then she looks up at Bodule. "Did Joshua do this?"

Bodule raises his shoulders helplessly. "We are close to the border here, Missus. There are bad people coming at night sometimes."

"We are all ruined. Without cattle there is nothing here. Just maize. And nobody wants to buy maize."

Bodule clears his throat in an obvious manner.

"Was there something else, Bodule?"

"Some strangers, Missus. This morning two men arrived and asked for shelter."

"Who are they?"

"They say they are going to Johannesburg. They are walking to Johannesburg."

Märit ponders the news a moment. "Do you think they had something to do with the stealing of the cattle?"

He spreads his hands in bafflement.

"Are the men still here, Bodule?"

"Yes, Missus. You wish to speak to them?"

"No." She shakes her head. "No. But they must not stay on the farm. Especially if they don't have their papers in order. I will have to call the police about this theft. You must tell them to leave."

"I will tell them to leave, Missus."

Märit walks back to the house with her head low, feeling the ominous presence of some malevolent force that has singled out this farm. She telephones the police. The man who answers tells her matter-of-factly that she should not hold out any hope for recovering the cattle. Then he asks questions about recent visitors to the farm, and the number of workers who live there—questions which seem irrelevant to her. The policeman tells her that the theft will be investigated. She has the feeling that he does not care. When she hangs up the phone she feels friendless and isolated from the world.

35

IN THE DRY, hard place where the garden lies hidden, Tembi brings her bucket of water. The earth must drink, the plants must drink. As she walks around the side of the koppie to the secret place that is hidden by rocks and scrub, her heart lifts in anticipation of seeing the flowers that grow. She sets the bucket down and flexes her arm to remove the ache in the muscles and clambers over the rocks—and the gladness in her heart is removed in one swift blow.

The flowers are gone.

She pushes aside the barrier of scrub, heedless of the thorns that rake her arms. The plants are there, yes—all is not lost—but where are the flowers? Has some animal found its way into the enclosure? Her hands reach in among the leaves, gently parting the vines, and her fingers touch the unfamiliar shape of small round objects, smooth to her careful touch. She bends lower to the ground, her heart beating, and in wonderment touches the new fruits that have sprouted. Small, green, flecked with yellow. The new life, strong and healthy.

She feels the trembling in the soil under her hands, she hears the pulse and beat of life in the air. The tremor in the air is loud, coming in quick surges that seem to push the air forward, and the vibration becomes a beat, then a steady mechanical shudder.

Tembi looks up to the sky.

In the fields where the cattle used to graze, the small boys also look up to the sky.

The women who bend to clear the weeds from the rows of maize straighten their backs and lift their heads and look up to the sky.

The men who pull the strands of wire tight as they repair a fence let the strands go slack in their fingers and look up to the sky.

The finches in the willows beside the river dart deeper into the screen of branches, and the doves in the bluegum trees beside the farmhouse flutter and wheel in confusion.

All look up to the sky, to the metallic roar hurtling towards the farm.

Sweeping low over the koppie, three squat helicopters drop down out of the sky. Three dark machines, the color of mud, squat, bristling, hard-shelled like swollen locusts. The sky shakes with their metallic clatter. One helicopter hovers above the house while another banks and circles over the kraal. The third makes a fast, sweeping pass down to the river and back, bristling with aerials and gun barrels, like some menacing giant insect.

The doves wheel and flutter in panic over the roof of the farmhouse. In the fields the small boys shake their willow switches at the helicopters and shout up through the grind and groan of the engines.

From the kraal a figure breaks from the entrance to a hut and runs in the direction of the river, through the orchard towards the screen of willow trees on the banks of the river. He runs quickly, desperate in his flight.

One of the machines tilts up and dives in pursuit like an angry insect, rotors whining. As it arcs over the koppie, almost on its side, Tembi looks up and sees the men in the open door of the helicopter, helmeted, gog-gled, arms pointing at the fleeing figure—the insect men inside the belly of the locust. The blades of the machine hack at the air, the smell of fuel is a rain from the sky, a gun barrel sweeps back and forth as the helicopter plummets upon the figure in the long grass.

The guns speak, and their words are the rapid chatter of steel against flesh. A man stumbles, then runs on. Now the running figure is in the last patch of empty ground before the shelter of the riverbank, and the machine swoops down, spitting flames. The running man falls, flung to the ground as if by an invisible fist, his feet and his hands and his face bro-ken by the bullets that spit down from the machine.

Tembi crouches in her small acre of the world, an acre that spans only the distance between her two spread hands. She crouches against the hot wind of sand and pebbles whipping across the soil, and the smell of machine fuel everywhere, and the voice of the bullets. She crouches with her body hunched over her green seedlings.

Märit is at the desk in her office with the accounts ledger spread open, her mind fixed on the financial future of the farm. How will she handle the finances alone? How can the farm survive without the cattle? She has telephoned the police in Klipspring about the theft of the cattle, and they have promised to investigate, but nothing has happened. Losing the cattle will mean that there is no future income for the farm. The mealies and the fruit, when ripe and harvested, will bring next to nothing. There are too many other farms with the same crops.

A faint tremor passes through her body, then the pencils in the jar on her desk begin to rattle. A boom and shudder shakes the house. Märit pushes her chair back and rushes to the window. Is it a storm? An earthquake?

But the sky is clear except for the high haze of cloud. A sound like hail falling on a tin roof rattles above, just as a dark shape flies over the house.

As Märit runs out to the veranda, a machine swoops low across the pasture, spitting little tongues of flame that make a chattering noise, like hail striking iron. A second machine is hovering just above the kraal. And now a third helicopter descends, larger than the others, and settles itself heavily near the house, the long blades spinning dangerously close to the trees. Before it has even touched the ground, uniformed men bearing weapons are spilling from the helicopter. Some scatter towards the kraal, while others make for the house.

Märit is stunned speechless. Everything is happening so quickly.

It is war, she thinks. But war is outside her knowledge except as pictures in magazines, old newsreels from another time, stories from elsewhere. This is different—the noise and the stench of the machines, the shouting, the purposeful and urgent men in khaki uniforms spreading across the gardens, and everywhere the ugly weapons, some even pointed at her now. She stands in a stillness at the center of this vortex, detached from this sudden tornado of activity, and her mind cannot grasp what she sees.

But it is war—for what other word is there to describe the violence that has descended so swiftly from the sky?

Tembi appears, running towards the house from the direction of the kraal. In her hand she carries a red plastic pail, and Märit's mind focuses on this one detail, as if in a dream, wondering why Tembi carries a pail, wondering why it is a red pail and not some other color.

The soldiers see Tembi, and one of them shouts and runs to intercept her, grasping her arm roughly as she passes. Tembi stumbles, dropping the pail, then manages to free herself. But with a curse the soldier is quickly upon her, and this time he jerks her to the ground.

"Leave her alone!" Märit screams. She leaps off the porch and races across the driveway. But before she can reach the struggling Tembi, other hands grab her, pin her arms tight against her side; a rifle barrel digs into her back.

"Let me go!" But the arms squeeze tighter, lifting her slightly off the ground, pressing the breath out of her lungs.

"Genoeg! Verlos haar." A sharp voice of command. Enough. Leave her.

The arms let Märit go. Tembi scrambles to her feet and runs to Märit's side.

A man emerges from amongst the soldiers in the khaki uniforms with their weapons and radios and equipment—a man in a light blue safari suit and dark sunglasses. The soldiers draw back, making way for him. He walks unhurriedly towards Märit, and a step or two behind him is a young soldier with a bulky radio on his back, the long aerial waving in the air, a mutter of voices and static emanating from the radio.

The man removes his sunglasses, revealing pale eyes, but Märit has already recognized him—Gideon Schoon.

"Mevrou Laurens." He nods. He takes in her appearance and shakes his head, his lip curling in disapproval.

"This is outrageous!" Märit's fright comes out in a surge of anger, her voice trembling. "What is the meaning of this? What are you doing to my farm?"

"Forgive the manner of our arrival, Mevrou, but it is necessary."

"What are you talking about? What's necessary?"

Schoon withdraws a sheet of paper from his jacket pocket and unfolds it.

"Under Section Four of the Emergency Measures Act, I am here to conduct an antiterrorist action. Specifically, to locate and arrest any subversive elements that represent a threat to the state."

"Terrorists? For God's sake, this is a farm. What terrorists? Do you mean us? This is absurd."

Schoon refolds the paper and fastens it back into his breast pocket.

"I have information, Mevrou Laurens, that certain individuals, who have no legal status in this country, are being harbored on this farm. Certain individuals whom we consider to be engaged in criminal activity prejudicial to the stability of the state."

"Your information is wrong. You're talking rubbish. I want you off my farm!"

"I think it would be in your best interest to cooperate with us, Mevrou." Schoon permits himself a little smile, but his voice is hard underneath the elaborate politeness of tone.

Märit remembers the way Eloise Pretorius spoke to her outside Patel's store in Klipspring, the same veiled politeness, the same threat.

"It is not in my interest," she retorts. "There are no criminals or terrorists here, unless you're referring to me. Is the way I live now an illegal act?"

"This document," Schoon says bluntly, tapping his pocket, "empowers me, should I so wish, to arrest every individual on this farm, Mevrou. Yourself included. So let's have no more of your nonsense." He is impatient now. "With your permission, Mevrou, we will have a look around." He turns to the soldiers, directing them to begin their search. "*Ondersoek die huis. Kyk wat is daar.* Search the house!"

They push past Märit and up the steps of the veranda. Märit half raises a hand in protest, then lets it fall. They are too many, they are too strong. And this is what soldiers are for—to subdue those weaker than themselves.

"You won't find anyone in the house," Märit tells Schoon. "Only Tembi and I live here."

"For the moment I am not concerned with you or your *meid*." The radio carried by the young soldier crackles a burst of words. The soldier listens a moment, then says something to Schoon, who snaps his fingers at Märit and Tembi. "Come with me, please," he says, striding off.

One of the other soldiers takes Tembi by the arm.

"Take your hands off her," Märit snaps at him. "She doesn't need your assistance."

As they follow Schoon, Tembi whispers to Märit, "What do they want?"

"There's nothing for them here. Don't worry."

"They were shooting, from the helicopter, into the fields."

"Shh. We'll see what it is."

There are soldiers everywhere, like a pack of dogs scurrying about her land, and everywhere is the crackle of distorted voices from the radios, as if there is no language other than this mechanical static.

Near the kraal the farmworkers are gathered into a tight huddle surrounded by a ring of soldiers. As Schoon strides past the group, who turn frightened eyes to Märit, Tembi tries to break away, but her guard roughly pushes her back.

Schoon is making for the lower pasture, near the river, where one of the helicopters has settled, its long rotor blades drooping like the wings of an insect. Just past the helicopter a small knot of soldiers has formed. They stand aside as Schoon arrives.

Märit sees the man lying on the grass, legs outstretched, and she sees the blood on his clothes, and the big puncture wounds on his body, as if he has been stabbed repeatedly with some crude spear.

She looks at him uncomprehendingly. The soldiers nudge the two women forward.

Tembi gasps in horror. A dead man, the blood almost violet on his dark skin, and on the ground where the blood has seeped the soil is stained black.

The bile rises in her throat and she turns away.

The soldiers stare at Märit and Tembi. And this is the first time that the soldiers seem human to Tembi, when she can meet their eyes, look into the faces of men who seem little more than boys. But in their eyes she sees only contempt, because she is not one of them. They despise her, she realizes. She is the enemy. And she wonders what they have been told to make them look upon her in this manner.

The grimness of these faces terrifies her, and she feels herself in the strangeness of a dream, where events unfold with a logical progression, but to some terribly wrong purpose. Has she been brought here to be shot and placed in the grass beside this butchered body? She wants to cry out, Stop! Something is wrong! But as in a dream she cannot find her voice, and her feet propel her inexorably towards the waiting horror.

Schoon steps up to Märit. "Do you know this man, Mevrou?"

Märit shakes her head, unable to speak.

"Look at him!" Schoon commands.

She half turns her head, with dreadful fascination. The ugliness of what she sees frightens and disgusts her, the obscenity of it, the ugliness of violence done against flesh.

She averts her eyes, but Schoon is insistent. "Have you ever seen this man before?"

"I don't know him."

The soldiers look down at the dead man with mute curiosity, apathy almost, as if at the aftermath of a traffic accident.

"Who is he?" Märit asks.

"They call themselves soldiers of liberation." Schoon snorts with contempt. "A bandit. Nothing but a terrorist."

"He doesn't look like a soldier," she says. Not compared to the soldiers who surround her. This man has nothing—just a pair of dirty sneakers and tattered clothes. Nothing that distinguishes him from the workers gathered near the kraal. No uniform, no radio, no helicopter.

Schoon snaps his fingers at the soldiers. "Show her. Show her the proof."

One of the soldiers holds up a weapon, an old battered rifle with a worn barrel and stained stock.

"AK-47," Schoon says. "Mass-produced, cheap, and dumped on this continent in the thousands. But a weapon all the same, no less deadly than ours." The soldier holds the weapon high like a trophy.

"This bandit was found here on your farm, Mevrou, in the kraal of your farm."

"Is that a reason to kill him?"

"I am surprised at you, Mevrou, surprised to hear *you*, of all people, take such a tone. Perhaps you have no feelings about the burning of the Potgieter farm, and the burning of their crops, and the killing of their dogs. Those dogs were pets of the Potgieter children, and their throats were cut and the bodies left in the driveway for the children to see. Perhaps you never met the Potgieters, so why should you feel sorry for them? But, considering your own personal tragedy, Mevrou Laurens, that is why I am surprised." He shakes his head in feigned wonderment.

Märit forces herself to look at the dead body again. Was it him? Did he set the bomb in the road? Did he murder Ben? But she cannot see this man as a murderer, this ragged malnourished corpse—one of the dispossessed who live on the fringes of her country.

"Perhaps you know this man, Mevrou Laurens? Is he one of your workers? Look closely, Mevrou."

Märit shakes her head. She remembers what Bodule said earlier this morning—that there were strangers on the farm, two of them.

Schoon waits for her to speak. "Well, if he is a stranger here then let us go and talk to the rest of your employees and see if there is anyone else who doesn't belong."

In the vegetable patch next to the kraal the squat brown helicopter sits amongst the rows of vegetables. The pilot has found a tomato and he leans against his machine chewing it, looking at the herded inhabitants of the kraal with a bored expression.

The faces are turned to Märit, not to Schoon, although they are all aware of his authority and power, but it is upon Märit that their hopes lie. It seems like only yesterday that she stood before them full of her own hopes and announced that she would run the farm. She had reassured them, as well as herself. But how quickly her weakness has been revealed.

"*Maak hulle in 'n ry staan.* Line them up!" Schoon orders. "*Vroumens daar, mans daar.*" He waves his hand. "Women to one side, men on the other. Now, Mevrou Laurens. Please identify each one of your workers."

She walks slowly along the line.

"By name, Mevrou."

Märit mumbles a reply, and Schoon says, "A little louder, please."

"I don't know all their names," Märit answers, turning away from the workers, ashamed to admit her ignorance in front of them.

"Then, perhaps you can tell me if there is anyone amongst them that is not familiar. Take a good long look, Mevrou. Just tell me if there is anyone you haven't seen before."

The men are standing in a loose line before her, clutching their green identity books, and the first face Märit looks at is one she does not know. His eyes meet hers and he does not look away. Is it defiance she sees in his face? Or a challenge? Or even a pleading?

That's him, she wants to say. Take him away. Does she not have the right of judgment, the right of revenge? Shouldn't someone pay for the death of her husband?

She looks away from the man's face. "They all belong here."

But Schoon has been watching her, and he turns slowly to see whom her gaze has lingered on.

"Do you see a stranger amongst these men, Mevrou?"

"I am the stranger here, Captain Schoon. These people lived on this farm long before I came. I don't know their names and I don't know anything of their lives. What is it that you want from me?"

"I will remind you, Mevrou Laurens, that under the terms of the Emergency Measures Act it is a treasonous offense to harbor criminals."

"Arrest me, then."

Instead, Schoon points at the man. "*Gee my jou pass*. Your papers!"

The man takes out his identity document. As Schoon stretches out his hand, the pass falls to the ground. Schoon puts his hands on his hips. "*Optel dit, kaffir.*"

The man hesitates, then bends to pick up the green booklet at Schoon's feet and hands it over. Schoon leafs through the pages and gives it back, but as the man reaches for it, Schoon lets the booklet drop to the ground again.

"Pick it up, *kaffir*," Schoon says again.

The man crouches in the dust again, and as he rises, Schoon nods to the nearest soldier. "*Weg met hom*. Take him away."

Two soldiers grasp the man by the arms and quickly march him towards the helicopter.

"Where are you taking him?" Märit says.

With his hands on his hips Schoon walks slowly down the line of men. "*Elkeen wil ry met hom?* Anybody else want to ride in the helicopter?"

"Where are you taking that man?" Märit demands.

Schoon turns back to Märit, and the contempt is naked on his face. "He is being taken for questioning. He will be released later. Unless, of course, he is guilty. Then he will take a different kind of journey."

Märit has a sudden vision of a body falling through the clear blue sky.

"You have no right to do this."

"Don't worry yourself about my rights, Mevrou Laurens." He moves away and speaks to the radio man, then strides towards the helicopter.

The machines rise into the air, throwing waves of dust and fuel smell onto the people on the ground. The machines clatter away with a rhythmic beating of the air. And then even the echo of their passage fades, and the sky is empty again.

36

FOR THE REST OF THE DAY and evening the inhabitants of the farm, in the kraal and in the house, exist in a stunned silence. Their actions and their movements are done by rote, as if there is no meaning in them. If words are exchanged they are whispered or delivered in a monotone.

What will happen now? Anything can happen now.

The next morning, early, when Dik-Dik the rooster crows in the chicken coop, a timid tapping sounds at the front door. Märit has just risen and put the coffee on the stove. Tembi's door is still shut.

Bodule, the foreman, stands on the porch, his hat clutched in his hands. He bows his head to her. "*Sawubona*, Missus."

"Good morning, Bodule."

"The weather will be fine today, Missus."

"Yes. No rain."

"No rain. But the mealies are not needing rain."

"That's true. They don't need rain."

Bodule nods his head a few times, twisting his hat in his hands.

"The fence by the bottom field, it's fixed now."

"I'm glad to hear that, Bodule. Good work."

"Yes."

Another silence. He shuffles his feet and drops his head. Then he takes a deep breath and raises his eyes. "Missus, I am sorry."

"I am too, Bodule. Terrible things are happening."

"I must leave, Missus. I cannot stay here. It's trouble for my family."

"Why? Has someone told you to leave?"

"Nobody is telling me, Missus. But I must take my family and leave."

He steps aside, and she sees a donkey cart in the driveway, loaded with bundles and a few items of furniture. A woman sits at the reins and three small children stand near the cart, watching their father.

"This is your land too," Märit says. "You don't have to go."

He nods his head and looks her in the face, distressed. "The troubles here, Missus, it's not your fault. You are good. Baas Ben was good. But . . . my family." He makes a helpless gesture, indicating those who wait.

"But where will you go, Bodule?"

"To my wife's people." He tilts his chin over his shoulder, as if that explains his destination, as if she will know where it is. Märit doesn't ask more, better that she does not know. Her heart sinks with the finality of it, with the inevitability.

"All right, Bodule, just a moment."

In the office Märit opens her ledger, finds Bodule's name, and does some quick calculations on a pad. She counts out some banknotes, and on an impulse she adds a few more and seals them into an envelope.

Bodule tucks his hat under his arm and cups both hands to receive his wages.

"*Usale kahle*, Missus. Stay well."

"Go well, Bodule."

Märit watches the cart trundle down the drive, the woman sitting up on the seat and the man leading the donkey, and the three children walking a few steps behind.

Märit has barely finished her coffee before a knocking raps again at the door. She hurries to open it, thinking Bodule has changed his mind. But it is one of the younger women standing on the veranda, and behind her in the driveway Märit glimpses family members with their bundles and luggage.

"You are leaving?" Märit asks, knowing the answer.

"Yes, Missus. We are going from this place."

"You are Lebitsa, aren't you?" Hers is one of the names Märit remembers.

"Yes, Missus, I am Lebitsa."

Märit writes down the names and the amounts paid and hands the envelope of wages to the young woman. She does not watch the family walk away, but shuts the door and goes back into the house.

Tembi is standing in the doorway to the kitchen in her nightgown, clutching a cup of coffee.

"They are leaving," Märit says.

"I know."

"You knew this would happen?"

"Last night. I was in the kraal, I talked to some of them. That man, Schoon, he told them that soon this district will be for the white people only and that it would be better for everyone to go now, before the soldiers come back."

"How can he do this!" Märit rages. "He can't just come on to someone's property and do what he likes—kill people from helicopters. It's savage. It's wrong."

Tembi stands silent. She has seen what men like Schoon can do. They come with their papers and make a declaration, and then they destroy.

Märit ceases her pacing and sits down, turning her face up to Tembi.

"And you, Tembi?" Märit asks the question that is uppermost on her mind. "Are you leaving too?"

"No."

"You don't have to stay here."

"Where must I go?"

"Your father lives in Johannesburg."

"Yes, he works in the mines in Johannesburg. But there is no place there for me. I cannot live in the shanty town near the mines. Those are bad places."

"Do you have no other family anywhere?"

Tembi only shakes her head.

THROUGHOUT THE DAY a steady stream of visitors comes to the house, always standing like supplicants at the door. Märit brings the ledger and cash box to the living room for easier access, and ticks the names off in the columns. With an increasing apathy and a sense of inevitability Märit watches the money dwindle away as the population of the farm depletes itself. At one point, almost overcome by fear of what the farm will become now, she lifts the phone to call Connie van Staden, to ask for help, for advice. But the phone line is dead, not even a hum on the line, just silence.

In the evening there is no longer the haze of cooking-fire smoke hanging over the kraal like a mist. There is no longer the scent of wood smoke in the air, the smell that is as much a part of the place as the smell of the soil, that clings to the skin of the people and binds them to the farm. The kraal is an empty place.

High overhead in the sky, the last rays of the sun glint off the wings of aircraft flying towards the border, and the roar of their engines is only a distant thunder.

WHEN MÄRIT RISES EARLY the next day, ready to make her rounds of the farm, she is struck by the silence: the mist still hangs above the river and the outlines of the trees are soft and the light on the veldt is pale and honey-colored.

How still everything is, how empty—how strangely beautiful.

A light breeze stirs the air and the vanes of the windmill begin to revolve with a slow creak. She looks back at the low farmhouse with its thatched roof and whitewashed walls that gleam in the morning sun. A thin stream of white smoke rises from the chimney, signaling that the kitchen stove has been lit, that Tembi is awake. She is alone, but not abandoned. There is still home.

Tembi is standing on the veranda, sleepy-eyed, still in her nightgown, waiting for Märit.

"I dreamed that you had gone," Tembi says. "You walked to the river and you disappeared."

"I'm still here, but everyone else is gone."

Tembi looks across to the kraal. "It doesn't matter. Let them go. Now we have the farm to ourselves."

After breakfast, Märit switches on the radio, to hear the weather report, to hear the news, to know something of the world outside the farm. But like the telephone, the radio does not work: the only sound is static.

When she takes her coffee out to the veranda and joins Tembi, Märit says, "What are we going to do?"

"Farm, of course."

"Can we do it by ourselves?"

"We have to." Tembi sets her cup down on the railing. "Come, let us go and look at our farm and see what is to be done."

Their first stop is the kraal. The ground around the huts is swept clean, the fire pit is cleared of ashes, a single piece of cloth hangs on the clothes-line near the washhouse—a handkerchief, forgotten in the exodus.

Tembi notices that even the big black iron cook-pot has been removed. That pot had always seemed to her to be rooted in the earth, as much a part of the farm as the huts and the trees.

"Which hut was yours?" Märit calls, peering into the doorway of a *rondavel*.

Tembi shows her, bending to enter through the low doorway. They stand together in the gloom, the empty gloom, until their eyes adjust to the meager light from the small window opening.

"Were you ever happy here, Tembi?"

"It was my home," she answers with a matter-of-fact tone. The interior is empty except for an upturned crate near the marks on the floor that show where a bed stood. Even the bed has been taken. Lives uprooted, another Relocation.

Now there is nothing here, as if nobody ever lived enclosed within these walls, as if she herself were never sheltered here. Only memory remains. Tembi wonders if she too should have joined the exodus. Is there not something of a betrayal in not following her people?

Noticing the flicker of doubt in Tembi's face, Märit says, "But you have a better house now. The farmhouse is your home. You know that, don't you?"

With a nod Tembi goes out into the sunlight again.

The silence upon the farm is like a cloak: no sharp whistles from the herd boys chasing cattle, no chugging from the tractor as it navigates the fields, no lowing of cattle in the pasture, no voice to call her name. All is silence except for the slow creak of the windmill, a slow, repetitive exhalation of breath, like a person in sleep.

"We are alone," Märit says, just to hear the sound of her own voice, suddenly fearful that the silence will swallow her as well.

Tembi catches an edge of fragility in Märit's voice. She knows that she is stronger than Märit, and this knowledge places a burden of responsibility upon her shoulders and upon her heart. Tembi knows that if ever that fragility is broken, Märit will be lost.

"We will manage," she says.

"How?" Märit says, turning to look at Tembi with panic in her eyes. "How?"

"By making the farm smaller. We will only give water to the strong and healthy vegetable plants, and we will only tend a few rows of maize. There is fruit in the orchard. And there are chickens for meat and eggs." She has noticed the fowls pecking through the underbrush behind the huts. "At least they didn't take the chickens."

"There will be a lot of work for just the two of us."

"We can work! This will be a farm for two women. Aren't we strong? Like lions!" She curls her hands into imaginary claws. "Watch out all who come here. This is the farm of the lion women. *Grr!*" Her hands rake the air. *"Grr!"*

They continue their inspection of the farm.

Outside the milking hut Tembi says, "The cattle are gone. All the cows. No milk or butter."

"We don't need it. We will drink water."

They walk over to the shed where the generator is housed. Märit opens the door and regards the machine, smelling the oil and diesel fuel. Ben had installed a new generator when they bought the farm, as well as batteries that are charged by the turning of the windmill vanes so that the fuel consumption will be less. The electricity for the lights and the refrigerator in the house are powered from this generator. She has no idea how any of it works. What will happen if it fails? With a shake of her head she shuts the door again. At least there is paraffin for lamps in the house, as well as candles. And there is plenty of firewood. They will manage.

Later that afternoon Märit makes an inventory—of the food in the house, of the money left in the cash box. She takes down the box of shells for the shotgun and counts them too. She makes a silent calculation, counting the days for which there is enough food, as if laying in for a siege.

When the heat of the afternoon is heavy on the house, Tembi and Märit walk down to the orchard and sit under the peach trees. Märit lies on her back, gazing up through the leaves. Far above the trees is the occasional glint of light on metal and the faint rumbling of aircraft. But it is distant.

She wonders about the other farms in the district. Have their workers left also? Are the men and women who remain also counting the days?

DURING THE NEXT FEW DAYS the two women begin to reshape the new boundaries of the farm. Much will be neglected, out of necessity, but there is also much they can do. Together with Tembi, Märit spends the mornings digging with a hoe between the rows of vegetables to remove the weeds that never cease to grow. They block off some of the irrigation channels that will now stream to unused beds and divert the water to where it will do the most good.

"We must make sure the chickens stay in their pen now," Tembi tells Märit as they examine a gap in the mesh fence. "Without the children to look after them, they will wander off and maybe get eaten by animals. And we won't find the eggs if the hens lay all over the place."

With a roll of wire mesh found in one of the sheds they repair the chicken coop. The rooster, Dik-Dik, watches from his perch on a nearby branch, emitting a threatening cluck every time Märit ventures near him.

"I don't think he likes me," Märit says.

"He's a man. He doesn't like to see women doing things without his permission."

The chickens are herded into the pen, which is a small hut surrounded by a patch of ground, enclosed in the wire-mesh fence. Märit shoos the last hen in. The rooster is still on his perch.

"What about him?" she says.

Tembi takes up an old broom and advances on the rooster. "Come on, Dik-Dik, join your women." The rooster spreads his wings and darts his beak at the broom that Tembi waves at him. With a deft movement Tembi dislodges the rooster from his perch. "Hold the gate open," she calls to Märit, as Dik-Dik flaps his wings at her.

For a minute there is a contest of wills, but the broom wins, and Dik-Dik is urged into the coop. He flutters up to the roof of the shed and crows mightily at the two women.

"All right, all right," Tembi says. "We know you are the king."

When it is time to collect the eggs, Dik-Dik accepts Tembi's presence in his domain, but if Märit enters, he swoops down from his perch and challenges her, crowing, flapping his wings, trying to peck at her calves. So Märit lets Tembi collect the eggs in the mornings while she stands at the gate, making sure that none of the hens wander out.

ONE EVENING AT DINNER, which is potatoes and beef stew, Tembi says, "That was the last of the meat."

"Is there nothing left in the freezer?" There has always been meat in the freezer. Ben had made sure of that.

"This was the last. We will have to slaughter one of the hens from the coop."

Märit grimaces. "We can have just vegetables and mealie-pap." But a diet of maize porridge and vegetables soon pales, and they realize they will have to butcher one of the chickens.

They stand together outside the coop surveying the fowls, which crowd against the wire thinking that the women have come to feed them. Tembi has a long knife in her hand.

"How do we do it?" Märit asks. "I've never had to kill a chicken. Do you know how?"

Tembi nods. "I've seen it done. You have to take the hen in your arms and put your hand over its eyes, and then it goes quiet. And then you must twist the neck and cut the throat."

"I suppose we have to do it," Märit says with some trepidation. "Which one will it be?"

Tembi opens the gate and they enter the coop. She surveys the hens. "This one, I think. She doesn't lay much anymore."

Dik-Dik observes Märit with a cold eye, emitting deep warning clucks.

"We can't do it here, where the others can see." Tembi hands the knife to Märit. "Hold this." She goes amongst the milling chickens and scoops the hen up into her arms, holding the unprotesting bird close against her body.

As Märit shuts the gate, Dik-Dik flings himself from his perch with an angry squawk and batters his outstretched wings against the mesh. Märit backs away quickly.

Tembi carries the hen to the back of the house and waits outside the kitchen door for Märit to catch up.

"What do we do now?" Märit says.

"Do you have the knife?"

Märit nods. Gritting her teeth, Tembi places one hand over the chicken's head and makes a sharp twist with her arm. Immediately the hen squawks and flaps its body wildly. Tembi lets go and the bird flutters to the ground, but quickly Tembi pins it down with her knee and grabs the head again, bending it back to expose the throat.

"Help me!" she calls to Märit.

The bird is thrashing now, and Tembi tries to hold it steady. With another convulsive twist the hen frees its head and pecks at Märit's hand.

"Do it!" Tembi shouts.

A squirt of greenish dung spatters onto Märit's dress.

Märit puts her hand on the neck, aware of the warmth in the feathered body. She plunges the knife into the hen's breast, feeling a sudden hate for the bird—the ugly squawking, the flapping, the stink of the dung. Why won't it just submit?

"Cut its neck," Tembi cries.

The long blade is very sharp, and slices through the feathers and bites into the flesh and gristle beneath. A terrible cry erupts from the hen as Märit saws through the neck frantically. The bird's head flips back and a great gout of hot blood spurts across Märit's hands. Tembi falls back and the hen springs free, its head dangling to one side as the dying body jerks back and forth.

Märit scrambles out of the way in terror as the convulsing bird flings itself against her legs. Then the chicken topples sideways, legs and wings twitching. Märit approaches gingerly. She is covered in blood and feathers and dung. The cold eye of the hen looks up at her from the severed head. She turns away, ashen faced, trembling, and lets the long knife drop from her fingers.

From the direction of the coop the piercing, alarmed cries of the rooster resound in the air.

"I never want to do that again," Märit says. "I would rather starve."

Märit spends a long time at the bathroom sink, scrubbing her hands to remove the smell of the chicken from her skin. Later, when she walks in the garden, she still detects the smell on her fingers and she rubs her hands in a mint bush, breaking the leaves and grinding them into her skin. It is Tembi who retrieves the carcass, who sprinkles sand over the blood-stained earth, who boils a pot of water and plunges the bird into it and then plucks the feathers. It is Tembi who slices into the belly and removes the dark entrails, the liver and heart and lungs, and wraps them in paper and stores them in the freezer.

Märit watches from the doorway with her mouth twisted in an expression of distaste. When Tembi says, "I'll make a stew. You can help me," Märit prefers to wash and slice the carrots and onions, reluctant to touch the chunks of meat.

Tembi slaps a breast onto the cutting board. "Cut this for me." Märit bites down on her lip and tries not to breathe as she slices the knife into the pale flesh.

Afterwards, when the stew is simmering on the stove and Tembi calls her to dinner, Märit finds to her surprise that the aromas in the kitchen bring a quickening of anticipation to her tongue. She eats the stew, and despite the memory of the afternoon, she has an appetite. "It's very good," she says, reaching for the dish to fill her plate again. Tembi shakes her head and smiles.

Koos van Staden comes over from the neighboring farm. He drives up in his battered old Mercedes, and when he gets out of the car Märit sees that Connie is not with him.

"*Goeie dag*, Mevrou Laurens."

She acknowledges his greeting hesitantly and watches as he goes around to the back of the vehicle. "I have brought you some things. Connie told me you might be short." Like most of the farmers in the area, he is blunt and to the point. He begins to unload some boxes of groceries onto the ground.

"How is Connie?" Märit says.

"She is well," he grunts as he lifts a box of canned goods. "You will find coffee, salt, sugar in those sacks. And there is a carton of cigarettes. Connie said you like to smoke."

"Thank you. We are running short of things here. Please thank Connie for me. I did try to phone, but the lines are dead."

Koos straightens up and looks directly at Märit. "I know about your troubles, Mevrou. I know about the difficulties you have had, in town, with the police. And that is another reason why I have come here. We are leaving the district. At least until the troubles are over. We are going to Cape Town. Connie says to tell you that you must come with us."

"Why? Why are you leaving?"

He shrugs and looks up at the sky, then turns his eyes towards the distant hills. "The border is just over there," he says. "A whole continent against us. The army is advising those of us so close to the border to leave. It's not safe."

"And if I come with you, what about Tembi?"

He frowns quizzically.

"My *meid*," Märit explains. "She lives here with me."

Van Staden shakes his head. "No, you can't bring any blacks with you. Certain areas are being declared 'whites only.' She must stay here."

"Where it's not safe."

"I'm sorry, Mevrou, I don't make these rules. Our destiny is not in our hands anymore."

Märit takes a step backwards. "No, I can't leave." His words fill her with apprehension, but she will not run from the farm now and leave Tembi behind.

Koos opens the door of his vehicle. "It's your choice, Mevrou. We are leaving on Wednesday if you change your mind."

37

IN THIS PART of the country there is a bird, not often seen, that favors the most dense foliage, whose song is seldom heard, except in the early mornings. The sound of its song is three repeated notes followed by two shorter tones in a higher register.

One morning as Tembi returns from her daily watering of the plants behind the koppie, she notices as she passes the vegetable garden that some of the tomato plants have been trampled in the night. At the same time she hears the distinctive birdsong from the bluegum trees beside the house, and she pauses to listen, searching the leaves for a glimpse of the bird.

The song stops abruptly, and then, to her amazement, the notes are sounded backwards—two short, three long. A moment later the whole sequence is repeated. Tembi steps forward carefully, peering at the branches. Just as she catches a glimpse of a flash of red high in the thickest part of the leaves, Tembi looks down and sees the man.

He is sitting at the base of a tree with his back leaning against the trunk, and in his hands is a small musical instrument. As she stops in her tracks, the man plucks at his instrument and echoes the trilled notes of the hidden bird.

She stares at him in astonishment.

He stops his music making and reaches for a tomato from a small heap next to his leg. The juice trickles over his chin as he bites into the tomato, and spatters his shirt. He chews slowly, then wipes the juice from his face and reaches for another tomato.

Those are our tomatoes, Tembi realizes. That we work so hard for.

"What are you doing?" she shouts.

The man looks up, acknowledges her presence with a smile, and reaches for another tomato, proffering it in her direction.

At the sound of Tembi's cry, Märit runs out to the veranda, sees the man, and calls to Tembi, "Who is it?"

"I don't know." She faces the man again. "What are you doing? Those are our tomatoes."

He nods his head and smiles.

The two women approach cautiously.

"Who are you?" Märit demands. "What do you want here?"

He is dressed in a grimy pair of trousers and an overcoat draped across his equally grimy shirt. He gives Märit a wet smile, offering the tomato in her direction. She sees there is something foolish in his eyes.

"Where do you come from?" Märit asks. "Why are you here?"

In reply he takes up his little instrument and plucks out a tune that mimics the cadences of her voice.

In spite of herself, Tembi gives a small chuckle. "What is your name?" she asks. "*Sawubona, mnumzana. Uphumaphi?* Where do you come from?"

He nods enthusiastically.

She tries again, speaking Xhosa. "*Ngubani igama lakho?*"

With the flat of his hand the man clears a space in the dust between his bare feet and with one finger carefully prints the letters MICHAEL.

Märit leans forward. "Michael?"

He makes an inarticulate sound in the back of his mouth and looks up at her with a pleased expression.

"Why are you here, Michael?" she asks.

He makes the incoherent sound again and smiles at her. His tongue comes out, and it is a stump, pink and wet, amputated. She recoils, shocked. How does a man come to have his tongue amputated? Märit wonders.

"He cannot talk," Tembi says, quick to realize his plight. "You don't speak, *mnumzana?*"

He points at the word in the dust, then reaches for his instrument and plays a quick succession of notes that could be taken for the seven letters of the alphabet that spell his name.

"He has come to us," Tembi says. "We must help him."

Märit shakes her head doubtfully. She raises a hand to her throat, staring at the man's mouth.

"Yes. He is hungry."

"We don't have anything extra."

"He has come to us," Tembi says with a finality that brooks no argument.

It is not Michael himself that Märit is against; she is filled with anxiety against any further intrusion into their lives. Every time strangers come to the farm there is trouble, destruction, killing.

"Come," Tembi says, extending her hand to him. "I am Tembi. This is Märit."

He gathers the tomatoes into the pockets of his overcoat and takes up his instrument, which is an ingenious contraption fashioned out of an old pilchard can and what appear to be the strings from a tennis racket.

"Come to the house," Tembi tells him. "You can wash the dust from your face and you can eat with us. Are you hungry, Michael?"

Michael smiles his smile, which is both emptier than that of other people and also shining with something that is not often in the smile of other people. He plucks at his instrument, and there is joy in the music.

In the kitchen Tembi serves up a bowl of cold porridge to which she adds a little canned condensed milk, and gestures for Michael to sit at the table.

He eats quickly, with evident hunger, the porridge trickling down his chin, his damaged tongue making futile efforts to lick away the milky residue. Märit finds it difficult not to stare at that pink stubby tongue darting between his lips.

He eats like a child, without the nicety of manners, intent on his hunger. Märit has no idea of what his age could be, for his smooth, round, guileless face is childlike. But his hands are those of a man.

"Where do you come from, Michael? Where is your home?"

He turns and points with his spoon to the land beyond the window.

Anywhere, Märit thinks. One of the wanderers, the relocated. "Are you lost?" she asks.

Michael nods, his attention on his plate.

Tembi pushes a cup of tea across the table. "You can stay here." Her eyes meet those of Märit with a questioning look.

"I suppose so," Märit says. "He can stay here. You can help us on the farm, Michael. Would you like to do that?"

He grins eagerly as he finishes his porridge and slurps down the tea. Märit clears his plate away and rinses it in the sink. "Come, Michael, we'll show you around."

Märit and Tembi try to explain the farm to Michael, but they are not sure how much he understands—sometimes his expression is attentive, at other times he just smiles. Märit gathers the hoe and garden fork from outside the kitchen door and leads the way to the vegetable garden. Weeds seem to spring up overnight between the rows, and if left to grow will quickly steal the moisture from the plants.

Märit frowns at the trampled tomato plants and does her best to straighten them, then hands a long-handled hoe to Michael. "Do you know how to weed? Like this." She digs lightly between the plants to uproot the weeds, bending every now and then to toss them to one side. "You have to make sure you get the root out. But the small plants only, not the vegetables, okay? Like so."

His smile and his constant nodding is foolish, and she wonders how much he understands.

"Try it, Michael," Tembi urges.

He sets to work eagerly, moving between the plants.

"He can do it," Tembi says.

"Yes, very good, Michael. That's the way. Carry on like that. We will be just over there, in the mealie patch."

Tembi and Märit work at clearing one of the irrigation ditches that has silted up where the channel has collapsed. When this is finished, and the water runs free again, Märit goes to check on Michael.

She finds him digging energetically at the spinach plants with the hoe.

"No, no, Michael! Not like that." She shows him again. "Just the small weeds between the vegetables." When he shows no comprehension, Märit sets down her own hoe and places her hands over his and demonstrates the gentle motion he must make. She feels the roughness of his skin, like the bark of a tree, and she looks down at his calloused feet, and she wonders what his life has been, and where he has come from like this, out of nowhere.

When Michael seems to have grasped the idea of how the weeding should be done, Märit picks up her own hoe and walks back to the mealie patch. As she turns back to look at him she sees that he has already discarded the hoe and is squatting on the ground with his music box in his lap. The strange repetitive music begins its rhythm.

Tembi looks up when Märit rejoins her. "Is he all right?"

Märit shrugs helplessly. "He is like a child."

"But I am glad he is here. He is harmless."

Throughout the morning he sits near the women as they work, sometimes playing his strange music, and sometimes just sitting contentedly in the sun, like a cat, his face upturned to the light.

THE MIDDAY MEAL is taken on the veranda, out of the direct sun. Michael sits on the steps, and when the two women talk he looks at their faces, but if they address him he only smiles.

After eating, Michael wanders off, but his hoe is lying on the ground still, so Märit does not worry that he might do further damage in the vegetable garden. She dozes a little bit. When she opens her eyes she watches lazily as a couple of chickens peck for worms in the freshly turned soil of the garden. Their clucking is subdued and has a gentle, soothing cadence.

Then she shakes herself awake and sits upright. "The chickens," she says, nudging the dozing Tembi with her foot. "The chickens are loose."

They leave the shade of the veranda and walk slowly towards the coop. "Maybe Michael let them out," Tembi says as they notice more chickens wandering around. There is no urgency in the women's motions, since the chickens are kept penned more for convenience than anything else, and to herd them together now is a diversion from the gardening.

The sudden alarmed crowing of Dik-Dik breaks the stillness of the afternoon, followed by the thudding of feet on the ground. The chickens scatter as the rooster appears, squawking wildly with wings outstretched. And in pursuit is Michael, brandishing a hoe in one hand.

"Michael!" Märit cries, breaking into a run. "Michael, stop. No!"

Dik-Dik is darting from side to side, wings flapping, trying to evade the pursuing man. Then Michael drops the hoe and lunges at the bird. Märit watches in horror as the rooster tries to fly into the safety of a low tree, but too late, for Michael is quick, and grabs Dik-Dik into his rough hands.

"Leave him alone, Michael!" Märit shouts over the alarmed cries of the rooster.

By the time she reaches Michael the rooster has ceased his squawking and is limp in the man's arms.

"Oh, Michael, what have you done?"

He has the bird cradled in his arms, one forefinger stroking the feathers along the underside of its neck. Dik-Dik opens one eye and regards Märit with his beady stare, then shuts it again, stretching out his neck like a cat. Dik-Dik is unhurt. Märit is astonished to see the fierce rooster so passive in the man's arms.

In his throat he makes a soft clucking noise, the way a chicken does when it sits on its perch, contented, and the rooster stretches out his neck and answers with the same soft clucking, content, like a pet in the man's arms.

"Dik-Dik likes you," Tembi says. "He is your friend. Looking after the chickens can be Michael's job, don't you think, Märit?"

"Would you like to do that, Michael? You can feed them and make sure they stay in the coop. Come, I'll show you where the grain is kept. But first we have to make sure that all the chickens go back into the pen."

The two women herd the chickens together and steer them in the direction of the coop. Michael watches, then sets the rooster down and joins in, crouching low and moving with his arms widespread, making a deep clucking noise. And wherever Michael moves, Dik-Dik follows behind.

When the chickens are back in the pen, Märit lifts the lid off the feed bin and beckons to Michael. "This is where the food for the chickens is kept, Michael. You can fill this pail and sprinkle it out on the ground for them. Once in the morning and once in the evening. Can you do that?"

He nods and plunges his hands into the bin of grain, coming up with two fistfuls, then he squats down and holds out his hands to the chickens. Dik-Dik is there first, spreading his wings to keep the hens at bay, pecking quickly at the grain in Michael's palm. Only after he has had his fill does he allow the hens to approach. As Märit crouches next to Michael, Dik-Dik flares his wings at her, darting for her ankles with his beak, so that she has to retreat.

"He just doesn't like me," she says.

"He's jealous," Tembi replies.

WHEN IT IS TIME for the evening meal, Tembi goes to fetch Michael. She finds him sitting outside the chicken coop, his musical instrument in his hand, the strange music filling the air. The hens peck and scrabble in the dirt near him, and every now and then they pause and cock their heads to one side, as if listening.

He is more at home with the chickens than with us, Tembi thinks. And she wonders what terrible thing in his past has set him to wander alone on the veldt with only a musical instrument made from a tin can.

"Time for supper, Michael. You can come to the house now and eat."

He reaches into the pocket of his coat and withdraws a battered alarm clock, holding it up for her to see.

"Yes, it's supper time," Tembi says. "Come to the house now."

Märit has set three places at the table and is serving a vegetable stew into bowls.

"You can sit there, Michael," she says, indicating a chair. But Michael takes his spoon and the bowl of food and walks back out to the veranda. The two women look at each other and shake their heads. Märit slices some bread and puts it on a plate, then carries it out to the veranda.

"Michael, you can eat with us in the kitchen. You don't have to sit out here."

He looks up at her but does not stir. She shrugs and sets the plate of bread down next to him. "It doesn't really matter. You can eat out here."

LATER, when the women are washing the dishes, Märit says, "Where will he sleep tonight?"

"I could make up a bed for him in the living room."

Märit sets aside the plate she is washing and dries her hands on her apron. The way she bites at her lower lip betrays her thoughts to Tembi.

"You don't really want him in the house, do you?"

"We don't know him, Tembi. He seems harmless and innocent, but we don't know anything about him. I would be nervous having him in the house while we are asleep."

Tembi continues drying the plates without making a reply.

Märit heaves a sigh of agreement. "All right."

From the linen cupboard Märit takes down blankets and pillows, and arranges them on the couch. On the floor of the cupboard she notices an old pair of boots that belonged to Ben. She takes these out and sets them next to the bed.

Michael is sitting in contented silence, watching the last rays of the sunset. The generator chugs to life off to one side of the house, as it does every night when the timer activates the motor. Michael looks in that direction and imitates the sound of the generator with his lips.

"I've made up a bed for you, Michael. You will be able to sleep there comfortably."

He imitates the sound of the generator again.

"That's the generator," she tells him. "It's a machine that gives electricity for the lights." He tilts his head and listens, but his expression shows no understanding of what she says. "Come and see your bed, Michael. In the house. Come."

Märit says, "I've found a pair of boots that might fit you, Michael. They seem to be about your size. Would you like to try them on?"

She lifts the boots and presents them to him.

Michael takes the boots and clutches them to his chest.

"Try them on. Put them on your feet, Michael."

He beams his smile at her and nods vigorously, then reaches into his pocket and presents his old alarm clock to Märit.

Märit shakes her head. "Thank you, Michael, but I already have a clock. You keep yours. Thank you, anyway."

As she herself prepares for bed, a soft tapping sounds at Märit's door. "It's me, Tembi."

Märit turns the key in her bedroom door, which she has locked.

"Michael is gone."

"He's left?"

"The bedding and the boots are gone too."

"Maybe he went out to sleep on the veranda," Märit says.

"No, I looked."

Darkness is not absolute yet; the silhouettes of the eucalyptus trees and the windmill are still faint outlines against the deep blue of the sky.

"Do you think he has left the farm?" Märit asks. "But where could he go in the night?"

Tembi puts a finger to her lips. "Listen."

Faintly in the night they hear the plink, plink, plink of Michael's music box.

"He has gone to sleep with the chickens." Tembi says. "He is happy with them."

38

THE GRASS GROWS tall in the fields now that there are no longer cattle to crop it. In the orchard the fruit begins to fill the branches. The maize plants rise higher each day and the cobs thicken on the stalk. In the vegetable garden the tomato plants thrive alongside the lettuce and the carrots and the spinach.

Märit no longer wears a watch, or counts the days, but she knows by the changes in the crops that months have passed since that day when her life changed with a stranger knocking on her door.

The farm has become smaller. Around the house many more birds are visible in the trees now, and their song is a constant music. Sometimes Michael teases the birds by mimicking their calls on his music box.

At night the generator chugs gently, and during the day the blades of the windmill turn slowly in the breeze. The women do not stray far from the house and the immediate fields. By unspoken agreement there is no talk of what might be taking place beyond the confines of the farm. Both Märit and Tembi know that their position here is fragile, but because there is peace and silence and harmony, they preserve the illusion that life is as it ought to be.

In the hot afternoons, sudden thunderstorms bring a brief deluge of rain. The fruit ripens, the maize grows tall and green, the vegetables and the flowers thrive. A kind of peace has isolated the farm—the outside world no longer troubles itself with this insignificant patch of soil.

Märit stands taller now, her face and arms are browned by the sun, her muscles show beneath the skin of her wiry frame, her eyes are bright. Her hair has started to grow out again, but she takes the scissors to it regularly so that it will remain short like Tembi's.

In the kraal, some of the thatch on the roofs of the huts is falling into disrepair and many of the huts have that particular air of abandonment that dwellings take on so quickly when the inhabitants leave.

Once or twice at dusk, just as darkness falls, Märit thinks she has glimpsed an animal on the property, perhaps a jackal or hyena, but since she is not certain what she sees she does not mention it to Tembi. Nevertheless, she makes sure that the shotgun is loaded and accessible on the top of the cupboard in the office.

Tembi still goes often to her hidden garden behind the koppie, carrying a pail of water to moisten the growing fruits. Sometimes Tembi asks herself whether she should tell Märit about her garden, even whether she should move the plants into the vegetable patch closer to the house where it would be so much easier to care for them. But she always hesitates. She cannot say clearly why she keeps the garden a secret, only that she knows it is tied to some other, inner life of hers that has nothing to do with Märit or the farm. She only knows that she must continue to possess this secret. A secret, when shared, is a gift, but still she holds back, perhaps because it is the only gift she has, and in the giving of it there will no longer be a gift or a secret. So she holds the garden to herself.

Märit does not count the days—she lets them pass, content within the enclosure of the farm. In her body she feels a new strength as she goes about her daily tasks. Some days there is the frequent flash of aircraft high above the land, streaking north to the frontier, but here on the farm the outside world has no meaning. The telephone is silent, the radio is silent. The outside world is absent.

Michael sleeps every night in the kraal and appears at the kitchen door each morning, announced by the tinkling of his music box. And each morning Dik-Dik follows Michael to the house.

"I think they have adopted each other," Tembi comments as she sits next to the window cradling her morning coffee.

When Michael enters, the rooster tries to slip in as well, and Märit has to shoo him away with a dishcloth. "Out, out," she admonishes, flapping the cloth at the rooster.

Michael collects his bowl and spoon from the counter.

"Did you sleep well?" Märit asks him. "Are you comfortable in the kraal?"

He sets the bowl down and puts his hands together in a pillow shape against his cheek, and his round face breaks into a particularly radiant smile.

"You are happy this morning, Michael," Tembi observes. "Why are you so happy?"

His reply is a mischievous chuckle. As soon as Märit serves the porridge, he grasps the bowl from her hands and sits quickly at the table. The porridge is spooned into his mouth rapidly, and when Märit places a cup of tea in front of him, Michael gulps it down just as fast, then moves to the door and beckons eagerly to the women.

"What is it, Michael?" Tembi says. "Do you want to show us something?"

His head bobs up and down.

"Can it wait a minute?" Märit asks. "At least until we finish breakfast?"

Michael giggles and shakes his head. He advances and grasps Märit's arm in a light tug. When she rises from her chair, he reaches over and urges Tembi from her seat as well. As the women follow, Michael darts ahead, turning every few moments to make sure they are behind him, gesturing for them to hurry on.

When the procession reaches the chicken coop, where the hens are milling about in the dirt, Michael unlatches the wire gate and hurries into the shed where the chickens roost at night.

He emerges almost immediately and beckons for Märit and Tembi to enter. Märit follows Tembi, keeping an eye out for the rooster. Michael crouches down and crooks a finger at Märit. He pats the sand, indicating that she should kneel next to him. With another glance around for the rooster, she does so.

Now Michael reaches with both hands into the straw and brings them out cupped together. Pursing his lips, he holds his hands out towards Märit and makes a high peeping noise with his mouth. When he opens his hands, a small fluffy yellow head appears and a peep, peep, peep comes from the little beak of a chick.

"Oh," Märit exclaims. "Oh, look at the little thing!"

Michael offers the fuzzy little chick to her, and she cups her hands to receive the warm, soft body, closing her fingers gently around the yielding down. The little chick nibbles at her finger and peeps up at her.

"How sweet!" she murmurs. "How lovely it is. Oh, how sweet." Lifting the tiny creature to her lips she plants a gentle kiss on the diminutive head. "Tembi, come look!"

A hen appears at the entrance to the shed, and when Michael makes the clucking sound that he uses to talk to the chickens, she waddles towards him, and from behind her four more yellow balls of fluff hurry after.

"Look at the little babies!" Tembi exclaims as she kneels in the dust with her hands extended, and the chicks come to her with a quick, darting motion, hurrying on their spindly legs. The mother hen hovers solicitously around the chicks, but she lets the women handle her brood.

The chick in Märit's hand struggles to join its siblings, but she is reluctant to let the warm creature out of her grasp. Raising it to her lips she kisses the soft head again. "There, there," she murmurs. "Mother is nearby. There, there." And the chick makes a peep, peep, peep sound in reply.

Märit holds the tiny beating life in her hands. So soft is the fluff, and the small body, and the beating of the new life in it. So soft and eager for life. Then she releases the chick gently to the ground, and the hen bends herself low, spreading her wings to enfold the small creature, which immediately huddles into the welcoming feathers.

Märit's heart breaks with tenderness. The tears fall from her eyes and splash into the dust. "Mother wants you," she murmurs to the small yellow face that looks out at her. And the mother hen clucks from deep inside her breast.

Suddenly, Märit is jealous. Jealous of the mother hen, jealous of her protective love. She has what Märit does not have. If she only had her own child to love now, her heart would not break so. The tears fall from her cheeks onto the dust as she stretches her hands with longing towards the little yellow chicks.

"Go to Mother," she murmurs to the chicks as they nibble at her fingers. "Mother wants you."

Then, from the doorway to the shed, rises the angry crowing of Dik-Dik. He catches sight of Märit and spreads his wings, rushing at her, but Michael is quick to intercept him, scooping the rooster up into his arms.

Märit retreats behind the wire-mesh fence. Even this little bit of tenderness is denied her by the possessive rooster. She hates him. She kicks at the fence, then wipes the tears from her face and walks back to the house.

At night, when the chickens have been rounded up and closed into their pen, and when Michael and Dik-Dik have retired to the hut in the kraal, and the chicks are safe with their mother, Märit and Tembi sit together in the living room of the house. The generator chugs with a comforting rhythm, the night air is mild and sweet, the lamplight falls in yellow pools on the heads of the two women. Sometimes, in the evenings, Märit tries the radio, longing for music. But there is never anything but static.

Tembi is reading a book, and Märit has some sewing in her lap, but her hands are still and her attention is elsewhere. She is remembering the feel of the delicate, fuzzy little chick in her hands, and she feels in her heart an obscure sensation of loss.

Tembi sighs and closes her book, stretching out in the chair. "It is so peaceful here. We are like a family now. The three of us. Even Dik-Dik is part of the family. And now we have some babies!"

Märit composes her face and tries to smile. "Yes, they're so beautiful."

Tembi studies Märit across the lamplight, her brown eyes inquiring.

"You are sad, Märit?"

Before Märit has a chance to answer, the lamplight flickers, then dies, casting the room into sudden darkness.

Tembi reaches for the switch next to her chair and flicks it back and forth. "What happened?"

"Listen."

"I don't hear anything."

"The generator. I don't hear it." Märit rises and goes to the window and listens for the chug, chug of the generator motor. "It's definitely stopped. I'll have to go and see what's wrong."

"But it's late now. You can do it in the morning."

"No. There is food in the refrigerator that will spoil by morning."

Märit finds the flashlight in a drawer and when she turns it on its white beam lights up the room. "Will you come with me?"

Outside, the night is cool. There is no moon, but the stars are a dense weave of sparkling points, flickering in the velvet sky. The white beam of the flashlight cuts a path through the darkness.

When they reach the generator shed and enter it, Märit plays the light over the engine. "I don't really know how it works. This is the fuel tank, for the diesel"—she taps the container—"but there is also a battery that is charged by the turning of the windmill. Ben always took care of it. I never learned how it works."

"Maybe there is no fuel. Shine the light here." Tembi unscrews the lid of the tank and Märit shines the beam down. "No, it's got fuel. There must be some other problem."

They spend the next minutes tracing pipes and wires, but to no avail. The workings of the generator remain a mystery.

"We'll have to leave it for the morning," Märit concludes.

As they walk back to the house, the chirping of crickets is as dense as the stars overhead. From the direction of the river a chorus of croaks and warbles competes with the crickets. And beyond that is a vast silence.

MÄRIT WAKES to happiness, because she remembers the little yellow chicks, and she wants to see them again, and she wants to hear the small music that Michael makes on his music box, and she wants to hold the sweet, soft life in her hands again.

But she also remembers the generator failing in the night. She doubts that either she or Tembi will be able to fix it, and now, without electricity, without a telephone, without a radio, their lives will be that much more difficult. Will they even be able to remain on the farm?

She rises quickly, hurrying to stoke the kitchen stove into life.

Tembi stretches like a cat when Märit brings the breakfast tray to her room. "You bring me breakfast again! You don't have to."

"I know. But I like to. Stay in bed a little longer." Märit takes pleasure in this occasional ritual, when she can sit on the edge of the bed and watch

Tembi sip her tea. These moments of intimacy give her comfort and a sense of normalcy.

"I didn't hear Dik-Dik this morning," Tembi says. "He usually wakes me up with his crowing."

"Perhaps Michael has taught him to sleep a bit longer in the mornings." Märit sits a while longer, then says, "We have to see about the generator. The food is going to spoil in this heat."

Tembi throws back the sheet. "I'll get up now."

"I want to go and look at the chicks first."

"Yes! I love those little babies."

Outside, the blades of the windmill turn in the warm breeze as Märit makes her way to the chicken coop. She pauses when she notices Michael, sitting with his back against a tree, in the same place where she first saw him. On the ground at his side is his music box, his old alarm clock, and the pair of boots that he never wears.

"Good morning, Michael. Where is Dik-Dik today? I didn't hear him when I woke up."

Michael barely glances up as she approaches, and as she steps closer Märit sees the lines of tears etched on his dusty face.

"Michael! What is it? Is something wrong?"

Märit crouches down next to him. There is mucus gathered in his nostril, and she wants to reach across and wipe his nose, as one would for a child.

"Michael, what's wrong. Is it Dik-Dik? Has something happened?"

Michael looks up at her and tries to speak, the words not forming on his damaged tongue. A groan escapes from his throat.

Märit stands slowly and stares in the direction of the chicken coop. "You're frightening me, Michael. What has happened? Is it the chickens? Is it Dik-Dik? The babies?"

Michael tilts his head and wails at her, showing the stump of his tongue in his open mouth.

Märit sets off at a run.

The breeze lifts and blows around her, and she sees the white rose petals blowing in the wind, and her mind refuses to believe what she knows is coming, and she sees white petals in the wind—and the white feathers that rise on the wind are stained with blood. The wire gate to the coop is wide open, and everywhere are white and red feathers and the smell of blood, and she sees the carcasses, entrails spilling onto the dust.

Märit rushes into the shed, and there are bloody feathers everywhere. Frantically she searches through the hay, her only thought for the chicks, her hands touching old droppings, the smooth surface of eggs, but no chicks.

Outside again she searches at the back of the shed, and there she sees the hole at the bottom of the fence, and the dug-up earth where some animal has come in. And here she finds a few puffs of yellow down, and here is the body of Dik-Dik, limp, torn, his head almost severed from his neck.

Märit recoils from the devastation. Every single chicken has been killed. Butchered. The bodies have been scattered everywhere by some ferocious presence that passed amongst the hens, ripping and clawing and slashing at random.

Märit staggers away from the carnage and the guts and the smell of death. And on the breeze a small tuft of yellow down drifts past her and then is gone. She clutches her hands over her eyes and wails, and the sound that breaks from her mouth is the same inarticulate cry of grief that came from Michael's damaged mouth.

When Tembi arrives, still in her nightdress, her brown face goes ash gray at the sight of the destruction. Clutching her arms against her body as if the day has suddenly turned cold, she sinks to her knees.

"I don't understand this," Tembi moans. "This wasn't done out of hunger. It couldn't have been. What animal could have done this? What evil? I don't understand why everything has to be killed." She grabs a handful of soil in her fists and flings it away from her. "I hate this country!"

Märit digs the pit in the earth while Tembi shovels together the carcasses and loads them into a wheelbarrow. Both women tie scarves across their lower faces because now, as the sun becomes hotter, the odor of putrefaction is a stench. When the remains of the chickens have been tipped into the pit Märit begins to shovel soil over the carcasses.

"This won't work," Tembi tells her. "Animals will come and dig it up. Hyenas, jackals. We must burn it."

"There is gasoline in the tractor shed. I'll fetch it."

She walks past Michael on her way to the shed, and he does not even look up, but sits slumped against the tree with his head hanging.

"Michael?" she says gently.

He raises his head and looks at her with dull eyes that show no glimpse of recognition.

She fetches the can of gasoline and brings it back to the pit. Tembi douses the chicken carcasses, then sets the can back at a safe distance. "Do you have matches?"

Tembi coils together some strands of dry grass, then lights it and tosses the burning coil into the pit.

The gasoline ignites with a bright orange whoosh, and the women shield their faces from the sudden heat. A pall of smoke rises quickly into the air, carrying with it the singed smell of burning feathers. The smoke is white, and then it is black, and the smell now is of burning flesh. Märit presses her scarf tighter against her face, suppressing the urge to gag.

When the flames die and the smoke dissipates, the women spread soil over the charred embers, and then they carry soil in the wheelbarrow back to the coop and sprinkle it over the dark bloodstains that are everywhere on the ground.

"We should burn this too," Tembi says, her voice grim. "The whole shed and everything. I don't want to see it here every day and think about the evil."

Märit pours what remains of the gasoline onto the wooden boards of the shed and trickles a trail out to the gate of the coop. Then she fashions a coil of grass as Tembi had done and sets it alight before tossing it onto the ground.

A tongue of fire darts up and races towards the shed, then licks up the side of the dry boards, and the flame consumes them. A dull thump blows out from the interior of the shed as one wall collapses inwards and the hay inside sparks alight. Tembi and Märit stand some distance away, in silence, until the shed has collapsed, and the smoke drifts away, and only charred timber is left.

All day Michael does not stir from his place under the tree. Not even the fire seems to have grasped his attention. When the women have been to the house, and washed and changed their clothes, and Tembi brings Michael a mug of tea and a bowl of porridge, he does not acknowledge her.

"Michael, you must eat something." Tembi touches him gently on the shoulder, raises his chin with her fingers, but she sees in his eyes that he is distant from her. "We will get some more chickens. And a rooster. A beautiful rooster, just like Dik-Dik."

But the distance in his eyes does not lessen. Tembi sits down next to him. She wants to see his smile, and hear the small melody from his music box again. And even though her heart is heavy she tries to find words to comfort the stricken man.

"Sometimes things like this happen, Michael. Sometimes wild animals will come after the stock on a farm. The wild animals get hungry too."

Michael shakes his head adamantly. Tembi wonders what evil he has witnessed before, and she wonders if here on the farm Michael had believed that he had found a haven from evil. She too wants to believe the farm is a haven, and she knows that Märit does also. But there is so much death on this soil.

She puts her hand on Michael's shoulder again. "We will buy some more chickens, and a fine rooster. I promise you that we will do that, Michael. And then we can build a new chicken coop, with a strong fence." But the distance is in his eyes and she has the feeling that he is not listening to her.

Michael does not stir from his place under the tree. Not when porridge and tea are brought for him, nor when Märit goes to sit with him.

Tembi watches from the window. "I'm worried about Michael. He won't eat, he won't move. And when he looks at me his eyes are in some other place. Those chickens were his family, Dik-Dik was his brother, and now he has lost them. His loss is greater than ours."

Märit slumps back into her chair. "Oh, Tembi, sometimes it all seems so hopeless. We're not strong enough for this place. I don't know how to help Michael. I don't even know how to help myself. We are running short of food—without the chickens it's going to be worse—we have no electricity now."

"We have the garden, we have maize that is almost ripe, there is fruit in the trees, we have water to drink. Even if it seems hopeless, this is our place."

Märit tries a wan smile. "You always have hope, Tembi. You know more about suffering than I do, yet you always have hope. Without you here I would die. I feel that I will never leave this farm. I will die instead."

"Don't speak such nonsense. You think too much. Go and see to Michael. Maybe he will listen to you. Try to make him eat something."

Michael still sits slumped against the tree, his hands lying limp on either side of his body. A trail of ants has found the bowl of porridge, and Märit tries to brush them away but then gives up. What can she say to him that will ease his loss? She cannot find the words to convince even herself to hope.

She reaches for his music box and plucks out a few notes, then places the instrument on Michael's lap. "Will you make some music for me, Michael?" But his hands remain limp in the dust.

He remains sitting in place all through the day and into the evening. The women bring food and tea periodically, and talk to him, but the food remains untouched except by the ants. When darkness approaches they both urge him to come into the house. But he seems unaware of them now.

"Michael, you cannot sleep out here. You will be cold. It's not safe." Tembi tugs at his arm. "Please, come to the house."

"He doesn't know us any longer," Märit says. She returns to the house and fetches blankets to drape over his shoulders. When darkness falls the women stand on the veranda of the house, looking out to the shadows that gradually obscure the sick and grieving man.

Märit brings a paraffin lamp and places it on the veranda. "I'll leave it here in the night. That way he will see it and know we are here."

IN THE MORNING when Tembi wakes she is immediately struck by the quality of the silence. No crowing from Dik-Dik, no clucking of chickens, no chug from the generator, no twanging music from Michael's music box. Michael is gone. The silence tells her.

On the veranda the paraffin lamp has long since burned out. She walks down to the place where Michael sat all the previous day and night. She sees only the pair of old boots under the tree. And a single palm print outlined in the dust, as if he had placed his hand there when he rose at last. Tembi does not go to the kraal to look for him, or to any other place on the farm. The silence tells her that he is gone. Only the boots remain. He came with nothing and he has left with nothing.

Part Three

The River

39

SOMETIMES MÄRIT WALKS in the cool air of the morning, with the breeze moving the blades of the windmill and the doves cooing in the eucalyptus trees and the rows of maize plants green in the sunlight and the distant mountains violet against the blue sky, and for a moment she forgets.

She stands at the bottom of the veranda steps and takes in the view. The landscape, so pure, the whisper of the breeze, the echo of birdsong.

She forgets the deaths that have marked this place called Kudufontein, or Lebone, or Duiwelskop, or nothing at all. She forgets the death of Grace, the death of Ben, the death of the stranger who was shot from the air, the death of the chickens. She forgets that Michael wanders out there in the wilderness.

But then she remembers, and the veil of sorrow descends. Then Märit is convinced that this farm is the last place on earth, that the rest of the world has been destroyed, and that destruction is lurking just beyond the horizon, in the brooding silence, knocking at the doors of Kudufontein. And then there will be no place left on earth.

If not for Tembi, Märit thinks, she would fade into the void that lies beyond the farm and give herself up to the silence. It would be so easy to give up, to cease the struggle, to let the veil descend. Only Tembi anchors Märit now. Tembi with her bright and optimistic smile, her courage to face obstacles, her brown skin that is a mixture of the veldt grasses and the dark soil so that she sometimes seems created from the veldt. I could fade into the pale light, Märit thinks, and I could disappear, because I am made from something insubstantial. But Tembi is made from the soil, she is this land.

When Tembi joins Märit on the veranda, and looks to see what Märit gazes upon so far away, and sees the distance in her eyes, she asks, "What are you looking at? What do you see?"

"Nothing. I'm looking at nothing."

"We must harvest the mealies. They are ready. And we must pick the fruit. Otherwise, the birds will eat it all."

"Won't it go rotten anyway?"

"Not if we dry it. You can do that with fruit. But first you have to take out the pits, and slice the flesh, and set it out in the sun. A lot of work."

"And what will we do with all the maize cobs?"

"Set them in the shed to dry. And then we can grind the ears to make meal, and then we will have mealie porridge. A lot of work!"

Tembi puts her hand on Märit's shoulder. Then Märit shakes off her thoughts, and smiles, and resolves to be courageous too, like Tembi. "I'm daydreaming. Is it time to go back to work?"

The women work through the morning. The work is hard and tedious, and it makes the hands ache, the skin rub and crack. The maize cobs are pulled from the tall plants and piled in small heaps down the center of the rows. There is no talking, because talking is an effort. Sweat collects and chafes where cloth meets skin. The breeze rasps like a hoarse whisper through the dry leaves of the maize and it whispers the song of the earth—that all must labor, that all must struggle.

The women take turns loading the cobs into the wheelbarrow and wheeling the harvest to a shed, where the pile on the floor grows ever larger.

"Maybe we have enough now," Märit says after returning from one of these trips to the shed.

Tembi studies the remaining rows of maize and shakes her head. "I told you it would be a lot of work. And we still have to peel them—otherwise, they will rot."

"But will we ever need this much?"

"We must harvest everything."

Märit sighs and bends again to her work.

The harvest takes two days of steady, repetitive labor that leaves both women aching in their bodies. Then there is the shucking of the dry outer husks, which is even harder on the hands, so that at night Märit complains about her chafed skin.

Tembi fetches a bottle of lotion from the bathroom. "Sit here," she commands, pointing to a chair. By the dim glow of candlelight she kneels before Märit, taking her hands in her own and gently massaging the lotion into Märit's skin.

When Tembi looks up she sees the glisten of tears in Märit's eyes. "Why are you sad?"

"No, I'm happy, Tembi. I'm happy, because you are such a good person, and you are here."

"And I am happy if you are happy."

"This farm should be yours, Tembi. You should be the one sitting in this chair, not me."

"It is our farm, together. And your hands are stronger every day. You are stronger. Not so much the weak woman who first came to this farm."

"Was I weak? Yes, I suppose I was. I'm stronger now. From all this struggle."

Tembi shrugs. "That is the way of the world. Struggle."

Märit sits up and clasps Tembi's hands. "Let's take tomorrow off! No work for a day."

"But we must pick the fruit. The birds will eat it if we don't."

"How much can they eat in one day? We need a day off. We'll have a picnic and go swimming in the river! Can we?"

Tembi laughs. "Why ask me? You can do what you like. If you want to swim, we will swim."

IN SOME PLACES the river is green, the color of bottle-glass. In other places it is coffee-colored, like Tembi's skin. Sometimes it is clear enough to see the pebbles and sand beneath the surface, and sometimes it is an opaque mirror, reflecting the sky and the trees.

Where Märit and Tembi have come, upstream from the house, the river flows amongst low flat rocks that lead out from the bank, and in between the rocks are pools of varying depth. Here the river makes a bend in its course, and on the opposite bank the rocks rise steeply, forming a wall of stone that is spotted with bushes and low trees that rise to screen the sky. The place is sheltered, calm, concealed.

Tembi is perched on the edge of a rock, dropping bits of leaf into the eddies, where they swirl in a circular motion before shooting off downstream. Märit reclines nearby with her face turned up to the hot sun, dabbing her toes in the water.

Tembi watches a blade of grass arrow into the current. She imagines herself tiny, small enough to sit on it, as if it were a boat. She imagines the boat traveling down canyons, through villages and towns, even through the cities, coming at last into a lagoon that spills out to the ocean. She imagines a yellow beach and crashing waves and ships offshore.

"I wonder where this river goes," Tembi says.

"Down to the sea," Märit murmurs. "Like all the rivers."

This single blade of grass, a strand plucked idly in passing, will float down this single river, and join a larger river where other streams flow into it. There, Tembi imagines, they will become one river, and plunge into the sea, all becoming one.

"I want to visit the sea one day. It's my dream."

"Yes," Märit answers. "I loved it there. I think I had my happiest moments by the sea."

"Tell me about it. Tell me what it was like."

Märit sits up and props her chin on her knees. "Ben and I went there, just after we married, for our honeymoon."

"To Durban?"

"Near Durban. The place was called Mussel Sands. We stayed in a small hotel. We always had our breakfast in bed—it was brought up on a tray—then we would go out and walk along the beach for hours. I loved the sound of the waves, and the smell in the air, the fresh, salty smell."

"Did you swim?"

"All the time. I wasn't a very good swimmer at first; the waves frightened me a bit—they could get quite big at times. But I felt safe with Ben. I would hang onto his back as he waded into the breakers, and he showed me how to duck under the big ones and how to ride over the tops of the swell before it broke. I loved it when a wave took me and carried me up as if I had no weight at all. It was like flying. Just for that minute when I was on the crest of the breaker, speeding towards the beach, it felt like flying, weightless and free."

She stares down at her toes, flat on the rock, remembering.

Tembi says, "I want to go to the ocean one day. I want to fly in the waves. But I cannot swim."

"No? Well, then, I will teach you." She springs to her feet. "Come on."

"But I have no bathing suit."

"We'll swim naked."

"Yes?"

Märit looks around. "Who could possibly see us?" She unfastens her sarong and lets it drop at her feet. Then she slips off her underwear and wades into the nearest pool. She splashes water up at Tembi. "Come on!"

After a quick glance around, Tembi follows suit and scampers into the pool, quickly dropping down so that the water rises to her shoulders.

"Over here," Märit tells her, moving into the deeper stream. "Give me your hands."

Tembi grasps Märit's fingers.

"The first thing is to kick, like a frog, just keep kicking, that's it." Märit moves them both a little closer to the center of the river, feeling the current now. "Keep your head up. Now you have to use your arms."

"Don't let me go!"

"I've got your waist. Now, use your arms as if you were parting the long grass, and kick at the same time." She releases her hold on Tembi's waist and lets her move away. "You're swimming!"

Tembi's head dips below the water and she surfaces spluttering, casting an anxious eye around for Märit. "Keep your chin up," Märit calls.

With a determined expression Tembi strokes into the current purposefully. She feels the strength of the water under her, and she matches it with her own strength, pushing against it upstream.

For a moment the struggle is equal, then the current spins Tembi around so that she is facing downstream. She is weightless, she is a feather. But the river is strong. It pulls her with a will of its own, and there is nothing below her feet as the impersonal power grabs her body. Her head drops below the surface and her eyes see the green depths.

"Märit!" she cries.

"I'm here, I'm here." Märit's hands catch her, stronger than the river, taking her to safety.

When she has caught her breath, spread-eagled on the rocks, Tembi says, "I wasn't frightened."

Märit stretches out next to her. "No. You're brave."

"I was a little bit frightened. Next time I will beat the river."

They lie naked, letting the sun dry their bodies. Tembi rolls over onto her stomach and rests her head on her folded arms so that she can look at Märit. "Tell me some more about when you were married. What is it like to live with a man, to sleep with him next to you every night, to wake next to him in the morning?"

"You feel safe. I never slept so well as I did next to Ben. His chest was broad and strong and warm, and when he held me I slept like a little girl."

"Is that what it is like to be married, you feel like a girl?"

Märit laughs. "No, there is more to it than that."

Tembi moves her arm so that her eyes are hidden. "Tell me about the other part. Tell me about the other things."

"Often you feel like a girl, but then there are the times that a man makes you feel like a woman. In a special way."

"You mean loving—when he is loving you in bed?" Tembi's voice is shy, her face hidden.

"A man's body is like your own in so many ways, but where he is different his body is something wonderful. And the difference gives you pleasure. Such sweet pleasure to touch him."

She falls silent.

"And he loved you?"

"I suppose he did. Although I don't think he knew anything more about love than I did. Perhaps we might have grown to love each other in a better way if he had lived."

Tembi asks no more. Finally, she says, "I want to be married someday too. I want to swim in the ocean. I want to have a man. I want to know these things too."

"You will, Tembi. You will. It will be sweet for you. And it will also be bitter sometimes."

Tembi shifts position onto her back and closes her eyes, lapsing into silence.

Märit leans on one elbow and lets her eyes move over Tembi's body with frank curiosity. She has never seen Tembi naked, or any black woman. How much a part of the rocks and the sun Tembi seems, her breasts and stomach as smooth and rounded as the stone, the pubic patch of tight curls only a tone or two darker than the surrounding skin.

Märit touches her own hair, which is growing out unevenly, and looks down at her light-colored body, so pale, so naked, the triangle between her thighs so visible and obvious. I look better clothed, she thinks, and Tembi is better naked.

"Tembi?"

"Mmm?"

"Do you think we will be able to continue living here? How much longer can we go on?"

Tembi opens her eyes, unclouded with doubt. "We can live here forever if we want to."

"I don't know if I am strong enough. I don't mean in my body, but in my heart."

"You have to be strong, Märit. For my sake. I need you also."

Märit leans over and clasps Tembi's hand. "Do you? Do you really? You don't know how much it means to me to hear you say that. I have nothing to hold me to this life otherwise."

Tembi raises herself and leans to splash water onto her feet and then wipes her face. Where her wet hand has rested on the hot rock, the perfect shape of a palm and fingers is delineated on the stone. Märit watches as the imprint begins to evaporate and fade, then quickly places her own hand over the outline. She feels the mixture of coolness and warmth emanating from the rock, as if from a body.

Tembi looks down at Märit's hand where it covers the palm print on the stone. "Without you, I too would be lost in this place."

40

DURING THE NIGHT the weather changes and an unseasonable, sluggish heat descends upon the farmhouse, pushing away the usually cool breeze and replacing it with a torpid, airless atmosphere. Tembi wakes in the darkness with her nightdress twisted and bunched into a painful knot under her back. She kicks off the blanket and sits up on the edge of the bed, breathing heavily.

Why is it so hot? The nights are never this hot, not even in the thick days of late summer. With the edge of her nightdress she wipes away the thin film of perspiration from her face. Even the normally cool flagstones are warm under the soles of her feet as she rises and walks out to the corridor, feeling her way against the thick farmhouse walls.

At Märit's half-ajar door Tembi pauses and listens to the soft sounds of breathing, then goes on to unlock the front door and step out to the veranda.

Out here the air is just as stifling. A hot wind moves across her face, blowing out of the night from the east somewhere. Above her head not a glimmer of starlight breaks the thick darkness, as if the sky too is heavy with this blanket of dead air. Not a sound disturbs the night, and the hot wind moves in silence.

The wind blows steadily with a constant flow, the air pushing forward in relentless streams, and in this flow there is a faint odor of decay, of something rotten out there in the night, a corruption that the wind brings on its unceasing current.

Is it the chickens? Tembi wonders. Does the odor of their slaughter still linger about the farm, almost three weeks after Michael disappeared? Or is there a death somewhere else in the night? She moves around on the veranda, seeking escape from the sour wind, but there is none, and eventually she sinks down into one of the chairs.

Where are her people this night? Where is Michael? She fears for him, alone out there. He needed so little from life, he demanded so little from the world, he stepped so lightly on the earth. Yet even the little he asked for was taken from him. She remembers the deadness that replaced the light in his eyes, and she fears for him. Because it is the dead hour of the night now, because she is alone and it is the hour when the human soul feels its solitude most, Tembi succumbs to her fears. Her own breath seems insignificant in the face of this nameless wind. Her own desires and hopes seem small. The night crushes her.

She has always accepted the world as it is—the veldt, the sky, the birds and animals—always there, part of some eternal wholeness that is constant. When tragedy and death and the presence of evil have come into her life she has borne them. She has always had faith and hope, and she has believed in something called God, some goodness at the heart of life. But can God take away her mother, and her father, and Märit's husband—all without reason? Can God cut down the lives of the strangers who came to the farm? Can God send an innocent and harmless man like Michael to wander speechless into a troubled land?

In this black and infinite night, with its smell of corruption and decay, when her own weak heart beats feebly in the void, Tembi fears that there is no God, and that this wind blows from a place where God is absent—from a place where there is no hope.

A soft footfall sounds from the doorway, and Tembi turns her head to see the pale presence of Märit.

"Can't you sleep either?" Märit asks.

"It's too hot," Tembi answers, hearing her own voice as if it comes from far away.

When Märit collapses into the other chair, Tembi reaches out and takes her hand, reaching for hope, and for faith, for life. "Your skin is cool, my sister."

"Is it? I don't feel cool in the least."

"Do you smell this wind?"

"Yes, it's strange, isn't it. And it smells bad. What do you think it is? Where does it come from?"

"From a bad place, where there is nothing."

Märit starts to remove her hand, but Tembi grasps it, pressing it against her forehead. "Leave your hand here. It's nice and cool."

"Are you feeling ill? You sound so strange."

"It's nothing. I'm hot."

After a moment Märit says, "What do you mean, 'from a place where there is nothing'?" She leans forward trying to see Tembi's face.

"Do you ever wonder what is happening out there? How is it that nobody has come to the farm in all these months except for Michael? Not the neighbors, not anyone from Klipspring, not even the police have come back. In all these days only one person has come to this farm—a man who cannot speak. There is something wrong out there. The whole world feels empty. Perhaps the world has passed us by, forgotten us."

"I hope so," Märit says fervently. "I don't want other people to come here again. We don't need anybody else. We don't need anything from the world. It just brings suffering. I just want us to be alone here, on our farm." She removes her hand from Tembi's forehead and reaches into the pocket of her night coat for her cigarettes. There are fewer each day and she rations them now.

She lights the cigarette, and holds the match up for a moment, trying to see Tembi's face. Tembi turns her head away. The scent of tobacco obscures the smell of decay in the night.

Märit extinguishes the match. "Do you think I'm being selfish to want these things? I know that there are others living terrible lives. It's easy for us here, really. We have food and drink and shelter. There are many others who must be without that. But is it selfish to just want some peace? Haven't we suffered enough?"

"I don't know," Tembi says in a strange and faraway tone that frightens Märit because she has never heard this tone in her voice before. "I don't have answers to these questions."

Märit smokes in silence. The taste of the smoke in her mouth is hot and stale, and when she exhales, the wind takes the smoke into the night.

Tembi rises and says in a numbed voice, "I think I will try to sleep again. You must too."

Märit stubs out her cigarette on the railing. "We still have the fruit to pick tomorrow." She follows Tembi into the house, pausing to bolt the front door. At Tembi's bedroom door she says, "If it is still hot like this tomorrow we can swim again."

From the darkness Tembi says, "Yes, we can swim if you like," and her voice is flat and listless.

Silence returns. The heat remains. The wind blows, hot and relentless, and always with the undercurrent of decay.

THE SKY is a bleached gray color when Märit steps out to the veranda in the morning. A long yellow smudge lies across the horizon. The air is thick and heavy, a weight upon the land.

When Tembi appears a moment later, Märit says, "Did you sleep?"

"A bit." Her face has an unhealthy pallor that shows her exhaustion. "It's so hot."

"The wind has stopped. The smell from last night is gone, at least."

"I think there is a storm coming."

"But there are no clouds."

Tembi points to the layer of yellow haze low in the distance. "Did you see that?"

"What is it?"

Tembi massages her face with both hands, sighing wearily. "I think we should bring in as much of the fruit today as we can. We must gather in what we can. And the vegetables. I have a strange feeling."

"What kind of feeling? A bad storm? Hail?"

With a shake of her head Tembi goes back into the house.

The women work slowly because of the heat, pulling the peaches and apricots from the branches in the orchard and piling them into baskets. When the baskets are full, Märit loads them into a wheelbarrow and carries the load to the sheds. Here she lays out the fruit on wooden shelves, leaving a small distance between them so that they do not touch. Otherwise they will rot, Tembi has told her.

Every so often Tembi pauses in her labor and looks to the east. There is a suspension in the air that precedes a storm in the country, a pregnant hush, as if all the earth were holding its breath, waiting for some event to unfold. Yet there are no clouds, only an uncanny light that seems to flow out of the dark smudge on the horizon.

Märit looks up at the sky and says, "I don't think rain is coming. There are no clouds. Maybe it's a bushfire."

"Maybe. I'm going to climb up the windmill and have a look."

Märit waits at the bottom as Tembi clambers up the rungs in the center of the structure. The blades of the windmill are not moving, their usual creak and whirr stilled in the oppressive atmosphere. From the small platform beneath the blades Tembi peers out across the veldt.

In the distance she can make out a house, the van Staden farm, the road to Klipspring, and the river winding beneath the trees that line its banks, showing as a green path in the brown veldt. But there is no movement anywhere, and when she turns to survey the other directions there are only the koppies and the gullies and the acacia trees and no sign of human life.

The smudge on the horizon has changed, is moving, expanding, trailing ragged edges as it rises, the way rain clouds do when seen from afar. But the color of this cloud is not the color of rain, it is that of yellow mud, like the clay that is sometimes found along the riverbanks. And in the center of the cloud is a darkness.

As she clings to her perch high above the deserted country, Tembi sees a ripple flutter across the grass and the trees as a wind moves across the veldt from the east, from the direction of the obscured horizon, and the wind reaches her, the hot wind, bringing with it the odor of decay.

Something flits past her in the air, like a leaf, then another. A grasshopper lands on her dress, clinging for a moment before she flicks it away into the wind, its wings making a quick papery sound. The windmill blades above her give a slow turn.

"Tembi! Come down. It's dangerous up there," Märit cries from the ground.

With a last glance at the cloud, which seems to have spread and moved closer, the darkness at its center expanding, Tembi hurries down the ladder.

There are more grasshoppers down here, flitting through the air. Märit is brushing them away as they try to settle on her dress and arms. "What did you see? Where are all these grasshoppers coming from?"

"The wind is bringing them. I don't know what it is."

The light changes suddenly, the mud-colored cloud obscuring the sun. A large grasshopper lands on Tembi's arm with a rattle of papery wings and she shakes it off quickly. The insect falls onto its back, wings quivering.

"These are locusts!" Tembi exclaims. She stamps her bare heel onto the insect and a yellowish ooze leaks from the crushed body, and the smell rises, the smell of decay that is also in the wind.

"We have to close the shed doors and get into the house! Come on!" She grabs Märit's hand and pulls her along. "It's a swarm of locusts."

The cloud is almost upon them and the air is full of khaki shapes fluttering past their heads. In the center of the cloud the darkness seethes with turbulence.

The women reach the shed ahead of the swarm and bolt the doors, then start towards the house. Tembi suddenly stops and turns in the opposite direction. "Go into the house and shut all the windows!"

"Where are you going?"

"Go in the house! I'll meet you there." She sets off at a run towards the kraal.

And then the swarm is upon the farm, blotting out the light.

The moment that the swarm appeared Tembi knew what was happening. She has heard the stories from the old people, how a yellow cloud appears suddenly from the east, before the harvest, a cloud made up of thousands of insects that cover the surface of the land. And the plague consumes everything in its path, every blade of grass, every leaf, every stalk.

Her first thought is to try to save the fruit and maize that is in the other sheds. She runs to fasten the doors. Then she remembers her garden, her five small plants, and she races desperately towards the koppie. She can bear to lose almost anything—but not her garden! Her fear gives her strength and speed as she runs towards the koppie. Insects flash past her head, descending upon anything that is green, some of them even lighting on her shoulders, on her hair, but she does not pause to brush them away.

The swarm has not yet reached the koppie, but some individual locusts have already found her plants; already their hungry jaws are upon the tender shoots.

Too late, she thinks, too late.

Without heed for the barrier that protects the garden, Tembi pushes her way through the thorny branches, her fingers pulling the locusts from the plants, crushing the insects, flinging them aside. Her eyes fall upon the plastic water bucket and she upends it, settling it over the plants as a cover. With her bare hands she scrapes pebbles and soil up around the edges of the bucket, sealing it so that no insect can enter.

By then the air is thick with the locusts, but still she takes the time to find some heavy stones to weigh down the bucket. She wants to stay here, to protect her garden, but the swarm is too heavy. Locusts are crawling on her neck and arms, down the front of her dress, across the face.

She runs back towards the house, which she cannot even see now through the yellow cloud. Everywhere the air is choked with whirring insects. The steps and veranda are slick underfoot, the door is covered with locusts. But the handle is locked. With the side of her palm Tembi wipes away a space and pounds on the door.

"Märit! Märit!"

There is no response and she thumps both hands on the door. "Märit, let me in!"

INSIDE THE HOUSE, Märit runs from room to room, slamming windows and doors shut. There are locusts in the kitchen already, where the back door is ajar. Grabbing a dishtowel Märit flails at the insects, but it is useless, so she bangs the door shut.

In the living room the air is thick with insects, their bodies squashing beneath her feet. Where are they coming from? Then she sees the stream of locusts pouring from the fireplace.

There are matches in her pocket, there is kindling and paper in the grate. Quickly she bends to the fireplace and touches a flame to the paper. Smoke rises as the kindling catches, and the stream of insects parts to avoid the flame. Those in the grate sizzle and crackle in the heat.

A solid mass of insects pours down the chimney and the sheer weight of their numbers extinguishes the flames.

Märit scurries on her hands and knees for the cushions from the couch, which she stuffs into the fireplace. But it is not enough. Insects stream down. In a near panic, she bundles up the rug and forces it into the opening, but wherever there is a gap, locusts struggle through. Märit grabs sheets of newspaper from the box next to the hearth and pushes the crumpled pages into all the gaps until at last the fireplace is sealed.

Inside the room locusts buzz frantically from wall to wall. The windows are crawling with insects, blocking the light; the room is dark as twilight. There are locusts on her arms and legs, on her head, on her face. The smell of decay chokes her.

Märit cowers under the weight of the locusts. She feels the weight of the swarm pressing on the windows, pressing on the doors, pressing on the roof. In a moment they will force the roof beams to sag, will force the doors to buckle, will shatter the glass in the windows. In a moment the swarm will suffocate her. Already she can hear the groaning of their weight upon the house, the thudding against the front door.

The banging at the door is loud in her ears, rapid, insistent. Märit cowers in a corner. She hears a thin, high sound. Her name.

Tembi! Oh God, Tembi! Tembi is still out there!

Märit shakes herself free of her panic and springs towards the door, rattling the bolt free. Tembi stumbles into the room, a rush of locusts entering around her before Märit has time to slam the door shut again.

Tembi beats wildly at her clothes, trying to shake free the insects that cling to her.

"They're in here too," Märit wails. "What should we do?"

"Into the bedroom! Quick."

Because the windows are closed, the locusts have not managed to enter the bedroom and the women find shelter. They brush away the insects from their clothes and stamp them underfoot.

Exhausted, Märit slumps down on the corner of the bed and clutches her arms around her torso.

"What is happening?" she whispers, her eyes fixed upon the crawling mass of insects on the other side of the window. "Will we ever be able to get out again?"

Tembi draws the curtain shut and flicks at the light switch, then remembers that the generator has failed. She finds matches on the bedside table and strikes one. The flare of the match is bright in the gloom. Lifting the lid of the paraffin lamp she holds the flame to the wick, but it will not catch.

"There's no paraffin," Märit says. "I forgot to fill the lamp."

Tembi extinguishes the burning match.

"Will they be able to get in?"

"No," Tembi answers.

They listen, breathing softly.

"I think there are some candles in the cupboard," Märit says quietly, as if the sound of her voice might alert the locusts to her presence. "On the top shelf."

Tembi crosses to the cupboard on the opposite wall and fumbles along the top shelf. Her fingers touch the glass of a bottle, then the slim shapes of two candles. She lights one, holding it tilted until the wax softens in the heat, then drips the hot wax onto the lid of a cosmetic jar and sets the candle upright. When she reaches for the second candle on the shelf her fingers again touch the bottle, and she brings it down into the light, the amber liquid revealing that the contents are brandy.

Tembi lights the second candle and sets it on the dresser. The glow is meager, but comforting. She sits down again next to Märit and unscrews the lid of the bottle. When she tips it up to her lips and swallows a small amount, Tembi notices how much her hands are trembling.

"What is happening out there?" Märit says. "Where do they come from?" Her face is haggard, the lines of strain exaggerated in the candle's light.

"Drink some of this," Tembi says, handing the bottle to Märit, who has begun to shiver. "It will warm you."

She drinks, coughs, sips again, then holds the bottle clenched between her thighs.

"Where do they come from?" Märit says again.

"They just come."

"But why? Why here?"

Tembi glances up at the rustling thatch. "I have heard stories from the old people. Some years too many eggs hatch at the same time, and there is not enough food, so the locusts fly off to look for food in another place. And because there are so many of them, when they find a place that has food, like this farm, they eat everything."

"What do you mean 'everything'?"

"They will eat all the flowers, and the leaves, the grass, the fruit."

"Our gardens? The orchard, the maize? All our food?" Märit holds her head in her hands. Now there will be nothing to eat, it will be a desert, they will finally have to leave the farm. "But will the locusts stay here?"

"No, they will go when there is nothing left to eat. They are always hungry, so they will go somewhere else. The swarm will move on, some will die, some will be eaten by birds, some will be blown away by winds, some will drown in rivers and dams. But they will lay their eggs, and in another year, somewhere else, there will be a swarm like this one, falling on some other farm."

Turning her glance to the window, Märit asks, "Is there nothing we can do? It's so awful."

"We can only wait. For tomorrow, and what it will bring."

Märit takes another sip of the brandy. "I felt I was going to be eaten alive. They were all over me, under my clothes, in my hair, nibbling at my skin." She shudders and brushes at her lap. "I feel dirty, like they've left their eggs on me." She clasps her hands together as they begin to tremble.

"I will run a bath for you," Tembi says. "It will make you feel better."

When the bath has been filled, Märit undresses and sinks into the water. Tembi shuts the door softly.

"Tembi, leave the door open," Märit calls.

She lies in the bath, weeping quietly, and the tears roll down her cheeks into the scented water, and when at last she gets up, she finds Tembi fast asleep. Märit climbs under the quilt and folds herself against Tembi's warm back. Finally, she sleeps.

Märit wakes to a pattering against the window. She hears the gurgling sound of water pouring from a gutter. She slips out from beneath the quilt, careful not to wake Tembi, and draws the edge of the curtains open.

It is night still, darkness beyond the window panes. She listens again, then opens the window carefully, just a minute crack. A thin stream of fresh moist air blows across her face and the sound of falling water is louder. Rain.

Opening the window another couple of inches, Märit stretches her hand outside. The clean cold air blows across her face and she tastes the sweetness upon her lips. The locusts have gone.

Leaving the window open, Märit returns to bed, curving her body again next to Tembi, pressing her cheek against the sleeping warmth.

This is how she used to sleep with Ben, against the solid comfort of his back. The memory of it brings a pang of loneliness. It has been so long since she felt the touch of another hand, since she was embraced. She knows that a part of her spirit is withering from the lack of touch.

She presses herself closer in against Tembi, who murmurs a question in her sleep.

"It is raining," Märit whispers.

41

AT FIRST LIGHT the two women creep out of the bedroom and down the corridor to the front door.

"Ugh, it smells bad in here," Tembi exclaims, covering her mouth against the lingering odor of rot and burned cloth. She steps delicately, trying to avoid the bodies of the locusts littering the floor, some of them still wriggling with life.

Märit, who has put on a pair of sandals, unbolts the front door and pushes it wide open to let in the clean morning air. The first thing she sees on the veranda are the bare stalks of the potted geraniums—every leaf, every petal has been stripped from the stalks of the plants, leaving them like winter skeletons.

The sky is overcast and gray and a thin fog hangs over the fields. From the misty distance near the river a plover calls gently, and a moment later, from the opposite direction, a second bird answers. Märit's eyes move across to the lawn, the flower garden, the vegetable patch. She gasps.

"They've eaten everything! Everything! Oh, Tembi, look what they've done!"

Märit and Tembi walk out into the devastation. A swath has been cut across the land, as if some strange machine has swept over the farm in the night and left ruin in its wake. Trees denuded of leaves, showing bare branches against the sky, maize plants that are nothing more than scraggly stalks with a few bare cobs, a once green lawn that is now bare earth, muddy and slippery underfoot.

Tembi pauses at the remnants of the vegetable garden and shakes her head in disbelief. "Every single plant," she says with despair in her voice.

"The beans, the tomatoes, the squash." Crouching down she fingers the few stalks remaining. "Nothing left. All our food—gone!"

The locusts have devoured everything in the vegetable garden, stripped the maize fields, the flower beds, the potted plants on the veranda, the trees around the house, the lawn, the hydrangea bushes against the walls.

Märit stands in front of the flower garden, staring at the destruction, at the wantonness of it, at the thoroughness of it. Ben had worked so hard to build this garden and the lawn surrounding the beds, and she and Tembi had struggled to maintain the flowers, to have something colorful in this land of brown and ochre.

But perhaps the whole thing was too artificial to survive. These imported flowers, the roses, the snapdragons. Like me, she thinks, something artificial imported here.

She notices a locust crawling in the soil and she raises her foot, then brings it down hard on the insect, crushing and grinding the body into the earth with the sole of her sandal.

Tembi sees the pain on Märit's face as she surveys the damage, and the anger as she raises her foot and stamps it on the ground.

"Don't worry, Märit, things will grow again here. It is good soil."

"Is God trying to destroy us, Tembi? Does God hate us?"

Tembi shakes her head. "Look, the mulberry trees are untouched. God has spared us. You are too harsh in your thoughts."

Märit looks down at the soil, at the crushed insect, and then raises her eyes to survey the damage done by the swarm. "Once, a long time ago, I was on the other side of the fence, there beyond the koppie, when a kudu came right up to me, so close that I could feel its breath on my fingers, and I had the thought that nature is good, that animals are good, that there is an order and a harmony to nature. But now . . ." She shakes her head. "Now when I see what nature has done I wonder if there is any goodness or harmony in anything."

"We cannot understand everything that happens," Tembi says. "The locusts came because there was a hunger in the swarm, and they came to our farm because it was here. It could have been any farm, at any time. How could the locusts know we were here, and that we are struggling to live?"

"Oh, Tembi, I wish I had your wisdom. You are right. God has put goodness in us. He has put it in you."

Tembi smiles shyly and takes Märit's hand. "Come. Not everything has been destroyed."

Tembi walks away in the direction of the windmill and climbs up a few of the metal rungs. "Märit, the orchard! Come and look. Everything is still there."

Märit runs to join Tembi on the rungs of the ladder, both of them climbing as high as they can.

The fruit orchard is untouched, the rows of trees still with their leaves and the peaches and apricots hanging on the branches. But around the house there is only bare soil.

"As if we were singled out," Märit observes.

"No. It was just chance, and maybe because we had maize and flowers and green things that the locusts saw in their hunger. What happened was not against us."

"I suppose you are right."

Tembi nudges Märit's shoulder with her foot. "Of course I am right. Now go down, we have to clean the house."

The women spend the rest of the morning sweeping up the bodies of locusts from the rooms, many of them still alive and fluttering. Märit is filled with revulsion as she wields the broom and carries the bin of wriggling insects out to the fire pit.

Tembi mops the floors with soap and water and washes down the walls where insects have been crushed. Märit drags the burned cushions and rug out to the refuse heap. Later, wood has to be chopped and brought in from the shed.

In the afternoon the drizzle ceases and sun breaks through the cloud. Birds have descended on the fields, feeding on the remaining locusts.

As Märit sweeps the veranda, a distant movement catches her eye, something on the periphery of the farm. She peers in that direction for a moment but sees nothing and continues with her sweeping. An antelope probably, she thinks, but that quick glimpse has imprinted a human shape on her eye. Could it be Michael? she wonders. Does he still wander the land, somewhere on the edges? Or is it someone else? She and Tembi have been so completely alone on the farm that she has forgotten about neighbors, about the town. What is happening in the rest of the country? As she works through the afternoon she looks up often, and does not see that movement again. She convinces herself that what she saw was an antelope.

When the sun descends in the sky, when the shadows begin to lengthen, Tembi calls Märit in. As she goes up the steps of the veranda Märit turns one last time to look back to the borders of the farm, and sees something move in the stillness, something darting furtively out of sight. But so quick that once again after a moment of peering intently towards the trees she is not sure. She enters the house, where Tembi has lit the lamp in the kitchen and the fire burns warm in the stove.

Before retiring for the night Märit sits on the veranda for a while. The lamps have been extinguished, the stars flicker in the sky, the frogs croak down by the river, nearby the crickets chirrup with the same rhythm they take up every night.

We have come through, Märit thinks. The vegetables will grow again, there is still fruit in the trees, and in the storeroom there is still maize meal. We will survive.

She rises, breathes deeply of the night air, and stretches her arms above her head as a yawn overcomes her. And there in the darkness of the veldt a light flickers. Just once. A single point of light in the darkness of the night, like the flicker of a star, then gone.

She stands a long time staring into the darkness. She can't tell how near or how far that flicker of light appeared; whether it was the flare of a match or a flashlight, a vehicle or a lamp.

Is someone out there, watching the farm, watching them?

When she goes back into the house Märit makes sure that the front and back doors are bolted tight, and that the window catches are fastened in all the rooms. And that night her rest is troubled and her sleep is light, because she listens, and she thinks about the figure out there, the point of light in the darkness, and she knows that she and Tembi are not alone.

* * *

In the morning, Tembi appears in the bedroom doorway. "Märit, there is no water."

Märit sits up, groggy, tired from an unsettled night. "No water? What do you mean?"

"There is no water from the taps."

Märit rises from the bed. "What is it now?" she says. "What else can go wrong?"

"There is no water from the kitchen taps, nothing from the yard tap either. I don't know why."

In the bathroom Märit turns on the sink taps, then those in the tub. A few spurts of water gush from the faucet and then cease with a shuddering of the pipes. "It must be the windmill, the pump or something. We'll have to take a look." She rubs her face wearily. "Is there any coffee?"

Tembi shakes her head. "Without water I can't make coffee."

"All right, I'll get dressed."

The vanes of the windmill are turning as usual in the light breeze, each revolving blade of metal catching the morning light with a brief reflected flash.

"It turns but there is no water," Tembi says.

Märit stands with her hands on her hips looking up at the windmill. "It seems to be working all right up there. It must be the pump. Did you check the tap in the kraal?"

"Not yet," Tembi says.

"Well, let's look at the pump first," Märit says, moving towards the small shed at the base of the windmill where the pump is housed.

After a moment of studying the pipes and valves and rods, she shakes her head. "I've no idea how any of this works. Do you?"

"I don't know anything about machines."

"Go and see if the tap in the kraal is working. I'll try and figure this out."

None of the metal parts that make up the pump mechanism are moving except for the long rod that extends upwards to the vanes. Märit traces its passage into the pump, trying to understand which wheel turns which cog. She finds the pipe that carries the water up from the ground and leads out of the pump house. But in between this pipe and the windmill is a bit of intricate machinery housed inside a bolted cover.

When Tembi returns with the information that the kraal tap is not functioning either, Märit taps the pump housing and says, "The problem is in here, I think. Maybe we can open it."

Märit tries the nuts and discovers that they turn easily, with just a touch of her fingers, as if someone has recently unfastened them. When she gets the cover off she sees immediately that a thin copper rod between two cogwheels has snapped in two.

"That's the problem. The solution is another matter. I don't know where we will find a replacement part, or how we will fit it together. Unless we go to Klipspring."

Tembi shakes her head. "We don't need the pump. We can fetch water from the river. We can wash in the river and bring our drinking water back in buckets."

Märit stands up and dusts her hands clean. She takes a last look at the pump mechanism before replacing the housing cover. Somewhere on the farm she will find a piece of metal, and somehow find a way to fit it in place of the broken rod. Yes, she can bathe in the river, and they can bring drinking water up to the house, but without the pump there is no way to irrigate, and there will be no way to grow vegetables again.

With two buckets each, they make their way down to the river and return more slowly to the house with heavier loads. The water is poured into basins and kettles.

"Shall we make coffee now or fetch another load?" Märit asks.

"You make the coffee, I'll fetch more water."

"No, we'll do one more together."

This time when they return, the buckets are emptied into the bathtub.

"I think we have enough for now," Märit says.

"Yes, we can get some more later."

When they have eaten their breakfast and drunk their coffee the two women make a third trip to the river. Halfway to the house Märit sets down her buckets and flexes her shoulders. "I'm aching already."

"We will have to get used to this."

"I know." But she resolves to try to fix the pump later. She will not let this latest setback defeat her.

42

Märit is in the kitchen preparing a cup of tea when she sees Tembi walking past the window with a red plastic pail in her hand.

Märit opens the window and calls out, "I'm making tea. Do you want some?"

"Later."

"Where are you going?"

"To the river." She raises the red pail.

"Don't we have enough water for now?"

"Just one more," Tembi says. Just one for her garden.

Märit carries her cup through to the living room and eases her aching body into an armchair. The carrying of the buckets together with her lack of sleep in the night has left her very weary. She shuts her eyes, dozing, her cup of tea forgotten, weariness overcoming her.

A shape appears in the doorway, a silhouette dark against the outside glare, waking Märit.

"Tembi?"

The figure steps into the room. A man.

The sudden fright brings her out of the chair. "Who are you?" she exclaims in a sharp, alarmed voice. "What do you want?"

He steps farther into the room and she shrinks back from him.

"What do you want?" Märit cries, squinting against the light to see his face.

"*Ek soek werk*, Missus." It is the phrase that every wanderer uses when accosted by a landowner, by an official. It is what every black person in an unaccustomed place says when questioned by a white person in this country—I'm looking for work.

"Work? There is no work here."

He takes another step into the room; Märit retreats, but still blocks his way. He is visible to her now—a young man, slim, with ropy muscles in his arms, dressed in a checked shirt, quite new, and a pair of khaki trousers.

He studies the room, trying to see into the rest of the house over Märit's shoulder. His eyes have an alert, inquisitive look.

Märit is frightened of him, but her fear makes her bold.

"Don't you know to knock when you come to a house?"

"No, I knocked, Missus. Maybe you didn't hear me." He smiles at her, white teeth bright against his smooth, dark face.

She knows without doubt that he is the one she saw yesterday, the quick darting movement out there on the veldt. He has been watching the house, and now he has come.

"Well, you should knock louder. What do you want?"

"Like I said, Missus, I'm looking for work, here on this farm."

"There is no work here. I told you. We don't need anyone." She takes a step towards him, her tone resolute, trying to force him to step back, because she is afraid of him, of his insolent smile, and her fear makes her determined. But he does not step back. He looks around the room again with his earnest curiosity, and he smiles at her again, confident, almost mocking, so that she is aware that her boldness and her authority mean nothing to him. He knows she is alone.

"I'm noticing, Missus, that there is nobody working on the fields in this farm. Nothing is growing. I see that the locusts have been here. There is nobody cleaning up around the place. I can do these things. I can help you do these things."

"We don't need help. The Baas does what needs to be done."

"Only I'm not seeing the Baas. I don't see him."

"He is in town, with the field boys. They will be back soon. He will tell you that we don't need any help."

"I don't see anybody for a long time, Missus. There is no smoke from the kraal; I don't see the men in the fields. No cattle. Where are they? I ask myself. No, I don't see them. I'm thinking you are alone on this farm. You are needing my help."

How many days has he been watching the farm? she wonders.

He steps farther into the room, no longer on the threshold, crossing a line, and she can't prevent herself recoiling from him. She smells him now, the smell of countryside, of wood smoke, of sweat, of the dust of travel. And she cannot help but shrink away from him.

He smiles again, confident. "You are alone."

She darts her eyes towards the office. The shotgun is there, above the cupboard. How many steps will it take to reach the gun? But is it loaded? She can't remember if she replaced the cartridges after she fired at Joshua.

The stranger follows her glance, attentive, curious.

Her heart is racing and she tries to keep her voice from shaking. "You must leave at once. Don't you know that you'll have trouble if they find you here?"

"Trouble?"

"The police. The soldiers. They are here all the time looking for people."

A slight frown of doubt flickers across his face. "I'm not seeing any soldiers. For a long time. I think they have gone also."

"No, they were here just the other day. They took the workers away. They shot a man."

He considers this news, regarding her with a suspicion that pinches his face, and he suddenly looks very young to Märit, a boy only.

But then he shakes his head impatiently, and his voice changes, and there is an edge of menace in his voice.

"This is a big farm, maybe you have something for me?"

Not a question, but a demand. And the threat beneath it, the implication that he can take what he wants.

Is it money that he wants? She restrains the impulse to look towards the office again, where the last of the money is hidden. Should she give him some money and send him on his way? But what is to stop him taking it all, taking everything? Where is Tembi? Should she call for Tembi?

"There is nothing here. You can see that. It's a poor farm."

"I am hungry. You can give me something to eat, Missus."

In normal times she would say, Yes, go round to the kitchen and I will tell the cook to give you something. But those times are over. He knows it as well as she does.

"Anything," the stranger says. "A sip of tea. I am thirsty, I have walked a long way."

"Where do you come from?"

A jerk of his chin over his shoulder. "That way."

Anywhere, everywhere.

"All right," she relents. "All right, I'll find something for you to eat. But then you have to go, you can't stay. The police are always here, looking for people. They could come at any time."

He looks past Märit at a sound from the corridor behind her. She spins around. Oh God, she thinks, there is more than one of them! Images flash through her mind—of the worst that can happen to a woman trapped alone in a house by desperate strangers.

The figure in the corridor materializes as Tembi. Märit's knees almost buckle with relief. "Tembi!"

Tembi looks from Märit, alarmed at her almost pitiful cry, and to the young stranger, who now smiles at her and raises an open palm.

"*Sawubona*, sister. I greet you."

He speaks rapidly to her, leaning forward, but his language is unfamiliar to Tembi; it is a language from the north, which she does not understand. She replies in her own language, asking him where he has come from, and what his name is. But he shakes his head. He does not understand her.

"He speaks English," Märit says.

"Yes, we can speak English," he says. "I am Khoza." He extends his hand to Tembi.

When he turns to Märit, she pointedly puts her hands in her pockets.

Tembi frowns at her. "And this is Märit."

He holds out his hand, waiting, smiling faintly, until Märit has no choice but to shake it.

"Where are you coming from, Khoza?" Tembi asks.

"I have walked from Swartkloof, from across the border."

"Such a long way! And where do you go?"

"Anywhere. Away from the war." He seems just a boy now, no threat or menace in him—just another wanderer.

"I was just going to give him some food," Märit interrupts. "To take with him. Before the soldiers come back."

"What soldiers?" Tembi asks. "The soldiers have been again?"

"They could come back at any time."

"I haven't seen any soldiers for a long time now, Missus," Khoza says. "You don't have to worry. There are no soldiers in this district."

"They could come back at any time," she repeats. "We will make you up some food for your journey."

"But he can't go back out there if the soldiers are around," Tembi objects. "Did you see soldiers today, Märit?"

Märit pushes past them towards the kitchen. "Come and get your food," she calls to the young man. Tembi hurries after her.

In the kitchen Tembi moves the kettle over the burner and throws a couple of pieces of coal into the stove, then stokes up the fire.

Märit brings rusks and jam from the pantry. "I don't want him in the house longer than is necessary."

"I can do it," Tembi says, grabbing the plates from her.

Märit shrugs. "Suit yourself." She sits down at the table.

Khoza leans in the doorway. "You have a cigarette for me, Missus Märit?"

His voice has a slight insolence. He is aware that a rift has opened between the two women, and he is aware that he is the cause.

Märit slides the cigarette package across the table. He takes one and bows slightly to her.

"Can you give me a match, Missus?"

Tembi turns and looks at them, sensing the tension. "You don't have to say 'Missus' all the time."

Märit slides matches across the table. Khoza lights his cigarette and blows out a stream of smoke. "Thank you, Märit."

Tembi sets out a plate with rusks and a sliced apple. "Please sit, Khoza. I'm sorry, we don't have much."

When he sits, Märit moves to stand at the counter.

Tembi sits across from him as he eats hungrily. He devours the rusks in a couple of bites and she sets out more for him. And when he has eaten the apple, she fetches another one from the bowl and slices it onto his plate.

"Thank you, Tembi," he says courteously. "I have been hungry these past days."

She smiles at him, and Märit sees that she is flattered by his courtesy. "What is happening out there? What have you seen?"

"There is war."

"Where? What kind of war? Have you been near the town—Klip-spring?"

He shrugs and avoids her eye. "Everywhere it's the same. War."

"Are there people in the town, on the farms?"

"There are no people. That is why I am coming here, Missus." He looks up at Märit. "Because I am hungry and thirsty." He says this with a kind of pleading in his voice, and she sees the boy in his face again, the boy masquerading as a man. When he looks at Märit there is something impudent in his grin, as if he knows that she cannot tell him to leave now.

His presence in the room is an affront to Märit. She does not want him here with her and Tembi. She does not trust him, because she remembers the way he looked around the room when he first came into the house, and she remembers the way he came in on silent feet, and the way he talked to her, almost with a threat in his voice. She does not want a stranger in her house.

When he has finished eating he wipes his mouth with the back of his hand and tilts his head back to drain the last of his tea. Both women watch the working of his smooth brown throat as he swallows.

Tembi glances quickly at Märit, then rises to gather the plates and cup and carry them to the sink.

"I can wash those," Khoza says, jumping to his feet and taking the plate from her hands. He turns the taps on over the sink. The faucets gurgle.

Märit moves away slightly. "There is no water," she says. "You have to use the water in the bucket."

"Why don't you have water?" he asks.

"We do. We bring it up from the river."

"No, but you don't have water in the taps."

"Something is broken in the pump," Tembi interjects. She points out the window. "There in the windmill. The pump isn't working so the water doesn't come out of the taps here."

Khoza steps over to the window. "I can fix that. I know machines. I can fix that for you." He turns back to them. "Then you won't have to go to the river."

"Don't bother yourself," Märit says. "It's no trouble for us to go to the river for water."

"No, but I can fix it for you. You have given me food and now I can do something for you."

"Come on," Tembi says to him. "I'll show you where the pump is." She glares at Märit, offended at her evident rudeness, and goes out with Khoza.

43

FROM THE WINDOW Märit watches the two figures at the base of the windmill.

The young man turns and points at the house and Tembi nods. Are they talking about her? Märit wonders. He puts his hand on Tembi's shoulder for a moment. Märit can almost see his smile, the insolent smile when directed at her, but now charming when he turns to Tembi. He leans closer to Tembi and says something to her, and they both look up at the house. Märit scowls and steps back from the window.

When Tembi enters the kitchen, Märit turns her back, pretending to be busy with the dishes.

"He says he needs some tools. A wrench and a hammer."

"Why?"

"He is going to fix the pump for us. Don't you want that?"

Märit shrugs. "There are tools in the generator shed. On the bench by the door. And see if he can fix the generator too if he is such a genius."

As Tembi turns to leave, Märit rushes over and grabs her arm. "I don't want him here!"

"But why not?"

"Why is he here? What is he doing wandering the countryside on his own? You don't know who he is. Or what he wants."

"Does he want anything?"

"He's probably on the run from some trouble that he's got into."

"If he is in trouble then we should help him."

"I don't trust him. I think he's been watching the house the past few days. I've seen someone."

Tembi looks at Märit disbelievingly. "Why do you say this now?"

"I didn't want to worry you before. It was for your sake, Tembi."

"And you said that the soldiers had been. Did you see any soldiers?"

"He cannot stay in this house, so don't invite him."

"Why not? There is room—that small room where the sewing machine is. You can put a bed in there."

"No. If he wants to stay then he can sleep in the kraal."

"Why are you like this, Märit? You were kind to Michael."

"That was different. I don't trust this Khoza."

Tembi shakes her head and slams the door as she leaves.

Märit watches from the window, sees Tembi bringing him the tools, and the familiar way he puts his hand on her shoulder again. The girl standing there ready to hand the man the tools—patient, helpful. And when Tembi hands him the tools, Märit imagines the touching of their hands.

Oh, he is a sly one, she thinks. He knows exactly what he is doing. Of course Tembi will side with him, against her. Tembi will trust him, will treat him as a familiar.

She watches as he crouches at the machinery of the pump, and Tembi leans over him, resting her hand on his back as she peers forward.

Why should Tembi not trust him? After all, she only sees his smile, not the sly darting glances around the room when he first entered the house, not the silent way he sneaked in. Nor did she hear the veiled threat in his voice when he asked for food.

A sudden hissing sound behind her makes Märit jump. The taps above the sink give a splutter and gurgle, then water gushes out the faucet. From the pump house a shout of triumph sounds across the yard.

The stream of water from the tap is silty brown, with the faint smell of iron, but in a moment it runs clear, and Märit puts her hands into the flow, into the cool, earth-deep flow, and she scoops the water onto her face, glad to have the cool, sweet water again.

Despite her mistrust of Khoza she is glad to have the water again, glad not to have to carry buckets from the river and to boil the river water before drinking it. She is glad not to have to clean herself in the river, or wash her clothes in the river. But she resents him still, as she hears the laughter and the triumph in his voice as he returns to the house, laughing with Tembi. Even though he has brought the water back she resents him.

He walks in laughing, proud. "You see, Märit," he exclaims, pointing to the flowing taps. "I can fix it. I told you."

She resents his pride, his boasting, and she cannot bring herself to thank him. And when he moves towards the sink, she steps away from him.

Khoza plunges his hands into the flow of water. "See!" he exclaims. "Aren't you happy now?"

Märit shrugs.

"You should be," Tembi mutters. "You should be glad."

"I am," she answers grudgingly, then turns to Khoza. "Where did you learn your skills with machinery?"

"I have been to school. Technical apprentice."

"And where was that?"

"In another place." He laughs, reaching for a glass, which he holds under the tap before raising it to his mouth. When he drinks, tilting back his head, a thin stream of water trickles along his chin and down his smooth, upturned throat.

Märit looks away, offended by the vitality and the health that emanates from him, offended by the vigorous male life in him. She does not want to acknowledge him. She leaves the room.

Later, in the coolness of the dusk, she wanders aimlessly through the orchard, asking herself how things are going to change now, for she knows they will change. But she finds no answer and eventually walks back up to the house. She does not enter but sits in the wicker rocking chair on the veranda.

Night is coming, another day ending. Swallows dip and dart in the air like bits of shadow themselves, feeding on the insects hovering in the fading light.

She senses rather than sees when Tembi comes to stand in the open doorway. After a while Märit turns and looks at her but cannot gauge Tembi's expression in the fading light.

"Where is your friend?" Märit says.

"He is working again on the pump. It needs more fixing."

"Did you ask him about the generator?"

"He looked at it. He will try to fix it tomorrow."

"I suppose that means he is going to sleep here tonight."

"And why not?" Tembi says.

"He can sleep in the kraal."

"No, we have room enough here. Khoza can sleep in the house."

"Tembi, I don't trust him."

"If it was one of your neighbors, would you turn them away? If it was one of your people from the town?"

"You know that's not what I mean. It's not about his color. I just don't want any more trouble here. For us."

"Then don't make any trouble where there is none." She swings away, and Märit slumps back into her chair with a sigh of defeat.

Dinner is maize porridge, carrots, and canned beef. Märit prepares the meal. She counts the few remaining cans on the shelf. Soon there will be none. And now another mouth to feed.

"Can I help you, Märit?" Tembi asks, poking her head through the door, her tone conciliatory.

"You can peel the carrots, please. Where is Khoza?"

"I think he is on the veranda."

"You should call him in for dinner."

"Märit?"

"Yes."

"You mustn't worry about him. He is not a bad person. He is here because he has nothing. He is like Michael, lost. It's not so hard to be nice to him, is it?"

"I suppose you are right, Tembi." She smiles wanly, resolving not to let her anxiety get the better of her. "It just makes me nervous to have someone else in the house. I'm not used to it. Go and call him to dinner now."

"WHERE DID YOU GROW UP, Khoza?" Märit asks as they sit at the table. "What is your home language?"

"I speak Shona."

"But your English is very good."

"I have had some schooling. I have worked at many jobs. I have been to a lot of places. I know many things."

"What sort of things?" Märit says, unable to keep an edge of sarcasm out of her voice.

"You ask me a lot of questions, Märit." He pushes his chair back and carries his mug to the sink.

"I'm just curious."

Later, before she retires to her room, Märit says to Tembi, "You can make up a bed for him in the sewing room. There is a folding cot in the cupboard." She locks her door. Just before she blows out her candle she rises from the bed and presses her ear to the door, listening to the low murmur of Khoza's voice and the soft laughter of Tembi. She makes sure the door is locked, then blows out the candle.

KHOZA IS AT THE STOVE, an apron tied around his waist, when Märit enters the kitchen.

"Good morning, Märit! You have slept well? Tea is ready."

She nods at him, not particularly pleased at this image of domesticity, and leans over to see what he is cooking. Six eggs are jostling in a pot of boiling water.

"Eggs! Where were you able to get eggs?"

"I saw a chicken in the bushes, I followed her, I found her nest." He points at the pot. "And I found eggs for you."

"An ordinary chicken? Not something wild?"

"Just a hen like you find on any farm. But I see that you don't keep any chickens on this farm."

"We did have some. They were all killed by some kind of animal." For a moment she looks at him suspiciously. Could he be responsible for killing the chickens? But then she dismisses the thought from her mind. It happened ages ago. If Khoza had been lurking around the farm back then he would have shown himself much sooner. Her suspicion brings back a memory of looking at the windmill pump and finding the workings loose, recently unscrewed. Could he have staged the whole thing, broken the pump, and then repaired it to ingratiate himself here?

Märit pours herself tea. "So cooking is another one of your talents?"

"There are many things I can do. You need a houseboy on this farm, Missus? I can do everything."

"No, we don't need a houseboy."

Tembi appears in the doorway, bleary-eyed. "Good morning," she mumbles, and yawns. When she reaches up to cover her mouth, her morning robe falls open, revealing a glimpse of smooth belly and the roundness of one breast.

Khoza's eyes are quick to notice, Märit observes. How long, she wonders, did they stay up last night, talking together? How late did Tembi sit up flirting with this stranger who comes from nowhere?

"Can't you dress before coming to breakfast, Tembi?" Märit remarks.

Tembi yawns again and looks at Märit uncomprehendingly. "Breakfast is ready," Khoza says. "Sit down, Tembi, my sister. I have made you breakfast."

Tembi looks pleased, and flattered, as he brings her a plate of rusks and eggs, then pours her a cup of tea. He sets a second plate in front of Märit.

They eat breakfast in silence, Khoza looking from Tembi to Märit with his eager glance. "The eggs are good?" he asks.

"Very good," Tembi answers. Märit merely nods.

When she has finished, Märit gathers the plates and cups and carries them to the sink. Khoza springs up and take them from her hands. "I can wash these for you."

"I'll do it myself." She is determined to resist him. "If you are so keen to do something then you can help us in the garden," she tells him. "You did say you were looking for work, didn't you?"

"Yes, Missus. I am looking for a job."

"Now that the pump is running again we can make sure that the vegetable garden gets water. And the irrigation ditches have to be cleared again. We have to undo the damage that the locusts did. I'm sure you know how to do garden work. And our generator, it's broken."

"Of course, Märit. I can fix it. I can do everything."

"You'd better get dressed now, Tembi. We all have to work."

44

THERE IS ALWAYS work to be done on a farm, even a farm as diminished as this one. The land will not feed even three people without constant attention. The vegetable garden must be reconstituted, more seeds must be planted. The dried cattle manure in the fields has to be gathered as fertilizer; fallen branches must be collected for firewood; the mealies in the storage shed must be set out in the sun to dry so that the kernels can be ground into flour for porridge. And now that the water runs again from the pump, the irrigation ditches have to be maintained so that the water can feed the plants.

"Have you looked at the generator?" Märit asks Khoza when he appears later. "Can you fix it?"

"No. The alternator coil is burned out. It must be replaced. Something like that cannot be fixed. Even I cannot fix it." He spreads his hands apologetically.

"Never mind, we don't need it. There is lots of paraffin for the lamps. And we have candles. It's more important to get the vegetables growing again."

Khoza is adept with the spade and the hoe. He works quickly and methodically, faster than both women. Märit increases the tempo of her labors, determined not to be outdone.

The day progresses, the sun rises higher in a cloudless sky, the heat beats down on the three people with a steady, relentless intensity. Märit loses herself in the motions of her labor, in the repetitive actions, the growing heat, the sense of nothing else existing except this patch of land where she shovels and digs. The sweat trickles down her face, a white haze seems to surround her, the landscape disappears.

The sound of Khoza's spade comes to her through the white haze, and she matches her own motions to his, trying to surpass him. If he works hard, she will work harder. She will not let him have even a small victory over her.

The sweat runs into her eyes, stinging, and she shakes her head, rubbing her forehead across her upper arm. When she raises her eyes the sun is there, a white-hot disk beating down. Her throat is dry, aching. Dizziness suddenly overcomes her so that she drops her hoe and sinks to her knees. The earth seems to spin beneath her feet and she has to put her palms on the ground to still the motion.

She looks up and sees that Khoza has taken off his shirt and is leaning on his hoe looking into the distance. His face is lost in shadow.

Tembi stands some yards away, a slack, dazed look on her face, her mouth half open. The heat is unbearable.

Khoza seems unaffected by the heat, although the sweat shines on his skin. Everything centers on him now, Märit realizes. His presence is at the core of their awareness. He stands, seemingly unaware of them, in the heart of the white haze of heat. A gleam of perspiration shines in the narrow channel down the middle of his back, following the contour of his spine, and disappears beneath the waistband of his trousers.

Märit wipes the sweat away from her eyes and squints at the man standing in the sun. She sees him in the abstract, not as Khoza, but only as a man, his body bared, the thin gleam of moisture trickling down his spine, shining on the brown skin. She forgets who he is and sees only a man, and he is beautiful to her, a thing of beauty.

The sweat blurs her vision and stings her eyes, and she sees the dark shape of the young man standing in the center of the world with his skin shining. The same way that Dollar's skin glistened when he came out of the pool, when she was a girl, when she touched his skin and he smelled of mimosa.

Märit wipes her dusty hand across her eyes, and she smells mimosa blossom in the air and she sees the naked man.

Turning her head slowly in the white haze that surrounds her, Märit looks at Tembi. Tembi too is gazing at Khoza as if mesmerized. Then she shifts her eyes and they meet Märit's. Something unspoken passes between the two women—a knowledge of themselves as women, defined by their relation to the man. They see the knowledge of his nakedness in each other's eyes.

Then Tembi lays down her shovel, and goes to the man, and says to him, "Are you thirsty? I will fetch some water."

He turns to her, and his eyes focus and become aware of her, and he nods.

"I will fetch you some water," Tembi says, touching his arm. As she steps away, it seems to Märit that Tembi's hand trails across Khoza's back—a brief touch, almost casual. But a touch. She does not look at Märit as she walks past.

Märit struggles to her feet and wields her hoe energetically, hacking at the weeds with fury, the blade of the hoe ringing on the cement of the irrigation ditch. Cicadas buzz in the long, dry grass—a piercing, grating sound, like metal grinding on metal. The noise fills her head, the serrated legs of the insects rubbing against each other like the teeth of a saw, teeth meshing on metallic teeth. The sun strikes the blade of the hoe as she wields it against the earth. Light hammers on steel, a steady hammering that pulses with the beat of the blood in her head. Around her the landscape shimmers and bends and tilts. The figure of the man at the center of it. The heat of his skin, the stickiness of the perspiration, her fingertip touching the sweat. And somewhere the scent of mimosa.

Märit turns her head up to the white sky and sees its emptiness descending upon her. She succumbs to it, sinking to her knees, bowing her head to the ground. Then the world tilts and the white sky strikes her flat, so that she falls, and tastes the bitterness that is in her mouth.

Märit smells mimosa. There is a pool of blue water, and the mimosa blossoms surrounding it, and from the blue depths of the water the man's face surfaces.

"Märit, Märit!" he calls to her from the cool, blue water, with his laughing eyes.

She lifts her head to go to him, but the haze envelops her and she falls back into the dry heat.

He lifts his hands and cups the water for her. "Drink."

The liquid touches her lips and spills over, and his fingers brush away the spill and touch her lips, and his palm is cool against her lips.

"Please," Märit says, appealing to him as the haze descends upon her.

Khoza and Tembi carry Märit into the house and lay her down in her bedroom. Tembi draws the curtains shut to block out the daylight, throwing the room into shadow. She fetches a bowl of cool water and a cloth, and sits next to Märit, bathing her face gently with the cool water.

"Bring me a glass of water," she whispers to Khoza.

He cradles Märit's head, lifting it slightly, and she sips the water, then moans and falls back. Tembi smoothes the damp cloth across Märit's fevered brow.

"Is she sick?" Khoza asks quietly.

"Too much sun," Tembi murmurs. "She must rest indoors, away from the sun."

In the white-hot light, in the long, dry grass, the cicadas shrill, like metal beating on metal, and somewhere, the smell of mimosa lingers.

MÄRIT WAKES and glances at the bedside clock. Nine o'clock. Experiencing a moment of confusion at the hour, she draws aside the curtains and sees the sun in the east, not overhead where it had been. She remembers fainting. But how long has she slept? She is dazed, but curiously alert to her surroundings, and very hungry. In the kitchen she finds fruit, rusks, cold mealie-pap, and she eats ravenously. There is tea in the pot.

Khoza is on the veranda, lounging in the rocker with his feet up on the railing, when Märit comes out with her cup. She feels a tremor move across her skin at the sight of him, a strange pang of apprehension and anticipation.

"Where is Tembi?" she asks.

He makes a lazy gesture with his arm. Märit sits down in the farthest chair.

"You are better?" he asks after a moment. "You slept a long time."

"Yes."

"Too much sun." He chuckles. "Your skin is the wrong color for the African sun. Maybe you should wear a hat."

She looks away from him and sips her tea.

"You like that tea, Märit? I made it for you."

"It's fine."

"But I didn't make any breakfast for you."

"I'm perfectly capable of making my own."

"Yes." He sits in silence for a while, turning his head every so often to look at her. She does not look back. Then he says, "Soon there will be no more food. Just mealie-pap and what you have in tins."

"In that case I will go to Klipspring and find some more."

"No, you won't find anything there."

"Why not?"

He turns the corners of his mouth down. "The people who lived there, they took all their food with them when they left. Everything. From the shops, from the houses."

"You were there? Why did they leave? What's happened?"

"Too close to the war. So everybody is leaving."

The news frightens her, even though she has suspected something all along from the total absence of a single visitor all these months. An image comes to her mind of the church in Klipspring, and the graveyard where Ben is buried, now abandoned, weeds growing, the town deserted. Except for the wanderers—like Michael, and Khoza.

"I can find you food," Khoza says.

"How?"

"I can hunt. For meat. With your gun."

"My gun?"

"Every farm has a gun. You can give me yours." He smiles at her now, the insolent smile that says he knows her. "There are antelope out there in the bush. I can go and shoot a *rooibok* if I have a gun."

"There is still lots of mealie meal, and fruit."

"A man needs meat. And a gun."

"You know about guns?"

He extends a finger at her. "Bang, bang."

"Is that something else you learned in school?"

The smile drops from his face. "You still want to know about my life, Märit? You want to know about life across the border? You want to know about the freedom fighters and the war?"

"Oh, are you going to tell me now that you are a freedom fighter? Is it something heroic like that?"

"Fighting for the land—to take it back. All of it. Even this farm here."

Märit sneers. "Why aren't you off fighting for freedom now?"

He gives a knowing nod. "I was trained. Many people have died already."

"At your hands?" she asks. "My husband was killed not that long ago. By terrorists. Saboteurs. You know that word? They put a bomb in the road and when his car drove over it he was blown to pieces. I suppose some freedom fighter put it there. Someone who was trained. They probably didn't even see who they killed. It could have been a busload of children, or a group of workers being taken to the fields. Anyone, really. Luckily it turned out to be a farmer, one Afrikaaner less! Isn't that what they say, your freedom fighters—one bullet, one Boer?"

Khoza says nothing.

"Is that what you were trained in?" Märit asks. After a moment she adds, "I don't think you were trained in anything. You probably stole something from your last employer and had to run away. And now it's easier for you to come and live off two women."

In one swift movement he swings his feet off the railing and springs to his feet, advancing on her with clenched fists. His look is murderous.

Märit flinches, but does not move from her chair.

Then he laughs. "You want to make the black man angry, eh, Missus? Be careful, he is angry enough." He collapses back into his chair, relaxing his legs on the railing again.

Märit leaves him sitting there and walks through to the office, where she retrieves a key from the back of the drawer and unlocks the cupboard. The yellow box of cartridges is on the top shelf. Märit takes out the shotgun from the back of the cupboard and counts out three cartridges. One to miss, one to hit, one to make sure.

Khoza looks up as Märit steps out onto the veranda with the gun in her hands. His eyes widen, because the long barrels are pointing straight at him. He swivels his upper body to face her and grips the armrests of the chair, but remains seated.

Märit stops about six feet away and points the weapon at Khoza. Where is your smile now? she wants to say. You think you can come here and have this farm? On your feet, she could say, and go back to wherever it is you came from.

Her face is cold, hard, and he sees the intent in her eyes. The fear is visible on his face. Perhaps he has gambled on her and lost.

Märit feels it would take nothing to shoot him. One gesture, one word. She could shoot him for Ben. She is ready, poised, calm, like an ax ready to fall.

She waits for him to prompt her, to give her a reason to shoot.

The fear in his face is naked, because he sees the intent behind her eyes.

Märit sees his fear, the fear of a boy who has blustered that he is a man, and has failed at his gamble. She sees the boy who has left his home and wanders across the veldt, a stranger. With an abrupt gesture she swings the barrels upright and thrusts the gun towards Khoza. He jerks away from her.

"Take it," she says. "You wanted a gun. Take it."

He reaches for the gun, gingerly at first, looking up at her. He sights along the barrel, aiming out across the veldt, then slowly swings the gun around to point at Märit.

This is a different story, she thinks, with a different ending.

"Is it loaded?" he asks, the beginning of a sly smile spreading across his face.

"What do you think?"

His finger curls around the trigger. "I don't think it's loaded."

"Try it and see."

Khoza studies her over the barrel. Märit waits. He is unsure of her now.

"You would have shot me?" he asks.

Märit smiles finally, and opens her hand, revealing the three cartridges in her palm. Khoza blinks and squeezes the trigger, and the hammer falls with a click that makes them both flinch.

Märit lets the cartridges fall into Khoza's lap. "Go and see what you can kill with these."

"Only three?"

"One for each of us. You said you were a crack shot."

He loads the cartridges into the shotgun and sights down the barrel again, then pats the stock with his hand, and beams at her like a boy with a new plaything. "I will bring us meat. You will see, Märit."

He shoulders the gun and steps off the veranda.

Märit watches him go. This is what it is now, she thinks—a young man hurrying across the veldt with a gun on his shoulder. This is how the landscape will look from now on.

45

ALL MORNING Märit listens. Is he out there hunting? She has not heard any shots. Perhaps he will not come back. Perhaps she has seen the last of him. Now that he has his gun, he can run off and join whatever ragtag army he can find.

She feels vaguely disappointed by this notion, in a way that she cannot quite reconcile with her feelings of hostility towards Khoza. After all, she wants him to be gone. Yet she feels a little abandoned, suddenly aware of how much impact his presence has.

Is it because he is a man, and they are women? she wonders. A man on a farm seems natural, but she doesn't want a man here. The farm belongs to her, her and Tembi.

"Where is Khoza?" she hears Tembi call.

"Why does it matter to you where he is?" Märit answers, without being able to keep an edge of resentment from her voice. She knows why she speaks this way, even though she would deny it. It is because Tembi has put her hand on the gleaming skin of the naked man, and because she has asked after him.

"Why should it not matter?" Tembi says, giving Märit a puzzled look.

"He's gone."

"You sent him away? Why did you do that? Is this farm not big enough for the three of us?"

"Why are you so quick to take sides against me now, Tembi?"

"You don't like him. You show it."

"It's quite obvious how much *you* like him."

Their eyes meet, and that secret knowledge is there again between them. Märit sees a flicker of hostility in Tembi's eyes.

"I didn't send him away. He went off by himself."

"I don't believe you."

"He asked for the gun, to go hunting. I gave it to him and he went into the veldt."

Tembi turns and scans the distance. She gives Märit a distrustful look. "Where? Why did you let him go alone?"

"He said he was going to hunt and bring us some meat. But I wouldn't be surprised if he doesn't come back. Now he has his gun, what is there here for him?"

"He will come back."

"For you? Is that what you hope?"

"Because there is no other place for him."

"What do you know about him? Has he told you anything about himself?"

"He doesn't like it if you ask him questions. He doesn't tell you things if you ask him."

"Do you trust him? I know you like him, but do you trust him?" Märit softens her voice. "Tell me honestly."

Tembi shrugs and chews on her thumbnail. "I don't know . . . He is nice . . . I think he is good. Maybe he doesn't tell us about himself because he is ashamed. Maybe he has come here because he was frightened . . . you know, with the war out there. He can't tell us he is frightened because we are women and he is a man. It is shameful for a man to ask women for shelter." She nods. "He is lost in himself. I think that is why he is here."

"Oh, Tembi. I worry about what will happen between us now, if he stays on the farm. It won't be the same. I worry that he is the kind of man who will not be satisfied until he has power over you and me. And now he has the gun. Guns always give men some illusion of power. They want to use it. I worry that he will use you, that he will be against me, and against the farm. He wants this farm."

Tembi ponders this, her brow wrinkling, looking at Märit with a certain

293

distrust. Then she gives a decisive shake of her head. "No, Khoza is not like that."

"I know you like him," Märit continues. "Do you want him to come back?"

She sees a kind of longing in Tembi's expression, a hope. "Maybe you are falling in love with him. Just a bit. Hmm?"

Tembi turns away, offended.

A thought occurs to Märit and she says, "You haven't been with him, have you?"

"What do you mean?"

"Did you sleep in your own bed last night?"

Tembi swings around, her face angry. "Is it for you to ask me that? Maybe you are the one that wants him. I saw how you looked at him yesterday. I am not just a stupid girl. You want him too. Just like you want everything. This farm, this country. You want to be the boss of Khoza. And of me. Maybe you want *me* to leave the farm!"

"That's not true! Who has put these ideas in your head?"

Tembi moves away from Märit, hunching her shoulders. "You can't be the boss of anything anymore. Nobody has to ask you for anything on this farm. You are just one person, like Khoza, like me. If he wants to stay here then he can stay. And if you want to go, then you can go."

Märit hears in Tembi's words a denial of everything they have both struggled for. She has given up so much already, but it is not enough. There will be more to give up. Perhaps she will have to give up everything.

"Tembi, this is not the way for us to speak to each other. After everything that's happened, this is the wrong path for us. I'm sorry if I doubted you. We have to remain friends. Whatever happens." Märit reaches across and takes Tembi's hand in her own. "If Khoza returns, we must not let him come between us. Promise me that."

"I don't know . . . we were better friends before. Now . . . I don't know." She shakes her head slowly and looks out over the veldt. "Maybe he won't come back, then." Her voice trembles slightly, betraying two conflicting hopes.

A shot echoes across the veldt. The doves in the bluegum trees take flight.

"Where did it come from?" Tembi asks eagerly, almost with relief. She pulls her hand loose from Märit's clasp and moves away a few steps. "Do you see him?"

A second shot sounds from near the koppie. The doves wheel and flutter. The women hear a shout, a distant cry of triumph.

Tembi starts forward towards the voice, shading her eyes against the sun.

Märit lets her go. The moment is lost, the outcome is undecided.

The silhouette of Khoza appears on the koppie. He raises one arm, brandishing the rifle, and hails the women. The hunter, victorious.

Märit follows Tembi, slowly, walking towards something that she knows will bring no joy in the end. But she walks in that direction nevertheless, because there is nowhere else to go.

THE LIMP CARCASS lies in the dust at the foot of the stairs behind the kitchen door. A young *rooibok*, tawny, sleek, almost as if sleeping with its long-lashed eyes shut. Except for the red stain on the white fur at its neck, and the dried blood on the muzzle where a fly crawls.

Märit kneels and brushes away the fly.

"Now there will be a feast tonight," Khoza proclaims proudly, standing with the shotgun draped across his shoulders. "Eh, Märit. Eh, Tembi! A feast!"

Märit does not watch the skinning and cleaning of the antelope. She cannot bear to watch the belly being cut open, the innards dragged out into the dust, the skin peeled back from the flesh. She knows that she will not be able to eat from the flesh of this animal, sacrificed to the hunter's vanity, to Khoza.

When evening draws on and the fire is made in the *braai* pit, and the meat is placed above the hot coals, the smoke drifts into the house through the open window. Märit shuts the window, but the smell of the grilling meat wafts into the house, and saliva fills her mouth involuntarily, and she remembers how long it is since she ate meat, and she remembers the taste, because the taste is in the air that drifts in with the smoke.

When Tembi calls Märit to come out to the *braai* pit, she relents; hunger overcomes her. To show her goodwill to the hunter, Märit takes from the cabinet in the living room a bottle of peach brandy and brings it with her to the fire that crackles bright and warm in the fading purple light, where the hunter stands, eyes bright from the flames, and the aroma of the meat is thick in the air.

AFTERWARDS, when their hands and faces are greasy with the fat and the juices from the barbecued meat, and their bellies are full, and their limbs are relaxed, they recline around the glowing fire under the stars, sated, content.

The brandy bottle has made its rounds; the sweet and fiery liquid complements the charred, smoky meat. Tembi declines the bottle when Märit passes it to her. Märit drinks, even though she is already light-headed, then passes it to Khoza. He swallows, smacks his lips, and settles the bottle between his feet.

Khoza then produces a small leather pouch from his pocket and pours dark tobacco into a sheaf of cigarette paper. He rolls the tobacco into a thin cylinder, licks the seam of the paper to seal it, and then lights the cigarette with a flaming twig. The cloud of smoke he exhales is pungent, like the smell of *khakibos* when it is burned off the fields.

"Give me one of your cigarettes, Khoza," Märit says. "I don't have any more."

"This is strong tobacco, Märit. *Dagga*. Are you sure?"

"You always smoke mine, so now you can let me have one of yours."

Khoza shakes out tobacco into the paper and repeats the process of rolling it into a cylinder. Just before he licks the seam of the cigarette he looks up at her and says, "You don't mind that your lips will touch a cigarette from the mouth of a black man?"

"I'm not asking you to kiss me," she retorts.

Tembi giggles.

"No, of course not," Khoza answers with a chuckle, handing the cigarette to her.

Märit looks away, irritated that she has responded so flippantly.

The taste of the tobacco is harsh, resinous, like burning leaves, and sends her into a fit of coughing when she inhales.

"Too strong for the white lady?" Khoza says.

When she has recovered, Märit takes another puff, smaller, and inhales less deeply. She suppresses a cough when she sees Khoza is still regarding her with amusement.

A chill has settled on the night and Märit edges closer to the fire. The flames dance and flicker amongst the red coals of the fire. No other light breaks the darkness around the three people. For all Märit knows, theirs is the only fire burning in the night that lies over the country. This flame here, burning softly on the African veldt in the African darkness, as it might have burned aeons ago in the same way—only the stars, a fire, the figures huddled close around the warmth.

When she raises her eyes the stars seem a long way off. "It's cold," Märit says. Her voice echoes oddly, as if muffled and coming from outside her. She looks over at Tembi and Khoza, but neither of them answers. Did she speak? she wonders. Or did she only think she spoke?

She draws again on the resinous tobacco, and the smoke seems to lift her limbs so that they become light, weightless. If she turned and looked into the darkness she would see herself floating out there.

"Do you want some *dagga*, Tembi?" Khoza says. Märit watches as Tembi takes the cigarette and inhales a small puff.

"I didn't know you smoked, Tembi," Märit says.

"I don't." She breaks into a fit of giggles.

Khoza begins to laugh too.

"What's the joke?" Märit asks, and her own voice seems almost foreign to her. Across the fire his eyes sparkle red, and his laughter is impish. He looks like a creature of the night, crouched there by the fire.

Märit turns her head and looks at Tembi, and the gesture of her turning seems to take a long time, as if the air is thick and viscous. It's the cigarette, she thinks, it's distorting my senses.

Tembi is leaning forward over the fire with absorbed concentration, a serene expression on her face. Her skin is tinted gold by the small flames, but her eyes are lost in caverns of deep shadow.

What do you see? Märit wants to ask, but the effort of forming the words defeats her; the words will not come. She turns her head slowly in the thick air and looks down into the embers, following Tembi's gaze.

In the heart of the flames, where the coals glow crimson, she sees to her astonishment a miniature city, all aglow in crimson, with ancient turrets and towers and burning walls. The city seems familiar, a city that she knows, where she might even once have lived. A city remembered, but from a dream. As she watches, the coals shift in a little burst of flame and the towers and turrets collapse and crumble into fire.

A small cry of distress escapes from Märit. The walls crumble and the towers disappear into flame. Like a city from the Bible, she thinks, like the story of Sodom and Gomorrah, remembering it from Sunday school when she was a girl. She sees the city from above, the burning city on the plain, as God must have seen it, the vengeful God who destroyed the city and turned the woman who looked back at the flame into a pillar of salt. The vengeful God, who destroyed the cities on the plain. Will we now be destroyed like the city in the Bible? Märit wonders.

She shakes her head. The cigarette is making her even more confused. She looks across the fire and sees the red eyes watching her. His black skin and his red eyes and his red tongue.

"Märit." His voice comes, soft, a honeyed whisper.

"What?" Her voice too replies in a whisper, as if she will be overheard.

"You feel it, Märit?"

"What?"

"You feel the *dagga*, the herb? You floating up there yet?"

She looks down at the cigarette in her hand.

"That's what you're smoking," he whispers. "The herb that the small people grow in the jungle."

"What?" she repeats, unable to bring forth more than that one word.

"Märit," he whispers, insinuating his voice into her consciousness.

Märit tosses the cigarette into the fire.

"Hey!" Khoza exclaims. "If you don't want it you can give it back. What a waste!"

Tembi begins to giggle again. They seem to Märit like children, Tembi and Khoza, like two small malicious children, laughing at her with impish faces. Little demons, laughing at her.

Märit is suddenly anxious. She does not know who they are, these two people. She thought she knew them, but now she realizes she doesn't. She rises to her feet, suddenly afraid, aware of their conspiracy against her. She is afraid and lost and she stumbles backwards, anxious to be away from them. But there is nowhere for her to go.

She hurries towards the house, silent and dark and cold, yet she cannot enter, because it too is strange, with all the details and evidence of her false life. The woman who lives in there is not her. But if the Märit who lives in the house is not her, then who is the Märit that stands in the night outside?

She creeps up the steps of the veranda and curls into the rocking chair, folding her knees up to her chin and clasping her arms tight around them so that she is curled into something small and hidden and sad, with her back to the fire and the demons and the night.

Märit looks up to the stars for comfort. They see me, she thinks. The stars see me and thus I can never be lost.

A sudden realization comes to Märit, curled up and small as she is in the vastness of the night. She will never leave the farm. It is the one place on the earth for her. It is here where the stars know her. She will die in this place. The knowledge that this will be her destiny is absolute.

Märit takes some comfort from the knowledge, because it means she is home. The farm is where she belongs. This is all there is—this is all of the world, here in the chill of the night under the stars.

But can she endure such a fate alone? Does she have the strength and the courage?

At last she rises and walks back to the glow of the fire, to the two people there, who are the only ones that share this night with her.

46

THE STARS ARE JUST THE STARS, the night is just the night. The boy and the girl sitting by the fire are not devils but just a boy and a girl—just Khoza and Tembi.

Märit sits down across from them and stretches her hands towards the warmth. There are no burning cities in the coals, no demons. The effects of smoking the *dagga* have worn off.

Tembi yawns. "It's late. We should go in."

But none of them stirs from the fire.

Eventually Tembi rises to her feet. "I am going to bed."

"Hamba kahle," Khoza says. He stands next to her a moment and lets his hand rest on her arm. "Sleep well."

"Yes," Märit adds. "Good night, Tembi."

Tembi looks down at Märit, a slight frown creasing her brow. "Aren't you going to bed?"

"Soon."

Tembi suppresses another yawn and moves away towards the house.

They watch her shape retreat into the darkness.

Khoza collects a few more twigs and branches and tosses them into the embers, then crouches to blow the flames into life. Märit studies his face. She sees no threat there, no evil—he is only a young man, and his bravado is that of a man who is young.

"Who are you, Khoza? Where do you come from?"

Khoza pokes at the fire with a stick, then tosses it into the flames and turns to face her. "I will tell you a story, Märit. It's a kind of ghost story. About another man in another place. We can call him Sizwe. In the time of this story he has a job, as a waiter at a hotel in the countryside, where there is a river and a swimming pool, and people come to take safaris.

In the mornings, on his first break of the day, Sizwe likes to go and sit on the slope above the river, where he can see into the distance. He sits there and smokes a cigarette and thinks his thoughts. The view reminds him of the country of his childhood, in another time, in another place.

One morning a man comes out of the trees that surround the river and walks straight up to where Sizwe sits. The man carries an AK-47 rifle in his hands, the kind that soldiers have. He wears a ragged camouflage shirt and a pair of torn shorts, and on his feet a pair of sneakers, too small for him, so that he has cut away the tips to give his toes room.

Sizwe looks at this man coming from the trees with his gun and then he looks away. He sits very still.

'*Sawubona*, brother,' the man says to Sizwe. 'Greetings.'

When Sizwe makes no reply, the man stops and the barrel of the gun shifts so that it points at Sizwe. 'Don't be afraid,' he says. 'Are you alone here?'

Sizwe says nothing. The cigarette in his hand is burning his fingers. He lifts it carefully to his mouth to take a puff. He sees clouds forming on the peaks of the distant mountains and he knows there will be rain soon. If not this day, then tomorrow. Or the day after.

'Don't be afraid,' the man says, and his eyes search the bougainvillea bushes behind Sizwe. 'Do you work up there, in that hotel?'

Sizwe lets his cigarette fall to the ground and he grinds it out with the tip of his polished black shoe.

The man says, 'I am hungry, brother. Do you have any food with you?'

He is more of a boy than a man, but he has tired eyes and there is the knowledge of killing in them.

Carefully, Sizwe takes from his pocket a pouch of tobacco and his rolling papers. He stretches and puts the tobacco and papers

and matches on the ground. The young man crouches, still pointing the gun at Sizwe, and scoops up the tobacco. He limps away a
few paces, then leans his gun against his thigh while he makes
himself a cigarette.

'We were five in the beginning,' the boy says. 'Three days ago.
They caught us at the Tugela, when we were crossing the river.
An ambush. We never even saw them, just the bullets coming
across the water like hailstones, and my comrades falling. I heard
the soldiers on the riverbank laughing afterwards.'

On the side of his calf there is a deep gash. He sucks at the cigarette with hunger. Sizwe can smell the tiredness on him, and the
sour smell of his fear.

'I need some food, I need something to eat. You can get me
some food from the kitchen. I know you work in that hotel.' He
points to Sizwe's starched white jacket and his black trousers and
shiny shoes—the uniform of a waiter. 'I don't care if it's from the
rubbish bins. Anything I can eat, brother. Nobody will miss some
food from the rubbish bins, will they?'

Sizwe doesn't answer. He is looking at the distant hills and the
clouds that remind him of the mists that came up the valley in the
mornings when he was a boy.

'What's the matter with you?' the boy with the gun says to
Sizwe. He springs forward and presses the barrel against Sizwe's
cheek. The metal is warm from the boy's hand. 'Don't you know
how to talk?'

Sizwe looks down at the tips of his own shoes.

'I could kill you,' the boy shouts. 'Right now.'

Sizwe knows that sometimes it is possible to kill someone without considering whether the person deserves to die.

Then the boy's finger curls down on the trigger and the hammer
falls with a click. Sizwe's heart stops. When it beats again it beats
like an antelope running, hooves drumming on the ground.

The boy staggers backwards with a cry of strange laughter. 'I
don't have any bullets. They only gave us three each . . . I used
them all up . . . trying to shoot a fucking antelope.' He screeches

with laughter, then slumps down on the grass and pulls off his beret and scratches hard at his scalp.

Sizwe gets to his feet. He brushes away the bits of grass from the seat of his pants. The boy is shivering in the hot sun, and flies have settled on the sores at his ankles. He has the look of death on him. He is already dead. He is a ghost.

Sizwe leaves his tobacco and rolling paper and matches on the ground near the boy and walks back up the path to the hotel.

He is in the kitchen, washing his hands at the big sink, when the manager calls and beckons for Sizwe to follow him.

On the gravel driveway outside the hotel is a Saracen armored car, and soldiers, and an officer in a slouch hat with a pistol strapped to his waist. The rest of the staff are lined up on the gravel driveway. The officer points at Sizwe.

'You. Come here, hey. Where are you coming from just now, hey?'

'By the river, Baas.' Sizwe keeps his eyes down, careful not to look the officer in the face.

'And what are you doing there down by the river?'

'I was looking at the land.'

'What business do you have looking at the land?'

'It reminds me of the country of my childhood, Baas.'

'Who else is down there? Did you speak to anyone? A man with a gun? Hey?'

Sizwe shakes his head. 'I did not see a man.' And that is true. He might have seen a ghost, passing briefly before his eyes, but not a man.

'What did you tell him? That you would help him? Where is he hiding?'

'I did not see any man.'

The officer snorts with disbelief and shoves Sizwe away. 'You monkeys are all the same. Bloody liars.'

The armored car starts up and the officer climbs aboard.

'Back to the dining room,' the manager tells Sizwe as the vehicle departs. 'It's time to serve lunch.'

Only one table is occupied in Sizwe's section, for this is not the high season—an older couple and a young woman he supposes to be their daughter. She is close to his own age. Sizwe sets the menu in front of them, and three glasses of ice water, and a bowl of spiced groundnuts. Each time he reaches across the table, the young woman turns her face and edges her body away from him. He has the impression that she is holding her breath.

When Sizwe brings the salads and sets a plate in front of the girl, she wrinkles her face and mutters to her mother, 'Ugh, he smells. They should make the staff here bathe more often.'

Once out of sight behind the kitchen door Sizwe lifts his sleeve to his nose and inhales. Is it the scent of the boy by the river she smells? Or his own fear?

A brief series of loud bangs sounds from the direction of the river. Thunder already, Sizwe thinks. The rain will come soon.

The chef rings the bell to notify Sizwe that his order is ready: two roast beef for the man and woman, grilled chicken for the girl. Sizwe carries out the two plates of roast beef. Back in the kitchen he fetches a silver tray, puts the plate of grilled chicken on it, along with silverware, ice water, a basket of breadsticks, and a linen napkin. He carries the tray out the back entrance, around the side of the hotel, and down to the place where he likes to sit and look at the distant hills and remember the time of his childhood.

The boy is not where Sizwe left him. The tobacco pouch and the cigarette papers are lying in the same place on the grass, but not the boy. Sizwe carries the tray further down the slope towards the river until he finds the boy's body under a wild fig tree.

There are three gaping holes in the boy's shirt, each one ringed with a circle of blood and burned cloth from where the muzzle of a rifle must have pressed against his chest.

Sizwe sets his tray down carefully on the grass. He unlaces the boy's sneakers and removes them, then tugs the ragged khaki shorts from the thin hips, and lastly unbuttons the shirt, until the boy lies naked.

Then Sizwe removes his own starched white jacket, his own

shirt, his pressed black trousers, his shined shoes. When he too is naked he dresses himself in the boy's rags. With the tip of a finger he touches his own chest through the bullet holes in the shirt. Now he dresses the dead boy: pressed pants, clean white shirt, starched serving jacket, shined black shoes.

The boy's sneakers are too small for Sizwe, even with the toes cut away, so he goes barefoot, the way he did when he walked through the mists beside the river of his childhood. He carries the tray back to the hotel, entering through the front doors this time, then across the carpeted lobby and straight into the dining room.

An abrupt silence falls upon the room. All the talking stops as Sizwe marches past the diners in his ragged uniform. At the table where the young white woman sits waiting for her lunch, Sizwe sets the tray down. He pulls out a chair and seats himself across from her.

He waits for the young woman to look at him. She glances around the dining room, holding her head to one side, as if it pains her to face him. And when she looks at him, only then, when she is looking straight into his eyes, does Sizwe begin to eat.

WIND CRACKLES through the flames, sending sparks towards Khoza. He coughs and moves away, finding a seat on the same side of the fire as Märit, but without looking at her, his face turned to the night.

She ponders the story he has just told. Not for the truth of it, for she believes it to be true. Neither for the question of whether Khoza is the man in the story, for she believes he is. No, she ponders the story for her place in it.

The question waits. She feels that Khoza waits for an answer from her, but when she looks across at him, he seems lost inside himself. Because it is her question. It is she who sits across from the man.

His scent, of fire, tobacco, and something else that can only be characterized as his maleness, touches her. It is the smell of a man, which has not been in the house since Ben died.

Märit inhales and fills her nostrils with the scent of the man. Staring into the fire, she sees once again Khoza standing under the sun, his back glistening with sweat in the furrow down his spine. She sees his nakedness, and she wants to taste the smell of him. She wants to put her hand on the place where the moisture shines in the furrow of his back and touch his sweat on her fingers and taste the scent of him.

She has never touched him. She shares the same food, smokes the same cigarette, uses the same knives and forks, but she has never touched him.

Märit looks at his hand where it rests on his knee. His hands are slim, with long fingers, well proportioned. So easy to put her hand on his, to touch him, to bring him away from the strangeness that separates them.

Yet she cannot. Even as she stares at his hand she cannot. Everything in her life forbids it.

But did she not touch Dollar, the pool boy? Did she not wrap her arms and her legs around his torso in the pool? What forbade her then?

Her eyes are fixed on his slim wrist, on the smooth skin above his wrist, on that delicate place where the hand narrows into the wrist, then flares slightly into the thickness of the forearm. His body radiates a kind of magnetism, so that without realizing it, she leans towards him.

Märit reaches out and puts her fingers on the smooth skin of Khoza's wrist. Her fingers are pale on his dark skin, and his skin is cool under the heat of her touch. Yet it burns her, so that she leans into him, into the heat. The beat of his pulse echoes in her body, so that her own pulse becomes his.

Here in the glow of the small fire, on the wide plain in the valley, in the small place on the immense continent, under the greater immensity of the stars in heaven, nothing forbids the man and the woman. A man and a woman—it is the simplest fact there is.

Khoza turns to face her, and she presses her body to his, and she takes his kiss, his lips, her tongue seeking his; all the taste of him is in her mouth, all the dust of his wanderings come home into her. She takes his hand and lifts it to her breast, to the pulse in her breast. Märit lifts her head and seeks Khoza's eyes, to see the desire there, to see that he wants her.

He glances quickly at the house.

And in that quick movement, his eyes leaving hers for a moment, Märit recognizes something that causes her desire to suddenly retreat. She remembers how he sneaked into the house that day he arrived, furtive and watchful. She remembers him watching her from the other side of the fire—the mocking devil with the red light in his eyes.

Yes, he wants her. But what else does he want?

From the moment that he first stepped into the house she knew she desired him. Beneath her shock and her fear of a stranger in her house, even then she knew him as the man and herself as the woman. Even then.

He wants her, and when he has had her, then what? He wants power over her, and he wants Tembi, and then he wants the farm.

Märit pushes away from him; his hand falls away from her breast. She rises to her feet, looks down at him, then turns and flees towards the house. Swiftly she runs into the house and straight to her room, where she locks the door behind her. She sits on the bed, listening to the beat of her fearful heart.

After a while she gets up and unlocks the door. She is ashamed. Not of her desire, but of her fear. Will she ever be free of fear? So she unlocks the door and returns to sit on the bed and waits.

Eventually Märit hears his step on the veranda, and the closing of the door, and the bolt sliding home. She imagines his tread on the slate floor as he sidles down the corridor to her room.

At the last moment she springs across the room and turns the key in the lock. She holds her breath, sensing him on the other side of the door. The handle turns slowly and the door moves a fraction, as if from the pressure of a hand. Märit stares at the handle.

The handle is released. Märit waits, hardly breathing. Slowly the handle turns again, and then is released.

She stands a long time at the door, listening, frightened of herself, of what she has done, of what she wants. And when her desire is gone, and when her fear is gone, and when the night is just a night, she crawls into bed with a sense of betrayal and bitterness. With a sense of failure.

Now she knows how the story ends.

47

Märit does not speak to Khoza in the morning. She does not look at him. He does not speak to her, he does not look at her.

When she enters the kitchen and sees him at the table with Tembi, Märit pours herself a cup of tea and carries it to her room, where she waits until she hears Khoza leave the house. Only then does she go back to the kitchen.

Tembi says, "What is between you and Khoza?"

"Nothing. What do you mean?"

"You don't say 'good morning' to him, you don't look at him, you act as if he is not here."

Märit shrugs.

Tembi says, "What is between you?"

"There is nothing."

"But Khoza does not say anything to you either. He looked at you with anger when you took your tea."

"Ask him."

"No, I am asking you."

Märit reaches for a rusk.

Tembi says, "What happened between you last night?"

"Nothing happened. We sat by the fire for a while after you went in, and then I came in to bed myself."

"And Khoza, did he come to bed with you?"

"Don't be ridiculous. Why are you questioning me like this? You're imagining something that didn't happen."

Tembi moves so that she can see Märit's face. "You are not honest with me."

"Stop this, Tembi."

"I see it in your face. You have something to hide."

"Don't be silly."

"I heard Khoza come to your room last night."

"My door was locked." Märit cannot prevent the blush rising to her face.

"Your face betrays you," Tembi says with sudden venom in her voice. "You lie to me."

Märit turns on her. "All right! You want the truth? Khoza tried to kiss me, he tried to force himself on me after you had gone to bed. That's what happened!" The lie is out, too late to retract. But the truth is impossible to tell.

"And you let him."

"No, I did not! I came into the house and locked my door. Yes, he tried to get in, but the door was locked."

"You want him. I see the way you look at him."

"Don't be ridiculous! I wouldn't lower myself to his level."

"Why? Because you think he is not good enough for you?"

"You're putting words into my mouth. Either I want him or I don't want him—make up your mind."

Tembi shakes her head in disbelief and turns away. Beyond her, a figure crosses the garden, framed for a moment in the window—a man in a slouch hat, her husband's hat—and for an instant Märit sees Ben.

Tembi also notices the resemblance. "You have had a husband, now you want Khoza too."

The truth is impossible to tell. "Tembi . . . I promise you . . . he was not in my room last night. I slept alone." Half a truth.

In a wounded voice Tembi cries, "Your face betrays you!"

She slams the door behind her as she runs out.

KHOZA, wearing the slouch hat and a pair of old corduroy trousers that once belonged to the farmer, finds Tembi standing at the foot of the vegetable garden, her arms folded tight against her body, her chest heaving with rapid breaths. He carries the shotgun on his shoulder.

He stops and smiles at her, but she jerks her head away and stares in the opposite direction. "You are fighting with Märit? Things do not go well with you and Märit?" He sounds almost pleased.

"I wonder what things go well between her and you!"

Khoza kicks at a pebble.

Glaring at him, Tembi says, "Maybe you would like it more if I left this farm so that you can be with her."

Khoza shifts the gun to his other shoulder. His voice is low with offended pride. "Why do you say that to me? You know that Märit does not like me."

"But you like her. You prefer her. Maybe you want to have a white woman."

"Never!"

Tembi studies his face. "Märit says that you tried to kiss her last night, that you tried to force yourself on her."

Khoza laughs and makes a spinning motion with his forefinger next to his temple. "That one, she is all mixed up in her head. Smoking the *dagga* has made her thoughts crazy."

"You shouldn't give it to her." She softens her voice. "You didn't try to kiss her?"

He makes a grimace.

"You don't want her? You don't want to be with her and have this farm?"

He recoils. "You are crazy! Maybe the *dagga* is in your head too. Crazy women!" Shaking his head he stalks off.

Tembi bites her lip, frowning with doubt. Then she runs to catch up with him.

They walk apart a little distance, in silence, skirting the river. Suddenly a guinea hen breaks from the underbrush and flutters into the air across the water. Khoza raises the shotgun and tracks its flight until it drops into cover on the opposite bank.

"Why didn't you shoot it?"

"We don't need any meat yet. And I need to keep the bullets for other things." He walks on, then stops. "Maybe I should shoot Märit?"

"Khoza! Don't say such a thing!"

"No, I don't mean it. But why should she own all this?" He extends the gun with one arm, making a wide arc. "All of this farm just for her? You should be Missus here, not Märit."

"But Märit and her husband bought this farm. They paid for it."

"Did they pay the people who lived here and worked the land?"

"They bought it from the previous farmer. The other family had been here a long time."

"And who did they buy it from? How did *they* get the land?"

Tembi follows the path that curves towards the gate.

"They stole the land," Khoza calls out after her. "They took it by force. There were people living here long before the whites came, all over this country, and the whites stole it from them. Märit bought this land from people who had no right to sell it. Were any of us allowed to buy land here? No. We can only have land where the soil is hard and dry, where the rains never come. Or else we have to go to the slums of the cities." He strides past her towards the farm gate and stops there, looking at the name painted on the gatepost. "Kudufontein!" he exclaims disdainfully, poking the gun barrel at the sign.

"This place is also called Isitimane," Tembi says. "The Place of Shadows." She points. "For the big rock there, because it puts its own shadow on the land."

"They change the names of everything and put their own names on things, and then they tell you there were no names before they came. They took away the name of our country. They make up history. They don't even call us by our proper names—it's just boy or *meid*."

"But Märit is not like that."

"You don't think so?"

"She is different. There is goodness in her."

Khoza disregards her observation. "Everything will be different soon. The land will go back to the people who work it, not those who can buy and sell. It is our land now." He swings the gun barrel again in a wide arc, encompassing all the farm. "All of this is ours." He points up at the house. "That house is yours, Tembi. You can call it whatever you want." Setting the shotgun against the post he says, "Wait here, I have to get something."

She leans against the gate with one foot on the lowest rung, slowly rocking back and forth.

Perhaps there is some truth in what Khoza tells her. There were people in the kraal before she came, before Märit came, before the other farmers came. This much she knows—that people like her have always lived on this land. Is not her own mother resting in this very soil now? Does she not belong to this place? And does it not follow then that this place could belong to her?

Her life here has always been defined by whoever lives in the farmhouse, whoever owns the land. Yet she lives there too now. And not only because Märit has invited her. The house and the farm belong to Märit. But if they did not?

For a moment she allows herself to see a new life on the farm: the land fertile and green once more, cattle in the fields, the mealie fields thick with plants, the orchard ripe with fruit. There will be no kraal, no washhouse with cold water taps, no open cooking fires.

She sees herself living in the house, wearing fine clothes, driving a fine car into town, where she will enter any shop she pleases and the shopkeeper will call her "Missus."

But who else will live on the farm? Where is Märit in this picture? Where is Khoza? This part of the picture is hazy. And what does Khoza mean when he says this land is "ours"? Does he mean the country, or does he mean the farm? Does he mean it is his?

Tembi is still musing on these questions when Khoza returns with a can of paint in his hand and a brush tucked under his arm.

"What are you going to do?" she asks.

"This is our farm now, and we will give it a new name." He opens the can, dips the brush into the paint, and with a few rough strokes obliterates the word *Kudufontein*. "Here." He thrusts the brush towards Tembi. "Write a new name."

Tembi hesitates. She looks up at the house.

"But what name shall I give it?"

"Call it 'Khoza and Tembi,'" he says, only half in jest.

Should she paint in the old name, Isitimane? But she cannot name the farm with a word of darkness. There is too much shadow on all their lives already.

"Go on," Khoza urges.

Tembi takes the brush, dips it into the paint, then just above where the other name had been, she writes.

Carefully she paints in the letters, as carefully as when she was a small girl writing her own name in her exercise book. And when she is finished she steps back and looks at what she has written, with the same wonder as that of a small child who writes her name for the first time. With the same wonder that a child realizes when she claims her own name by writing it down. Tembi writes the letters with wonder, claiming the world by her own hand.

"What is that word?" Khoza asks.

"*Ezulwini,*" Tembi says. "The Valley of Heaven."

48

Märit sits in front of the mirror at her dresser. Have I been wrong in everything? she asks herself. A bitterness is upon her, and the sense of having failed in some profound manner.

She studies herself in the mirror—her African dress, her shorn hair that is growing back unevenly. What is she supposed to be? Who is she supposed to be? I have tried to be something other than what I am, she concludes.

Leaving the mirror she goes to stand at the bedroom window. The man in the slouch hat walks past on his way to the sheds, and her heart gives a queer lurch in her chest. Who is he? What does he want? If only it were Ben, she tells herself, and nothing had happened and nothing had changed, and the world was the same as before.

The interloper who walks across the land in her husband's hat, with the gun across his shoulder, walks as if he already owns the farm. She knows that he wears the hat for her, to signal his intentions.

Looking beyond him, Märit sees Tembi, in her bare feet and simple clothes, a copper necklace at her neck and the blue bracelet on her wrist.

They are part of the landscape, the man and the woman, while she hides in the house.

Märit turns away and sees her reflection again. What have I tried to be, she asks herself, with my colored sarong and my beads and bangles? I can never be like Tembi, I can never be like them.

She removes the bracelets from her wrists and drops them onto the dresser. She unfastens the sarong, the brightly colored sarong from Durban, bought in the African market, and divests herself of this too, peeling it from her body like a skin that does not fit.

She bathes, washing the dust of the farm from her limbs, rinsing the scent of wood smoke from her hair, scrubbing the traces of soil from under her cracked fingernails.

When she has bathed, Märit dresses in her cream-colored suit—so strange to wear these clothes again—and sits at the mirror to apply makeup to her face. Her hands have not forgotten the art: mascara on the eyelashes, a line penciled in to accentuate each eyebrow, a touch of faint blue on the eyelids, so that her eyes become larger, almond shaped, intense. She rubs rouge into her suntanned cheeks, emphasizing the contours of her cheekbones. Finally she applies lipstick, red, her mouth becoming lush and full.

To each earlobe Märit clips a small pearl earring, and around her neck a necklace of pearls. A dab of perfume behind each ear and on her wrists, to cloak her in a scent that is neither dust nor wood smoke nor the sweat of labor. She paints her fingernails red to match her lipstick, covering the broken and ragged edges, and when the varnish is dry she eases her stockinged feet into a pair of high-heeled shoes, then walks up and down the room a few times to accustom herself to the forgotten sensation. There is nothing to be done about her hair except to trim a few ragged strands.

Dusk brings a fading of the light. Somewhere else in the world people are sipping cocktails, an orchestra is playing dance music. Somewhere out there people are living normal lives.

Märit goes through the house and lights all the paraffin lamps, and from the liquor cabinet she takes a bottle of gin, pouring herself a good measure. She sips the liquor, and for a moment she hears the music and the laughter and smells the scent of another world.

WHEN TEMBI ENTERS the house she does so sheepishly. She wants to tell Märit what she has done about the name on the gate—to apologize, to explain.

She finds the old Märit.

The Märit that she expected to find has disappeared behind a barrier of clothes and lipstick and jewelry. She sees a woman from another world, the world that she has never entered. This is the Märit who is everything Tembi is not. Her gesture of painting a new name on the farm gate seems childish and puny now.

Khoza enters behind Tembi, pausing to set the gun in a corner. He straightens up and gives a low whistle of appreciation.

"Would anyone like a drink?" Märit says.

Tembi looks upon Märit and her face burns with shame—for everything that she is not, and for what Märit has suddenly become. The betrayal is complete. She burns with shame at the betrayal. Angrily she pushes past Märit and runs to her room.

Khoza looks Märit up and down, then leaves her alone in the room. She swallows her gin and pours a second one.

There is a movement back and forth in the corridor, low whispers. Märit pointedly ignores the sounds. She pours a third drink.

Then Tembi appears—but a Tembi that Märit has never seen before.

A pale pink dress patterned with small flowers, earrings, necklace, high heels that she teeters on, handbag. Märit recognizes all of these, for they are her own. But the face is that of a stranger—powdered, lips bright with red lipstick. The dress is tight, cut low in the front to reveal the fullness of Tembi's breasts. The effect is crude, almost a parody of herself. But the outcome is undeniable, radiating a raw sexuality; the clothes and makeup accentuating what is hidden.

Tembi takes a glass from the table, fills it, and stands next to the fireplace, posing.

Märit suddenly feels that it is she who is the parody, the grotesque. She feels old.

She remembers the day she came into the house and found Tembi asleep in the bedroom, wearing the blue dress. And she remembers her sexual jealousy. Now it is complete. On that day Tembi seemed just a young girl dressing up, but now she has a new confidence, an awareness of her body that is obvious.

Khoza saunters into the room, and his appearance is like a blow, for he has found Ben's suit and one of his white shirts and has dressed in them.

Märit staggers unsteadily to her feet. "How dare you! How dare you wear those clothes. Both of you! What right do you have?"

"You don't need them. You have so many things," Tembi says, and glances at Khoza quickly for confirmation.

"Don't look to him. Those are not his clothes, this is not his house."

Khoza says, "You think you own everything, even us. But not anymore."

"Neither of you belongs in this house. You are here because of me. And what you are wearing belongs to me."

Tembi wavers, looking to Khoza for reassurance. "Before, when I came to this house, you wanted us to be the same. You wore clothes like mine. But now, if I wear your clothes, you don't want that anymore."

"You forget your place, Tembi."

"It is not for you to tell me where my place is."

"He put you up to this, didn't he?" Märit says.

Khoza laughs.

"Get out of here," Märit says coldly. "Both of you. Get out of my house and off my farm."

Tembi turns on her and, to Märit's great astonishment, says, "*You* get out!"

"What? What did you say?"

"If you don't like us, then you can go."

"Yes," Khoza says. "This is not your place anymore."

Before Märit can react, Khoza has grasped her by the arm and propelled her towards the door. He pulls it open and shoves her out. The door closes and the bolt rattles home behind her.

Stunned, Märit stands on the threshold gasping. Her head spins. She turns and leans her face against the door, then suddenly pounds on it with both fists.

"Open this door immediately! Tembi, do you hear me? I said, open this door!"

She hears laughter from inside.

Enraged, Märit marches around the side of the house to the kitchen entrance. She hears the key turn in the lock as she reaches the top of the stairs. Her fists beat on the door. "Get out of my house! Both of you! How dare you?"

When she tries to peer in through the side window, rapping on the glass, the curtain is quickly drawn.

"You devil!" Märit screams. She strides away from the house, fuming. Devil, devil, devil! Both of them. Devils! How dare they throw her out of her own house!

She paces furiously back and forth along the driveway, kicking at the gravel. The house is pale in the dusk, the glow of the lamps yellow in the curtained windows. She imagines revenge—setting fire to the house, finding a gun and forcing them out, making them beg for her mercy.

A chill wind blows around her. Night is coming; already the veldt is losing its color. Anger surges back—she will not let them keep her out in the coming night.

Märit pounds on the door with both hands, hard, again and again. There is no answer. She walks all around the house, shaking the windows, finding each one locked and curtained. At her bedroom window, a chink of light shows between the curtains. "Tembi?" She taps lightly on the glass.

Khoza's face appears. *"Voetsak!"* he yells. The curtain is pulled shut.

The word is like a slap in her face.

She stumbles away from the window and her feet bump against a rock. Without a second thought Märit bends and lifts the rock in both hands, high above her head, and with all the force in her arms she hurls it at the bedroom window.

The glass shatters with a tremendous bang, like a bomb exploding.

In the silence that follows she shouts, "Go ahead, wear my clothes, sleep in my bed. I give you my permission. Go and fuck him on my bed, you little *kaffir* bitch!"

No sound comes from the house. The curtain flutters across the broken glass. Then suddenly the barrel of the shotgun is thrust through the window. Märit screams as blue flame leaps from the gun, and the bang of the shot deafens her. She flings herself to the ground as the second barrel fires, pellets whining over her head like hail.

She crawls away on all fours, very sober now, and truly terrified. Her skirt catches on something, rips. She yanks it loose, and then she is on her feet and running into the night.

* * *

WHEN the night is fully dark, and only then, Märit crawls out from her hiding place in the trees and makes her way to the kraal, seeking refuge in one of the huts. By the faint flickering illumination of her cigarette lighter she finds a hut with a rough mattress and an old chest of drawers in the room—nothing else. She drags and pushes the chest in front of the door to make a barrier, then curls up on the mattress.

Sometime in the night she wakes to hear the snuffling and snorting of an animal at the door of the hut, and she sits up, waiting for it to go away. She is not afraid. Not of animals. It is people she fears.

IN THE SOBER HARSHNESS of morning, Märit rinses her face at the washhouse tap and swallows a mouthful of water. Carrying her shoes in her hand she follows the path back to the kitchen and tries the door. Still locked.

She knocks, and after a moment Khoza appears in the doorway.

"Are you looking for work?" he says.

"No. I want a cup of tea. Not your games."

"If you want breakfast then you must work."

"What kind of work?"

"Cleaning, cooking, washing. *Meid*'s work."

She tries to push past him into the house, but he bars her way with his arm.

"Where is Tembi? I want to talk to her."

"Tembi doesn't want to talk to you."

"Let her tell me that to my face. I want to see her."

Khoza shakes his head.

"I won't work for you. Why should I?"

He slams the door in her face.

Märit sits down on the upper step. Her skirt is torn along the hem, the thread unraveling. Absently she twines the strand of cotton around her finger, then snaps it off.

"All right," she mutters. She knocks on the door again.

"All right, I'll work," she says when Khoza opens the door.

The trace of a smile crosses his face. "Yes. And you can change your clothes as well. Put on your *meid*'s clothes."

Märit bows her head, penitent, and edges past him.

She enters her house as a stranger.

In the bedroom, glass litters the floor under the broken window. The curtain has been stuffed into the hole. The bed has not been slept in, she notices with relief.

"You can clean up that glass too," Khoza says from behind her.

Märit closes the door, then finds her sarong, her beads, her bracelets. She puts a *doek* over her hair. Her soiled and torn suit she stuffs into the closet, along with her shoes and her jewelry. At the bathroom sink she washes the remnants of makeup from her face. When she is dressed again, the only incongruous element is the red varnish on her fingernails, a reminder of another self.

With a few quick steps she crosses to Tembi's room.

As Märit enters, Tembi quickly pulls the sheet up to cover her face.

"Tembi?"

No answer, just the slight rise and fall of the sheet from Tembi's breathing.

"Look at me, Tembi. Is this what you want? For me to be your servant?"

No reply.

"This is what *he* wants. We both know it will be his farm if you let it happen." The sound of Khoza in the kitchen prompts her to draw back. "I wonder how long he will let *you* live here," Märit mutters from the doorway.

She strides through to the front door and leaves the house. As she passes through the orchard she grabs an apricot from a branch and bites into it hungrily. She pulls down a few more and carries them with her to the river.

White and brown and violet dappled light on the water, the whistling and chirping of the birds, the gurgle of the flow across the rocks. Patches of sunlight breaking through the leaves. Beauty that she does not see.

She is tired of the struggle. She is hungry and she is thirsty and she is tired. She doesn't care what happens to the farm, or who lives in the house. Better to let go, to give in, not to struggle and fight anymore.

In the willow branches that hang low over the water, weaverbirds flit back and forth between the nests, which hang like little gourds of woven grass, suspended from the thinnest and most inaccessible of the slender boughs, each with its own round entrance by which the green birds come and go.

Märit counts the nests—at least ten—a small community of families, busy living their lives high in the trees, unconcerned with her. Although they seem to squabble at each other constantly and defend their individual nests fiercely, the birds live in harmony. They make no war, they don't banish their own kind. Why must we? Märit wonders.

She remembers that Ben liked to watch the birds at their nest building. He wanted the farm to be like this—a small community, living in harmony. Why did it have to end?

Becoming aware of the apricot in her hand Märit lifts it to her cheek and rubs the silky texture of the fruit skin against her own skin, inhaling the scent. The old half-conscious reverie descends over her as the tension lifts from her mind, lulled by the texture of the birdsong and the gurgling of the river flow—that old dreamy state of being outside herself, of being somewhere else.

She bites into the apricot, crunching on the firm flesh, but it is sour on her tongue.

As she stands to toss the unripe apricot into the river, Märit sees the men coming towards her through the trees.

49

THERE ARE THREE MEN, spread out in a loose line, cutting off any path of escape. Soldiers. She sees that immediately—the guns in their hands, the habitual manner in which they carry their weapons, the way they point them in her direction.

The soldiers advance through the trees, camouflage tunics dappled olive and khaki in the light and shade that speckles through the leaves. Their path towards her is stealthy, intent—a tension suddenly vibrating through the air like electric current.

Märit realizes that the birds have fallen silent. The half-eaten apricot drops from her fingers.

Her dreaminess is now dread, for the soldiers have a weariness about them, their tunics are dusty and stained, their faces are gaunt and unshaven. They have the weariness of men who have fought for, and lost, something. Her dreaminess becomes dread, because the war has finally come to the farm.

Those distant sounds sometimes heard far off, heard as a whispering across the sky, or the faint rumble of thunder on a cloudless day, those sounds she pretended not to hear, have finally come to the farm.

It is not fear that Märit feels as she stands to face the soldiers, but dread at what was inevitable. Now she will have to look into the faces of these soldiers and know that war has come to the farm at last—not a plague of locusts or a broken generator or a faulty water pump, not a squabble about who will wear whose clothes, or who will cook and who will eat.

The inevitable harm will come now to her, to Tembi, to Khoza, and to the farm. Even to the soldiers themselves. Märit knows this with a terrible certainty as the soldiers come for her. She sees it in their gaunt and weary faces. They bring harm. Despite themselves, they bring an end to something with their arrival.

She turns, to the right, to the left, looking behind her where there is only the river. Some futile hope in her wants to stave off the future, and she turns towards the river, seeking a path along the shore beneath the willows.

She has taken only a few steps before she comes face-to-face with a bearded man, so close that she can look into his eyes. A blur of camouflage, the soft cap, the glint of silver buckles, the dark sinister shape of the pistol in his hand, and the blue eyes peering into her own.

He grabs her arm and pulls her towards him.

"Mevrou!" he whispers. "Mevrou Laurens, be still!"

Hearing her name like this, her old name that nobody has spoken in a long time, shocks her. Beneath the man's beard and the dust on his face and the fatigue that has etched itself into the lines of his skin, Märit recognizes the blue eyes.

"You!"

"Gideon Schoon, Mevrou," he says in a low voice.

"Why are you here?"

With a jerk of his head in the direction of the house he whispers, "Who else is up there?"

"Tembi. My *meid*. And the houseboy."

"Anybody else?" His grip on her arm is hard, hurting her.

"We are the only ones left on the farm. The others all left, a long time ago." She does not know how long ago; the days have become months. "They all left, after the last time you were here."

His grip on her arm relaxes slightly but does not loosen. "You are hurting me," she tells him.

"Excuse me." He steps away a couple of paces.

The other three soldiers have spaced themselves out in a loose semicircle around her and Schoon, favoring the shadows, two of them facing outwards, the other watching her. Märit feels the tension emanating from the men, she smells it in their sweat as something metallic and acrid.

"Has there been anybody here to this farm lately?" Schoon asks in a more normal tone.

"Who?"

"Any soldiers? Military personnel. Other visitors?"

"No. There hasn't been anybody."

"Good, good. Let's go up to the house, shall we?" He says this casually, as if they are going for a stroll, but at the same time he makes a quick gesture to the soldiers. "Kruger, Malan, watch the back of the house. And careful, hey?"

"Come," Schoon says to Märit, speaking with some of his old authority as the soldiers melt away through the orchard, but she sees the wariness in him, the anxiety. "Nobody up there but the *meid* and the houseboy, you said?"

"Only them."

The remaining soldier walks just behind her and Schoon, his head moving to left and right, eyes scanning everything.

In the back of Märit's mind there is something new now, a relief. That they are white soldiers. On her side. And something else—a feeling that, if she were to analyze it, could only be characterized as a sense of righteous revenge. She will be reinstated in her house now. Khoza will be put in his place.

Schoon mounts the veranda steps with her and stands to one side, away from the door. Märit hesitates, then, when he nods, tries the handle.

The door is locked.

Schoon frowns—not entirely trusting her, she sees.

"It's locked," she says. "For safety."

"Knock," he whispers.

She does. Then again.

After a moment from the other side of the door Khoza's voice says, "What do you want?"

"Khoza, it's me."

"Go away."

"Open the door. We have some visitors." She makes a gesture of apology to Schoon.

"Take them to the kraal and entertain them there," Khoza chuckles.

Schoon leans in front of Märit and raps hard on the door.

The bolt rattles open, the door swings wide; Khoza stands blocking the entrance with his hands on his hips.

"I told you . . ." His eyes widen as he sees Schoon.

"This is . . . these are . . ." Märit stammers, then gathers her composure. "We have visitors, Khoza. Go and put on the kettle and prepare some tea."

But he just stares dumbfounded at Schoon.

"You heard the Missus, boy," Schoon says, pushing into the house.

Khoza retreats. He stares wide-eyed at Märit, as if this is some trick she has played on him.

"Don't just stand there," Schoon says with irritation.

As Khoza turns towards the kitchen, the other soldiers appear and he backs away from them looking wildly about him, like a trapped animal seeking escape.

In a calm voice Märit says, "Make some tea please, Khoza."

Schoon directs his attention to the soldiers. "Anybody else in the house?"

"A girl—sleeping in one of the rooms."

"That's Tembi, the *meid*," Märit says quickly. "I'll wake her. Please, sit down. Rest. Khoza, make the tea." She gives him a slight push towards the kitchen.

In the corridor she whispers to Khoza, "Do what they tell you. Don't make any trouble." She propels him towards the kitchen and enters Tembi's room.

Tembi has the sheet drawn up over her face. Märit pulls it away and leans over her.

"Tembi! There are soldiers in the house. I want you to get up now. Quickly!"

Tembi gives her a sideways, doubtful glance. There are still smudges of makeup on her face.

Märit grasps her chin and gives it a shake. "I'm not playing, Tembi! Get up immediately. There are four soldiers here. The same ones that came before. Get dressed now. And put on your clothes—your own clothes."

Tembi seems about to say something, when her eyes slide past Märit. She pulls the sheet over her face suddenly.

Schoon is watching from the doorway.

"She's been a bit unwell," Märit explains. "But she's better today." Moving forward she blocks Schoon's view, then shuts the door behind her. "She will be up in a minute."

"The situation seems a little unusual around here, Mevrou," Schoon mutters.

"I'll just see how the tea is coming along. I'll bring it in directly. Are your men hungry? Would they like something? There's nothing fresh. Mealie-pap, a bit of leftover *rooibok* stew."

Schoon smiles. "Good *boere* food. That would be very generous of you, Mevrou Laurens." He makes a little bow.

In the kitchen Märit busies herself preparing the food. Khoza stands near the window, tapping his teeth with a fingernail.

"Who are they?" he asks quietly. "Why are they here?"

With a warning nod at the door Märit whispers, "I don't know any more than you do."

"But that one with the beard, he knows you."

"He was here once before." She reaches past him to get cutlery from the drawer. "Don't just stand there. Is the tea ready?"

Hearing her own words, the unintentional echo of what Schoon had said a minute ago, gives her pause.

"Listen carefully to me, Khoza. The bearded one, Schoon, is not someone to fool around with. He is a hard man. Don't try your games with him. Do you understand?"

"He knows you. He's your friend. Now you can do what you like again."

Märit grits her teeth and shakes her head. "Sometimes I think you are nothing more than a fool." She lifts the lid of the teapot to make sure there are leaves, then fetches the last tin of condensed milk from the pantry and punctures the lid with two holes before pouring the milk into a jug. As an afterthought she adds some water and stirs it into the milk.

Khoza folds his arms across his chest, glowering.

"Try to be sensible, Khoza. For Tembi's sake, at least. Now take this tray into the dining room. I'll bring the food. And you and Tembi stay out of sight here in the kitchen."

Märit calls the men in to the dining room. They leave their packs in the living room but carry their weapons with them and set the guns next to their chairs, close at hand.

Schoon watches Khoza as he sets the plates down on the table. He notices the way Khoza studies the guns leaning beside the chairs. He notices this because he watches everything, and he says to Märit, "This houseboy, has he been working here for long? I don't remember him from before."

"He came just after you were here the last time."

"He seems the cheeky type to me," Schoon says, staring hard at Khoza. "A little too clever for his own good. These are the ones you've got to watch, Mevrou."

It occurs to Märit that a word from her would remove Khoza from the house and from the farm. All she has to do is ask Schoon. But what would they do with him, these weary, dusty soldiers who come from nowhere? In her mind's eye she has an image of a lone figure running across the veldt, running like an antelope, then the single crack of a shot, and the legs stumbling, the fall, and afterwards the vultures, the hyenas, the scavengers that come for carrion.

"No, he's a good worker. There isn't a problem."

"Well, it's your house."

The soldiers bend over their plates with evident hunger. Their faces seem slack, eyes dull; everything about them speaks of weariness. Hardly more than boys, Märit thinks. Boys who should be on the farms or laughing with their comrades on the rugby field. Yet when they raise their heads, she sees the boyish faces and tired men's eyes.

"I'm sorry we can't offer you anything more," Märit says. "We don't have transport to go into town. The generator is broken. It's a bit isolated here."

"Yes, I see that the farm is not as it once was."

"A locust swarm destroyed the gardens, the crops."

"But you are lucky to be off the beaten track," Schoon comments. "There has been worse destruction on other farms. Worse than a few locusts."

She notices that he has not joined the others at the table. "Aren't you hungry?" Märit asks.

"Not at the moment, Mevrou. Thank you. I'll just have some tea." He pours a cup and carries it out of the house to the veranda.

Märit follows a minute later. Schoon is sitting in one of the wicker chairs. He does not look at her when she sits down next to him.

After a while Schoon says, "A beautiful land. That's what they say of us abroad. You might not think it, Mevrou Laurens, but I've traveled in other countries. Europe, America once. 'Ah, but your land is beautiful,' they say about us. But they only see the veldt, and the blue mountains, and the herds of antelope. Yes, they see the beauty—who can deny the beauty?—but they don't see what it rests on. Do you know what this much talked-about beauty rests on, Mevrou?"

Märit makes no response, for Schoon seems almost to be talking to himself.

"I'll tell you," he says. "Blood. All this beauty rests on spilled blood. Blood feeds the flowers and the grasses. The spilled blood of our forefathers, and of their forefathers. Every beautiful thing that the tourists see is fed by blood. Yours and mine too, Mevrou. Yours and mine now."

He is thinner than the last time she saw him, much thinner. Not as neat and groomed as he was then. She remembers the faint scent of Vitalis hair oil that lingered around him. She had thought him vain then. Now his uniform is dirty, worn, the boots scuffed. He seems to have lost his vanity. Or relinquished it. And something else is lost too, she realizes—his confidence. He still retains his authority, but it seems empty now.

"I didn't recognize you at first, down by the river," Märit tells him.

"Nor I you, Mevrou. Nor I you." He points at her sarong and bare feet. "Has it come to this now? That you dress like them?"

Märit blushes and looks away. "Things change. We're isolated here. Nobody comes to the farm. . . ."

"Yes, things change," he says, and lapses into silence again.

"How are things . . . out there? What is happening?"

Schoon turns the corners of his mouth down. "Things are not what they were. That much I can assure you of, Mevrou. There have been setbacks."

His tired eyes meet hers and he takes a long time to continue. "I don't know how much longer we will be able to call this country our own. The government forces are holding strong in the south, but up here . . . well, it's a difficult situation. Defeat is a possibility that we must consider at last."

"Have you been to Klipspring? What is happening there?"

"Abandoned. And the nearby farms. All your neighbors. The towns have been attacked. For all your isolation here, Mevrou, your situation is better."

"Where will you go now?" Her voice gives away her anxiety to have the soldiers off the farm.

Schoon stands with a sigh and leans on the railing.

"We will only impose on your hospitality a brief time, Mevrou Laurens." He stands with his back to her, in silence, hands clasped behind his back. "I wonder why you are still here."

"Me?"

"Yes." Schoon turns to face Märit. "What is there for you on this farm now? You are alone. Do you not have family somewhere, relatives, in a safer place?"

Märit shakes her head.

"You are not safe here."

"Where would I go?"

"You can come with us, to the south. Leave this farm. Leave it to them. They are too strong for us, they are too many."

"I have nowhere else to go," Märit says quietly, more to herself than to Schoon.

The door behind them opens and Schoon spins around immediately, his hand reaching for the pistol at his waist. When he sees it is only Tembi, he shakes his head in irritation.

"I would advise your servants to return to their huts when their duties here are finished. My men are a bit jumpy. We wouldn't want any accidents to happen." He shakes his head again and walks down the steps and across the garden.

Tembi waits until he is out of sight before coming farther onto the veranda.

"You will have to sleep in the kraal tonight," Märit says. "Both of you. You heard what he said."

"How long are they going to stay?"

"I don't know."

Tembi folds her arms and looks out at the distant figure of Gideon Schoon as he paces across the mealie patch.

"Now you have your house back again. And I must live in the kraal again."

"It's not me, Tembi. You know that. The soldiers won't let you stay in the house. You heard him."

"And now I will be the servant again."

Märit feels a wave of anger come over her. "What did you expect? Is it better for me to live in the kraal while you and Khoza live in the house? Shall I tell the soldiers that is what you would prefer and ask if they can arrange it for you?"

Tembi turns away without a word.

The evening meal is prepared and served by Tembi and Khoza. Märit does not enter the kitchen. She eats with the soldiers, a mostly silent meal; they answer her questions in monosyllables, and after a while she gives up trying to converse with them.

When the dishes have been cleared away, Märit steps into the kitchen, where Tembi is drying the last of the cups. "Remember what I said—stay in the kraal tonight. It will be safer for you. Where is Khoza, have you told him?"

"He is outside somewhere."

"You had better tell him not to wander around after dark." Märit moves closer and lowers her voice. "These men can be dangerous, Tembi. Make sure that Khoza understands that."

When Gideon Schoon steps onto the veranda after dinner he finds Khoza sitting in one of the wicker chairs, feet up on the railing, a cigarette in his fingers. The chair is tilted back on two legs, rocking slightly. Khoza takes a puff of his cigarette and tips his head back to let the smoke trickle skyward.

Schoon stands and watches him without speaking. Then he says, "What are you doing?"

"I am smoking a cigarette. Your food has been served to you and the cleaning is done. Now I am smoking a cigarette after my work."

With two quick steps Schoon crosses the veranda. His boot lashes out and kicks the bottom legs of the chair away, and as Khoza flails for balance, Schoon grasps him by the collar and hauls him upright. With the palm of his other hand he slaps Khoza once across the face and then pushes him down the steps.

"Go and smoke your cigarette where I don't have to look at you."

For a moment it seems that Khoza will try to remount the steps towards the other man.

Schoon lets his hand rest on the butt of the pistol at his waist and grinds his heel into the fallen cigarette.

"*Voetsak!*" he says.

SOMETIME LATE IN THE NIGHT Märit awakes, hearing a noise outside her window. She lies silently, holding her breath, and hears it again, the slow tread of footsteps. Could it be Khoza or Tembi sneaking back to the house? She gets up from the bed and throws a robe over her shoulders before slipping into the corridor. In the living room the soft snores of the soldiers asleep on the floor are the only sounds.

As she steps through the front door, a voice asks, "Can't sleep, Mevrou Laurens?"

With a start Märit turns and sees Schoon sitting in one of the chairs. "I heard someone outside my window."

"That will be Malan, he is on sentry duty. Go back to bed, Mevrou. You are quite safe."

"Yes. All right."

Then he calls her back softly. "Mevrou?"

"What is it?"

"Explain something to me. Were we wrong? Was everything we believed in wrong? What we were taught, how we lived, our whole way of life? It all seems misguided now. A waste."

Märit has no answer to his questions.

"Think about coming with us," his voice says quietly from the shadows. "It will be better for you."

"No," she answers. "I have nowhere else to go."

50

In the morning the soldiers are gone. They have disappeared as silently as they arrived. As if they had never been in the house at all. Nothing remains of their presence except the lingering smell of dust and sweat and something metallic.

Märit is alone in her house. The emptiness strikes her like a blow. She runs to the veranda and peers across the veldt in the hope of seeing the four men, her last link with a different life. Nothing. As if they had never been. She should have gone with them, to safety, away.

She dresses. The sarong, the beads and bracelets. And bare feet—to feel herself on the slate floors, to feel her soles on the dust of the farm, to walk the earth with nothing between her skin and the soil.

In the kitchen she kneels and scoops out the cold ashes from the stove, then begins her morning duties.

In the kraal, in the hut, the morning enters the shadowy interior as a shaft of sunlight falling through the window upon the smooth brown skin of the sleeping Khoza. Tiny motes of dust hang in the beam of light above his back as it rises and falls with the gentle motion of his breathing.

Märit stands in the doorway of the hut.

Khoza shifts in his sleep, turning, and from behind his shoulder, where the light falls, the face of Tembi looks out at Märit. There she is, huddled down into the warmth of the sleeping man, nestled against his chest, sheltered, protected. Her eyes are wide, dark.

Märit is held by the intensity of Tembi's black eyes.

Then, between the two women passes the knowledge, unspoken, but saying everything. Finally, Märit gives an imperceptible shrug of acceptance.

"The soldiers are gone," she says softly. "You can come back to the house."

Still Tembi gazes at her, still the dark eyes hold Märit, full of their new awareness. Märit turns away, not wanting the intimacy of the knowledge in Tembi's eyes to touch her anymore.

KHOZA IS THE ONE who appears at the house first, hat crammed onto his head, a peculiar energy seeming to vibrate around him.

"When did the soldiers leave?" he asks without greeting Märit.

"They weren't here this morning when I woke up. Do you want some breakfast?"

Khoza pours himself some water, gulps it, then sets his cup down with a bang in the sink before striding quickly out of the room. He is still angry with me, Märit thinks, realizing that the energy he emanates has nothing to do with Tembi.

She hears him in another part of the house, cupboard doors opening and closing. When she goes through to the living room, he is there with the shotgun tucked under one arm, stuffing shells into his pocket.

"Are you going hunting?"

"Which direction did they go? Did you see where they went?"

"What are you going to do?" she asks, beginning to realize that there is another cause for his anger. "Where are you going with that gun?"

There is a hardness in his eyes that she has never seen before.

"I am going to look for that bearded one. Your friend."

"Schoon? Why?"

"You can knock a man down, you can beat him with a stick, you can whip him, you can even shoot him. All of this, and he will accept it. But you cannot slap him in the face with your hand." He shakes his head vehemently. "This you cannot do! To shame a man in such a way puts something in his heart that will eat him forever unless it is removed."

"Is that what Schoon did to you? When did this happen?"

"I have to kill him. Until I kill him I can never be a man again." He shoulders the shotgun and walks out to the veranda.

"Don't be stupid, Khoza! What can you do? They are soldiers. It is you who will be killed."

He ignores her.

"What about Tembi?" Märit calls after him.

Khoza's step falters, he turns. "An eye for an eye, a tooth for a tooth." Then he strides away.

Märit watches him go. And when he is almost out of sight, a man with a gun on the veldt, she says to herself, "What will I say to Tembi?"

TEMBI APPEARS, coming to the kitchen door where Märit sits at the table waiting. She enters with her hands cupped before her, and extends them towards Märit, as if making an offering.

"Look."

In the bowl of her palms are three eggs, dust-colored and speckled.

"What are they?"

"Guinea fowl. For our breakfast. I heard the hen clucking in the grass, and when I went to look I found the nest."

"But should you have taken them?"

"I did not take them all. The mother hen will have enough."

Märit studies Tembi as she prepares the eggs. When she looks over at Märit she smiles in a particular manner, an inward smile. It is a look only a woman can have, Märit thinks, not the look you would find on the face of a girl.

There is a radiance and contentment around Tembi, a radiance that comes from within.

"Where is Khoza?" Tembi asks as she sits down.

"He went out . . . hunting."

Tembi smiles, the smile of a woman who is no longer a girl. "He will come back soon."

* * *

IN THE FARMHOUSE, as the two women clear up the breakfast dishes, Märit cannot keep her eyes from following Tembi; she glows as if in a shaft of sunlight.

Märit feels a mixture of sadness and something else that is both bitter and sweet. But she no longer feels jealousy. All of that has drained away from her. She is not jealous of the woman for her possession of the man, nor is she jealous of the man.

She marvels a bit at this, for she remembers the past days, all the days since Khoza came to the farm. He has looked upon Märit as a woman, and has touched her, and she has touched him. But what has happened was inevitable. A part of her knew it would come, ever since that first moment when Khoza came into the house as a stranger and Tembi's face lit up in greeting when she saw him.

And so Märit feels something else now, something bitter-sweet, both a sadness and a joy. She looks upon Tembi with joy, for the girl who has become a woman, and she looks upon Tembi with sorrow, because the innocent girl she has known is gone. Her own innocence too. Sometimes Märit feels that she was born old, with the melancholy of age, with a soul that has never known innocence.

When Tembi says, "I wonder what is taking Khoza so long?" Märit looks upon her with sadness, because now Tembi will know the bitterness that love always brings.

51

IN THE ORCHARD Tembi waits. She picks idly at the few apricots and peaches that are ripe and begins to make a small pile of the fruits she has gathered.

All the while she keeps her eye on the veldt beyond the farm, waiting for the shape of the man to appear, the man who will come back to her. There is no thought in her mind that he will not come back. How could he not, after the tenderness of last night? No, her man has gone into the veldt to bring back food, and he will come back to her. So she waits, content in herself.

When she hears the slight rumble of thunder Tembi raises her eyes to the sky, the blue sky that is empty of clouds, and she turns to look to the veldt, because the thunder vibrates in the earth under her feet.

The horsemen are almost upon her before she sees them. Her eyes register uniforms, the glint of guns. Soldiers on horseback. But at the same time her eyes recognize the color of their skin, and it is the same as hers. Her fear lessens slightly, but a soldier is still a soldier, and in a time of war this is always a sight to fear.

Then she sees Khoza, on foot, trotting behind the horsemen.

The gladness in her heart to see the man coming back to her is overtaken by dread. Why is he bringing soldiers to the house?

She is torn between running to Khoza and running back to Märit. She turns back to the house and runs inside.

"Märit! Märit! There are soldiers!"

Märit sticks her head out of the bedroom. "They're back?"

"But Märit, they are black soldiers. And Khoza is with them."

Märit's shoulders slump. "Have they come from across the border?"

"I don't know. But they mustn't find you!"

"What does it matter?"

"But we don't know what they want here."

"Soldiers do whatever they want," Märit says with resignation.

"They mustn't find you." Tembi grasps Märit by the arms. "You have to hide. The kraal! You can hide there in one of the huts."

Märit stands in the center of the room passively.

Tembi hustles her to the kitchen and peers out the back door. "Go on, Märit! Hide in one of the huts until they are gone." She gives her a push. "I'll come for you later."

Without urgency Märit walks down the path and through the trees.

Only when Märit is out of sight does Tembi turn and go to meet the soldiers, and Khoza.

The horsemen come to a halt at the foot of the veranda. Khoza does not come forward, and she realizes by the expression on his face that something is wrong. Have they captured him for some reason? But they are black soldiers. They are not the enemy.

One of the men urges his horse forward.

He is thick in the chest and shoulders, his uniform clean and neat, and he sits in the saddle with an air of authority. He is not like the soldiers who were here last night, who had a desperate and unkempt look about them and watched every little move she made.

"*Sawubona*, sister," the man says. "I greet you."

"*Sawubone*, Nkosi," Tembi answers, using a title of respect. She inclines her head slightly.

He smiles down at Tembi. "What is your name, sister?"

"I am called Tembi, Nkosi."

"You may call me Captain. Do you live here? With this young man?"

"Yes, Nkosi. We live here."

"Just the two of you?"

Tembi tries not to look at Khoza. What has he told them? "Yes, Nkosi. Just the two of us now."

"We have come a long way and we are thirsty. You will invite us into your house?"

"Of course, Nkosi. Please."

He dismounts. "Yes, why don't we sit in your comfortable kitchen and drink a cup of tea together? And this young man as well—Mr. Khoza. Come and join us, Mr. Khoza."

Tembi hurries to the kitchen to put the kettle on. She sees through the open door that there are soldiers at the back of the house too, but they seem to be taking no interest in the kraal.

The captain enters the kitchen, his boots loud on the floor, and pulls out a chair. "Sit here, Mr. Khoza." He takes a seat on the other side of the table.

Tembi prepares the tea.

"So," the captain says, "just the two of you living here in this nice house."

Tembi shoots a quick glance at Khoza but his face tells her nothing.

"The farmer died. And the workers left. The Missus too. After that we moved into the house."

"You didn't want to leave with the other workers?"

"There was nowhere to go."

She sets two cups of tea on the table and a plate of rusks.

The captain dips a rusk into the tea and chews it slowly. "Very good. I like rusks with my tea. Did you bake these yourself, sister?"

She nods.

He reaches for another rusk and looks up at her, his hand poised over the cup. "You must be glad to have some visitors, you and your young man all alone out here, so far from everything?"

"Yes, it's nice."

"And who else has been to see you lately?"

Tembi looks at Khoza.

"I ask you, not him," the captain says, still very polite.

"There have been no visitors, Nkosi." She looks down at her hands.

A figure passes by the doorway, a head looks in briefly and withdraws. There is something familiar in the glimpsed face, but her attention is drawn back to the captain.

"When I came into the kitchen I noticed three cups in the sink, not two. Why is that, if there are only two of you?"

Khoza is the one who answers. "Because I took a cup of tea to Tembi this morning when she was still in bed. Later, when we had breakfast, she took a clean cup from the cupboard."

Now Tembi knows that Khoza has said nothing about Märit. But she still does not know why Khoza has brought the soldiers. It dawns on her that it was they who brought him, not the other way round.

"How nice," the captain says, "just the two of you living here, and bringing each other cups of tea."

A man steps into the room. "She is lying!"

A soldier, but less well outfitted than the others, although he wears a beret and has a bandolier of bullets across his chest and a bayonet in a scabbard at his waist. He pulls off his beret with an angry gesture. "She is lying, Captain."

And now Tembi knows why the gesture of that head poking into the room a moment ago was familiar. She knows this man.

It is Joshua.

"They are both lying," Joshua says. "Where is the white woman? She wouldn't leave this farm."

The captain regards Tembi mildly. "Well, sister, do you have anything to say?"

"She left, a long time ago."

"Maybe they killed her," Joshua says, showing his discolored teeth in a sly leer. "And buried her in the fields, or in the kraal."

"It's this matter of the third cup that bothers me," the captain tells Tembi. "It bothers me just a little bit too much, so that I don't entirely believe you. And Mr. Khoza here, he seems to me to be quite nervous. Joshua, you know this farm—take some men and search the place."

Tembi gets up from her chair.

"No, sister, you can stay here. We will have some more tea. Just the three of us, since there are three cups."

They sit in silence. Every now and then the captain dips his rusk into the tea and chews slowly.

At last Khoza cannot hold his silence any longer. "Is there war? What is happening out there?"

"Yes, there is war."

"Are we beating them? Have you killed many? I would like to be out there, making them beg for their lives."

The captain studies Khoza with a bemused smile. "Why is it that young men are always so eager for killing? Is that the only purpose of war?"

Khoza scowls, and again Tembi wonders what he has told them. Do they know about the soldiers who were here last night? Will they find Märit?

MÄRIT SITS on a metal chair in the darkness of the hut, in the shadows, looking through the open door that frames the landscape—a rectangle of light cut out of the darkness. A bird flies across the canvas of light, perhaps a dove; a small cloud makes a slow trajectory from one corner of the sky to the other. In the thatched roof above her head she hears the faint scratching of a mouse in the straw. Dust motes float in the beam of sunlight like the slow drift of stars. A bead of perspiration trickles slowly down her ribs, as slow as the movement of dust and stars.

They will find her. Of course they will find her. It is inevitable. So she waits for them. And out there in the daylight is the farm. Just a place. No longer her farm, no longer anybody's farm. Here in the stillness and the shadows of the hut she waits for what will happen.

There have been times when Märit has found herself at the center of a stillness, in a quiet place in the landscape where the only sound is the bending of the blades of grass in a breath of wind, when she has imagined a world emptied of human voices. This farm, this country, this continent, this earth. It has not seemed to her then a difficult thing to leave it all, to go to a place that is nowhere.

She waits, feeling neither fear nor hope. She waits, because all living things wait. But her waiting is without hope. At the end of all her waiting is the end of hope.

Inside the hut the air is close and hot with the smell of straw. A tiny red ant crawls across her forearm. It meanders down across her fingers and then onto the cloth of her sarong. The motion of the ant seems futile to her, as futile as the drift of the dust motes in the beam of sunlight, as futile as the endless turning of the stars behind the thin fabric of the sky. She is without hope, she is without fear.

The shape of a man fills the doorway, darkness blocking the light, and even though she expects this, the suddenness of it makes her flinch—the quick eclipse of the daylight, the violence of another body entering the stillness of the hut.

Märit stands up. The man in the doorway points a gun at her. He has no identity for her, his face is a blank—one of the many, the countless, a child of the locust, come to claim his heritage.

"Here she is!" he cries.

Märit steps forward from the stillness into the storm.

"I told you we would find her," the soldier shouts. "Now we will see who is lying."

Märit knows this voice, so victorious at finding her. Yes, she knows him, and he knows her. He rushes towards her, triumphant, and she raises her head in defiance. He lifts his arm above his shoulder and slaps her across the face.

"Now we will see. Eh? Now we will see."

She raises her head again, in defiance, but he means nothing to her.

She recognizes the old cunning servility in his eyes, like a mark that he can never free himself from, even in his triumph.

"Don't look at me!" Joshua shouts, and raises his hand again.

Märit turns her back on him and begins to walk towards the house. His footsteps hurry after her, and she feels a shove in her back.

"Your friends are waiting for you. Now we will see, eh!" So close that she feels the spray of warm saliva on her neck.

In the kitchen Märit sees Tembi, and her heart lifts out of the stillness into which it has retreated. She smiles reassuringly, because Tembi's face is drawn and tight with worry. She smiles to show that she is unhurt and without fear.

Joshua, who has edged in right behind her and now has a tight grip on Märit's arm, says, "We found her, Captain. Hiding in the kraal. Just like I said. Hiding from us."

The man at the table looks Märit up and down, taking in her sarong, the *doek* on her head, the beads and bangles, her bare feet.

"And what are you supposed to be? An African?"

The soldiers laugh and Joshua prods her in the back.

"Who are you?" Märit demands.

"You can call me Captain Simba."

The men laugh again. She knows this word, it means Lion.

"My name is Märit Laurens. This is my farm."

"Your farm, you say? For a moment I thought you might be the *meid*, come to sweep the floor."

"What do you want here?"

Even as Märit speaks the words she knows it is the wrong thing to say, the tone of her voice is all wrong; it is a question she has asked before, a question any farmer would ask of a stranger on the property, of a black stranger.

"I don't like that kind of comment," the captain says. "I have heard it too often from your type."

She wonders if he too has been a servant in the past. But unlike Joshua, the servility never took root in him.

The captain taps his fingers on the table. "Are there any more of you out there in the kraal? Where is your husband, Missus Laurens?"

"Ask him," Märit says, shaking herself free from Joshua's grip. "Isn't he the one who brought you here so that he could have his revenge on us?"

"There was a husband, sir," Joshua says. "But he died. A casualty of the military struggle."

The captain lifts his cup and studies the dregs in the bottom for a moment. "We are not here for anybody's revenge, Missus Laurens. At least, not upon you." He looks up. "Although, as the poet has written, 'if you wrong us, shall we not revenge?'"

Märit frowns at him, unsure of where his conversation is leading.

"You don't know the reference?" the captain asks. "*The Merchant of Venice*. The Jew Shylock speaking."

She gives a small shake of her head, which the captain acknowledges with a smile.

"Does it surprise you that a nigger like me can quote Shakespeare? It must be something of a novelty to you Boer farmers, I suppose. But not to worry, we are bringing civilization with us. There is hope for you yet."

Märit feels out of her depth with this man. She could understand Schoon, whose intentions were always clear, but not this man, who seems not to say what he means, and to disguise what he means by talking of other things. Yet she senses that he is far more dangerous than Schoon ever was.

"What is it you want from me?"

The captain sits up straight, all irony leaving his voice. "Suppose you tell us about your friends, for instance."

"What friends?"

"Mr. Gideon Schoon."

"He is not a friend of mine. I barely know the man."

"But he has been a visitor here, more than once."

"Only on official business."

"Oh, I know all about Mr. Schoon's official business. He has been a busy man up and down this district. But now I have some business of my own to conduct with him." He stabs a finger at Märit. "There were soldiers here yesterday, your kind of soldiers. How many were they? Where are they going?"

"There were four of them," she answers readily. "Three soldiers and Schoon. They stayed only through the night. This morning they were gone."

"Ah." The captain turns to Khoza. "Yet this young man, this Mr. Khoza, tells me that there was nobody here. When I found him wandering through the countryside with a gun, he told me that he was hunting. Now, who should I believe?"

"Tell him the truth, Khoza," Märit says.

Khoza looks down and mumbles, "Yes, they were here. I was hunting them when you found me. I didn't tell you that because I am the one who will kill Schoon."

The captain laughs humorlessly. "So you have made the acquaintance of Mr. Schoon." He turns to Märit again. "Where were they going?"

"South. That's all he said. The war was going badly here and they were going south."

"Yes. It is going badly, especially for Mr. Schoon. Well, now, I am certainly eager to meet up with Mr. Schoon. And if there is any question of revenge I will be glad to discuss it with him. But let me ask you another question, Missus Laurens. I am curious—why did you not go with them?"

"There is nowhere to go."

"Yes, of course. No place to hide." The captain stands and stretches. "We will rest here a while, Missus Laurens, with your permission. Perhaps you can offer something refreshing to my men?"

"Take whatever it is that you need. Why ask me?"

A flash of anger crosses his eyes, then is gone. He chuckles. "Because we prefer to be civilized. We don't want to take. Isn't it much better if you offer hospitality, the same as you did for your friends last night?"

"They are not my friends."

"No, of course not. At the moment I fear that they are quite friendless." With his hands on his hips the captain surveys the kitchen. "Well, since you are so eager to dress the part of the *meid*, Missus Laurens, let us see how well you can play it. My men are hungry and thirsty."

Tembi pushes her chair away from the table and stands. "I will help you, Märit."

The captain shakes his head. "Oh, no, we can't have that, Miss Tembi. Not at all. Märit will be the *meid*. She will do the work. Anything else would be letting the side down. Come, leave her to it." He beckons with a finger at Khoza. "And you, Mr. Khoza, I would like you to stay within my sight."

IN THE EVENING, the captain commands Märit to prepare a meal for his men. He again forbids Tembi to enter the kitchen.

Märit measures out the fine white mealie meal into a pot. As she tips the last of the flour from the bag she realizes that this is the end of it. She adds water to the pot and sets it on the stove to boil. How many meals would this have made if she didn't have to feed the soldiers?

The soldiers have made a campfire outside the house. Märit brings the plates, the cutlery, the cups. She brings the pots of mealie-pap, any vegetables she could find, rusks, some strips of jerky. She brings everything.

When Tembi tries to help, the captain restrains her. "Sit down. She will serve."

She moves amongst the men silently, handmaiden to them. She spoons food onto their plates, she pours water into their cups. Her eyes are downcast, her step light. After the food is served, she returns to the kitchen and sits at the table to wait. She is invisible, she is a ghost.

Around the fire the soldiers eat the food of the farm. The liquor cabinet has been opened, all the bottles are brought out. The liquor is passed around amongst the men. When they have eaten, Märit collects the pots and the plates and the cutlery and the cups. The men lounge on the ground, smoking, passing around the liquor bottles. Märit walks with downcast eyes.

She washes the dishes and the cups and puts them back into their places on the shelves. From outside the house she hears the sound of music—somebody has a concertina, somebody has a harmonica. There is laughter, there is sudden singing.

If she wanted to she could walk away into the night. The guards are nowhere to be seen. She is alone, invisible.

The soldiers have stoked up the fire on the lawn and are gathered in a rough circle. The light glints on bottles being passed around. Three of the soldiers are moving in an impromptu dance, shuffling back and forth, then raising their legs and stamping them in time to the music.

Märit leans against the stone wall of the house and watches from the shadows. She steps away from the wall and approaches the fire, trying to see if Tembi is there.

One of the soldiers notices her. "Come and dance for us, Missus!"

Märit ignores him.

The soldier reaches for Märit's wrist and pulls her into the circle of light. "You can dance now, Missus." The smell of brandy is on his breath.

She breaks away and tries to retreat into the shadows again, where she can be invisible, but the circle closes around her, hands push her back towards the flames.

"Dance, Missus!"

She begins to dance, mimicking the shuffle and stamping of feet. The

346

music increases in tempo; the men clap their hands, speeding up the dance.

Märit stumbles and is caught and pushed towards the fire. Someone presses a bottle to her lips and she tries to move her head away but the liquid is poured across her lips and when she opens her mouth to gasp for breath the brandy spills down her throat.

Märit lurches away, her eyes searching for Tembi.

Hands spin her around, the men clap and chant. Somebody holds her arms and pours liquor into her mouth. The music and the clapping and the chanting and the men's feet stamping out the rhythm on the earth and the dancing flames and her spinning feet—everything whirls faster and faster. The night blurs and gyrates, and the stars tilt in the sky and slide towards the horizon.

She stumbles again and falls against arms that swing her upright. As she is pushed into the circle of light again, a hand snatches at her sarong. Märit slaps the hand away, but someone else grasps her shoulders and twirls her off balance again, and another hand pulls at her clothes. She staggers out of their reach, but the circle closes in on her, pressing tighter, a circle of hands snatching at her clothes.

"Dance, Missus! Dance!"

Märit tries to break through the press of bodies, to get out from the circle, but now she is being pushed back and forth roughly, back and forth between the hands. Someone grasps the hem of her sarong and jerks hard. The force spins her towards the flames and the sarong comes loose. With a quick tug it is pulled free from her body and she falls towards the fire, at the last moment twisting to avoid the flames.

And suddenly the heat is on her bare skin and the sarong is tossed past her head. Märit makes an ineffectual grab for it, but too late. It bursts into flame on the blazing coals. She falls to her knees in her underpants. The men whistle and shout. She turns in one direction, then the other, clutching her hands over her exposed body. Everywhere the faces of strangers, laughing at her. She cannot hide. Whichever way she turns, they see her, see her nakedness.

Märit tries to curl into a ball. The circle tightens around her. Hands pluck at her arms, pulling her upright, exposing her body to their mockery.

"Leave her alone!"

The cry is shrill, cutting through the laughter and the whistling, silencing the music.

Tembi forces her way through the jeering soldiers. "Get away!" she screams. "Leave her alone!" She puts an arm around Märit's shoulders and pulls her outside the circle of men.

Head down, tears streaming down her cheeks, hands clutched across her front, Märit stumbles away from the fire.

"Come away from here, Märit," Tembi urges. "Come away."

Then the captain is there next to them. "Let her go," he says, separating the two women roughly. He sneers at Märit scornfully, "You, go on. Get away from us."

Sobbing, Märit flees into the darkness, then veers back to the house in a panic. In the bedroom she grabs clothes, any clothes, frantically trying to cover her shame, before she bolts back into the night.

If only Ben were still here, to protect her, to order these invaders off her land, to kick them back out into the veldt.

Somehow she finds the hut in the kraal, somehow she manages to drag the battered dresser across the entrance, then she retreats into the farthest, darkest corner she can find and curls herself against the mud wall, pulling the old mattress up around her, cowering down into the darkness where nobody can see her, where there is only the desperate thud of her own heart.

Exhaustion finally envelops her and she burrows deeper under the mattress, closing her eyes.

IN THE DARKEST HOUR a scuffling comes at the entrance to the hut, a creak as the dresser is shifted.

Märit jerks upright.

A barely audible whisper from the darkness. "Märit? Märit, are you in there?"

"Tembi?"

"Märit!"

"Tembi," she whimpers.

The dresser moves and a shape slips through the gap, fingers searching for Märit's face. A racking sob bursts from Märit's chest and she flings herself into Tembi's arms.

"Oh, Märit, I'm sorry. I'm so very sorry for this." Tembi's hot tears splash down, mingling with Märit's own. "I wanted to help you. Oh, Märit!"

Märit weeps like a child; her heart breaks and convulses, the sobs shaking her body. Tembi's fingertips soothe away the tears from Märit's cheeks.

"I want to die," Märit moans.

"Shh." Tembi cradles Märit's head against her breast. "I'm so very, very sorry."

"I want to die."

Tembi strokes Märit's face and her tears fall. "Weep instead. Weep."

And Märit weeps. Until, like a weeping child, she is depleted and emptied and exhausted, and like a child, she lays her head on Tembi's breast and falls into weary slumber.

52

TEMBI WAKES in a place that is at once familiar and strange. The events of the night before come back with a stabbing clarity that makes her want to press her eyes shut and retreat into sleep. Carefully she eases away from the sleeping Märit and edges past the dresser in the doorway and into the empty kraal. How desolate the farm seems! Where can she go? Who must she be? As she stands on the morning-cool ground, Tembi feels as if she is being tugged in two directions at once. Behind her in the hut is Märit, wounded and broken. In the house is Khoza. If only life were different. If only it were Khoza who slept in the hut now, and there were no farmhouse, no soldiers, no history of pain on this farm. If only it were Khoza who slept peacefully in the hut now while she made the morning fire, and cooked the breakfast for him. And afterwards they would go together into the fields and the gardens, man and woman.

Her body goes warm and weak inside when she remembers the night she spent in the hut with Khoza, and the tenderness in his hands as they caressed her. And then her heart chills, because she remembers the scorn in Khoza's eyes when he watched the men force Märit to dance, and she remembers that he stood by and did nothing to stop the torment. Her heart chills even as her body remembers the tenderness.

She is being pulled in two directions at once, and neither place will ease the loneliness that has descended upon her as she stands in the desolation of the deserted kraal.

*   *   *

Tembi seeks refuge in the only place she can—her garden. Each time she visits here she is afraid that some small animal will have discovered a way through the barrier, and she will find nothing but cheweddown stalks. Always her heart beats a little faster in apprehension as she moves the thornbushes aside.

But all is safe. The plants have spread across the whole surface of the little plot—thick stalks of vine winding over the soil, and the glistening dew upon them—and from these vines branch off smaller stalks and leaves. Distributed amongst the vines are the five fruits, each in its own place, quite separate from its neighbors, as if each has found its own best place.

Each fruit is now the size of her bunched fist. And each fruit is a pale yellow, darkening slightly where it is joined to its stalk, soft to the gentle pressure of her fingers, almost ripe.

Tembi has no name for these fruits; she knows only the taste they will have when ripe.

Lifting her bucket she pours out water, an equal measure for each of the yellow fruits, the water trickling down towards the roots. Her careful fingers snip off any dried or discolored leaves. Then she arranges the barrier of thornbushes to protect her garden, making sure no gap exists to tempt entrance.

Her heart is lifted by the growth of these five yellow fruits, for through all the hardship and change they are constant in their purpose—to ripen and grow in the sun, to bring forth sweetness out of the earth.

The time will come, one day, when she will gather the fruits in her hand and bring them to Märit, and to Khoza—a gift. The day will come.

Tembi raises her face to the sun, and the warm rays dispel the fog and chill that grips her heart. She raises her face to the sun, and the warmth brings hope to her soul.

The morning sun rises above the hills and above the trees, and the warmth of the sun falls upon the fields and the grasses. The birds call to the sun newly risen, and somewhere the beasts of the field lift their heads to the scent of the warmth that falls upon them. And somewhere, the women and men of the earth find hope in their hearts.

The grass in the orchard is thick underfoot, littered with fallen peaches, and a sweet jam-like smell hangs in the air. In the dappled yellow and green sunlight, bees hum and buzz in the patches of sunlight, gorging themselves on sweetness.

Once, as a small girl, Tembi walked somewhere through a grove of fruit trees like this one, hand in hand with her father, in an orchard similar to this one, where the perfume of peaches and the humming of bees was like a paradise hidden in the dry veldt. The fruit was high above her head, too high for her, and her father reached up to a branch to pluck a ripe peach for Tembi. From his pocket her father brought out a small penknife that sparkled bright in the sunlight. With the knife so delicate in his large hands he carefully peeled the peach, turning the fruit in his hand as the small blade sliced the skin into a long curving spiral. He held the spiral up for her to see, then cut a sliver of the fruit and placed it delicately on her lips.

Tembi remembers the brief sensation of the knife blade on her lip, followed by the exquisite sweetness of the peach flesh on her tongue.

She loved her father for this. She admired him beyond measure. She loved him for his skill, his assurance, but mostly for the fact that he would bring down the peach from its branch and peel and cut it so cleverly, all for her. Even though she was a child she knew his devotion, and even though she was a child she realized that it was possible to love a man for the kindness in him. Her heart breaks for his absence. Here in this leafy enclosure where the smell of ripe fruit is in the air and the bees hum in the dappled light, her heart breaks for his absence.

A horse is loose in the orchard, one of the soldiers' horses, cropping at the grass near where she stands. She hears the sound of its teeth pulling at the grass, and when she moves forward, it looks up at her with mild and gentle eyes. Oh, where is her father, that he cannot ride up to this house on his own horse, and call her name, and taste the sweetness of the gift that she grows for him in her garden.

Tembi moves towards the horse, her hand extended to stroke its warm flank, to feel the gentle life in it, to touch the long smooth neck.

The horse jerks its head suddenly.

A man steps out from behind a tree. When she sees his face Tembi's heart freezes.

Joshua.

He moves out from behind the tree, where he has been watching her, and heads straight towards Tembi. The skin on her arms prickles in alarm. Then she sees the bayonet in his hand, the blade that catches the sunlight and reflects it back in a silvery gleam.

Tembi runs. She does not pause to cry out, or even to draw a breath. She runs. For her life.

He darts to block her passage towards the house. She turns the other way, towards the river, but again he anticipates her and dashes forward, suddenly in front of her.

Tembi races towards the kraal. Joshua's breathing is hoarse behind her, almost upon her neck, and the drumming of his feet on the ground is as loud as the drumming in her heart.

Joshua kicks one of her heels so that her legs tangle and she pitches upon the ground. Tembi rolls away, trying to regain her feet, but he is quickly upon her, the bayonet flashing in front of her eyes. He straddles her waist and brings the blade of steel down towards her neck, the sharp point pricking at her flesh.

"Shut up or I'll kill you!"

She shrinks from the blade.

His eyes are wild, yet determined. Tembi knows in this instant what he wants, even though she has never experienced this look from a man before. She knows it instinctively, as a woman. There is no other thought in his eyes.

The tip of the bayonet cuts her skin—a small cut only.

She submits because of the determination in his eyes and the inhumanity of his gaze, and she submits because of the bayonet at her neck. She knows that if she struggles, or screams for help, he will kill her. She submits, because it is better to live than to die. If she is nothing to him, then this will be nothing to her—less than nothing. She will not give up her life to this man, no matter what else she must sacrifice. She is not Tembi to him, not an individual. She is just a female animal, to be hunted, to be taken. She is nothing to him. Nothing more than this.

Tembi lies inert and submits as his knee forces her thighs apart and his hand pushes up her dress and tears away her underpants. She stills herself and endures as he unbuckles his belt and forces her thighs wider apart.

She turns her head away.

A fallen peach lies near her head, the flesh exposed on one side where birds have pecked at it. She smells the faint sourness of the decaying fruit. A small green caterpillar is making its slow and deliberate way across the surface of the peach. And then there is a sudden buzzing as a wasp lights on the fruit. The caterpillar lifts its head, antennae querying the shape in front of it. The wasp falls upon the caterpillar.

Joshua shudders above her, his hoarse panting loud in her ears. Then he rolls away.

She hears him fasten his belt and stand up.

"If you speak of this, I will find you and kill you," he says. "You and your Missus. All of you."

His footsteps recede across the grass.

Still she watches the wasp devouring the caterpillar, and she lies there under the indifferent sky with the semen drying on her thighs.

AT LAST Tembi lifts herself from the grass. She does not look to see where the man is. He is nothing to her.

With slow steps she makes her way out of the orchard. At the riverbank she removes her dress and wades into the water, forward into the river until the flowing current rises to her neck, to her lips, over her eyes. Deep into the water she plunges. How easy now to just open her mouth and let the river fill her and take her away. The shame is upon her like a great weight, heavy enough to carry her down into the depths. Her lungs cry out for air, but she holds herself below the surface, holding the weight of the pain in her chest. But she cannot. She kicks her feet against the bottom of the river and surfaces, gulping down air, even though there is no sweetness in the air and there is no music in the voices of the birds and there is no warmth in the sun. She breathes only because she must, to live, and it is better to live than to die.

If she could go naked when she emerges from the river, naked across the veldt, she would, but she must clothe herself, even though her dress is a garment of shame to her now. But she clothes herself, then walks away from the river, away from the orchard, away from the house, and up the slope of the small hill to the place where the graves of her people rest.

And here is the resting place of her mother.

Tembi stands there with her hands clasped together. "I greet you, my mother," she says.

And in her mind she hears the answering, *"And I greet you, my daughter."*

Tembi stands for a long moment with sorrow in her heart. For all that she has lost, for all that will never be. Only her mother and the company of the dead will ever truly have a place on this farm.

And where is God?

She weeps at last. Tembi weeps as she kneels at her mother's grave, placing the palms of her hands flat on the ground. She prays, and the words of the prayer are bitter with her tears.

The morning light rises above the hills and above the trees, and the warmth of the sun falls lightly upon the fields and the grasses. The birds call to the sun newly risen, and somewhere the beasts of the field lift their heads to the scent of the warmth that falls upon them. And somewhere, in some other place, even the women and men of the earth find hope in their hearts. But not in this place.

53

Märit can no longer bear to remain hidden in the hut. Whatever the consequences, she must return to the house. Even if she must be a servant and suffer the derision and scorn of the soldiers.

Outside the house the soldiers are gathering their horses together and loading up their weapons and packs. The remains of last night's campfire are cold ashes, a couple of empty bottles tossed onto the remnants. Märit avoids looking in that direction and stands to one side, partly hidden, watching a soldier loading a mule with bundles that he brings from the house. They are taking what is left of the food, she realizes, they are taking everything. But she cannot run forward to stop them. She is afraid of the soldiers, of their casual brutality.

Khoza struts back and forth amongst the horses with an air of self-importance, inspecting bridles and saddles, stopping here and there to pat a horse on the rump and exchange a word with the soldier seated in the saddle.

When all the soldiers are mounted, the captain makes a quick inspection of his troops. Then he turns to Khoza.

"You can lead the mule."

"What? Why?" Khoza looks around in befuddlement.

"Didn't you tell us last night of your bravery and your ability with a gun? What a good shot you are? Don't you want to kill Schoon? Well, you can come with us."

Khoza backs away with a sheepish grin on his face.

"No . . . I should stay here. . . ."

"Not so brave after all," says the captain, and a couple of the men laugh mockingly.

"I should stay here to look after the farm," Khoza responds.

"Ah, you want to stay with the women and do women's work. Or is it that you are afraid?"

Khoza mumbles, "I'm not a soldier."

The captain walks to the mule and unfastens a coil of rope from the saddle, which he then ties into a loop at one end. He approaches Khoza with a smile on his face and with a quick motion drops the loop around his shoulders and jerks the knot tight, trapping Khoza's arms flat against his body.

Before Khoza can react, the captain mounts his horse and tugs at the rope, causing Khoza to stumble forward.

"I will teach you how to be a soldier," the captain says. He kicks his horse into motion and Khoza has to run to keep from being dragged to the ground.

"Stop!" a voice cries with such authority that all activity ceases.

Tembi comes running up the driveway.

"What are you doing? Where are you taking him?" she demands, planting herself in front of the captain's horse.

He ignores her and nudges his horse forward.

Tembi runs to Khoza and begins to work the loop free from his shoulders.

The captain shouts an order to one of his soldiers and the man leaps from his saddle. He grabs the rope from the captain, and before Tembi can react, he wraps it around her as well. The soldier mounts his horse again and fastens the other end of the rope to the pommel of his saddle.

"I don't mind if you come too," the captain says to Tembi.

Only now does Märit rouse herself from her passive watching.

"Leave them alone! Let them go!"

Reining his horse back the captain shouts, "Go back, woman. Go back to your house. It is yours again."

Märit dodges between the horses towards Tembi. "They are just children. You don't need them in your war." She grasps the rope and tries to jerk it loose.

A rider detaches himself from the group and spurs his mount in Märit's direction. She tries to dart away, but the horseman wheels upon her. She sees that it is Joshua in the saddle.

"Bitch!" Joshua shouts, and urges his horse into a gallop. As he bears down on her he lifts a foot from the stirrup and kicks hard between Märit's shoulder blades. The impact throws Märit to her knees. The horse is charging down upon her again, the hooves flashing and whirling around her. She falls to one side, raising her hands to protect her face, hearing somewhere the screams of Tembi, then a sudden pain burns along her leg, a pain so intense that nausea rises in her throat, and then a light bursts between her eyes. She hears a sound like the rushing of wind, and the wind sucks the light away, leaving her in darkness.

MÄRIT'S FACE IS WET when she comes back to consciousness. For a moment she is outside of time, outside of all awareness except for the gentle comforting drizzle on her face and the cool, misty light.

Rain. It has been so long since she felt the touch of rain on her skin. She lies on her back in the damp silence, letting the drizzle bathe her lips and cheeks. And then the image of the horse charging upon her breaks through her stillness and she sits up abruptly. Where is Tembi?

A searing pain shoots up the length of her right leg, and she gasps in shock. She lies back and waits for the pain to lessen, and when it abates slightly, down to a persistent throb, like a terrible toothache, she gingerly leans forward and examines her leg.

Her ankle is cut, deeply gashed down the inner side, the skin purple and black. But there is no blood from the deep gash. She touches the cut, wincing again, and sees a whitish gristle. Nausea makes her turn her head away. How terrible to see her own bone beneath the skin!

She falls on her back again and waits for the nausea to subside, for the pain to lessen.

The sky is a uniform gray, the light without variation. How long has she been here? Where is Tembi, where is Khoza, where have the soldiers taken them?

I can't lie here, she tells herself. I must go after them. I cannot let them just take Tembi away like that. I have to do something. She sits up, then turns to her left and kneels, letting all her weight rest upon her left leg, then pushes herself unsteadily to her feet, the bile rising in her throat because the pain is so terrible—but she must stand, she must get to the house. As she takes a step forward, having to put pressure on her other foot, the pain makes her scream out loud, her voice the only sound in the silent drizzle.

The few yards towards the veranda steps are the most dreadful journey she has ever undertaken, each step excruciating, each step a weight that threatens to snap her ankle, each step filling her mouth with bile. But she must go on, she must reach the house. She will die if she does not, she will die lying in the dust outside her own house. And Tembi will be lost, cast into the hands of strangers.

Here is the railing; she clutches her fingers around the wood gratefully, then up the first stair, no, the pain is too much, she turns and sits backwards on the stair and levers herself up, then the next one, pushing with her good foot and using her arms as props, all the way up the six wide stairs; then, still pushing, she manages to get to the door, reaches up with one hand to open it, then into the hall, into the living room, here is the couch, one last effort to lift herself. She sits a long while with her eyes closed, waiting for her heart to stop its wild beating, for the fire in her body to cool.

When she opens her eyes and looks around the room, the familiar room, her breath is taken away. The radio has been smashed, the telephone ripped from the wall and flung across the room, the pictures shattered and broken, the furniture gashed.

The sight of it is too much, like a blow to her heart. A final wave of pain shudders through her. She collapses onto the cushions and slips into unconsciousness.

Märit wakes in the dark house. Her leg throbs with a pulsing, biting pain. When she places her foot on the floor she realizes that she will not be able to walk without some kind of aid.

Lowering herself onto all fours Märit begins a slow crawl towards the kitchen, using her knees, holding her injured foot up from the floor. She crawls all the way into the pantry and finds what she is looking for—the broom. Levering herself to her feet Märit upends the broom so that the wide part with the soft bristles can fit into the niche of her armpit, and the broom becomes a makeshift crutch.

She hobbles to the sink and holds a glass under the tap, waiting for the slow trickle of water to fill the glass. How thirsty she suddenly is! She gulps the water down and fills the glass again. The water trickles even more slowly, then ceases.

Now there is only the future. But the future is too terrible to contemplate. Märit stretches out on the couch and curls her head into the cushions and shuts her eyes. She is too weary, too weary of everything.

Her mouth is dry, her body aching, in darkness, not knowing where she is except that she is in some abandoned place. The texture of the cushion pressed under her check is unfamiliar, the feel of her face against her hand is unfamiliar, the ache down her side has an unknown cause and origin, the darkness is unfamiliar.

A cool waft of air drifts across her face, then a moment later the smell of something warm, something living, something animal.

She knows that she is alone in the house, that she is injured, that somewhere a door or window is open. A noise sounds from the direction of the kitchen, as if a cupboard door is slowly being opened. Something clatters into the sink. Someone in the house.

Märit sits upright, wide eyes trying to see into the darkness. The zoo smell—the warm living animal smell—is suddenly very strong. Märit stares towards the vague outline of the doorway leading to the corridor.

A soft cough out there. A shape in the doorway, darker than the darkness, something upright, shoulders, arms, a head. Moving slowly into the room towards her.

Märit fumbles on the side table for matches—somewhere here, didn't she see a box? Where are they? Her fingers close on the box, she draws a match out and strikes it across the phosphorous strip.

"Who is it?" she cries as the match flares.

A figure leaps past her, crashes into the front door, turns, upends a lamp. Footsteps down the corridor.

Märit screams. The match goes out.

Then silence, and the air in the room is full of the rank living smell.

What was it? So fast that she saw nothing but a figure. Was it an animal? Not a person, surely, to move with such agility. Yet it had a human shape, like a long-limbed child.

Märit strikes another match and holds it high above her head, but she knows the intruder has gone. Who was it, what did it want?

The flickering light from the match dies. How she hates this darkness! Märit bends down and finds the broom and levers herself upright. Pain banishes all other thoughts from her mind, and she stands a long time, leaning on the broom heavily, waiting for the fire in her leg to lessen. Slowly she hobbles down the corridor and into the kitchen. The back door is ajar, the night air drifts in. With one hand she slams it shut, then hobbles over to the table, remembering that a candle stands on the windowsill.

When it is lit she sinks down into the chair, her arms shaking. Her leg is throbbing, almost unbearably, and when she moves the candle closer to the edge of the table so that she can examine her ankle, what she sees sends a wave of panic through her.

Her ankle has puffed up like some bloated fruit, purple as an overripe plum, the gash from the horse's hoof a raw red line stitched across the swollen skin, and the rest of her foot is a sickly yellow color. She winces as her fingers probe the flesh.

Somewhere in the kitchen cupboards is a first aid kit, she remembers. She must get some aspirin, something for this pain. And disinfectant. The sight of her ankle frightens her.

With the aid of the crutch, and with the candle in her other hand, she hops over to the cupboards, wax spilling hot onto her fingers, and she groans with the agony in her leg.

There is nothing in the cupboard. Stunned, she stares at the empty shelves. Nothing. Not a single dish or cup. Nothing but the one glass that she drank from earlier, now standing in the sink. Her first thought is that the intruder has stolen everything. But how could it—wasn't it some kind of animal? The soldiers, she realizes, they have taken everything. She slams the cupboard door angrily. How could they! How could they steal everything like this? Her anger is replaced swiftly by a more pressing anxiety. The food!

Disregarding the pain, she scuttles into the pantry, pulling open cupboards, her hands touching nothing but bare shelves. Nothing. Not even the two tins of corned beef and the coffee jar that she had hidden on the top shelf. They have found everything, and taken it from her.

She remembers that there is maize and fruit drying in the sheds. Have they taken that too? But she cannot go now, in the darkness, with a strange animal out there. In the morning. In the morning when she feels better, when the pain is less. But without aspirin, without disinfectant, will the pain be less? The thought is too terrible to contemplate. Everything is too terrible.

Leaning on the crutch Märit shuffles back to the sink and turns on the tap, holding the glass under the faucet. A slow trickle appears, then ceases. She turns the handle back and forth and bangs on the pipe. A few more drops of water trickle into the glass. Have the soldiers smashed the pump as well?

Märit groans and rests her head against the cupboard. Now this too. No food, no medicine, no water. And crippled. Märit drinks the last half glass of water.

Making her slow and arduous way along the few yards to the bedroom, she reaches her wardrobe and opens the doors. Empty. The dresser is empty as well. They have taken everything.

54

FOR THE FIRST MILE or so after the soldiers leave the farm, both Tembi and Khoza are forced into a trot to keep up with the horse to which they are roped, no words exchanged between them, all their efforts directed towards not stumbling and being dragged across the ground.

An outrider comes galloping back and exchanges a few words with the captain, who then wheels his horse around and approaches Khoza. "You saw the direction those men were traveling in. Which way is it?"

Khoza nods towards the valley. "Somewhere up there."

The captain dismounts and unties Khoza. "Come on, you can go up front with the trackers and show us."

Khoza turns a helpless glance towards Tembi as he is pushed up to the head of the troop. The horses set off again, though at a slower pace, except for a group of fast riders that gallop ahead.

All through the day the soldiers press on. At one point the rope that binds Tembi is unfastened and draped around her neck in a loop, then tied to the mule that carries the soldier's supplies. Most of the soldiers have ridden on ahead, and she walks with only two guards, one in front and one behind.

Tembi turns to look back at the route they have covered, but the farm is long out of sight, the landscape is unfamiliar. For a moment she hopes that she will see the figure of Märit outlined against the top of a hill—Märit following. But there is nothing, there is nobody following beneath the gray sky, and Tembi is left only with that last image of Märit collapsed on the ground and the horse charging over her. Her heart aches. Is Märit lying there in the dust, hurt, unable to move? When Tembi looks at the column of soldiers moving ahead of her she wonders if she will ever see her home again.

The rope chafes at her neck, but when she tries to lift it, a harsh word from one of the guards warns her to stop. She thinks of trying to escape, of slipping free from the rope and dashing away, but she knows that on foot in this unfamiliar country she will soon be caught.

She walks on—thirsty, tired, dispirited.

In the early afternoon a halt is called. The soldiers dismount for a meal of cold mealie-pap and water from their canteens. Tembi sinks to the ground, weary, her feet aching. A plate of porridge and a tin mug of water are set in front of her, but she barely lifts her head.

Then Khoza sits down next to her and reaches across to squeeze her hand. "Eat something," he says.

Her spirits lift at the sight of him and she manages a weak smile. "How are you, Khoza? Are you all right?"

He glances over at the guards, then winks at her as he uses his fingers to lift the mealie-pap to his mouth.

"Where are they taking us?" Tembi asks.

"They want to catch that man. The one called Schoon."

"Are they going to kill him?"

Khoza shakes his head. "They should. But they want to put him on trial in a courthouse. He has committed crimes."

Tembi picks at her food, swallowing morsels of the cold porridge. "And us? Why does the captain want us? What have we done?"

"I think he just took us to spite Märit. Because we were friendly with her. He took us away to spite her. He doesn't like white people."

"How will all this end? What is going to happen to Märit all alone on the farm? She is hurt. You saw what happened."

Khoza shakes his head and shrugs, any answer he is about to make cut short by a command from the captain for the men to mount up again.

Once more Tembi is separated from Khoza as the rest of the troops range ahead of the slow-moving mule. Once more Tembi walks with the chafing rope around her neck under the watchful eyes of the guards, moving towards the unknown future. The mule plods on next to her, its large brown eyes long-suffering, resigned. Tembi reaches out a hand and strokes the animal's neck soothingly, a gesture that perhaps does more to calm her own distress than offer any comfort to the mule.

Through the long afternoon the journey continues. Tembi walks on at the same steady, resigned pace as the mule, aware only from the position of the sun ahead of her that they are heading southeast. The country here is unknown to her, with many shallow valleys surrounded by green hills where thin streams flow down to the valley floor. Sometimes she glimpses the soldiers up ahead as they crest a hill, and again on the floor of the valley as she herself descends the same hill. Sometimes she makes out the figure of Khoza.

Only when dusk approaches, when the group halts to make camp, is Khoza allowed to join her. There is a weariness and a disappointed air about the soldiers, their quarry still eluding them. One of the men unfastens the rope and brusquely orders Tembi and Khoza to gather firewood.

Tembi sighs audibly as she sets about her task, weary, but glad to have Khoza at her side again.

"Are you very tired?" Khoza asks.

She nods.

"We should try to escape," he says.

She looks back at the soldiers, who are unpacking bedrolls and weapons from their horses. "They'll notice, and chase us."

"I don't think so. They don't care about us." He lowers his voice. "Pretend you are getting wood and slowly move up into the trees. We can run when we are out of sight. You go first." As she moves away, he hisses, "Not so fast! Make it look like you are searching for the firewood."

Stooping every now and then to gather up a small branch or handful of twigs, Tembi works her gradual way into the copse of trees. Then, when she is hidden from sight, she hurries on a few more yards and stops to wait for Khoza.

A moment later he joins her. "Come on, let's go, quickly," he urges, grasping her hand.

Tembi lets the wood fall to the ground and runs with him. As they emerge from the shelter of the trees to a gentle slope that leads up out of the hidden valley, Tembi sees a soldier standing with his back to her.

She stops immediately and pulls back.

Khoza puts his face close to her ear. "We can sneak round him," he whispers. "Down this way through the grass. He won't see us if we crawl."

The man half turns, showing his profile, and Tembi immediately recognizes him. Joshua.

Khoza is tugging at her hand, jerking his head for her to get down and follow him. Tembi looks back at the man. She cannot move. She cannot take her eyes from the figure of Joshua. She stares at him with revulsion, with dreadful fascination, like a rabbit staring at a snake, unable to move.

The man clears his throat with a loud, ugly rasping sound, then leans forward and spits into the grass. Tembi feels as if she will faint. She steps back into the trees without removing her eyes from the figure of Joshua. Khoza is on his knees in the long grass, beckoning to her, frowning hard.

Slowly Tembi shakes her head, then turns and walks back to the camp. She finds her pile of wood, gathers it up into her arms, and walks back to the clearing.

When Khoza catches up to her he whispers, "Why didn't you come? What's wrong?"

What can she say to him, what can she tell him? The mix of emotions coursing through her is too confusing, too strong. Her body is filled with a sickness. Dropping her eyes she mumbles, "I am too tired. Too tired."

Tembi sleeps huddled close against Khoza. She feels numb, empty, and she nestles in against his chest for warmth. She is glad of him, glad of his enfolding presence and warmth.

"Don't worry," Khoza says softly, stroking her face. "This will end, then we can go home."

But where will home be? she wonders. Her heart aches for Märit, lying in the dust. Her heart aches for the farm, for her mother, for her father. Her heart aches for everything.

She presses her face close against his chest, burrowing closer, and she falls asleep to the sound of the slow beat of his heart.

55

HER MOUTH IS DRY. A rectangle of light is burning on the wall where the sun strikes the plaster, and the bright hot rectangle is like the doorway into a desert, a place of terrible thirst.

Märit sees small figures in the distance, shimmering and indistinct as they travel across the dry, salty plain. She calls to them, but the harsh light blinds her and beats her down to her knees, and when she raises her head the figures are gone. The taste of salt is in her mouth.

With an effort she sits upright on the couch and stretches to look out the window. Nothing but the blue sky and the brown earth. What time is it? Once a slim silver watch used to adorn her wrist, but it is gone now. She does not know what has become of time. There is only light and dark, hunger and thirst.

When Märit looks at the ransacked room, at the torn armchairs, the smashed pictures on the walls, the broken radio and the telephone, they seem foreign to her, outside of the consciousness she inhabits, objects in another world in which she no longer exists.

Once she lived here, with other people, but they are gone now. When was that? Who were they? Their faces will not come to her; she remembers only a brown-skinned girl.

Raising her hands before her face Märit studies her fingers. They don't seem to belong to her, they seem to be outside of time, in that other place along with the furniture and the brown earth. The woman that lived in this house, that walked across this land, whose name was Märit, is no longer here. That was someone else. Not her.

Slowly lucidity returns, and she remembers. She remembers everything. She looks down at her leg, at the ugly poisonous swollen thing that is her foot. Thin lines of red show on the skin, like veins, drawn up her calf towards the knee.

I am being poisoned, she thinks. There is something wrong with my thinking and it is because I am being poisoned by my own body. When these red lines reach my heart I will die.

Grasping the broom she struggles to her feet, accepting the wave of pain that wants to pull her into the desert. Pain is a condition of living, she thinks. There is always pain. First I will have a drink of water and then I will go and lie down in the desert.

No water pours forth from the kitchen taps. She runs her finger around the inside of the glass standing on the counter and dabs the single drop of moisture across her lips. I will go down to the river and I will drink and I will bathe and I will wash away the salt of the desert, she tells herself.

The river lies beyond the vast expanse of desert that Märit must cross, but cross it she must. There is no hunger now, there is no fatigue. There is only thirst.

How many hours does it take her to cross that vast distance? There is no time. There is only eternity. Sometimes pain and fatigue force her to stop and she sinks to her knees and bows her head, because the journey is too long, the river is too far, the desert is too vast.

When she looks back, the small farmhouse with its thatched roof is far, far away. When she turns her head in the other direction the willow trees are a vague shimmering green in the far, far distance. But go on she must, for she is thirsty, and she must drink; otherwise she will die.

Above her head is the blue sky, empty, and at her feet is a piece of the sky, fallen. Märit slowly bends down and touches the blue, her fingers closing around a bracelet of blue glass beads. She stands, dizzy for a moment, then fastens the bracelet around her wrist. She sobs quietly for a minute, because Tembi is gone, because she is lost in the desert, and her steps are small and slow and carry her nowhere.

The river is near, so near, yet so far. Her progress is slow and painful, her foot a constant searing flame, but she struggles on, for she must have water. The crutch is chafing in her armpit, her swollen foot is a shackle that binds her to the earth. She can smell the water, and she swallows the salty saliva in her mouth, and she goes on. She goes on through the desert of pain because otherwise she will die.

I am thirsty, she says, and perhaps she says it aloud, or perhaps there are no words. Words belong to time and there is no time now. There is only the matter of life and death. But who is dead and who is alive? All the others are dead, all the others who used to be here in this place—the man who loved her, the boy who came out of the veldt, the brown-skinned girl. Or is it she who is dead? Is it she who walks now with the hyenas?

Water! Like a wave breaking on the shore the sweet smell of water washes over her and she hears the gurgling of the river flowing over the rocks and she hears the birdsong in the trees.

Casting aside the crutch Märit tumbles down the bank and flings her body into the shallows. Oh, the cool water, across her face, into her open mouth, wetting her parched throat. Sweet, sweet water! She gulps at the water, immersing her head, drinking it down. Using her elbows she pushes herself farther into the stream, the water so cool and sweet along her body.

When she has drunk her fill, when thirst is no longer thirst, Märit rolls over onto her back and eases her injured leg under the water. The pain is there still, a constant companion, but it troubles her less now that it is no longer linked with thirst. She lies on her back in the shallows and lets the flowing river wash over her, soothing, cooling, restoring.

Hope returns, time returns, the future becomes possible once more.

A plan, a possibility, begins to form in her mind. Somewhere on the farm she will find food, dried corn, or fruit, and once she has rested she will go for help. Somewhere on one of the neighboring farms there will be help. Even if she has to walk all the way to Klipspring she will find help—food, medicine, people. There will be people somewhere. Even if there is war upon the land there will be people somewhere, someone left behind, someone hiding, someone like herself. She will find a vehicle and then she will go in search of Tembi.

The future seems possible, hope seems possible, Märit's plan seems possible.

She hobbles out of the river, finds her crutch, and with the wet clothes on her body slowly drying in the sunlight, begins the arduous journey towards the house. The minutes are long, long as hours, long as days. An eternity. But she goes on.

As she approaches, coming up through the trees, she sees the figures outside the house—black figures against the white walls.

People! They have come back! Is it the soldiers returned? Is it others? The sweat stings her eyes, the light is blinding, her head is spinning.

Suddenly the figures cease all their movement. Heads turn towards Märit. One of the figures that has been squatting on the ground rises to his full height and makes a loud, guttural sound of warning, almost a bark.

"Waagh!"

Märit stops and wipes the sweat from her eyes.

Again the hoarse shout sounds, *"Waagh!"* Just once, but she hears the threat in the sound, and senses the sudden tension in the other figures.

That single figure comes forward, half hopping, half loping on all fours, dark gray and black, a tail arched above the back. A baboon.

The baboon lopes towards her and raises his dog-like head, his long muzzle, drawing back his lips to show long yellow canine teeth.

"Waagh! Waagh," he snarls, charging down upon her like some strange dog-creature.

Märit flinches, raising the broom above her head, and lets out a wild scream.

The baboon skids to a stop in a flurry of dust. He stands resting his weight on his front legs, massive head lowered between his wide shoulders, then paces back and forth angrily. He turns and glances back at his companions before sinking to his haunches and glowering at Märit.

Märit slowly lowers herself to the ground.

The breeze carries the scent of the baboon towards her—a zoo smell is how she thinks of it—and she remembers the creature in the house last night. Not a dream or a delirium, that strange human-like shape leaping past her in the darkness, but a baboon.

She looks up to the house and sees the other baboons on the veranda, some of them going in and out of the house. She wants to run and chase them away. But this other one blocks her way, this one who must be the leader, protecting his companions. But what is there in the house for them anyway? There is no food, there is no water. Soon they will lose interest and wander off. She will wait, for there is nothing else to do, there is nowhere else to go.

She waits.

Sometimes she closes her eyes against the glare and sinks into a cool shady place where there is no pain, where there is neither hunger nor thirst. And when the daylight pulls her back she resists, she returns with reluctance.

Märit counts the baboons. Eleven, she thinks, watching as they scamper about in front of the veranda and go in and out of the house. Twelve, including the big one, the leader, who sits between her and the others.

Why have they come here? Have they watched the farm, and seen only this single aimless woman, and known that she is nothing? Why have they come? Is it to prevent her from going back to the house? Will they move into the house, as others have done, and possess it instead of her?

SOMETIMES HER THOUGHTS drift off, sometimes she dozes in and out of wakefulness. Sometimes she comes back to lucidity, brought back by the pain in her leg, and then she knows that she is sick, that her mind is sick with the poison coursing through her body.

I must get help, she tells herself, I must get up and go into the house and use the telephone to call for a doctor. When will Ben return with the car from Klipspring? He can take me to the doctor. Or maybe that woman from the neighboring farm will come—what is her name, the one with the little white car who spoke kindly to me? She will come and help me.

Tembi will be here soon, she thinks. Tembi will come and fetch me. She opens her eyes to look for Tembi and sees the animal watching her, his furrowed brow frowning over his yellow eyes. *What do you want from me?* she says, but he doesn't even blink, and she realizes that she does not know whether she has spoken aloud or only voiced the thought in her mind.

Behind the one who watches her, the other baboons have drawn nearer, curious, looking at her.

They are a family, she decides, looking them over. There is the patriarch, who watches her, and there is a handful of smaller animals with the same silvery coloring as the big one, but they are smaller, although still powerful, walking with that powerful gait. Then there are four others, whom she knows to be females because their movements are different, less swaggering, and they seem less interested in the presence of the big male. She knows they are females because there are two small baboons, small like little monkeys, who frolic amongst the females, and their attention is directed to these two small creatures.

The two small agile youngsters dart away from their mother, skirt the big male, and approach Märit with open curious playful faces. A warning grunt sounds from the mother and she sits up straight.

Märit smiles weakly as the two little faces study her with open curiosity, their round brown eyes so human and child-like. She lifts her hand to them and clicks her fingers. "Come, come."

The big male springs up on all fours and barks, lifting his head to show his yellow incisors.

An immediate outcry. The two babies flee screaming back to the females, leaping onto the nearest body and clinging to the thick fur with agile hands. The females form into a protective huddle. The young males charge back and forth, barking and screaming hoarsely, their cries echoing back from the koppie.

"I only wanted to say hello," Märit says softly. The big male barks again at her, like a shout of warning.

How strange they are, she thinks, looking at the baboons. Not like people, and not like other animals either. Yet somehow a bit of both. There is something ancient and dog-like about them, their long muzzles and the way they walk on all fours. Yet they seem human when they sit up and look at her with their intelligent eyes. The two babies are just like human children with their appealing faces. They are a family, a people, a tribe. Didn't someone tell her they were called the Rock People? They are a family, the way they touch each other with their hands, and talk to each other. An ancient tribe, with ancient faces, from the time before humans walked the earth, and their language is made up of words that humans have forgotten how to speak.

The sun moves across the veldt, shrinking the shade, the white light blurring everything around her.

When Märit opens her eyes again, one of the baboons is sitting very close to her, studying her with its intelligent eyes. A female, with a look of pity and sympathy in her eyes. Her two children sit close, leaning into her, regarding Märit with curiosity.

"Where are your people, sister?" the baboon asks.

"I have none."

"You have no one to belong to? Where is your family, sister?"

"I am alone on the earth."

"Without a people to belong to you will die."

"I am already dead," Märit answers.

"Not yet, sister. Not yet."

"What must I do? Where can I go?" Märit asks.

The baboon regards her with its wise and ancient face. *"You can come with us."*

"Yes, yes, I can do that." Märit sinks back on her elbows.

The sun moves across the land, time moves, the shadows are longer, and the baboons have gathered closer together in a loose group near the house. They seem to have forgotten Märit.

Now they move away, ambling, unhurried, the two small ones scampering back and forth, the young males in the forefront, the females next, and lastly the big silvery male.

Märit looks for the female who spoke to her. She squints and shakes her head and wipes the perspiration from her brow. Did the baboon speak to me? she wonders. Is such a thing possible? Or is it the sickness in me that causes me to imagine things?

She gets to her feet slowly, fighting off a wave of dizziness, and when she is upright she stands unsteadily, swaying on her crutch as she watches the tribe of baboons making their slow path in the direction of the koppie to the hills and valleys of the wild country beyond.

"Wait for me," Märit calls, her voice a dry croak. She stumbles after them, gritting her teeth.

The baboons seem unconcerned by her presence; they don't even look back—except for the big silvery male, who turns and watches her from his yellow eyes, then lifts his dog-like muzzle and barks once before turning his back on her.

She remembers a story, told to her long ago, when she lived on this farm with her husband, and people used to come and visit, about a man who had trapped a baboon and painted it with whitewash, so that when it tried to rejoin its fellows they fled from it in terror, as if it were a ghost.

Am I the ghost? Märit asks herself.

"Wait," she croaks, stumbling after them.

56

ON THE FAR VELDT, Tembi is in bondage amongst strangers. In the hottest hour of the day the company of soldiers lies resting in the shade below a ridge.

A low drone sounds above the trees. All eyes turn to the sky. A long-winged aircraft slowly passes overhead, high up. It turns to make a wide circle above the trees where the soldiers are hidden. The aircraft circles back, lower, its camouflage markings visible above the trees, then it rises and continues south.

Tembi lies on the hard earth and closes her eyes, glad of this respite, glad to cease the endless walking.

She wakes with a full bladder. Her back is damp with sweat, the cloth sticking to her skin. She can smell the dust of the journey on her skin, the wood smoke, the cigarettes that the men smoke, that Khoza smokes, and the smell of the horses, their sweat. She rises and pulls the damp dress away from her skin. The soldiers are dozing, the horses cropping at the scrub under the trees. She moves away, past outstretched soldiers, seeking someplace out of sight.

"Where are you going?" a voice demands as a sentry materializes in front of her.

"To piss," she says brutally. "Do I have your permission?"

"Watch out for snakes," he calls after her as she moves out of sight. "Don't let one bite your honey pot." His laughter is crude.

She steps carefully, although she has not seen a snake since that long-ago day when she killed the mamba that Märit found in the laundry room.

Märit! Where is she now? What will become of her? The last image of

Märit is fixed in Tembi's mind, of Joshua riding her down with his horse, and the figure lying on the ground in front of the house. What if she is so badly hurt that she cannot get up? What will become of Märit? What will become of them all?

When she is out of sight Tembi looks to see that the guard has not followed her before she squats behind some bushes to relieve herself. The reddish soil turns dark under the stream of liquid, dark as blood on the earth. What will become of her garden, thirsty in the dry earth?

Tembi becomes aware of the silence. There is no sound anywhere. She cannot hear the soldiers, or the chirp of birds, or the buzz of cicadas. There is an interruption in the motion of things, as if all living creatures have paused in their eternal motion, and hold their breath, like that moment before a storm when all the world catches its breath and holds it—in anticipation, in hope, or in fear.

In the pit of her stomach she has a sensation of foreboding, waiting for the storm to break. Only her own solitary heart beats, as all the rest of nature waits. But for what does it wait? Far off she hears the sound of an engine, and she cannot tell if it is an airplane in the sky or a vehicle on the ground. A faint tremor moves the air, as if some monstrous creature has sighed and lumbered to its feet.

She knows what the world waits for now, in this strange moment of anxious anticipation. That fluttering in the air is the motion of Death's cloak, and that distant engine is the announcement of a terrible presence beginning to make itself known.

Tembi waits.

A shout. A rapid booming noise shakes the earth. Something unseen rips through the leaves above her head like a scythe, scattering a spray of chopped leaves and twigs through the branches. A burned smell in the air. Then the guns speak—a hail of bullets smashing into the camp from all directions, men's voices screaming, smoke filling the air. Death announces itself.

A vehicle of some kind strains its engine on the ridge and whines into gear, then ceases suddenly as the booming of a heavy weapon reverberates through the thick smoke.

The suddenness of the eruption stuns Tembi. The shooting is coming from every direction, voices screaming around her, figures running, boots thudding on the ground, the air filling with a burning smell of battle.

She cowers with her hands over her head, trying to make herself small, to block out the banging of the guns and the terrible voices, to hide from the bullets cutting through the branches. The explosions and the shooting seem to go on forever, as if the entire earth is being destroyed.

A sudden pause, the clamor silenced—only the yellow smoke drifting through the trees. She rises cautiously to her feet. The chatter of a gun makes her flinch, but it is farther off, the shouting is moving away.

"Khoza!" Tembi calls.

Distant voices, too far away to make out the words.

Tembi runs back to the camp; the horses have bolted, the soldiers are gone. Some items of clothing lie on the ground—blankets, a single shoe.

"Khoza?" she calls. Then louder, "Khoza!"

The battle has moved up the valley—she hears the firing of guns, the cries of men. After only a few yards Tembi stumbles upon a body. A man lying on his back, as if sleeping, except for the way his legs are twisted under him, except for the fact that his uniform is stained below the waist, wet and dark with blood. Tembi looks quickly at his face, slack and dead, then turns away and hurries on.

The sounds of battle are growing fainter, distant. Tembi follows the tracks of a wheeled vehicle.

A second body. This man is shirtless—somehow he has lost his shirt—and in his throat is a gaping hole, the size of a fist. Already the flies are there, crawling into the exposed red flesh. Tembi retches violently.

She follows the tire tracks in the soil. The noise of the battle is gone, leaving an eerie, singed silence, broken only by an occasional distant shot, too far off to guess the direction.

"Khoza, Khoza," she calls. "Where are you?"

Tembi finds Khoza. He is sitting under a tree with his back resting against the trunk, a rifle lying next to his leg. His eyes are upon her.

"Khoza!"

They have not hurt him, Tembi tells herself as she rushes towards

Khoza. Like me, he was hiding in the trees when Death came. He is resting now, waiting for me. They have not hurt him, they did not see him when the battle started and Death came.

He sits under the tree like someone waiting. "Khoza, Khoza." She calls his name, so that he will know her.

As Tembi sinks to her knees and stretches out a hand to him, his eyes are upon her but they do not see her. "Khoza." She whispers his name. But what is a name? Once it was the word by which the world knew him, the sound of his presence in life, the sound by which the stars knew him. It was the word by which the world acknowledged his presence.

His eyes do not know her.

"Speak to me, Khoza."

She wants him to say, "Tembi, Tembi, where have you been?"

But his name has already become a memory to the world, and the world does not know him, the wind does not know him, the stars do not see him.

"Oh, Khoza," she says softly, and looks for the wound on him, for there must be a wound to have caused this stillness in Khoza. Her hands touch his face, tilting his head back slightly, and she sees the dark blood in his nostrils. Her hands pat his chest and unbutton his shirt, revealing the muscles of his chest well-formed and strong with life and youth, with all the strength of life.

On the right side, just below his breast—the breast of a young man that is flat, with a nipple small as a raisin, so unlike her own breast that he has touched with his strong hands—there just below the nipple, in the place that guards his heart, is a small hole, a small hole the size of a coin, the smallest coin. A coin that will buy nothing ever again, for all payment has been made, and the cost was the life of Khoza.

She embraces him, and his body slumps forward, revealing the bloodstains on the bark of the tree.

"Oh, Khoza," Tembi whispers. She holds him close and kisses his face, his lifeless face. She kisses his lips and his cheeks and his brow. She kisses his eyes, then reaches up and closes his lids with her thumb, for his eyes will no longer know her and there is nothing more in this world for him to see.

Tembi sits down in front of him and holds his cold hands in hers, rubbing them gently between her palms to warm them. He has ceased his wandering.

She cannot let him lie here at the mercy of the hyenas and the vultures. "I will bury you," she tells him, "and let you sleep now in the earth, in the one final place that is yours."

Tembi searches amongst the discarded equipment and packs scattered on the ground until she finds a small folding shovel. She digs a resting place in the earth. For a long time she digs the earth with her small shovel, and when there is space enough dug for a man's body to lie in the earth, she rolls Khoza into his grave, and covers him with the soil that becomes wet with her tears. Then she searches for stones and rocks, to cover the soil, to protect his resting place from the hyenas and the vultures.

When it is done she slumps down under the tree. She reaches for Khoza's rifle and cradles it on her lap. What is there in life for me now? she wonders, running her fingers across the metal. Nothing but this gun.

If she were to place this barrel against her temple and pull the trigger then the sadness and the sorrow would end, and she would join Khoza, and be free of sadness. She rests the cold muzzle of the gun against her forehead, pressing it hard against her skull, her other hand reaching for the trigger. All it will take is one small movement.

A shuffling noise makes her lift her head and look across the clearing. A man is limping towards her. One look at his face and she leaps to her feet. It is Joshua.

"You can give me that gun," he says to Tembi.

She shakes her head. "Go away. Leave us alone."

He stops, grimacing as he holds one hand pressed to his side, the sly glint in his eye that she knows from before.

"Give me that rifle. I will need it. You have no use for it."

"No."

In his eyes she sees the knowledge come to him that he can take anything he wants from her. If he has done it before then he can take again.

Joshua's hand drops to his waist and slides a bayonet loose from its sheath.

"Don't come any closer," Tembi says, raising the rifle. Her heart fills with anger and hate for all that he has taken from her. The gun is heavy in her hands.

He advances, sure of himself, sure of her weakness. In his eyes she sees the cruel pleasure. Some evil thing in him is enjoying this moment.

He raises the bayonet, his other hand reaching to grasp the rifle.

Tembi squeezes the trigger. The rifle jerks in her hand; she doesn't hear the bang.

A puff of dust leaps from Joshua's shirt, just below the collar. Surprise appears in Joshua's eyes as he jerks back from the impact.

Tembi thrusts the rifle towards him, almost as if offering it, and pulls the trigger again.

He looks down at the slow stain spreading across his stomach.

The surprise leaves his eyes, the life leaves his eyes. He topples over, dead already.

For a long time Tembi just stands there, shocked into emptiness—her mind empty, her heart empty, her soul empty. She becomes aware of the gun in her hands. All the sadness and the waste that is her country is in this gun, this instrument of hate. With an exclamation of disgust she flings the weapon away from her.

She turns and crouches down in front of the shallow mound of earth. "I'm sorry, Khoza. I'm sorry, I'm sorry, I'm sorry."

The vultures circle in the sky. Somewhere the hyenas lift their heads at the smell of carrion.

Along the path that leads through the valley and out of the hills towards the veldt the young woman strides with purposeful steps, making her solitary way. She does not look back. Somewhere ahead of her is a farm, a place with many names but only one meaning—home.

57

SOMETIMES MÄRIT LOSES SIGHT of the baboons. Even though their motion is unhurried, apparently aimless, with frequent stops for grooming or to investigate some nest of insects or tasty root that one of them has discovered, still she falls behind.

Sometimes she finds herself alone, except for pain, her constant companion. Behind her in the white haze stands the empty house, the ruined fields, already receding into memory, into the past.

Once more she sets off. To keep up with the baboons is her only desire, to not be abandoned by them. She rounds the side of the koppie and catches sight of the animals just disappearing into a narrow cleft that seems to lead into the tall rock.

Perhaps the baboons live inside the rock, where there is a pool of cool water in the rocks, and a garden with fruit trees. We can live there, hidden from the world, forgotten and ignored by the world. We can live there. Perhaps that is where they live, Märit thinks. Inside that rock that is called the Devil's Head, inside the shadow of loneliness.

The last of the baboons disappears into the crevice. Märit pushes on, anxious to catch up. As she enters the shadow that the tall rock throws across the ground she feels a chill in the air, as if the sun has never reached this place. The path is steeper and she must stop often. Once, she knocks her wounded leg against a stone and the terrible agony makes her cry out loud. Her voice is swallowed up into the rock.

She drags herself up the path, almost bent double, using her free hand to lever herself forward. The crevice narrows as the path flattens out.

Märit leans against the sheer rock and breathes deeply, gathering her fading strength before struggling on once more.

As she rounds the edge of an outcrop she comes face-to-face with the baboon, the big silvery one. He is planted squarely in her path, standing on all fours, his head lowered. But his yellow eyes under his furrowed brow are upon her. The warning grunt that rolls from deep in his chest makes Märit halt.

She looks past him, trying to see where the path leads, to see where the female is, the one who spoke to her, who said, *"Follow us."*

The baboon raises his head and barks at her. Märit understands his words: You can go no farther.

His eyes fix on hers and she understands. Then he turns and lopes off without looking back. But when he is out of sight around the curve, Märit starts forward again. He is waiting for her, as if he knew she would disregard his warning.

Without a sound he charges.

Märit falls back against the rocks as he leaps towards her, the long canine teeth bared. She shuts her eyes. Something swats her face, knocking her down. Then she is alone.

Märit opens her eyes. She is alone. Raising a hand she touches her cheek in the place where the baboon's hand has slapped her. The sensation of that leathery palm is vivid upon her skin. She sits on the path, holding her cheek, feeling the welt where the baboon's fingers have scraped across her skin. For the first time in her life a creature from the other side of life has touched her. And he has slapped her.

The disappointment wells up in Märit; her heart swells with humiliation, choking her breath. She begins to sob. High above her where the rock face rises is a small patch of sky.

Märit lies in her prison, the absence of hope as heavy as the rock that rises above her to the ragged patch of sky. Her soul is empty. Even the humiliation is gone. She watches the sky pale, then darken to violet, then turn black. Stars appear, but they are distant points of light, and their cold light cannot reach her in this crevice of rock, in this prison.

Daylight comes, as it must, as it always will. Märit does not know if she has slept or not. One day will be like another. Empty. Sunlight eventually reaches between the walls of rock and falls on the narrow track where she lies. Märit rouses herself. She looks down at her leg, touches it once, then averts her eyes from the swollen pustulant ankle. A faint smell of rot reaches her nostrils. I am decaying, she thinks. I will lie here forever, I will rot and decompose. But it doesn't matter.

She rouses herself, because she remembers the house, the river, because she still lives, because she thirsts, because the life still in her drives her to rise and find her crutch and hobble slowly back down the path. Somewhere across the immeasurable distance that is the day lies the river, and the life in her thirsts for the water, and drives her on.

As Märit skirts the edge of the koppie, head bent, picking her slow and painful way amongst the rocks, a small quick flash of green darts in front of her eyes.

She sees it again, noticing now a small green lizard, no longer than her index finger, perched on the edge of a rock in a patch of sunlight. A rapid pulse of life beats in the lizard's throat, the tiny heart beating. The lizard darts over the edge of the rock and out of sight. Märit shuffles forward a few steps, wanting to see that quick throb of life again, wanting some small image of hope to sustain her in the long, long journey to the river.

Her eyes fall upon a patch of green, speckled with some bright spots of yellow. She stumbles forward and uses her crutch to push away the brush that has been gathered around the plants. Here amongst the dry hard rock someone has built a little garden. A memory pushes at the edge of her mind; she remembers this place from a long time ago. When there was a farm lush with maize and cattle and fruit, someone had cultivated this little garden, hidden in the rocks, hidden in the midst of plenty. A child's garden.

Märit lowers herself onto a rock and reaches down for one of the round yellow fruits. As she breaks it loose from the stem a melon-like aroma is released, and immediately her stomach rumbles. She bites down into the fruit, through the soft rind to the sweet yellow flesh. A groan of pleasure escapes from her throat as she stuffs the sweet fruit into her mouth. Then she reaches for another one, pulling it loose from its vine, and gulps at it voraciously. She falls to her hands and knees amongst the plants, grabbing at the yellow fruits, stuffing them into her mouth.

And then there is only one fruit left, one of five, and she tries to eat it more slowly, to savor the texture and the sweetness and the nectar, but her need is too great, her hunger and her thirst are overwhelming. In a few bites and swallows the fruit is gone. Märit spits out a mouthful of seeds and runs her hand across her mouth, then licks her fingers, sucking up every last droplet of the juice.

A clarity forms in her mind, as if for the first time, as if all her life she has existed in a fog. She sees her life as if for the first time, and she knows now her destination. She begins to limp towards the farm, the pain in her leg nothing to her now. Every object seems drawn with a fine pen, delineated in clear crisp lines and colors. The clarity is sharp and hard and cold.

There is the kraal, the huts empty; there is the washhouse, the tap; there is the windmill, turning; there is the row of eucalyptus trees where the doves roost; there is the farmhouse, empty; there are the fields, the fences, the outbuildings; there is the road. There is the veldt, the hills, the trees, the sky. Once she lived here, with a gentle man who dreamed of a different life, and a young woman who gave kindness and love.

Here is the farm. And here is the river.

TEMBI WALKS one step at a time, one foot placed in front of the other; step by step she travels across the empty veldt. Behind her lies the end of the world—death, destruction, murder. She is hungry, she is thirsty, but her thoughts are directed to one place only.

She turns her thoughts forward, to home, to Märit. Goodness and mercy, Märit. Goodness and mercy.

The sun drops out of sight behind the hills, the sky pales into a washed-out violet, darkness falls. Tembi walks on. By starlight and by moonlight she walks on. She sings a song, from the days before, when her father walked up the hill to greet her in the morning light, when her mother sang on the banks of the river in her sky blue dress. She sings softly, to give herself courage, to give herself strength.

Ku yosulw' inyembezi, nokufa nezinsizi
Ayibalwa iminyaka, ubusuk' abukho.

God shall wipe away all tears, there's no death, no pain, nor fears
And they count not time by years, for there is no night there.
In the land that does not dry, you will never age,
for there is no night there.

At first light she is still walking. One foot placed in front of the other, one step after the other. The landscape becomes familiar, for she is out of the valleys now and into the flat veldt, dotted with acacias. A ridge, a bend in the road, the river appearing. And there is the tall rock rising above the veldt, the rock called Isitimane, where her garden grows, and the kraal, and the windmill that turns in the breeze, and the farmhouse with its thatched roof. And Märit.

HERE IS THE RIVER. It seems to Märit that her journey from the koppie to the banks of the flowing river has taken a lifetime. How many days has she been wandering across the parched and brown earth towards the river? All her life.

She does not turn to look back at the house, the distant house standing isolated in the glare, the white walls bright in the sunlight. She can never turn back, she can never go there again, because the journey is too long, the distance too far.

Märit lowers herself to her knees and cups water into her hands, washing the sweet stickiness of the fruit from her face. She drinks, but the cool water gives her no comfort, no sustenance. She is beyond thirst now.

Easing herself onto a rock she lets her wounded leg rest in an eddy of the swirling stream. On her calf and thigh the thin red lines have spread into a pattern of streams and tributaries. The coolness of the liquid on her burning foot gives no relief, for the pain is everywhere, a part of her now, a constant part of her body that she has grown accustomed to. Pain is life.

The river flows, always, through the dry landscape, between the hills, into the valleys and the plains, past the towns and the cities. The river flows, through the country that is not hers, until somewhere it reaches the sea and spills into the great wide ocean and loses itself.

I have always been lost, Märit realizes. I have never belonged anywhere or to anything. My life has been a dream. I have failed—at marriage, family, friendship, farming—at life.

She looks down at her hands. Her fingernails are caked with dirt, rimmed with black; in the fine lines of her knuckles is a map of darker lines, like a map that she carries in her skin. Even her body is unreal to her now.

On her wrist is a bracelet of blue beads, the color of the sky. Märit unfastens the beads and sets them on the rock. Tembi once wore those beads, but Tembi is gone.

She remembers Tembi, but the past is something that happened to someone else.

I have holes in me, she thinks, and all memory has emptied from me. I have lived in a world made of glass; everything around me is painted on glass that could shatter into a million shards at any moment. But what is behind the glass? Märit looks up at the sky. There is nothing behind the glass. The sky vibrates, the thin blue cloth is ready to rip and shred at any moment. When the sky rips apart will the light flood through, or will darkness pour down and bury her?

Leaving the rock where she sits, Märit eases into the river. Under her feet are pebbles and then sand, and then nothing, as she kicks off and swims out to midstream.

She will enter the water and become water, become air, become nothing.

Letting her limbs go slack, Märit allows the current to take her. She opens her mouth and swallows water, then coughs and struggles to raise her head above the surface.

She is afraid, afraid to do what she desires now.

She lets herself go limp again, giving in, not resisting. She begins to fall, and the pressure on her lungs grows, and momentarily she struggles against the fear.

She closes her eyes and the fear leaves her. A great weariness like sleep descends over her. The water embraces Märit, carrying her into the opaque depths. Darkness fills her eyes. Opening her mouth wide, Märit lets the river fill her, drawing her into a deep emptiness, turning and turning her into the vast darkness. She feels herself moving towards the sea, cradled and embraced in the warm and deep blue sea.

HERE IS THE FARM.

Tembi's heart lifts, and the weariness of her long journey lifts from her aching body as she sees the fields, the windmill, the koppie, the kraal, the farmhouse with its walls bright in the sunlight.

"Märit!" she calls. Her voice is small in the silence. "Märit! I'm back."

Tembi runs towards the house.

Märit is not in the house. The rooms seem weighted with an atmosphere of abandonment, as if nobody has lived here for a very long time.

Tembi hurries out the back door and follows the familiar path to the kraal. "Märit," she calls. From hut to hut she searches, and at each one she calls, "Märit, Märit."

As she stands in the clearing outside the huts, calling one more time, Tembi's eyes are drawn towards the koppie. A peculiar sense of foreboding comes over her. Heart beating with anxiety and misgiving, she seeks out her garden.

The soil is trampled, the vines are broken, the fruit is gone.

With an exclamation Tembi falls to her knees, her fingers searching amongst the broken stalks and leaves. The fruit is gone. The garden has been plundered. All for nothing. All the days of nurture, of carrying buckets of water, all the care and hope—all for nothing.

She slumps down in despair. Even this has been destroyed.

As Tembi gets to her feet she sees a scattering of seeds on the ground. Quickly she gathers them into her palm. Five seeds. All that is left of the sweetness that she tried to nurture forth from the earth.

In amongst the vines and leaves Tembi makes out the imprint of a hand in the soft soil—a very clear outline where someone has leaned heavily on the earth. She places her own hand on the shape that has been pressed into the soil. She remembers a day when she sat with Märit on the rocks by the river, a day of innocence, when she let her wet hand rest a moment on the warm surface of a rock, and the outline left behind was like a drawing on the stone, and as it faded, evaporating, Märit placed her own hand on the imprint. Tembi remembers how the two hands matched.

Märit has been here.

Tembi raises her head. "Märit!" Only an echo answers her call, only an echo thin and faint.

She stands, clutching the seeds, and looks towards the river. The foreboding shivers through her again, a feeling so intense it makes her tremble.

The river flows, silent, eternal, always moving. There are footprints and scuff marks in the sand near the shallows. Tembi does not have to examine them or place her own feet there to know that they belong to Märit. But the footprints lead in only one direction, into the river.

Tembi wades into the shallows. A flash of blue catches her eye—a bracelet of blue beads gleams on the rock. She holds it in her hand a moment before fastening it onto her wrist. Her eyes rest upon the smooth flow of the river for a long, long time. The premonition that she felt earlier is now a certainty. She knows it in her body, and in her soul is a sudden absence, as if something has been removed.

Tembi does not call out again. She knows with a terrible and final certainty that it is futile to call Märit's name.

She turns and slowly walks away from the river.

Here is the farm: the windmill silhouetted against the blue sky, the grass rustling in the breeze, the white walls and thatched roof of the house, all so still and quiet.

She opens her hand and studies the five small seeds in her palm. She bends down and carefully places the seeds on the soil.

Here she will grow that which does not as yet grow. In this small acre of the world. From here the sweetness will come. A gift.

But first she must plant the seeds.

Acknowledgements

I am grateful to my wife, Gunilla Josephson, for her love, her understanding, and her inspiration.

Thanks to my agent, Hilary McMahon, for her early support and encouragement.

Special thanks are due to Phyllis Bruce for her perceptive reading of the manuscript, her wise suggestions, and for finding the title in the text.

In its early stages the writing of this book was supported by grants from the Canada Council and the Ontario Arts Council.